RAVE REVIEWS FOR SANDRA RUTTAN!

THE FRAILTY OF FLESH

"*The Frailty of Flesh* tore me asunder. Rarely has a novel of such art and skill reduced me to a wreck. It moved me in ways I didn't even know I felt. It's a kick in the head that is underwrit with sheer compassion."

—Ken Bruen, Shamus Award–winning
Author of *The Guards*

"An unflinching look into the dark heart of family dysfunction, *The Frailty of Flesh* raises difficult questions and shuns easy answers. Sandra Ruttan writes with passion and honesty about every parent's worst nightmare and the result is an emotionally wrenching experience."

—Sean Chercover, Gumshoe Award–winning
Author of *Big City, Bad Blood*

"Brave, dark and utterly convincing, *The Frailty of Flesh* is guaranteed to break the hardest of hearts. An absorbing read."

—Allan Guthrie, Theakston Award–winning
Author of *Hard Man*

"*The Frailty of Flesh* is not only one of the best procedural thrillers I've read in a long time...but the ending knocked me right out of my seat. Ruttan captures the nature of crime in a way few thriller writers ever manage...this is vivid, impressive, gut-wrenching stuff."

—Russel D. McLean, Crime Scene Scotland,
Author of *The Good Son*

"Ruttan has a spellbinding style."

—*New York Times* Bestselling
Author Clive Cussler

"Ruttan's deft touch intrigues and satisfies, making her a powerful new force in the mystery field."

—JT Ellison, Author of *All the Pretty Girls*

CURIOUS BEHAVIOR

Ashlyn heard Richard Reimer mutter, "What the hell's going on?" but he didn't force the question. Tracy Reimer remained silent, as though there was nothing unusual about two plainclothes RCMP officers bringing her eleven-year-old son home.

Tain gestured at the door. "Perhaps it would be best if we spoke inside."

Richard gaped at him for a few seconds before he turned and moved toward the house.

Ashlyn started to follow. She'd taken a few steps when Christopher said, "Jeffrey's dead." Then he ran inside.

Tracy Reimer just stood there, face blank and colorless. She looked from Ashlyn to Tain without so much as a shrug of her shoulders, a widening of her eyes or the tiniest hint of wrinkles on her brow.

Her husband walked up to her and said, "I'll call the lawyer."

Ashlyn saw Tain glance at her, and she gave a small shake of her head. Let Richard Reimer call. She wanted to know why he thought he needed a lawyer when he hadn't even asked what had happened to his son.

Or where his daughter was.

Other *Leisure* books by Sandra Ruttan:

WHAT BURNS WITHIN

SANDRA
RUTTAN

THE FRAILTY
OF FLESH

LEISURE BOOKS NEW YORK CITY

For Uncle Charlie, taken from us too soon, sorely missed.

A LEISURE BOOK®

November 2008

Published by

Dorchester Publishing Co., Inc.
200 Madison Avenue
New York, NY 10016

ISBN 10: 0-8439-6075-2
ISBN 13: 978-0-8439-6075-4

Visit us on the web at www.dorchesterpub.com.

THE FRAILTY
OF FLESH

"Nothing softeneth the arrogance of our nature like a mixture of some frailties; it is by them we are best told that we must not strike too hard upon others, because we ourselves do so often deserve blows; they pull our rage by the sleeve and whisper gentleness to us in our censures, even when they are rightly applied."

—Sir George Savile, *Advice to a Daughter*

CHAPTER ONE

"It's just . . ." The woman's gaunt face tightened as she clenched the muscles, twisted her jaw and blinked rapidly. She sucked in a sharp breath and continued, "Just not . . . right, somehow. You raise 'em. You don't really think about buryin' a kid."

Her hands shook visibly as she pushed her strawlike hair behind her ears, then reached for the pack of cigarettes on the table. The trembling eased as she slipped a cigarette from the container, as though touch alone could transfer the nicotine into her system. Her motions were so fluid the cigarette was in her mouth within seconds, her eyes closed as the tension seeped out of her wiry body.

She almost smiled.

Then the facial muscles sagged again as she slowly removed the cigarette from her lips and stuck it back in the pack. Her actions had been instinctive and automatic when she was taking the cigarette out. Once she'd remembered the no-smoking ban in restaurants she'd devoted her full attention to the process of putting it back in the box, as though if she pried her gaze away for even a split second or dared to breathe it would break her concentration . . . as though tragedy might strike if she failed to replace the cigarette properly.

Craig Nolan processed all of this as he watched the woman who sat across from him. Before today he hadn't heard of her. When she asked if he could meet with her to discuss an old case he'd suggested she talk to someone who handled cold case files, but she'd been insistent. Not that kind of case. An old case Steve Daly had handled, years before.

That was when it clicked. Lisa Harrington had received notification from the parole board. Her daughter's murderer had applied for early release. Craig guessed Lisa had reached for the cigarettes first and the phone second. She'd called the Mounties in an attempt to locate Steve Daly, with no luck, until someone finally suggested she call Craig Nolan instead.

Someone who figured it was personal, not professional. Possibly someone too lazy to look up the name of whomever Steve had partnered with when he'd worked this murder.

Or someone who just couldn't be bothered to ask Lisa what she wanted to talk to Steve about.

Craig wasn't familiar with the case, but his present workload was light. His workload had been light for months, but that was a different issue. All that mattered was that there was no excuse for him to brush her off. It was just to grab a quick coffee, explain how parole hearings worked, and there was a niggling voice in the back of his brain that told him Steve would want to know he'd followed up on this. One small thing Craig could do to ease Steve's guilt.

Guilt about so many things.

A waitress filled a mug of coffee in front of Lisa and reached for Craig's cup, but he shook his head.

"You, uh, look kinda young," Lisa said as she wrapped her hands around the mug. "I-I don't remember you at all."

"I didn't work your daughter's case." He watched the truth hit home in her features as she set her drink back down abruptly. The question was forming on her lips as he raised his hand. "Steve Daly is teaching classes at The Depot." Her face remained blank, so he guessed she wasn't familiar with the name of the academy where Mounties went for their training. "Where they train new officers."

She nodded, as though this all made perfect sense, but the way her eyes pinched with confusion told him it was so far beyond her focus right now that she couldn't process it. Her mind was on one thing: Donny Lockridge.

Lockridge, the teenager convicted of murdering Lisa's sixteen-year-old daughter, Hope.

Lockridge, who, despite being bumped up to adult court and given a twenty-year sentence, had served ten years and was now eligible for parole. Life sentences in Canada seldom meant life, and in most cases convicted murderers never came close to serving the usual maximum of twenty-five years.

Release after ten years wasn't unheard of. Just another thing about the so-called justice system that made Craig's stomach turn.

"Nobody tells me nothin', you know? Just lock him up and move on. Steve, he was the only one who said much to me at all." She lifted the mug with both hands, her gaze on the contents as she took a sip. "I don't know what this means."

"Do you have a lawyer?" Craig asked. The quick shake of her head confirmed what he should have already known. This was a woman who, barely in her forties, looked like she'd turned into a compulsive chain-smoker when she'd finally kicked other habits. The way she scratched at her arms, her skin-and-bones body, her gray pallor and the vacuous stare gave it away. She was a shell, someone who'd tried to fill the void with one substance or another, and her best years were well behind her, despite the fact that she wasn't that old.

Lisa Harrington was someone who'd probably spent her life in and out of jail, dependent on court-appointed attorneys and government-assistance programs to make ends meet when she wasn't on the wrong side of a prison sentence. Not that any of that mattered at the moment.

"They sent the letter to let you know he's applied for early release. It tells you when the hearing is scheduled. You can choose to attend."

Her head snapped up and a rush of color filled her cheeks. "Why would I want to see that filth go free?"

Craig waited until he felt she was calm enough to hear him. "He won't be released right away. It's a hearing."

"W-why tell me?"

"The families of the victims are notified in case they'd like to participate. You can prepare what's called a victim impact statement. It gives you a chance to tell the parole board how his crimes affected you."

Lisa set the mug down. Her elbows were digging into the table as she reached back and smoothed the hair that was still tucked behind her ears. "What good does that do?"

"Well, you get to make sure they don't forget about your daughter. He'll be trying to show them how much he's changed and that he's a better person, and he'll say he's sorry and ready to rejoin society."

Her eyes narrowed. "Will that work?"

Craig took a deep breath. "If he's managed to stay out of trouble in prison and has good references, says he's found Jesus or something, yeah. He just might persuade them. I won't lie to you, it's possible he'll get out."

Her face fell. Craig hadn't thought it was possible for her to look worse than she did, but she managed to pull it off. Something about the way her cheeks sagged and how her bottom lip quivered . . . But the glint in her eyes told a different story.

It hinted at a woman on the brink of madness, of really, truly losing it. Probably the only thing holding her back was lack of energy. Her one small outburst seemed to have drained all her reserves. She didn't look like she had the physical strength required to go off the deep end. Instead, she lay whimpering at the edge of the abyss.

"That's why it's important for you to go, make a statement. You have to tell them who Hope was. You have to make them see the daughter you lost, understand what he did to her and to you."

"I just . . . just wish Steve would be there. Maybe he'd know the right thing to say."

"He's away right now, but he does keep his own notes on every case. I can take a look if you want, see if there's anything in there that might be helpful."

"Y-you could get those?"

Craig nodded. "They'd be at his house here. He's just on a temporary assignment." *I hope,* Craig thought.

She gaped at him for a moment, then forced her jaw up as she nodded. "Th-that would . . . Thanks." Lisa lowered her gaze as she pushed herself up slowly and slid out from behind the table, visibly shaking. She picked up her purse and tried to open it.

Craig stood and put up his hand. "I've got it."

Lisa kept tugging for a moment. The sharp jerks she was exerting on the zipper were probably the reason it had jammed and refused to yield. Craig reached out and touched her arm. "It's okay."

She released the zipper and took another deep breath while Craig took his wallet out of his pocket. He tossed a bill down on the table, removed a business card and passed it to her.

"I'll look at his notes, see if anything might help. If there's anything I can do, just call." Hollow words. She would go home, think about her dead daughter, try to get it together for the parole board hearing and then pace the floor, chain-smoking until she got word of the decision.

He'd go back to work, move on to the next case. Different names, different faces, same look of shock surfacing behind their eyes as they came to grips with the destruction crime had wrought in their lives.

Most days, Craig hid behind the idea that he could at least catch the criminals and put them away. Meeting with Lisa Harrington had been the first time in his career he'd had to face a victim on the other side, dealing with the possible release of her daughter's killer.

As he watched her walk away, shoulders hunched, gaze down, he realized he was kidding himself. He didn't help heal wounds; he just put a Band-Aid on them while they festered.

CHAPTER TWO

No course, no seminar, no self-help book filled with wise words and the best of intentions . . . Nothing prepared you to tell a parent their child was dead. *No parent should outlive their child.* It's not the way things were meant to be, not as nature intended. Children were supposed to be the legacy. You could comfort yourself, knowing when you passed on you left a bit of yourself behind, knowing you wouldn't immediately be forgotten.

Losing a child just wasn't right.

Tain had heard it all. He understood it. Every time he prepared to speak with a parent it was right there, churning beneath the surface. Let the memories come and all the anguish would be back, fresh, threatening to overtake him, to push him over the edge into a bottomless pit of despair.

The grief was enough to make you feel as though your soul was being put through a shredder.

There were few things worse than telling a parent their child was dead. Tain didn't just know that. He *knew* it. It wasn't textbook head knowledge or practical knowledge from the experience of watching the fallout. For him, it went far deeper.

Mrs. Reimer, we regret to inform you your son is dead. Your four-year-old boy, the one with the dark curly hair and big brown eyes. They hit him on the torso and back of the head but didn't mark his face. We all saw it, standing there, looking down at where he'd curled into a little ball, in the fetal position. He was still warm, the tiniest bit of pink in his cheeks. Put a blanket over him and it would have looked as though he was just sleeping, as though he'd just worn himself out playing and had curled up on the slip of pavement at the park to take a nap.

Just don't look at the back of his head or the dark stain on the pavement and you could hold on to the idea that he would get up soon and run off to play. You could pretend someone hadn't used him as a human piñata.

They couldn't tell her all of that. And this time, telling a mother her son was dead might just be the easier part of their task. Mrs. Reimer would likely think her world was falling apart, that she had already heard the most unbearable news imaginable.

Under different circumstances that would be correct. A parent's worst nightmare, until they managed to tell Jeffrey's parents the rest.

That their daughter was a suspect in the murder. And that she was missing.

Tain looked up as his partner, Constable Ashlyn Hart, appeared in the door to the ladies' washroom. She paused, lifted her hand to her forehead and stood still for a moment. No smile to light her face. Under the circumstances Tain wouldn't have expected one, but there was something else in her expression . . . Hollow cheeks, pallid skin. He watched her rub her temple, her gaze fixed on some spot on the grass.

They had worked on tough cases together before. This wasn't the first time they'd found themselves standing over the body of a child, but this time he'd seen the tears well up in her eyes for that split second. Then she'd swallowed it down, gotten on with the job, not even the hint of a tremor in her voice as she assumed control of the scene. That's what he'd come to expect from Ashlyn. She felt it as deeply as anyone, but she was a professional.

Every now and again she had her moments, though, like anyone else. He didn't blame her. If anything, he commended her for taking it off the field, making it a private moment instead of a public display. Now a raw look in her features hinted at a deeper pain.

And then it was gone.

He trawled through his memories of the past few weeks but

couldn't think of any indication that there were problems. Had he been so preoccupied with—

"Is it nice there?"

As his eyes focused on Ashlyn's face, now a few feet from his own, he frowned. "What? Where?"

"The fantasyland you're off in."

"Cheaper than Disney World."

Her tiny smile faded as she looked him straight in the eyes. "You okay?"

He bit back the words on the tip of his tongue and instead said, "Tough call."

They knew each other well enough to read subtle changes in expression. The way her left eyebrow rose for a split second in conjunction with the downward turn of the corners of her mouth said it all. Then her lips formed a hard line.

"It is odd," Tain said.

The distant stare was gone as she refocused on him. "I'm not overanalyzing?" she asked.

He shook his head. "Why would you even think that?"

She sighed as she pushed her dark hair back behind her left ear. "It isn't like we can do anything about it . . . It just is, if that makes any sense." She paused.

"It's okay."

A slow smile spread across her face. "You don't mind?"

"Are you questioning me?" He waited half a second, then continued, "Look, they searched the area and didn't find anything. It wasn't until the officers were returning to report in that they saw him." He knew she wanted him to run her through all the details of his interview with their witness. Other officers might take it personally, feel it was an attack on them, but he knew better. Ashlyn was reprocessing the details because something wasn't sitting right with her. And she was trying to figure out what it was.

"They found him near the water?"

He nodded. "In the woods, down by the shore. I believe the word used was 'skulking.'"

She raised an eyebrow but didn't comment.

"They couldn't get anything from him. When they brought him to me I managed to get him to give me his name and address."

"And you asked if he'd seen what happened."

"He said yes. That's it. So I asked if he recognized the attacker."

"And again, he just said yes." Ashlyn's mouth twisted. Her hands were on her hips. The longer Tain worked with her, the quicker her instincts kicked in. This case was already bugging her, and her issues centered on their one witness.

Christopher Reimer.

But she hadn't shared her thoughts with Tain. Not yet. He knew her well enough to know she'd voice them when she felt more confident about her conclusions. Around everyone else, other than Craig, she usually kept her musings concealed. He knew others who didn't like partnering with someone who wouldn't divulge their hunches, but Tain respected the fact that Ashlyn tried not to jump to conclusions. She was always processing information, turning the facts over in her mind, looking for the things that didn't add up.

She was sharp. And cautious, and he respected both qualities.

"Ashlyn?"

She turned her gaze back to him. "And you asked the name."

Tain nodded. "He said it was Shannon."

"And you asked her last name . . ."

"Christopher didn't volunteer a single word. He answered my questions directly, but with no additional information."

Her mouth twisted again, that uncertain, uneasy look distorting her features.

"I know, it's odd," Tain said. "I've had more information offered up by members of organized crime gangs up on soft charges."

"And Christopher Reimer is just a kid."

"But it was his brother who was murdered." A fact that raised another question in Tain's mind, and he felt certain she was wondering the same thing. Once Christopher had identified the attacker as Shannon Reimer, his older sister, Tain had asked if he knew the victim. There had been no change in Christopher's voice, no wavering, no hesitation, nothing. He'd said, "Jeffrey," and then, just before Tain could ask, added, "Jeffrey Reimer."

Christopher had removed a wallet from his pocket. Inside, ID confirmed his address, that he was just a few weeks short of his twelfth birthday, and there was a photo of three healthy kids, two of whom Tain could already identify.

Once Christopher had confirmed the girl in the photo was Shannon, Tain had given the photo to another officer with in-structions to circulate her description and begin searching for her immediately.

He'd left Christopher with two Port Moody police officers. They were watching him until Tain and Ashlyn finished at the scene and were ready to take him home and notify the family. Under normal circumstances Tain would have liked to take Christopher to the station for questioning, but he was a child. Tain couldn't sort out what he thought of the boy's behavior. The only thing he knew for certain was that he wanted Ashlyn there when Christopher Reimer was questioned again.

"Shock?" Ashlyn asked.

Tain shrugged.

He watched as Ashlyn turned and walked along the sidewalk, toward the parking lot where two uniformed officers were wait-ing for them.

Tain kept pace beside her. He knew she could have covered the short distance in a matter of seconds. Instead, she seemed to be drawing it out, giving herself time to let her thoughts gel.

Two officers were waiting near the front right bumper of their patrol car. One stood, the other leaned back, butt on the edge of the hood of the cruiser, legs spread apart, arms folded across his chest. The back passenger side door was open, the tousled brown hair on top of the boy's head barely visible.

The one leaning against the car, whose name was Parker, chomped on a piece of gum without dislodging the cocky grin. He had dark hair. From even the little gossip Tain heard he knew Parker considered himself a bit of a ladies' man, and a lot of female police officers seemed to agree with that assessment.

Tain resisted the urge to smile when Ashlyn ignored him completely and addressed the other officer.

"How is he?"

"Uh . . ." The officer, whose name was Bennett, stood with his mouth open as he glanced at Parker, who relieved him of the need to answer.

"We've taken good care of him."

Ashlyn slowly turned to look at Parker. "Got him something to eat, drink? Offered to put some heat on in the car?" She glanced at the open door and shook her head. Ashlyn straightened up as she turned back to Parker and lowered her voice. "Wonderful job, I'd say. Stellar."

There was no way for anyone to miss the sarcasm that saturated her words, and Tain watched as the cocky grin fell from Parker's face. "We did what we were told. We're ready to take him home, just waitin' on the official okay."

"We'll be talking to the family, so Christopher can come with us," Ashlyn said. "You guys are done here. You can check in with Sims and see where he needs you."

Parker's mouth hung open for just a second too long to go unnoticed, and then his jaw tensed. "But—"

"I am in charge of this case and this crime scene, Constable Parker." She glared at him for a moment, then walked toward the open door.

Tain watched as the officer's gaze followed her, and the corner of Parker's mouth twisted into a scowl. His, "Whatever you say, ma'am," response was barely audible, but the tone came through loud and clear.

"Is there a problem?" Tain asked him.

The officer's focus shifted to Tain's face, and after a second he started chomping on his gum again. Parker reminded Tain of one of those stereotypical U.S. patrol cops they always had on TV shows, with their dark sunglasses, willingness to use force even if unnecessary and inclination to see women as pretty li'l things in need of rescuing.

"No." The cynical smile was back in place. "No problem."

Tain leaned closer and said, "There better not be." His voice had just enough edge that, from the corner of his eye, he could see Ashlyn glance back at them, but Tain kept his focus on the man in front of him.

He'd worked with guys like that before. Head full of attitude and an undersized dick they were compensating for that was still bigger than their brain.

Kind of guy who was reckless. Who'd screw up on the job and expect his brothers in blue to close ranks to protect him.

Kind of guy who could get someone killed.

Ashlyn felt her cheeks burn but tried to suppress her annoyance. A few years earlier Tain's protectiveness would have pissed her off, but now it was Parker's attitude that got to her. She had a job to do, and so did they. Politics and prejudices shouldn't get in the way, but all too often they did.

There were far more important things to think about. Christopher Reimer was hunched in the backseat of the car, where he'd been for over an hour. His face was pale. Not ghostly white, just lacking color, the way skin did this time of year in an area where residents were denied exposure to the sun day after day.

She knelt down beside him. "I'm Constable Hart. We're going to take you home now."

There was no change in his expression. He didn't look up, just sat slouched down on the seat and stared at his feet, as though he hadn't even heard her.

"Christopher?"

"Whatever."

Ashlyn was glad he still hadn't looked up because she was able to push the frown off her face before he had a chance to see it. It was never easy to deal with kids, but this one was particularly tough to read.

"Come on. We're taking my car."

That finally got Christopher to look at her. His eyes were hooded, face still expressionless as he let out a deep breath and muttered, "Whatever."

If Tain hadn't relayed the details of his interview with Christopher, she would have wondered whether that was the only word in his vocabulary. She straightened up, stepped back and watched as Christopher Reimer got out of the car and walked across the parking lot. His baggy jeans were streaked with mud near the bottom, and from the knee down on the left side they were wet. The thin shirt he was wearing barely covered his thin frame, but from the way he carried himself Ashlyn suspected he was pretty strong. He was more of a lean, tough type emerging, rather than a scrawny weakling.

Ashlyn exchanged a look with Tain as she reached for the door, pushed it shut and followed Christopher to their car.

It was a short drive around the head of the Burrard Inlet. The city of Port Moody embraced the tip of the fjord on the one side and nestled up against the foot of Eagle Mountain on the other. Port Moody, City of the Arts, was a nature lover's playground. From where they'd found Jeffrey Reimer's body at Rocky Point Park a network of trails and boardwalks formed an extensive walking path. With the proximity to Belcarra Regional Park it wasn't unheard of for joggers and walkers to encounter bears. There had been problems in recent years with coyote packs living in the forest the walkways wove through, and there were even sporadic cougar sightings.

Traffic heading into Port Moody was light. Ashlyn had only a matter of minutes to compose herself before the next stage of the investigation. People always said stupid things, like practice makes perfect, but no matter how many times they handled notification it never got any easier.

Even Tain seemed unusually quiet, although she suspected that was because of their passenger. Tain's usual brand of irreverent humor could draw criticism from seasoned cops, but she knew there was no way he'd shoot off his mouth in front of a child.

Tain slowed the car. "Is this the right address?"

Christopher exhaled. "Yeah," he said.

Ashlyn thought over what Tain had said about his interview with Christopher, and what he'd left unsaid. Christopher had a reserved, cool demeanor, as though he was bored and inconvenienced by being detained by the police.

Trauma did strange things to people. She'd experienced it

herself and in her mind's eye could look back and see herself reacting to her fear, feeling as though she was looking at someone else. The intensity of her own reactions had surprised her, and she didn't recognize that person. It was a side of herself she was uncomfortable being confronted with, but now keenly aware of. Emotionally, she liked to be in control. The experience of actually being in shock, and losing her sense of power over herself had been as difficult to deal with as the events that had put her in shock in the first place.

Still, she couldn't put her finger on what it was, exactly, but Christopher's reactions didn't feel as though they were about shock. There was something else, and she was certain Tain shared her misgivings about their only witness.

As they got out of the car the front door to the house opened. A man appeared. He had black hair, cut short, and looked to be a bit below average height, in decent shape. One of those chiseled faces, dark eyes.

Ashlyn noted that in a split-second summary, but the scowl on his face as he marched toward them was what really stood out. "What's he done?"

The words weren't polite or born out of exasperation. They were laced with anger and accusations. Ashlyn and Christopher had walked around from the passenger side of the car, and the man she presumed was Richard Reimer walked right up between Tain and Ashlyn and grabbed the boy's arm.

Christopher pulled back, and for a moment they were locked in a tug of war. Richard Reimer tried to grab his son's other arm. Before Ashlyn could order him to stop, and identify herself as a police officer, Christopher swung. He planted a decent blow squarely on his father's jaw. Richard let go of him and staggered back, mouth hanging open as he stared at his son. Then he clenched his jaw as his cheeks turned purple, and he raised his fist. He looked like he was going to strike back. Tain stepped forward.

"I'm Constable Tain and this is my partner, Constable Hart. Sir—"

Christopher let out a yelp and ran toward the house.

Ashlyn released her grip on her gun, dropped her hand and felt her jacket fall over her weapon. A woman had appeared on the doorstep. Presumably Mrs. Reimer, she appeared to be an older, well-used version of her living son. Pale cheeks and wavy brown hair, Tracy Reimer was what Ashlyn would call solid. Not heavy but not slight, she appeared to be as tall as her husband.

Christopher's sudden display of emotion made an already difficult task that much harder. Ashlyn had expected him to flee into the house, but instead he remained on the front step, with his head lowered. He didn't reach out to his mother for physical comfort but just stood there.

Ashlyn heard Richard Reimer mutter, "What the hell's going on?" but he didn't force the question. Tracy Reimer remained silent, as though there was nothing unusual about two plainclothes RCMP officers bringing her eleven-year-old son home, or the need to break up a physical confrontation between her husband and child on their front lawn.

From the corner of her eye Ashlyn saw Tain's glance and could feel her eyebrows arch, even as she fought to keep her face blank.

Tain gestured at the door. "Perhaps it would be best if we spoke inside."

Richard gaped at him for a few seconds before he turned and moved toward the house.

Ashlyn started to follow. She'd taken a few steps when Christopher said, "Jeffrey's dead." Then he ran inside, the sound of footsteps fading as he sprinted up the stairs, legs quickly disappearing from Ashlyn's limited view inside the house.

Tracy Reimer just stood there, face blank and colorless. She looked from Ashlyn to Tain without so much as a shrug of her shoulders, a widening of her eyes or the tiniest hint of wrinkles on her brow.

Her husband walked up to her and said, "I'll call the lawyer."

Ashlyn saw Tain glance at her, and she gave a small shake of her head. Let Richard Reimer call. She wanted to know why he thought he needed a lawyer when he hadn't even asked what had happened to his son.

Or where his daughter was.

She wanted to know if this was the usual level of drama maintained in the Reimer household.

They followed Tracy Reimer inside. The house was neat and what Ashlyn would call showy. Just off the landing there were double glass doors that opened up to a living room, the kind with sofas that looked stiff and uncomfortable, as though they'd been taken out of plastic wrap the day before, and shelves with thick volumes of books that didn't have their spines cracked. There was no evidence of children in the room, not even family photos. The walls were a nondescript white, and there was no artwork to break the monotony. Ashlyn didn't sit down. Neither did Tain.

Tracy Reimer perched on the edge of the love seat, back straight, hands folded neatly on her lap.

From the hall Ashlyn heard the brusque words as Richard ordered his lawyer to meet them at their house immediately. Everything after that was answered with a "yes" or "no," so Ashlyn couldn't get a sense of the context. At one point Richard added, "family emergency," but that was followed by another "yes," and then he hung up.

"Our lawyer's on his way," he said as he entered the living room, without looking up. He sat on a chair that was beside, but at a slight angle to, the love seat, with such force that his wife glared at him for a moment. He was either unaware or ignoring her.

Ashlyn saw Tain's split-second glance but didn't intervene.

"Mr. Reimer, may I ask why you felt you needed your lawyer?" he asked.

Richard looked up, his hand mechanically massaging his jaw. "You can't question Christopher without a lawyer. He has rights."

"Mr. and Mrs. Reimer, we aren't here to question Christopher," Ashlyn said. "We're here to inform you that your son Jeffrey was found dead this morning at the water park at Rocky Point."

Richard stopped rubbing his chin and lowered his hand. "You mean, you haven't arrested Christopher?"

"Mr. Reimer, is there some reason why you'd assume Christopher would kill his brother?" Tain asked.

"Well . . ." He directed a wide-eyed stare at his wife, who quickly lowered her gaze, then held up his left hand, palm up, almost as though asking a question. "You brought him with you."

Would you have preferred we leave him at the park to walk home by himself? Ashlyn bit her bottom lip to keep from saying something she'd regret later.

"Christopher was found near the scene, and he identified Jeffrey. We—"

Tain was interrupted by a loud bang from upstairs. Richard and Tracy both sprang to their feet, but Ashlyn raised her hand and gestured for them to sit back down.

"Stay here," she ordered them as she reached for her gun.

Tain led the way to the foyer. Their visual checks were instinctive as they scanned the staircase and what they could see of the upper hallway. She followed Tain to the second floor, both with guns drawn.

These were the moments that required extreme mental focus. You never knew what you'd face around the next bend or behind a bathroom door. You hoped for the best, expected the worst and had to be ready to deal with anything.

Ashlyn was only a few steps behind Tain as he moved down the hallway and approached the first door, but she could see that it was open. Carefully, he looked into the room from the side of the doorway, then lowered his gun and stepped inside.

She still approached with caution, but when she glanced inside she could see enough from a mirror above the dresser to know it was safe to enter.

A child's room, obviously Jeffrey's. Unlike the sterile living room below this was a space that resonated with warmth. A car mat was on the floor beside the bed and a table with a train track on it was between the mat and the wall. Buckets in bright primary colors were overflowing with toys. The green walls were filled with posters of frogs, dinosaurs, Spider-Man, crayon drawings of spaceships, a photo of Jeffrey and Shannon laughing and hugging each other. In the far corner, between the window and the bed, there was a hammock filled with stuffed animals, and below that a shelf that had picture books spilling off it. Beneath the window there was a child's art desk and chair.

Christopher Reimer sat on the bed and held a string attached to a burst balloon. It was then that Ashlyn noticed the cluster of ribbons tied to the bedpost, one foil "happy birthday" balloon still bobbing in the air. The rest lay limp and lifeless in a pile on the floor.

The tear-stained cheeks were the only evidence of his earlier outburst. Christopher sat, slouched forward, gaze fixed on the floor, expressionless.

As Ashlyn reached back to holster her gun Tain said, "Wh—"

"Leave me alone!" Christopher sprang off the bed, ran out of the room, and seconds later they heard a door slam down the hall.

Tain looked at Ashlyn and shrugged. "That went well."

She shook her head and followed him back to the stairs. Richard Reimer had entered the foyer below and was opening the door. A man entered. The Reimers' lawyer had just arrived, and from their vantage point they could see enough to know who it was.

Byron Smythe.

A young lawyer who'd struck hard and fast with a high-profile case that had gotten him on speed dial with every criminal organization and lowlife with money in the Lower Mainland.

The kind of guy who never let his hair get a millimeter longer than he liked it, probably got a facial before every major court appearance, definitely invested in manicures, and the heaviest thing he'd ever lifted was his ego.

Ashlyn groaned. She'd made the mistake of thinking their morning couldn't get much worse. With a lawyer like Smythe on speed dial one thing was certain: the Reimers had things to hide. No wonder Christopher was acting strange. One of his siblings was dead, the other missing, and the first thing his parents did was call their attorney.

Byron Smythe.

And that meant their job had just gotten a lot more difficult.

CHAPTER THREE

"Where the hell were you?"

The man was perched on the edge of Craig's desk, one over-sized butt cheek spilling over the side like too much batter put on a waffle iron. He was leafing through the papers and file folders Craig had stacked on his work space. Craig looked away from Sergeant Frank Zidani as he removed his jacked and tried to will the tension out of his face.

Zidani persisted. "I asked you a question."

"Out." Craig set the coat on a hook and turned.

The sergeant glared at him. He was a solid guy with black hair. Zidani looked like he knew how to use his fists, and he sported a nose that had definitely been broken, possibly several times. He tossed the papers he was holding back on the desk and turned to face Craig directly.

"You forgetting your daddy isn't here to shield you anymore?"

Craig felt the rush of color coming up the back of his neck. "I never needed Sergeant Daly to protect me from anything."

"Right. Never got your partner killed either, did you?" Zidani slid off the desk, straightened up, turned and walked toward the door, then stopped and looked back, holding up his index finger as though he'd just remembered something.

"I was hoping your new partner would last a bit longer. Guess if you leave him here all the time I'll have nothing to worry about."

Before Craig had a chance to respond Zidani was gone.

Craig's new partner, Constable Luke Geller, stared at the papers on his desk just a little too hard to convince Craig that he found the contents riveting. Luke's brown hair was cut too short to conceal his intense expression, or to allow him to sneak glances without being easily detected.

Craig pushed his own "beyond regulation length" hair out of his face and sat down at his desk, which faced Luke's.

He'd been partnered with Luke Geller for a few months. A few quiet months. They were being fed vandalism complaints, the occasional domestic, and robbery. Nothing that would require them to work all hours of the day and night. Nothing high profile.

Nothing that would give them reason to draw their weapons.

Craig had bitten back his instinctive response when he was told he was going to be breaking in a rookie. With all the scandals in the news about the RCMP in recent years the bosses wanted him to take it "nice and easy" with the new boy.

Nice and easy with Luke Geller, bullshit. Craig knew what was going on. He was the one they were babying. For months his hands had been tied and he'd been kept from working on more serious cases.

Meanwhile, Sergeant Frank Zidani didn't miss a chance to take a shot at Craig, reminding him his last partner was dead.

The fact that Craig had almost died didn't seem to matter.

Acting sergeant, Craig reminded himself. A temporary fill-in. Until a final decision was made about whether Sergeant Daly would be returning to the Tri-Cities.

Since Craig had gone out to meet with Lisa Harrington, three messages had been left on his desk. He picked them up and skimmed the brief notes. One from Vish Dhaval, the boyfriend of Craig's deceased partner. Craig pulled the lowest drawer of his desk open and tossed the slip of paper in with the stack of other messages Vish had left over the months. Craig knew he should really throw those messages out.

He glanced up at Luke, who was still pretending to read at his desk, and thought maybe it would be a better idea to burn them.

The second message was from Alison, his stepmother. *Call me at home.* He thought she was supposed to be in Saskatchewan, but guessed she'd come back early to get ready for Christmas. Craig crumpled that one into a ball and tossed it in the empty garbage can beside his desk, and reached for the third message.

Craig leaned back in his chair. First Lisa Harrington. Now the man incarcerated for killing Lisa's daughter. Well, not the man himself, but his lawyer. Donny Lockridge's lawyer.

Donny Lockridge's sleazeball lawyer.

He could understand why Lisa Harrington had eventually been referred to Craig: His dad had worked the case, and his dad was currently out of the province. His dad's partner was retired, Craig knew that much. He didn't know what Ted Bicknell was doing these days. This time of year it was possible he was laying on a beach in Boca Raton.

Steve Daly didn't talk about his former partner.

Craig had never consciously concluded that before, but the truth hit home as he thought about it. He knew the name of his dad's former partner because of cop-shop talk, but he realized now he'd never heard Steve mention Ted Bicknell. Not even once.

"You want a soda, coffee or something?" he asked Luke as he stood and stuck the message in his pocket.

Luke didn't look up. "Thanks, I'll grab something later."

It only took a few minutes for Craig to leave the building and climb in his Rodeo. Once he'd pulled the door shut he took his cell phone out of his pocket and dialed the number for the lawyer.

Out of the office. He left a message saying he was returning Byron Smythe's call, and hung up. Then he dialed information.

"I'm looking for a number for Ted Bicknell. B-I-C-K-N-E-L-L."

"Which city?" the operator asked.

"Can you check the whole province?"

A sigh, followed by the clack-clack sound of keystrokes. "I'm sorry. No listing for a Ted Bicknell. And before you ask, no T. Bicknell either. I checked."

"In the entire province?" Craig asked.

The exhaled breath sounded less like a sigh and more like a huff this time. "I said I checked. If you have another name you'd like me to try . . ."

"No. Thanks." Craig hung up partway through the "Have a nice day" spiel. There were a few options. Ted Bicknell could be in BC, but just use a cell phone. He could have moved somewhere warm, or had family elsewhere in Canada and moved out of the province.

For all Craig knew, Bicknell had passed away and was permanently unreachable. Did it really matter? Odds were, Donny Lockridge's dirtbag lawyer was calling him as a last resort, for the same reason Lisa Harrington had. Because Smythe couldn't track down Ted Bicknell either and some lazy RCMP officer had directed him to Craig when he asked for Steve Daly.

Not lazy, Craig. That's not politically correct. You mean unmotivated.

But why would Lockridge's lawyer want to talk to the arresting officers after all this time? Craig had nothing to do with the case. His only tie to Lockridge was through his dad.

The cell phone buzzed and lit up. Craig flipped it open.

"Craig Nolan."

"Constable Craig Nolan?"

He didn't recognize the voice. "That's right."

"This is Emma Fenton, with the *Vancouver Sun*. I'm doing an article on Hope Harrington's mu—"

"No comment."

"Mr. Nolan, you haven't even heard—"

"I didn't work that case, and I have no idea why you're calling me."

"Alison Daly."

The name was blurted out in a rush, presumably as a way to keep him from hanging up. If that was Emma Fenton's intention, she succeeded.

"Mr. Nolan, it was Alison Daly who gave me your phone number."

The reporter paused. Craig could only assume she was hoping he'd say something, show some sign of curiosity, but instead he gripped the headrest of the front passenger seat with his free hand and bit his lip.

"I was hoping we could speak in person," she said.

Craig closed his eyes and counted to ten. When he opened his eyes he still felt the skin on the back of his neck burn. "If you have a question, ask."

He heard her draw a breath. "Fine. There's a rumor of legal action over the wrongful conviction of Donny Lockridge for the murder of Hope Harrington ten years ago."

And what does that have to do with me? Things were starting to make sense. Lockridge's lawyer, now a reporter . . . Had Lisa Harrington known something more before they met? Why hadn't she said something?

"Mr. Nolan?"

He rubbed his brow with his thumb and forefinger. "That wasn't a question, Ms. Fenton."

"Emma." She paused, but he didn't respond, so she continued. "Really, Mr. Nolan, I'm just trying to get to the truth. We could meet for lunch, on the newspaper's dime. All I want to do is get the facts straight."

Craig glanced at his watch. 11:28 A.M. "I've already eaten." A lie, but there was no way in hell he was meeting her, or saying anything until he knew what was going on.

"Coffee then."

"Ms. Fenton—"

"Emma."

"Look . . . I have no comment. I didn't work this case. I have no knowledge of any legal action."

"So you deny being contacted by Donny Lockridge's lawyer?"

Craig swore beneath his breath. Who could have told this reporter that Byron Smythe had tried to contact him? He hadn't even known about that himself until less than half an hour ago.

"I have no comment."

This time he lowered the phone and cut the call. Why the hell had his stepmother given a reporter his cell-phone number?

There was no time like the present to find out. He flipped the phone open and dialed.

Six rings later Craig snapped the phone closed. There was no answer.

"If it had just rained today. I never let the kids out in the rain. Shannon wanted to walk to school early, to meet friends . . . It's the Lower Mainland, it's December, it should be raining. Shouldn't it be raining?" Mrs. Reimer looked up from where she stood on the front sidewalk, her dull eyes suddenly wide, as though she'd just had a sudden revelation, received a flash of insight. Her lawyer spoke in hushed tones as Mr. Reimer locked the front door to the house, then hurried down the steps. He took his wife's arm, turning her away from Ashlyn and Tain.

Ashlyn knew grief did strange things to people. It derailed reason and made the mind latch on to the most trivial things. Like, *If only Bobby had let me give him one more hug, he wouldn't have been running across the street at that second and been struck by that speeding car.* Or, *If I'd just let Sally take the jeep she never would have been walking to the bus stop* . . . And sometimes the mind obsessed on one key point the person couldn't let go of. Some trivial detail about the crime, the events, or a ridiculous question born out of desperation and false hope. Her personal favorite: *Do you think he suffered?* The eyes pleading with you to tell them it was quick, that the victim likely didn't even know what was happening. *No, ma'am. Being murdered didn't hurt. Probably hardly noticed.*

Today it was about blame. *If it had just rained today. I never let the kids out in the rain.* As though the weather were responsible. Your child goes out to play because it isn't raining. Your child is murdered. If it had been raining your child wouldn't have gone outside. They'd still be alive. Therefore, it was the weather's fault. The mind's weird way of trying to make sense of the senseless, to apply logic to madness.

It took more than a break in the rain to create a murderer. Ashlyn knew that. Even days of going stir crazy with cabin fever

from being stuck inside because of the constant winter downpour didn't make a person run outside and beat someone to
death.

People tried to find something they could pin it on so that
they assign blame without confronting anything too uncomfortable. Blame the weather or the hugs or a split-second decision,
but don't blame the killer. Don't acknowledge that there are bad
people in the world who aren't guided by the same moral com-
pass as the rest of us.

People who would kill a child.

Ashlyn wondered if this was the product of some twisted form
of karmic logic. Put good out into the universe and it comes
back to you, so if bad things happen you must have done something to deserve it so it must be your fault . . . right?

With her job it just wasn't possible to buy into that. Crime
could touch anyone. Some people were at risk, and the average
person comforted himself with the thought that the victims had
done something to deserve it, that it made sense they'd been
raped, mugged or murdered because they shouldn't have been in
that part of town at night or been doing drugs or having a drink
in that kind of bar.

Bringing reason into it to assume control. What they were really saying was *It couldn't happen to me because I don't live like that.*
Using faulty logic to convince themselves they weren't vulnerable when sometimes crime is as unpredictable as a tornado that
reduces one home to a pile of rubble and leaves the house next
door intact. Why one and not the other? Why this street and not
the next?

In her relatively short time with the RCMP Ashlyn had
learned one thing for certain: When it came to murder, *why* was
usually pretty damn irrelevant. Oh, it mattered to her as a cop.
It was a question she usually had to answer to solve a case. But
knowing why wouldn't bring back the dead, and sometimes the
trivial reasons why one person would end another's life left you
feeling nothing but hollow. The reasons usually weren't good
enough to make sense of it.

At times Tain's gaze seemed to have the force of a magnetic

pull. Sixth sense kicked in, and she knew he was watching her with those dark eyes. She looked up.

He tipped his head to the side, just a bit. A nod toward the couple. She looked at Mr. and Mrs. Reimer.

They walked down the driveway solemnly. Although she'd been deep in thought, Ashlyn had been aware of them the whole time, of Mr. Reimer telling his wife it was time to go, of their lawyer advising them it was best they take some time to discuss things privately. Of Mrs. Reimer's wide-eyed expression, as though her revelation about the weather would somehow change things. The break in the stream of tears that had finally come, long after Christopher had blurted out the news, hinted at misplaced hope, as though it were possible to unwind time and do things differently, summon the rain in the morning and save her child's life.

The woman was in denial, not that Ashlyn could blame her.

Mr. Reimer hadn't said a word. His eyes hadn't widened or narrowed. No color dissolved from his cheeks. He had remained expressionless the entire time, and now he gripped his wife's elbow and steered her toward the car.

TV camera crews had descended in the past half hour. News had leaked out somehow, and Ashlyn had been forced to call in patrol cars to keep the press off the Reimer property, which had prompted the lawyer's decision to take the Reimer family away from their residence for the afternoon.

Christopher was already in the back of the vehicle. Once Mr. and Mrs. Reimer were strapped inside, doors closed, Byron Smythe walked back to the sidewalk where Tain and Ashlyn stood.

Even the way he carried himself made Ashlyn nauseated. Mr. Tall, Dark and God's Gift to Women with the cocky grin and what she thought of as rented biceps. Kind of guy who went to the gym and did his thirty minutes five days a week just to keep the image, but had never done any manual labor in his entire life.

Style over substance.

He flashed her his custom-designed smile. "I trust you'll keep me apprised of all developments on this case."

"You'll be notified of anything relevant to your clients immediately." She pushed the corners of her mouth up deliberately. "Assuming, of course, we can reach you."

He took a small silver case out of his jacket pocket and removed a card. "Work and personal numbers. Day or night, Ms. Hart."

"Constable Hart."

"Funny, I thought you'd been known to let the personal and professional intersect from time to time."

"It's the line between respectable and repugnant I don't cross."

He flashed his smile again and held the card out to her. "We'll have to assess your boundaries another time."

She bit back her retort and took the card.

Once Byron Smythe had returned to his car and driven away Tain said, "You know, it could be fun to slap a sexual harassment charge on that bastard."

"Fun for you, maybe. I'd rather not deal with the pompous ass, myself."

"Maybe I'm scarred because he didn't leer at me and give me his phone number."

"Oh, that's rich, coming from the guy who smacked my ass at a crime scene last summer."

Tain cracked a smile. "Guess I never could make that fly."

"And I hate to tell you this, but you aren't living up to your reputation as a sexist pig these days, either."

"You know how it is. If I come off as nice and reasonable for a while the women lower their guard."

Ashlyn laughed.

"Feels good, doesn't it?" Tain's smile faded. "But then you start to feel guilty."

Ashlyn looked back at the Reimer family home, at the upstairs window to what had been Jeffrey Reimer's bedroom. Now it was just a painful reminder.

"I don't think we'll have much to feel good about with this case," she said.

Tain looked up at the window as well. "No, I don't suppose

we will." He reached for his ringing cell phone. After a few one-word responses he hung up and paused as he looked her in the eye.

Ashlyn groaned. "Don't tell me."

Tain nodded. "Sergeant Zidani wants to see us in his office."

"May as well get this over with," Ashlyn muttered as she followed him to their car.

Craig felt the knots in his shoulders loosen when he saw the familiar figure leaning over his desk. He bent over her shoulder and glanced at the note she was writing.

"I know you can't make lunch. That's why we're eating out."

She turned and gave him a look. "Very funny."

He held up his hands as he sat down. "It wasn't a shot at your culinary skills." He smiled. "Or lack thereof."

Ashlyn's eyes pinched as she leaned back against his desk and glared at him. "My peanut butter sandwiches are as good as anyone's."

Said with jest, but there was something in her eyes. A weight. "You guys catch something bad?" he asked.

"A murder. Four-year-old boy."

"Domestic?"

She opened her mouth to answer, but said nothing. Craig was used to the vacuous look she got when she was deep in thought. In as much time as it took to snap your fingers the look was gone. She glanced at Luke and shook her head. "It's . . . messy."

Craig looked at Luke, who was again avoiding eye contact. He seemed to have an endless supply of fascinating paperwork to read. Couldn't the guy take a hint and go find himself a cup of coffee or a window to stare out of?

"And you haven't got time to eat?"

A thin smile. "We've been summoned to the sergeant's office."

"Lucky you."

Her eyebrow rose and the hint of a real smile tugged at her mouth for a few seconds, then faded. "It'll probably go further than that. This one's bad."

Children always were, for a variety of reasons, but something about the way she said it made him suspect this one was more complicated than usual. "You know where to find me."

She nodded. "What about you? Working on something interesting?"

He surveyed the thin pile of paperwork on his desk. "More annoying than anything." Craig made the mistake of looking up in time to see the softening around her eyes. The longer he was kept on the sidelines at work the more she worried about him.

Tain approached them and Craig offered a quick nod. "Tough case, I hear."

No hint of emotion on Tain's face, just a one-word reply. "Yeah." Tain had a way of packing so much meaning into one single syllable. When Craig, Ashlyn and Tain had first worked together Craig and Tain had barely moved from open hostility to thinly veiled loathing.

In the end, they'd both earned a grudging respect for each other. Then, when they'd all been transferred to the Tri-Cities they'd ended up working together. Ashlyn and Tain had been partnered, and when the case was finished they continued working together.

Once Ashlyn had been cleared to return to active duty.

"Zidani's waiting for us," Tain said as he glanced at his partner.

"Lambs to the slaughter." She straightened up and followed Tain out the doorway.

Craig rolled his chair toward his desk and picked up the note she'd started to write. She'd only written that she couldn't make lunch, nothing more. He'd interrupted her before she'd even had a chance to sign it.

She'd never leave anything too personal for him at work anyway. It wasn't her style.

He crunched up the slip of paper and tossed the ball in the garbage can beside his desk and was about to pick up the phone when he took a second glance.

Other than the note he'd just thrown in, the garbage can was empty.

A quick glance at the can sitting beside Luke's desk confirmed it was half-full.

He looked up. For once, Luke had made himself scarce and disappeared so quietly Craig couldn't even be sure if he'd left when Tain had arrived, or afterward.

Craig decided to take the opportunity to make one quick call before his partner returned. It only took a few seconds to dial his stepmother's phone number.

And it only took a minute to confirm there was still no answer.

When Ashlyn and Tain arrived at Sergeant Frank Zidani's office—his temporary office, which still had the name *Steve Daly* posted outside—Zidani didn't invite them to sit down or even offer a casual greeting. Instead, he glared at Ashlyn.

"Have you screwed this up already?"

Her only response was to stare back. The muscles in the back of her neck pulled tight, and she knew her instinctive retort would lead to more trouble than it was worth, even if it would feel so good for a moment to tell Zidani off, just once.

"Well, what have you got?" It was supposed to be a question, but he had a way of growling the words so they sounded aggressive, accusing.

"Four-year-old boy named Jeffrey Reimer. Found at the water park in Rocky Point Park in Port Moody. He—"

"How'd the call come in?"

Ashlyn swallowed. Zidani refused to just let them run through the details. He had to keep them off balance and jump all over the place.

"He was located by Port Moody police officers after an anonymous 911 call about an assault at the park."

"I take it you haven't tracked the source of the call yet." Zidani leaned back in his chair, arms folded across his chest, scowl firmly in place.

"We located a witness who's identified a possible suspect."

"Who's this witness?"

"Christopher Reimer, the older brother o—"

"How much older?"

"He's eleven." Ashlyn bit back the urge to slap a sarcastic "sir" on the end of that.

"Who'd he identify as the killer?"

"Shannon Reimer, age sixteen."

The scowl deepened. "Motive?"

Ashlyn paused. "We haven't been able to establish that yet."

Zidani leaned forward. "Constable Hart, what exactly have you been doing all this time?"

"What do you think?"

Zidani pounded his fist against the desk and then pointed a meaty finger at her. "I asked you a question. I expect a direct answer, not some smart-ass remark." He leaned back in his chair and proffered a heartless smile. "Now, I'm going to pretend you didn't just get mouthy with a superior officer. Let's try this again. What have you been doing all this time?"

"My job." Ashlyn felt her chin jut out. As hard as she tried to stay calm she could feel her cheeks flush with anger. Zidani had no right to question the quality of their work. A few hours into the call and they already had an eyewitness who'd identified a suspect. "We worked the scene and did an extensive search. Constable Sims is still on site, in charge. Once we located the witness and identified the victim and potential suspect, Constable Tain and I went to the Reimer house to make notification to the parents, but they insisted on calling their lawyer before we told them their daughter is a suspect and—"

"Who's the lawyer?"

"Byron Smythe."

"The dead kid . . ." Zidani snapped his fingers a few times. "What's his dad's name?"

Tain answered. "Richard Reimer."

Zidani didn't acknowledge Tain and kept his gaze on Ashlyn. "Known criminal connections?"

"We haven't been able to check yet. We didn't know Smythe was the family lawyer until he arrived and right after they left you called us in."

"What about the daughter? Is Smythe bringing her in for questioning?"

"She's missing."

"She's missing? What the hell are you doing here?"

"You called us and ordered us to report in." Before he could do more than snarl at her Ashlyn continued. "We have her photo and information in circulation. We're going to check her friends, extended family, talk to the teachers. A teenage girl is more likely to go to someone she knows, and the uniforms have the streets covered."

Zidani glowered at her for a moment. It appeared he couldn't think of a way to argue with that, but guessing what was going through his mind wasn't her main concern.

"How was the boy killed?" he asked.

"Beaten to death. Possibly a baseball bat. We'll be waiting on the coroner's report, but there was a note made at the scene about a splinter of wood in one of the wounds. Speculation is a blow to the back of the head is what ultimately caused death."

"Reporters are going to be all over this." Zidani tapped his fingers on the desk. "It may be best to reassign the case."

"On what grounds?" Ashlyn demanded. She felt her body stiffen.

"Are you questioning me?" Zidani stood, the scowl deepening.

"Damn right I am," Ashlyn said, ignoring the light touch of Tain's hand on her arm. "We've handled this case like professionals, and you have no grounds to remove us."

"What about the little matter of a series of child murders you two worked? Didn't end so well, did it? You shot the suspect, Hart, and he jumped out a window. To his death. And as though that wasn't enough for one day, you killed a cop."

"You make it sound like I'm trigger happy and reckless, and you are way off base." She could feel the heat in her cheeks. "I was cleared of any wrongdoing in both incidents, and you have no right to stick that in my face."

"I have no right? Well, what about those reporters out there? You think they made your life difficult before? You wait until they publicly question your ability to handle this. The RCMP doesn't need another scandal right now, and I don't think you're emotionally able to handle the pressure. How you've responded to me is proof of that."

"No, it isn't. I'm pissed off with you because I'm sick of your sexist bullshit. You pull me in here, prevent me from giving a proper report and then jump down my throat with accusations. Same crap we've had from you since day one. What you're re-ally saying is you aren't prepared to back me because you don't like me."

Zidani planted both hands on his desk and leaned forward. "You think you can handle this, Hart? Then you'd better. Because if you screw this up I'll actually enjoy watching the press and senior brass chew you up and spit you out."

She returned his stare for a moment. "Is that all?"

He glared back for another few seconds and then jerked his head in the direction of the door. She turned and yanked it open, and stomped down the hallway.

"Ash." She sensed Tain reach for her arm and pulled it from beyond his grasp, but did turn to face him.

"I'm sick of his garbage, Tain. I'm—" Ashlyn pulled in a shaky breath. Her eyes were burning with hot tears, unshed, and she blinked them back rapidly. Tain reached out and squeezed her shoulder.

"It's a tough case, and he's an asshole. You can't let him get to you. You're the best partner I've ever had."

"I'm the only partner you've had who's lasted." Her hand went to her mouth even as she spoke the words, as she realized what she'd said, and she squeezed her eyes shut. "I'm sorry. I didn't mean—"

"It's okay."

When she opened her eyes she could see the hurt, but there wasn't anger. Tain had earned a name for himself. He was known for being difficult to work with, and he was aware of what his colleagues thought of him. She knew that. He'd admitted once that he worked hard to maintain his standing as a hard-ass, and she was a threat to his image. One of the things she liked about him was that he didn't pretend it was unfair, either. He knew his reputation was more than justified.

But she also knew there was a lot more to Tain than the person he'd been a few years ago.

She released her breath and rubbed her forehead, which allowed her to look down for a moment and get herself together. When she looked back up he gave her a pat on the arm.

"What's next?" he asked her.

"Shannon's school. Let's see if we can find out if any of her friends missed class today."

Tain nodded. "School it is."

CHAPTER FOUR

"I have three possibles," Ashlyn said as she joined Tain near the school parking lot. "Don't take it personally."

"Why should I? Just because a man with an RCMP badge is still a man and girls are less likely to talk to him . . ." Tain shrugged. "It's no big deal. People often underestimate the strengths of partnering with a woman. You can charm the socks off anyone."

Ashlyn felt her nose wrinkle instinctively. "Not that I want to."

Tain nodded at the notebook in her hand. "So what did you find out?"

"Three good friends who aren't here today either. The teachers I spoke to confirmed Shannon should have been in class this morning, but wasn't, but they'd only speak to me strictly off the record." Ashlyn followed his gaze, which was now on the students returning from lunch break. "Any special reason you're here?"

"Looking for the boyfriend."

Ashlyn shook her head and smiled. "How'd you get that?"

"You know how it is. Guys will talk to guys. They'd be too busy hitting on you to think about your questions."

"Is that supporting sexism or just using it in your favor?"

"I've seen you flirt to get someone to talk to you."

"In your dreams, maybe."

"You know that's why guys like Zidani are afraid of you."

"What?" She said it so loudly a few heads turned and she

drew a deep breath. "First you call me a flirt and now you say Zidani's scared of me because of it. You're nuts."

Tain shook his head. "I didn't call you a flirt. You just use your charm to your advantage. It's no different for guys."

Ashlyn thought about that. "All those rape cases last year. The women all talked to Craig."

Tain nodded. "He made them feel secure. None of them would talk to Lori."

Although he suppressed it quickly, Ashlyn had seen the passing look of regret the moment Lori's name slipped out. She hadn't liked Lori much as a person, but she'd never had as much guilt over killing Lori as Tain and Craig thought.

Lori had shot and killed an unarmed man, and critically wounded Craig. Ashlyn did what she had to do. Lori died.

Ashlyn chose not to focus on that. "It's okay, you know. I'm not going to fall apart if you say her name."

"I know." Tain gave her one of his looks. During the months they'd worked together she'd learned to read him about ninety percent of the time, but this wasn't one of those easily decipherable expressions. It made her wonder if he worried about her, if he thought she'd been scarred by what had happened.

He nodded at a car pulling into the lot. She turned and saw an old Mustang with a personalized license plate on the front pull in.

"This should be him," Tain said.

Ashlyn let Tain take the lead and followed him to the parking lot. As the teenager got out of his car Tain held up his ID. "Matt Lewis?"

The gangly youth pushed his floppy brown hair back from his face, glanced at Tain's ID, then looked at Ashlyn. Matt held a small stack of books with one arm and stood with the door to the car still open.

"Yeah?"

"I'm Constable Tain, and this is Constable Hart. We'd like to ask you a few questions."

Still no sign of surprise, confusion or any emotion on Matt's face. "Uh . . . okay."

"Do you know what this is about?" Ashlyn asked him.

He gaped at her for a second, then shut his mouth and shook his head.

"Yet you have no problem answering questions for us." From the corner of her eye, Ashlyn noticed Tain giving her a look, and this was one of his looks she had no trouble reading at all. She ignored him.

Matt shrugged. "Should I? You going to jack me up on some bogus charge?"

Tain shook his head. "We were hoping we could ask you about Shannon Reimer."

Matt shifted the books from one arm to the other and pushed his car door shut. "What about her?"

"You know her?" Tain asked.

"Sure. She's my girlfriend." He shrugged again. "You wouldn't be asking me about her if you didn't know that already."

Ashlyn bit her lip. From another kid this would be pure wise-ass commentary, but Matt Lewis had a casual, unaffected way of talking that made it sound like an innocent observation. "Have you seen Shannon today?"

Matt shook his head. "She hasn't been in class."

"We're trying to track down some of her close friends. Can you tell us if there's anyone else we should talk to?" Ashlyn passed him the slip of paper listing the names she'd been given.

Matt looked at it and shook his head. "They're her best friends."

Ashlyn didn't reach for the list as he tried to pass it back. "Any of them missing from school today?"

For the first time Matt exhaled and his brow wrinkled, but he looked at the list and said, "Jody Hoath."

He extended his hand again, and Ashlyn forced the nicest smile she could manage. "Do you have their phone numbers or addresses, by chance? All of them, just in case."

Matt paused. He propped the books up on his knee, dug in his pockets until he found a pen. Then he fished in his other pocket until he pulled out a cell phone. He punched some buttons and then made a note on the slip of paper. After the third note, when he tried to hand it back to Ashlyn, she took it from him.

Street addresses and phone numbers for all three girls.

"If that's all . . ." Matt started to walk away from them, toward the school building.

"You know, Matt, most people would want to know why we're asking about their girlfriend. Most people wouldn't be too quick to give out phone numbers and addresses if they didn't know what we wanted to talk to their friends about."

He stopped but didn't look back. "Is that a question?"

"No," Ashlyn said. "Just an observation. Tell me something." She waited until he did turn around. His mouth was in a tight line, but his wide-eyed look gave it away. He was scared.

"You said you hadn't seen Shannon today. Have you spoken to her?"

They stood for a moment, staring at each other. She could see the color draining from his face. Then the school bell rung, and Matt jerked his thumb in the direction of the building.

"I've gotta go."

Ashlyn nodded at his car. "You might want to lock this first, though."

Matt swallowed but didn't say anything.

Ashlyn turned and walked away, trusting Tain to follow her. Her path formed a U. She went back to the entrance to the parking lot Matt had entered from, then she followed the sidewalk on the other side of the fence back toward where the Mustang was parked. Once she was close enough to watch him Ashlyn moved beside a large tree.

"What's gotten into you today?" Tain asked her.

She shook her head. "I don't know. Everything about this whole case seems off. Like someone playing a piano that's just slightly out of tune, you know?"

From where they stood they had two distinct advantages. They were close to where they'd parked, and the spot provided a clear view of Matt Lewis. Matt had returned to his car and locked the door after they'd left. He'd also taken the time to remove his cell phone and, after a quick glance in the direction of the entrance to the parking lot, made a call.

"Number seems to be programmed in," Ashlyn said.

"He's probably warning her. Which means he talked to her today. He knows something."

Ashlyn rolled her eyes deliberately as she gave Tain a look. "Duh. Did you hear how he was talking? He never even asked why we wanted to talk to him about Shannon. He knew."

"Well, maybe he doesn't know, exactly. How do you want to play this? We could go back—"

"Hang on." She nodded at Matt's car. He'd closed the phone, unlocked the door, tossed his books on the backseat and climbed in. As soon as the brake lights went on Ashlyn started to move. "Maybe he'll lead us right to her."

"I suppose stranger things have happened."

"We get along," she said as she flashed him a smile.

Tain said, "Point taken," as they opened their car doors.

It wasn't hard to follow Matt Lewis. The personalized license plates, INXTC, helped.

"Do you ever wonder what the hell parents are thinking, letting their kid get a plate like that?" Ashlyn asked.

"Be thankful. It's a public service. Combined with erratic driving I'm sure it's probable cause to search a vehicle."

She smiled. Matt led them to Anmore. One of four villages that were part of the Greater Vancouver Area, the Village of Anmore was a tiny area to the north of Port Moody, on the way to scenic Buntzen Lake. Although it wasn't far from the shores of the Burrard Inlet, the elevation made a considerable difference in the weather, and it wasn't uncommon to drive the few kilometers to Anmore and discover snow on the ground while most of the Lower Mainland remained damp and green.

Ashlyn looked at the addresses Matt had written down. "My guess is we're on our way to Nurani Patel's. Assuming he wasn't giving us false information."

After another turn Tain said, "Look's like that's the house." He slowed the vehicle and pulled over to the side of the road.

"That's the right address." She nodded at the figure coming down the long driveway, bundled in a heavy sweater pulled tight around her slender body. "Shall we?"

The roads were quiet that time of year, without the usual

steady stream of traffic heading out to the lake and the hiking trails surrounding it. In all likelihood Matt had heard their vehicle pull over. Despite the trees lining the property the hedge was low in front, providing them with a clear view of the driveway. If he turned around he would see them immediately, so there was no point watching and waiting.

They got out of the vehicle, both closing their doors quietly, and began to walk toward Matt's Mustang, which was pulled over at the base of the driveway. He had his back to them, and despite Nurani's height still concealed her from view.

"But how do they know?"

That's what Ashlyn heard the girl say first, because she'd raised her voice. The agitation was obvious.

"Beats me. They just showed up at school and started asking questions."

"And you talked to them? You—"

Ashlyn had come far enough around that Matt was no longer shielding her view of Nurani. The girl looked up and over, and went silent the second her gaze met Ashlyn's. Her brown eyes widened. "Oh, God."

Ashlyn and Tain lowered their IDs as Matt turned. His mouth hung open for a moment, and he tried twice to say something and failed. Finally, he took a breath. "What are you doing here?"

"You did give us this address," Tain said.

"You what?" Nurani glared at Matt and for the first time his cheeks filled with color.

"Look, I tried to get them to go to Jody's house."

"And it was a nice try," Ashlyn said. "Except we walk away and suddenly you need to make an urgent phone call. Either you phoned your friend Nurani here, or you phoned Shannon or one of the other girls to warn them. But since Nurani was expecting you I'm guessing you called her." She watched his face for a moment, but he said nothing. "Feel free to jump in and tell me if I'm wrong."

"Look, I didn't tell you anything. You asked if Shannon had any other real close friends. I told you the truth."

"And we asked if any of her friends hadn't been in class today, and you said Jody Hoath," Tain said. "Yet here you are, talking to Nurani Patel. Unless your class has a field trip to her house this afternoon, she isn't at school either."

"I didn't say Jody was the only one absent. I just said she wasn't there." Matt let out a breath. "I didn't lie."

"You didn't lie, but you may have hindered a criminal investigation," Ashlyn said.

"Criminal investigation?" Matt practically squawked the words. "What are you talking about? You guys are finally going to do something?"

Ashlyn stared at him for a few seconds, wondering what he meant. Finally do something?

"Maybe we can back up a bit here, clear this up," Tain said. "What are you talking about?"

It was Matt's turn to have his jaw drop open, and then he shook his head. "I-I don't think I should talk to you."

Ashlyn squeezed her eyes shut for a few seconds, counted to five and tried to push all the agitation out of her voice. "Listen, all we're trying to do is find Shannon."

"She's sixteen. She can do what she wants," Nurani said. "You can't make her go back."

"Whoa. We just want to talk to her." Tain's voice was calm, almost hypnotically soothing.

Nobody spoke for a moment. There was nothing but a slight breeze to break the calm. Ashlyn fought her urge to snap at the two teenagers. They had a dead boy and a missing girl. Whatever high school drama they'd stepped in the middle of, it was wasting their time.

Nurani started to shake her head and held up her hand. "You can forget it. I won't help you."

"It doesn't matter anyway," Matt said. "Shannon didn't tell us where she was going. She knew we might get in trouble so she didn't want us to know."

"But you did speak to her this morning," Ashlyn said.

Matt glanced at Nurani, who was staring at him wide-eyed. Ashlyn could just imagine the girl willing him to keep his mouth shut.

He shook his head. "No. I talked to her last night. After she'd packed."

Ashlyn looked at Tain. She wondered if he was as frustrated as she was.

If he was, he didn't let it affect his voice. "Why was Shannon packing?"

Matt looked at Nurani again. The girl blew out a big breath and rolled her eyes. "Why do you think?" Nurani said. "She was running away."

Craig finished up the last bit of paperwork from his latest case, if he could call it that. A stolen bicycle, which was generally a seasonal crime in the rest of Canada, but in the GVA winter meant rain. The occasional snowfall didn't usually last long. Give a child a bicycle in November and the minute the downpour turned to a drizzle he would be outside if his parents let him.

The theft was important to the boy, who'd been knocked off his bike and had it literally stolen out from under him. And it was a good thing they'd caught the little thief so that they could return the bike. They'd been able to give the young criminal the government-sanctioned frown, the only punishment considered appropriate for a kid that age in this country.

No wonder crime was on the rise.

"Nolan, my office. Now."

Zidani didn't wait for him to follow. As soon as the sergeant was gone Luke looked up from his desk. "I take it I'm not invited?"

"If he doesn't order you to bend over I wouldn't volunteer for a spanking." Craig got up and walked down the hall to his father's office, the one Zidani was using. A constant reminder that Sergeant Daly's future in the Tri-Cities remained undecided, even after all this time.

There wasn't much Daly had taken with him when he'd been reassigned, because he never kept much personal stuff in the office, but the space seemed darker, colder, almost soulless without him.

Zidani spat out a question the moment he saw Craig in the doorway. "You don't like me much, do you?"

Craig paused. It was a question with no right answer. The only "acceptable" response he could think of was a blatant lie, and Zidani would know instantly. He already knew what Craig thought of him. Some things couldn't be denied. The only question was whether or not Craig would play the game, try to be diplomatic long enough to avoid a confrontation, maybe earn himself some credit from his temporary supervisor.

Zidani stood and leaned back against the window ledge, behind the desk. Steve Daly's office was unusual in layout, because it was a corner room. From the entrance the desk was to the left, with a tall, narrow window behind it. Daly had kept one picture on the wall, to the side of the window, and otherwise the wall that bordered the hallway and the space on the far side of the window were filled with bookshelves and cabinets.

The far wall also had a window, but it was partially concealed by a freestanding whiteboard that had been brought in, when Craig, Tain and Ashlyn had worked together. Those cases had led to Steve's temporary reassignment, and the whiteboard hadn't been removed before his departure.

"Come in." Zidani remained perched on the window ledge, arms folded, scowl in place.

Craig stepped inside but left the door open.

"I asked you a question."

"Respectfully, I'll decline to answer."

Zidani grunted. "So now you think you can play nice?"

Another loaded question. Craig remained silent.

"You've been on the shelf for a while," Zidani said.

There was no sense denying it. Zidani could be baiting him, hoping he'd jump at the chance to get back in rotation with more serious crimes. Before he reminded Craig of all his perceived shortcomings and why that wasn't going to happen.

Or was he seriously thinking about resolving this stalemate?

"What do you think of Geller?"

Craig paused. "Seems competent."

The beady-eyed stare didn't waiver. "A few months in and that's all you've got to say?"

What do you expect when you hand us routine cases and make sure we spend more time at our desks than on the street?

It seemed as though Zidani had read Craig's mind, because something resembling a smile replaced the scowl. "Fair enough. You two need a chance to get on the street."

Zidani would get no argument from Craig, but he still kept his mouth shut.

"I want you to handle something." The sergeant nodded at two boxes sitting on his desk. "Convicted killer is applying for early parole. Since the cops who made the arrest aren't available I thought you could step in, make sure there won't be any problems. Scum like this should never see the light of day, if you ask me."

Craig stepped up to the desk and looked at the label on the box. Evidence in the Hope Harrington murder investigation.

"Think you can handle it?" Zidani asked.

"Isn't this a—"

"All you're doing is reviewing the material, checking up on any loose ends. Make sure we have nothing to worry about."

Craig returned Zidani's stare for a moment, then nodded. "Is Constable Geller working on this with me?"

Zidani pushed himself up off the window ledge and grunted again. "This'll only keep you busy a few days. Then you guys can hit the streets." He sat down in his chair and picked up the phone.

Craig grabbed the boxes and left. First Lisa Harrington. Then the lawyer and the reporter. Now Zidani. He felt his stomach twist. Something wasn't right about this. Since when did they review files to make sure a case was solid ten years after someone was convicted, unless . . . Craig thought about what the reporter had said on the phone and swallowed. He was being cut loose to work on his own for a few days on a case long closed, after being assured it was a routine task, so why did he feel like he was being set up?

* * *

Tain and Ashlyn sat in the car in silence for a moment before he stated the obvious. "I think we stand a better chance if you call."

She turned her head to the side so she could glare at him.

He shrugged. "You don't hate me. You hate that I'm right."

Her mouth twisted into a half smile as she removed the card from her pocket that she'd reluctantly taken hours before. It only took a moment for her to reach Byron Smythe and explain the reason for her call.

"You'd like permission to search the house." The way Smythe spoke, it wasn't a question. It was a regurgitation of her request, with attitude inferring the answer.

"Actually, we're only interested in searching Shannon's room at this time."

"And clearly, since you're asking permission, you don't have a search warrant."

Ashlyn rubbed her forehead. "In the spirit of cooperation I thought we'd ask, since it's in your client's best interests that we find their daughter quickly as possible. They've already lost one child. I'm sure they're anxious to have Shannon home safe and sound."

"However, they aren't anxious to have the police invade their privacy so that they can pursue unfounded charges against a sixteen-year-old girl."

"I—"

"I'm sorry, Ms. Hart. You'll have to find another reason to see me."

Ashlyn clenched her teeth. What she wouldn't give to wipe the self-assured smile she could hear in his words right off his face.

He wasn't finished. "Don't worry. I'm sure we'll be seeing a lot of each other very soon."

She terminated the call without another word, let out a deep breath and looked up.

Only the ghost of a smile lingered on Tain's lips. "That went well."

"Never expect a skunk to smell nice."

He laughed. "I thought the saying was, 'A leopard never changes its spots.'"

"I prefer to think of sleazy lawyers as closer to vermin." She leaned back against the headrest, eyes closed for a moment. "With Byron Smythe involved we're going to need rock solid evidence to get in the house. And now he knows we want to search."

"He can't tamper with evidence."

"Well, technically, he can. We'd just have to prove it in order to charge him." She rubbed her forehead. "He doesn't know what we're looking for."

Tain didn't answer. That was all the proof she needed: Her words had sounded as hollow to him as she knew they were. A lawyer like Byron Smythe would figure it out in no time at all. If he believed there was something in the house that could help them he'd try to find it first.

And he didn't need to tamper with anything to look. If he confirmed what was missing, he'd know the truth.

"We're losing time. All we really wanted to do was prove whether or not the kids were lying." Ashlyn opened her eyes and looked at Tain. "We need to find another way to do that."

"You can forget arresting those kids and taking them in for questioning. If you thought Zidani came down on you before . . ."

"It would waste too much time, anyway. You think Nurani's parents don't have a lawyer on retainer, with a house like that? We—" Her cell phone rang and she lifted it to look at the caller ID, answered and listened to the voice on the other end. "We'll be right there," she said, and hung up.

Tain reached to start the car. "Sims?"

She nodded as she clipped her seat belt. "He's found something he wants us to see."

Craig wondered how his dad had felt when he stood over the body of sixteen-year-old Hope Harrington.

It was easier than acknowledging how he felt himself, just going over the evidence.

The school photo in the file set the stage. A beautiful girl, slender, creamy skin, with silky black hair and gentle blue eyes.

Sometimes blue eyes seemed cold, but Hope's eyes were like a warm sky on a cloudless day. There was something in her shy smile, but even the hint of self-consciousness that crept in couldn't conceal the fact that Hope had been a lovely girl.

Underneath her simple beauty there was another story that came through. Perhaps it was the faded blouse, the lack of makeup or the absence of any jewelry other than a locket around her neck. Craig couldn't put his finger on it, but he didn't believe his assessment was tainted by his earlier meeting with Lisa Harrington.

They were poor. And there was something within Hope, just the tiniest touch of sadness in the lines around her eyes, that said she knew she wasn't destined for great things. It wasn't that her smile was forced, but it was bridled. You could tell this was a girl who didn't cling to delusions or childish optimism. Dreams were already fading as she accepted her place in society's pecking order.

Or was it that Craig was projecting himself into the equation? Something about Hope made him think of his half sister, and he swallowed hard. He pushed that thought aside.

He set the picture down and looked back at the crime-scene photos.

Craig had wanted to look at the photos before reading the details of Hope's death. The photos alone wouldn't tell him how many times she'd cried out for help or for how long she'd suffered before the fatal blow, but they were the only way he could see the crime scene for himself, through his own eyes, untainted by interpretations that would affect how the officers on the scene would record the details.

Hope's death had been horrendous. If a picture really was worth a thousand words, that was the first one the photos shouted. The next words that came to mind were brutal and vicious.

Photo after photo, more of the same. The shock turned to rage. How many times had Hope Harrington been struck? The once-creamy skin was a mass of purple bruises, and where the flesh wasn't discolored it was broken. In one photo there was a fly in the gaping wound.

Craig felt his stomach turn.

The coroner's report wasn't any easier to get through. Bludgeoned over five dozen times. Indentations made on the soles of the victim's feet were consistent with the shape of a twelve-inch crowbar, also known as a wrecking bar. One that was the right size had been located in the Harrington home. Two sets of fingerprints were found on the weapon. Lisa Harrington's and Donny Lockridge's.

Blood and tiny shreds of flesh were found still on the crowbar. Samples taken positively matched Hope Harrington's DNA.

The autopsy revealed other injuries. Broken fingers and fractures in the ulna, attributed as defensive wounds. Death had resulted from a particularly vicious series of blows to the head that cracked the skull, although the beating and blood loss may have been enough to kill Hope already. The coroner couldn't say for certain. If Hope had reached a hospital within a short period of time it may have been enough to save her, if she'd had a skilled surgeon and received immediate care. If, if, if. Hope's attacker appeared to have started at her feet and worked his way to the top, becoming more vicious and aggressive the more he struck her, leaving no portion of her body untouched.

And then there were the other wounds. As Craig read through the report, he realized there was no way his dad would want to talk about the specifics of this murder. This was the kind of case he wouldn't want to remember, but wouldn't be able to forget.

The murder had gone beyond personal. It was savage. The body had been dumped, the murder weapon hidden, the scene of the crime never discovered. That meant it wasn't a place they'd normally gone to, such as his house or hers. Both locations had been searched, and despite public appeals for information the murder site had never been located. The fact that Donny hadn't murdered Hope at home or any place their friends knew they hung out meant it was somewhere he'd taken Hope to deliberately. Not a crime of passion, not something that happened in the heat of the moment. Premeditated brutality. Someone capable of this level of violence would most likely kill again.

There was no way his dad would want to see Hope's killer released early.

Craig hadn't stood over Hope's naked, broken body himself, but he'd seen more than enough to know he didn't want Donny Lockridge to be released early either.

No wonder Lisa Harrington had been such a mess. What parent wouldn't be? Had she identified the body? Craig assumed so. Just as he started flipping through the paperwork to confirm that his phone rang.

"Constable Nolan."

"Craig, it's Alison."

"I tried to call you earlier."

"I was out for a bit, and I haven't been answering the phone. They just won't stop."

"Who won't stop?

"The reporters, the lawyers, they won't leave me alone."

Craig rubbed his forehead. "You mean the reporter you gave my number to?"

Her breath caught. "I'm sorry, Craig. I don't know what to tell these people."

Craig frowned. He'd thought their phone number was unlisted. "Aren't these people just looking for Dad?"

"Did you talk to her?" Alison's voice had risen. Level and calm—which was Alison's normal tone, even when upset—wasn't how Craig would describe her words now.

"Who? The reporter? Briefly."

"Craig, someone broke into the house."

He frowned. Nobody had mentioned a break-in, and he was the primary contact while Steve and Alison were out of the province. "Is that why you're back? Nobody told me anything about this."

"I was already back."

"Who's handling this?" Silence. "Alison, I want to talk to whoever's handling this."

"I . . . I haven't reported it."

"Alison, what the—"

"I phoned you."

He stifled a groan. Could he blame his stepmother? Not really. If Steve wasn't away, Alison would have called him. Craig would automatically be next on the list.

"Okay, look. I'll have to put this through properly if you want—"

"I want you to come and deal with this."

"I'm on my way. Okay? Lock the doors, sit tight. I have a key. I'll let myself in. Okay?" He waited a moment, then asked again, "Okay?"

She sounded calmer when she replied. "The bedroom."

"What about it?"

"I don't want to go downstairs, Craig. I locked myself in the bedroom."

"Okay. I'll be there soon."

Craig hung up and took the folders he'd been looking through and set them back in the box, on top, along with a separate folder, titled DESIREE HARRINGTON that he hadn't had a chance to read yet. He wondered why they'd have a file on Hope's younger sister, who hadn't even been born at the time of her murder, in with the case notes, but he'd have to find out later. He replaced the lid and stood up.

"Knocking off early?"

Craig didn't need to see who was behind him to identify the voice. Why was it every time he did something Zidani was looking over his shoulder? He turned.

"Not exactly. Someone broke into my parents' home."

Zidani's eyes narrowed. "Who got the call?"

Craig exhaled. "I did. From my stepmother. She hasn't reported it through proper channels." He held up his hand. "Spare me the lecture. She's used to my dad dealing with things."

"I thought your parents were in Regina."

"They were. Look, my stepmother is at home alone, and she's locked herself in her room. She's waiting for me."

Zidani almost looked thoughtful and then he nodded. "Take Luke with you."

Craig bit back his reply. From the corner of his eye he could see that Luke was already out of his chair, reaching for his jacket.

Zidani walked away.

Craig slid the boxes under his desk, grabbed his own coat and put up his hand. "I'll be back in a minute." He started down the hallway, as though he was following Zidani to argue with him. Then he pulled out his cell phone, called Alison and told her he was on his way but had to bring his partner.

When he returned Luke was putting something in one of his desk drawers.

"Ready?" Craig asked.

Luke slammed the drawer shut and looked up. "Sure." He grabbed a key and locked the drawer.

Craig led the way to the parking lot, thankful that at least Luke Geller had enough sense to keep his mouth shut.

Constable Sims was the kind of guy who could piss Tain off just by existing. He wasn't fallible flesh and blood; he was chiseled. Sims's uniform was always perfect. Why he hadn't been assigned to an airport or tourist attraction where international visitors lined up to have their photo taken with a real, live Mountie was beyond Tain. Sims could be the poster child for the fresh, young face of the RCMP.

He could certainly be on the recruiting photos aimed at getting women to join the force. Tain had heard more than enough from female officers already in uniform to know that.

Yet he had a grudging respect for the fact that Sims actually had a head for police work. When Ashlyn had gone undercover months before Sims had assisted Tain, and even Tain had to admit the pretty boy was more than just competent.

"Clothing and the possible murder weapon."

Another thing Tain could appreciate about Sims. No preamble, no theatrics, no bullshit. At least, not with him. Tain didn't indulge theories and prolonged explanations from most officers, and Sims knew that.

"Take me through it, Sims."

The boyish smile slipped from Sims's face. "Shouldn't we wait for Constable Hart?"

Tain turned and looked up toward the washrooms. Ashlyn had said she'd be right down.

"She's taken, Sims."

Sims was trying not to react, but his face fell just a bit. "It's not . . . I . . . I understood Constable Hart is leading—"

"Save it, Sims. My bullshit detector's working today."

"And some say you're a heartless bastard."

Tain smiled. "I actually tolerate you, Sims. Just imagine if I didn't like you."

Sims's gaze shifted and as he looked past Tain he frowned. "Is Constable Hart not feeling well?"

A glance over his shoulder was enough to explain why Sims had asked. Another officer had intercepted Ashlyn and she was rubbing her forehead as she spoke, her skin a pasty white, eyes weighed down.

"It's a tough case, Sims. We've been at it for hours and haven't eaten."

Tain didn't mean to sound as brusque as he did, but he wasn't about to indulge Sims in a conversation about Ashlyn. If Sims thought Tain was being curt with him on the subject, he should try broaching it with Ashlyn directly. Even if she was tired she'd find the energy to put him in his place.

Constable Sims didn't seem to know much better, or bought into the idea that he could charm anyone. He smiled at Ashlyn as she joined them, just as much as was appropriate, under the circumstances. "Constable Hart. How are you?"

Ashlyn's eyes narrowed just a touch as she said, "Fine." She turned to Tain. "I have officers going to question Shannon's other classmates who were absent, and to follow up on whatever family we can track down. We also have an indirect witness. Someone who saw the kids in the park recently, and has some information they think we might be interested in. Wouldn't tell the officer who questioned them more."

"Better than nothing," Tain said.

She nodded and turned her gaze back to Sims. "What have you got for us?"

"Clothing and the possible murder weapon. We've covered most of the wooded area on this side of the inlet. We did find some branches smeared with what looks like blood, and a large pool of blood on the ground."

"Show us," Ashlyn said.

Sims led the way, elaborating on the extraneous details of the search to Ashlyn as Tain walked behind them. He had to give it to the guy—he didn't give up easily.

It didn't take long to reach the spot, as it wasn't far into the wooded area to the south side of the woods, near Murray Street, which was the road that ran along the park up to Ioco Road, a major road leading to the north part of Port Moody.

Tain watched as Ashlyn knelt down beside the spot on the ground where they'd found the blood. It wasn't a perfect circle, but it definitely wasn't a line of blood drops either.

A baseball bat was on the ground, only a few feet away.

"What do you think?" Ashlyn asked Tain.

He was silent for a moment. "Most likely something with blood on it, set down. It doesn't look like someone was beaten here." Tain glanced around. "If someone had been injured here there should be a blood trail, but there isn't."

"If they had something to stop the bleeding there might not be a trail."

Tain nodded. "We don't have enough information to be certain of anything at this point."

"You said you found clothing?" Ashlyn asked Sims.

He held up the evidence bag. "On the shore. Damp, but the blood wasn't all washed away."

Ashlyn stood up and her gaze met Tain's. He didn't need to ask what she was thinking.

"You cataloged the items when you transferred them to the evidence bag?" Tain asked.

Sims nodded. "One of those hoodies. Extra large."

Tain looked at the other officer, who'd been at the site when they arrived. "I'll take some markers." Once he had them he turned to Sims. "Show us where you found the sweater."

This time, Sims led the way silently. Tain walked slowly, occasionally tagging a spot on the ground without comment, although he pointed out some of the broken branches to Ashlyn.

"What is it?" Ashlyn asked when he knelt to study the ground.

He didn't answer right away. With other partners there'd always been the inevitable slew of jokes about Injuns tracking in the wilderness.

"Tain?"

He glanced up at her and then pointed to a spot on the ground, a few feet to the left of where he was.

She squatted down beside him. "It's still damp in here. Mucky. The brush is too thick for one day with no rain to make much of a difference."

Tain nodded. "And that's a deep impression. We've hit part of the track, where branches have been broken, but we're going in a straight line. Our runner was zigzagging. The other spots I tagged were footprints."

"This looks more like someone tripped and went down on one knee."

"That's my guess." Tain put a marker by the spot they'd been scrutinizing and looked up at Sims, who'd walked back to where they'd stopped. "You need to have someone go to all the spots I marked and make casts. We've got shoe prints."

Tain turned to Ashlyn while Sims pulled out his cell phone and made the call. "This puts an interesting spin on things."

She nodded. "But let's not jump to conclusions. Even if we're right it could be hard to prove."

"One step at a time. I'm with you."

They stood up as Sims closed his phone. "They're on their way. I can't believe I missed this."

"You guys searched the woods and then came back. It wasn't until officers were returning to the park that they found Christopher Reimer," Ashlyn reminded him. "Everyone was moving from the park parallel to the trails and back. Nobody was searching from the water to the road."

Sims frowned. "We still should have found evidence of his movements."

Tain shook his head. "Not if he didn't run down here until

after the officers had already made their way through. Who searched the section near the road, where the bloody spot on the ground was found?"

"Port Moody police. The officers we assigned to wait with Christopher," Sims said. "They weren't the ones who found the blood and the bat, though. After we found Christopher I sent two of ours back out to take another look around, near the road, in case we could find any evidence that Shannon had gone that way."

Cocky and sloppy. Tain glanced at Ashlyn. Her eyebrows rose and she looked away.

"Okay, Sims. From now on, you keep the Port Moody police away from any of this. Double them up with our guys and if they bitch about it you tell them to talk to me."

Sims looked at Tain for a moment, then glanced at Ashlyn as though he was waiting for her to back up that order.

"You heard him," Ashlyn said. "If the PoMo officers don't like it, I'll deal with them myself."

"Most of the guys from PoMo have already gone," Sims said.

"Then it won't be a problem." Ashlyn nodded toward the water, indicating she was ready to continue.

Sims turned and walked silently. Ashlyn had her arms folded over her chest. Her shoulders sagged, and she still looked pale. When she looked up Tain offered her a small smile.

She half smiled back, one side of her mouth turning up. Those smiles lit her eyes differently. It wasn't happiness; it was amusement. In this case, wry amusement, probably centered on Officer Parker and his ego.

"Was the water this high when you found the bag?" Ashlyn asked once they reached the spot along the shore.

"It's risen a bit, but not much," Sims said. "We found the knapsack here." He pointed to a spot, pressed up right against the water, where a dead tree hung out over the inlet. "It was caught on one of the branches."

Tain didn't even need to look at Ashlyn to feel her smile. "Guess that's our quota for this case blown," he said.

She started to laugh. "And yet the sweater was wet, so the

evidence may be contaminated. A defense attorney can argue someone stuffed their sweater into a bloody knapsack, unknowingly. I'd hoped we'd find some evidence of Shannon's movements, if she came down here to toss the bag in the water.

"And what about her pants?" Tain asked. "Wouldn't they have blood all over them? Why dump a sweater and not the pants?"

Ashlyn shook her head. "Not a break in sight with this investigation."

Tain saw the question on Sims's face as he looked from one of them to the other. "Luck, Sims. I doubt whoever threw that bag meant for it to hook on the tree so we'd find it. They meant for it to be underwater."

"Where was Christopher found, exactly?" Ashlyn asked.

Sims led them up the shore a short distance. From there they had a clear view to the spot where the bag had been located.

Tain reached down and picked up a heavy stick. He threw it at the tree and bounced it right off the spot where the bag had been recovered.

"Any identifying marks on the baseball bat?" he asked Sims, who shook his head.

"No name."

"Okay, Sims. I want a detailed description of the bat on my desk when I get back to the station. You need to get the bat, the bag and the sweater to the lab right away. I also want a thorough description of the hoodie and anything that might indicate who was wearing it." Tain put his hand up when Sims appeared about to interrupt. "What kind of bag was it?"

"A black knapsack. Nothing on it to say who it belonged to, but I'll have a general description of it for you, along with the sweater and the bat. And as soon as we have information on the shoe prints I'll update you immediately."

"Good." Tain turned and started to walk, Ashlyn following him without more than a quick glance at Sims.

"I thought you liked him," she said after a moment. When he didn't respond she said, "Out with it."

He stopped. "Look, we have a job to do here. Maybe if he

wasn't so anxious to impress he would have found the trail through the woods himself."

"There are a lot of other people to point fingers at. The officers who searched the section of the woods nearest the road may have missed Christopher Reimer entirely." She paused. "You remember what they said when I ordered the search? We had no grounds to search the woods. We weren't just looking for possible witnesses; we were looking for a murder weapon. It's standard procedure to search the area, and since there are trails that go through the woods it's a logical place to try to hide a weapon, and it's also a possible avenue of escape."

The PoMo police officers, Parker in particular, had given Ashlyn attitude about her orders. She was right, but that wasn't even what nagged at Tain now.

Something Sims said, about why he sent men back out there, and something else about Christopher Reimer that wasn't adding up.

Before Ashlyn could ask what he was thinking he said, "Do you have an address for that witness?"

She nodded. "I just hope he has something useful for us."

Even this early in the afternoon traffic was already starting to build. In British Columbia's Lower Mainland, at this time of day rush-hour traffic flowed west to east, from Vancouver through the Greater Vancouver Area. The Tri-Cities of Port Moody, Coquitlam and Port Coquitlam were not just home to thousands of people. They were a traffic corridor to Maple Ridge and Pitt Meadows, even Mission.

And like so many Canadian cities the GVA was hampered by its habitat. With the Burrard Inlet, along with the parks and mountains, to the north; the Fraser River to the south; and cities on every other side there was no real room for growth. Like Burnaby and New Westminster, the Tri-Cities were bursting at the seams and the only way to expand was up, which could explain why high-rise condominiums reached to the sky wherever developers could gain access to enough land to build on.

The traffic would get much worse over the next few hours,

but it was already enough to test Craig's patience. That, and being forced to bring Luke Geller with him.

As they crossed the bridge over the Coquitlam River Craig's cell phone rang. He flipped it open and lifted it to his right ear as he shoulder-checked and switched lanes, preparing for a left turn.

"Craig Nolan."

"Emma Fenton."

It took him a moment to unclench his jaw. "I have nothing to say to you."

"How can you be so sure? You haven't even heard what I have to say."

The advance turning light flashed and Craig did a quick check to make sure the traffic from the other direction understood red meant stop before proceeding across the Lougheed Highway.

He lowered his voice. Luke could still hear him, but that wasn't the point. It made him sound less angry than he felt. "I don't have time for this."

"I—"

He snapped the phone shut without listening to more.

From the corner of his eye Craig could see Luke glance at the phone in his hand and then his face, but Craig didn't offer an explanation. He could feel the burn in his skin. Despite the fact that he was a younger officer he'd already dealt with his share of negative press and he had no desire for more.

Especially not when it involved his dad. And not when it could keep him from getting back on regular rotation.

Just before they reached Ulster Street he slowed down well below the speed limit and surveyed the area. He was approaching the south end of the road his parents lived on, and to his right was a wooded area with walking trails that led through Hyde Creek Nature Reserve.

Nothing seemed unusual or out of place. When he turned on to Ulster Street he continued slowly. Steve and Alison Daly's home was on a residential road, with a number of houses lining both sides. The south end was filled with newer homes in more modern, similar styles while the north end contained some of the older homes in the area that could not be classified as cookie-cutter houses. Each was distinctive enough in shape, siding or features to be easily identified. There were a few cars parked on the road, but not as many as usual, which Craig attributed to the fact that many people still hadn't returned from work.

When he reached the end of the street he turned on Apel Drive and drove a short distance. Luke frowned, looked about to speak, but in the end stayed silent. Craig turned the vehicle around.

Steve and Alison Daly lived in a home near the north end of Ulster Street. Craig's dad had a good eye for property and had bought a handful of houses over the years. After strategic repairs he'd been able to sell some and make a decent profit.

This had been an untapped area for a long period of time, and the Dalys had moved when houses were still cheap by Lower Mainland standards. It meant they had an older home, one that was unique.

It meant it wasn't likely an intruder got the wrong house if they were targeting Steve and Alison Daly.

Craig parked and got out of the vehicle.

Luke followed. "How do—"

"I have a key."

It only took a second for Craig to locate the right one. Once the door was unlocked he nudged it open. "Alison? It's Craig."

No response. He stepped inside and reached for his gun.

The ground level included a two-car garage, a laundry room, furnace room, two bedrooms, a full bathroom and rec room with a kitchenette. Similar homes utilized the rec room, bathroom and bedrooms as a rental suite, since there was a private entrance off a patio from the backyard. Steve and Alison had never rented out that section of the ground floor.

Upstairs there were three bedrooms plus a den, two full bathrooms, a dining room, kitchen and living room. Alison had said she'd locked herself in the master bedroom.

In the hallway leading from the entry there were drops of blood on the tile.

"No sign of forced entry, though."

Craig turned. Luke was standing in the doorjamb.

"There's another entrance in the back. Watch yourself." Craig pointed to the floor. The entry opened up to a staircase on the far left, against the outer wall, a hallway leading to the other rooms on the ground level, and to the right a wall bordered the garage, then the laundry room and furnace area. He moved to the wall that ran under the stairs, where a storage and coat closet were located. There wasn't as much blood there, but he still moved cautiously, careful not to disturb anything.

When he'd spoken to Alison he'd had the impression someone had broken in while she was out, that she'd returned to discover her home had been invaded. He'd allowed himself to be distracted by his annoyance that she hadn't reported the incident properly and hadn't pressed her for more details.

Now it all made sense. Alison had locked herself in the bedroom because she was afraid the intruder was still in the house.

Craig slowly made his way along the wall, careful to watch where he stepped while listening for the sound of movement from someone other than himself and Luke. The house was still. He opened the closet door and checked it. Clear.

When he got to the end of the hallway he moved to the other side and gestured for Luke to follow. They took positions outside the laundry room door, guns drawn, and opened it. Empty. The furnace room was also empty. Craig paused at the next door. When Luke was in position Craig reached across for the handle, turned it slowly and nudged the door open.

It led to another hallway on the other side. To the right the hallway passed two bedrooms. On the left side there was a full bathroom, followed by a kitchenette. The other end of the hallway opened up to the rec room. There were still drops of blood on the floor, scattered and uneven, but small enough to avoid easily.

It was easy enough to scan the long, narrow bathroom. The length ran parallel to the hallway, but the door was open and the shower curtain had been pulled back all the way. There was no place to hide, and there was no blood on the floor, suggesting the room hadn't been entered by the intruder.

The first bedroom was a guest room. Craig entered and Luke followed. From the mirror above the dresser Craig could see that most of the room was empty before he stepped inside. It took half a second to confirm that if someone was hiding there, they were under the bed or in the closet.

Luke looked at Craig, who nodded at the bed. There wasn't any blood on the floor that he could see, but he wasn't taking any chances. Craig waited while Luke drew closer and then pulled the bedspread back.

Nothing but the balls of dust that had built up during his stepmother's absence.

Luke looked at Craig, who tipped his head in the direction of the closet, which was on the far side of the dresser.

They took positions. Again, empty.

The next bedroom was used as a storage room of sorts. There was a desk and chair along one wall, a sewing table along another, and Craig already knew the closet contained most items they had boxed up. The room didn't have a large mirror, though, and that meant they took up positions outside the door and followed procedure.

Again, the room was clear, other than the visible blood drops marking the floor. The only thing left to check was the closet. The boxes were there, and what Craig suspected was more evidence of the intruder, although the closet door had been shut. One box had been pulled out and opened, the papers inside rifled through. It only took a quick cursory glance to know they were his dad's, and Craig knew Steve Daly would never leave his files stored in that condition.

However, someone who didn't know Steve Daly could be persuaded that the box had just been left there. It was inside a closed closet, and most people weren't meticulous with their paperwork. Assuming the intruder had touched it, it looked like they'd been careful. He couldn't see any evidence of blood.

Craig turned to Luke and quietly said, "Clear." He saw Luke look past him, to the box on the floor of the closet. Their gaze met and Craig nodded at the doorway. "One more room."

Luke glanced back at the box for half a second. Craig shut the closet door and although he hesitated, Luke followed without argument.

The rec room was a large area that opened up off the kitchenette and hallway. There wasn't much furniture in the room, and what was there was pushed up against the walls, so there was no place to hide. It only took a heartbeat to be sure the room was clear.

And in that same split second they confirmed where the suspect had entered the house. The obvious choice would have been to break the glass patio doors, but instead a window along the far wall was smashed. The kind of window that was in such an odd place it served no practical purpose, because it looked out to the fence between the Daly property and their neighbor's. It didn't really let in light, but it had served as the point of entry for the intruder. Shards of glass covered the carpet.

There was more blood on the floor where the glass was scattered, and there was also a smear on the windowsill.

Craig quickly scanned the area beside the house that was visible from the window. A cement walkway, grass and then the trees that bordered the back of the property. No sign of a trespasser.

He looked at his partner. "We need to check upstairs."

Luke didn't argue. They cautiously made their way to the landing on the second floor.

The house was remarkably still. Craig had been in and out so many times while his parents were away, and he'd barely noticed the quiet. It was expected. But knowing his stepmother was somewhere in the house made the silence seem threatening.

Halfway to the second floor the stairs curved to the right, putting them at the juncture at the end of the hallway, the start of the living room and the entrance to the kitchen. The hallway led past the dining room, two bedrooms, a bathroom and the entrance to the den before it reached the master bedroom. Every room would have to be cleared.

It didn't take long, and once they'd established there was no further evidence of the intruder upstairs Craig told Luke to wait in the living room, went back down the hall and approached the door to the master bedroom.

"Alison?"

Silence.

He knocked again. "Alison, it's Craig. We've checked the house."

At last there was the sound of muffled footfalls on carpet, drawing closer, then the click as the door was unlocked.

Alison Daly had only been part of Craig's life for just over a decade, but he was startled by how much older she seemed since he'd last seen her, a few months earlier. Less color in her dark hair, which was cut shorter than he was used to. Crow's-feet had spread out from the corners of her eyes, which were wide with worry.

Craig kept his voice low. "We're going to call for a team."

"No." She shook her head. "I don't want anyone else in the house."

Alison's mouth twisted with anger, but before she could say anything else a voice from behind Craig interrupted. "Perhaps you could tell us what happened?"

Craig felt the annoyance in the form of heat on the back of his neck. He hadn't been aware of Luke approaching, and there was no way Alison would cause a scene unnecessarily in front of a stranger, but he'd told his partner to wait.

Alison turned to look at Luke and folded her arms across her chest, then shifted her gaze back to Craig. Her eyes pinched just a touch, the way they always did when she was annoyed with him.

He ignored the look. "Why don't we go to the living room and you can tell us what happened?"

Luke and Alison introduced themselves as Craig watched Alison sit down on the sofa and cross her legs. She was wearing a pair of dark slacks and a sweater. Craig wondered if she'd lost a bit of weight, but brushed the thought aside. She'd been startled by the intruder, which explained her pallor, and the dark clothes made her white face more noticeable. It was just an illusion of color and circumstance.

Her story was simple. She'd come home early to get ready for the holidays. At first she thought she'd unpack and relax, but then she decided to go out and get some groceries.

When she returned she put the groceries away and went to her room to finish unpacking. That was when she heard the sound of glass breaking, and someone in the rec room.

"I locked my bedroom door, called Craig and waited for you to arrive."

Craig saw Luke glance at him, and he could see the questions in Luke's eyes. When Craig didn't comment Luke continued.

"I wasn't aware the intruder was in the house when you phoned."

Alison's eyes widened as she looked from Luke to Craig and back. "I guess I didn't say that. I just told Craig someone had broken in."

Luke looked at Craig again, and Craig gave one curt nod.

"Can I ask why you didn't call 911?"

A dark look flickered across Alison's features, gone in almost a heartbeat. "I've already had one intruder. I don't want another group of strangers invading my home."

She got up and walked across the room and down the hall. Her bedroom door closed. No scene, no confrontation, but it was unusual for Craig's stepmother to react that way. Still, someone had broken in, and Steve was in Regina. It was understandable that she was upset.

Luke stood up. "I'll call Zidani. Maybe we can be discreet." He pulled out his cell phone and pressed a couple buttons as he walked to the kitchen.

Craig wondered if Alison had called Steve.

There was movement in the kitchen, the sound of the airtight fridge door being pulled open, then shut. Craig entered the room as Luke opened the pantry door.

Without hesitation Luke said, "Zidani promised to send a

couple guys, quietly. Just photos, prints, blood samples." He closed the pantry. "I'm looking for the glasses. I need some water."

Craig turned toward the counter and opened one of the upper cupboards. He took out a glass and handed it to Luke instead of challenging the flimsy lie.

CHAPTER FIVE

Daylight had been waning during the drive to the Daly home, and by the time Luke and Craig returned to the station it was dark. Some said in Vancouver in December there really wasn't any such thing as day, only varying shades of gray and black. No matter what you called the hours that weren't black you knew when night had come. Unlike the prairies, where light could linger in the sky hours after the sun had officially set, in the GVA any light that remained was artificial. The darkness was the kind that hung heavily, like a blanket over the sky.

Craig cut the engine and got out of the vehicle. It wasn't until he started to follow Luke inside that he saw the figure emerge from the shadows. She stopped him by the sidewalk, in a well-lit area not far from the entrance to the building.

"You're a hard man to track down," she said.

He didn't need to ask who she was. The voice was enough.

"I have a report to write, Ms. Fenton. I don't have time for this."

"That's fine. I'll wait." She smiled. "Once you're finished your paperwork maybe you'll be able to give me something on the break-in as well."

He stopped walking and looked at Luke. "Go ahead. I'll just be a minute."

Luke glanced at the reporter for a split second, then turned and continued walking to the building without comment.

Craig waited until Luke had put some distance between them but still lowered his voice. "How do you know about that?"

"How does a reporter ever know about anything?" She smiled. From what he could tell the hair tucked under her beret was a lighter shade of strawberry blond and she had a few freckles on her cheeks, wide blue eyes, not a lot of makeup. He guessed she wasn't much more than five feet tall, which added to the overall impression. She didn't seem threatening.

But she was still a reporter, and Craig had had his share of run-ins in the aftermath of Lori's death and his own shooting. He heard another vehicle pull up, the engine stop, the doors open. The longer he stood there the more people who would see him talking to a reporter, and the more likely Zidani would hear about it . . . "What do you want, Ms. Fenton?"

The smile slipped from her face, but she didn't look angry. Instead, the corners of her eyes dropped just enough for her to look hurt. "Just let me talk. Hear what I have to say. If you still decide you don't want to comment"—she held up her hands—"no problem. What have you got to lose? Let me buy you dinner."

That was when he realized the footsteps had stopped. He looked up as Tain reached for Ashlyn's arm, tilting his head toward the door. Ashlyn stood frozen for a moment, looking from Emma to Craig before letting Tain lead her inside.

"Look, I've already told you I didn't even work this case. And I don't know how you heard about the break-in, but that's hardly front-page news. A few dozen homes are broken into every day in the GVA."

"But how many of those homes are owned by a ranking RCMP officer who just happened to get promoted after closing a high-profile murder investigation, the same murder investigation that is now under review? Word is, Donny Lockridge plans to file a lawsuit against your father over his wrongful conviction—"

"Alleged wrongful conviction. He was put on trial and convicted by a jury. That wouldn't have happened if there wasn't evidence to support it."

She smiled. "See? We're talking and you weren't struck by lightning. It probably didn't even hurt."

Craig blew out a breath and ran his hand over his head, pushing his hair back before pointing at her. "Look, I'm sure you're a nice person, don't take it personally. But you're jumping to conclusions without facts and printing such speculation would be irresponsible and unprofessional."

"Which is why I'm here, talking to you, trying to find out what did happen. Don't you want to know? Aren't you curious?" She looked him in the eye. "Is there any part of you that doubts Donny Lockridge murdered Hope Harrington?"

"How can I answer that? I've hardly even had a chance to look at the files."

Craig almost groaned when she smiled. "So, you admit you're looking into this?"

He raised his hand to stop her. "I am reviewing the case only because I have been ordered to. It has nothing to do with my father, the break-in, you, Lockridge's lawyer or anything else."

Craig started to walk to the building, but she wasn't deterred from following him. "Is that why you met with Lisa Harrington today?"

He grabbed the door and didn't even acknowledge her question with a glance as he marched into the building, thankful that she had enough sense not to follow him any farther.

"I'll catch up in a minute." Ashlyn pushed the door to the ladies' room open and disappeared inside.

Tain paused. Should he wait, make sure she was okay? They'd had a long, hard day with little to show for their efforts, but he hadn't seen her shoulders sag so low since they'd been working almost around the clock on the child abductions and murders. The "angel arsons," as the press called them.

He continued down the hall, knowing how she'd react if he checked up on her. Still, he wondered about Craig and the woman outside. Ashlyn had never been the jealous type. Then again, as far as he knew, Craig had never given her reason to be. His own instincts told him that whoever the woman outside was, she was far more interested in Craig than he was in her. The bit of their exchange he'd heard had been strained, the woman trying to sound casual, pleasant, but Craig's posture had been tense and he'd looked agitated.

"Did you get it?"

Tain looked up and almost wished he hadn't. Zidani was nodding at Luke Geller, whatever response he had kept low enough that Tain couldn't make out the words.

They were in an adjoining hallway, not the one Tain needed to go down. He just hoped they were too busy with their chat to notice him.

A small stack of notes waited on his desk. Updates from various officers following leads on the case. So far, no luck anywhere. Shannon hadn't been seen at school. Her friends had been questioned but hadn't offered anything useful. The 911 call had been tracked down, with the tape sent to Zidani, but they hadn't gotten any useful prints from the phone. Nothing that would allow for an identification that would stand up in court.

He clipped the notes together and put them on his "in" tray.

Ashlyn entered the room and stopped at the cooler to pour a cup of water. Tain watched her push her hair back from her pale face and take a sip. After a few gulps she dropped the cup into the wastebasket and walked to her desk, which faced his.

She dropped into her chair, propped her elbows on the desk, let her head fall into her hands and rubbed her temples with her fingers.

Tain pulled a bottle from the top drawer of his desk and passed it to her. "Here. I'll get you another drink."

She wasn't lacking the energy to glare at him. "I'm fine."

"Ash—"

He was familiar with the look she was giving him. The one that said *I'm not a child. I can take care of myself.* He forced a look of contrition. "You sure?"

She straightened up, forcing her body to hold the weight of her head as she dropped her hands. "I'm good."

He lowered his voice. "Just a word of warning, that headache's about to get worse."

Her eyes narrowed and then closed when she heard the words "My office. Now."

Zidani waited for them instead of letting them follow him, which meant they had no time to come up with excuses. He walked behind them and as soon as he'd followed them into his office he told Tain to shut the door.

They weren't invited to sit down.

Zidani passed a note to Ashlyn, who took it without comment. "No teachers, staff, volunteers, students or parents of students are to be questioned on school property without making arrangements with the principal and the school's lawyer." He sat down in his chair, leaned back and smiled. "Tell me something I want to hear."

Ashlyn glanced at Tain for half a second before she responded. "We did develop a useful lead. A few of Shannon's close friends were absent, and we spoke directly to one of them and Shannon's boyfriend, who told us that Shannon had planned to run away today."

Zidani frowned, but still kept the sarcasm out of his response. "She'll be even harder to find if she was prepared, won't she?"

Ashlyn nodded. "Yes. But we sent other officers to question her friends who weren't in class. We know she's not with any of them. This morning we thought it was spontaneous, that she was on the run. Now we know she'd made arrangements, probably had money saved. What we need is to figure out where Shannon would plan to go, if she has a friend who might have had a job for her to go to. We'll also be monitoring the boyfriend closely."

"He'll know where she is. They always do."

"I don't think so. He was pretty convincing. He said that Shannon wouldn't tell him where she was going so he wouldn't have to try to lie." Ashlyn paused. "I believed him."

"So did I," Tain said. "The kid was jumpy. I had the impression—" He looked at Ashlyn, then continued, "I got the feeling there were problems at home, that something was going on that prompted her to run away."

"Well, kids don't usually take off on a whim," Zidani said.

"Unless this was just a case of trying to get attention, maybe being unhappy because she thinks her parents love her brothers more and she wants a car for Christmas or something."

Ashlyn's mouth twisted and then she shook her head. "No, I agree with Tain. We tried to get access to the house, just to check Shannon's room. We wanted to see just how prepared she was, if there were bags missing, a lot of clothes and personal items, but the lawyer wouldn't let us without a search warrant. Without more proof we've only got what the boyfriend told us."

"Which was corroborated by one of Shannon's school friends," Tain added.

"Still . . ." Zidani smiled. "Young girls love drama. What better way to get attention? This friend you spoke to, was it a girl?"

Tain saw Ashlyn draw a breath. "Yes."

Zidani nodded. "And the witness? The one near the park?"

"Not home when we went there. We've been back twice."

Zidani leaned back, folding his hands behind his head. "So what's next?"

Tain saw Ashlyn glance at him again. They'd come in, prepared for a confrontation, and Zidani's demeanor seemed to be throwing her off as much as it was unnerving him.

"Sims recovered what's believed to be the murder weapon and clothing discarded near the scene that was stained with blood. We'll check with the lab to confirm that, see if we can link the items to the Reimer family. We'll try to get the lawyer to give us access to the family to question them. Of course, we can't expect much there. Smythe will have spent the day coaching them," Ashlyn said. "We do have officers monitoring the Reimer home, in case Shannon tries to return and will expand the search for her, question all relatives, acquaintances."

Tain waited, but it never came. He knew what he thought Ashlyn really wanted to do with the investigation, but even Zidani's attempts to play nice weren't enough to get her to take the bait, if that's what this was. She waited silently, hands now clasped behind her back, chin jutting out just a touch.

Whatever Zidani thought, he was keeping it to himself. No smile, no snide comment . . . Nothing. "Right. Sounds like you have things under control. It's pretty much a slam dunk anyway. Tragic murder of a young boy by his older sister, who clearly has some emotional issues. Go home, get some sleep."

Tain only hesitated for a moment before opening the door. Once they'd put a safe distance between themselves and the office he looked at Ashlyn.

"You know what this means, don't you?" she said. "This afternoon, while we were looking for Shannon Reimer, aliens landed and replaced our acting sergeant with a clone."

"They didn't get the personality right."

She smiled, and once they reached their work area turned around and leaned against her desk. "Part of me wants to ask what the hell just happened, but the other part's mumbling something about gift horses."

"Go home. Get some sleep. Before the Martians realize what a bastard Zidani is and swap him back."

This time she didn't smile. Instead, her eyes took on weight. "Tain, you know I want to look hard at—"

He held up his hand. "Yes. And you're right." He tilted his head in the direction they'd just come from. "And we'd best keep it quiet until we have more than the word of two teenagers to go on."

"So it wasn't just . . . ?" She shrugged.

"No. But it wasn't like he gave us a direct order, was it?"

He squeezed her shoulder and held her gaze for a moment. When he saw the flicker of a smile he let go and went to his own desk.

She said good night and left without further comment. Another message had come in since they'd gone to Zidani's office, and he picked up the slip of paper. It only took a few seconds to read it, and then he slipped it in his pocket and reached for the Tylenol he'd offered Ashlyn earlier.

Just another headache he didn't need.

As soon as Craig arrived at his desk his partner stood. "It's finished. Nothing left to do." Luke pulled on his coat. "See you tomorrow."

Craig nodded and sank into his chair, bumping his foot against a box as he did.

The Harrington case files. He sighed, glanced at his watch. They'd have to wait, unless he wanted to take them home. There was no way he was going to risk running into Zidani again after the day he'd had.

He pulled out the box he'd been going through earlier and opened the lid. On top were the files he'd been looking at, the ones with the reports and crime-scene photos. All the case notes, interviews, leads tracked down . . . All of that still waited in the folders below.

Craig realized he'd spilled a bit of information when he was talking to Emma Fenton, but she'd reciprocated. Legal action. It explained Zidani's interest. Anything that could taint Steve would help Zidani keep his job, and he'd no longer be "acting sergeant." The promotion would be finalized.

After a minute Craig stood, picked up the second box and stacked it on top of the first one. It wasn't until he was outside, boxes propped between his body and the Rodeo as he dug in his pocket for his keys, that he realized he hadn't talked to Ashlyn.

He opened the door, put the boxes on the front passenger seat and got in.

They'd talk when she got home.

Ashlyn pulled into her parking spot and stopped her car. She leaned back in her seat, listening to the drumming of rain on the roof. First it came down slow, erratically. Then it built to a steady rhythm, the kind of long, dug-in rainfall that demanded you take it seriously, coming down thick and fast.

Thick enough to distort her view of the house. Through the water she could see the warm glow from inside. Craig was home. He hadn't waited to talk to her at the station. She knew that, because she'd checked at his desk before heading for her car.

She closed her eyes as she rubbed her temples, wished the rain could wash away her headache. What was it about the nausea that was making her head feel like the inside of a mixing bowl with the beaters set on high? Her stomach wasn't even that agitated; it just sent a clear message that it was set to trampoline mode, that any time she even thought about eating it was ready to bounce up some lingering remnant from a previous meal to remind her it wasn't accepting contributions at the moment.

Throughout the day she'd felt Tain's gaze on her, sensed the unasked questions. If she couldn't shake this quickly . . .

She sighed and opened the car door. The idea that she wasn't in control of her own body, that she couldn't even coerce its cooperation, bothered her. There had to be a way for her to handle it.

The rain was cold and she felt a shiver run down her spine, but could still only manage to walk to the door. By the time she was inside and had hung up her coat the chill had seeped through her clothes and skin, right to her core.

The house was quiet. No music, no sizzle of the wok or whirring of the microwave to guide her to Craig. The only clue was the light spilling over from the living room. Her legs protested as she forced herself to walk down the hall, telling her they only had enough strength left to carry her upstairs to bed and that if she went this way she'd have to figure out another way to get to her bed, because they'd have called it quits for the day.

In the corner of the room, on the far side of the fireplace, the half-decorated Christmas tree stood, performing its fiber optic light show. Ashlyn had thought it would be so much easier having a fiber optic tree. No need to fiddle with strings of lights, to try to evenly disperse them throughout the branches. Just plug it in and hang the decorations. What could be simpler? They kept saying tonight they'd go to the mall or the afternoon of their next day off together, and then a case would get in the way. Always her case, never his. Not since Lori had died. She felt a sudden urge to make tree decorations a top priority. Part of her knew she wouldn't really feel it was Christmas until they had a tree decorated and had done something festive, but it was more than that. It wasn't something she could explain, but she was overwhelmed with a compulsion to make sure the routine holiday traditions didn't go undone.

Craig was in the living room, sitting on the chair beside the fireplace, two boxes on the floor, files stacked precariously on the coffee table. He said nothing as she sank down on the couch, but continued reading the report in his hands. Then he thumbed through a stack of folders on the table, pulled one out and flipped it open. After a moment his frown deepened and he set it down with the report on top of it.

He leaned forward, elbows on his knees, face in his hands. Ashlyn knew that look.

"What's wrong?"

His head snapped up and he stared at her for a moment before the color returned to his face. "You shouldn't sneak up on people."

"Craig, really," she said as she picked up the blanket that had been tossed over the far end of the couch and spread it over her legs. She put her head on the armrest. "You were so deep in thought you would have missed the second coming, trumpets and all."

"Hardly. This isn't even the first time tonight I've turned to find you watching me."

She sat up, the blanket slipping to the floor. "You're talking to some woman, in public, right in front of the building I work in, and I'm not supposed to notice?"

"I talk to women all the time. It never bugged you before."

"Who said it bugs me now?"

He glanced at her as he gathered the folders and put them back in the box. "Take a look in the mirror. You're choked."

"Not for the reason you think! You're the one who's being defensive. You looked upset when you were talking to that woman, tense. I was worried, not jealous."

"I can handle her."

"Fine. Whatever."

They sat for a moment, the beating of rain intensifying, drowning out even the crackle of fire.

She heard him exhale and from the corner of her eye could see him scratch his head. "Look, I'm sorry. I guess I was distracted, and it's been a lousy day and that's no excuse. Are you hungry? I was thinking of making a stir fry."

The words alone were enough to make her stomach protest, and she shook her head and raised her hand. "No. Thanks. I think I'll just go to bed." Whether it was the promise of sleep or the thought of her stomach reacting to the sizzle of vegetables on a wok she wasn't sure, but she found the energy to get up and start walking to the stairs.

He followed her. "Come on, Ash. I'm sorry for snapping at you. You don't have to punish me for it."

"Believe it or not, the whole world doesn't revolve around Craig Nolan. I'm just tired." She turned to look at him. "You aren't the only one who had a lousy day."

He stood perfectly still as he looked at her. No flicker of emotion on his face, nothing to suggest what he was thinking. After a moment he nodded. "Okay." Then he reached behind her head with his hand and kissed her forehead. For a moment he stood with his cheek pressed against her temple before letting her go. "Get some rest."

She turned quickly so he wouldn't see the tears pricking at the corners of her eyes and climbed the stairs.

It took a moment for her to get her bearings when she opened her eyes. Somehow, her body knew it wasn't late. She also knew she was in her own bed, the one she shared with Craig. The thing that struck her most was what was missing from within her. For the first time in days her head wasn't throbbing and her stomach didn't feel as though someone was using it as a juggling ball.

Rain was still falling, though the drumming had lost its intensity, settling for a soft tapping on the roof. A flicker of light was enough for her to get her bearings and see that Craig was standing by the window, rivulets running down the glass.

She slid off the bed, walked over to where he stood and wrapped her arms around his chest. Some of his tension seemed to dissolve as soon as she rested her head against the back of his shoulder.

The light shimmered on his bare skin.

"Candles?" she asked.

"The power went out."

"What time is it?"

"Not late. Just after ten. I brought you some dinner, in case you're hungry."

She realized then that she could smell the food, and even that wasn't bothering her stomach. "That's a good sign."

He turned to face her. "That I brought you dinner?"

"That the smell isn't making me queasy."

"If you're feeling better you should eat. You haven't had much of an appetite the past few days."

"Later."

His thumb stroked the small of her back as he bent down, resting his forehead against hers. "You're really feeling okay?"

"Well . . ." She smiled. "I feel pretty good, but I could still feel better."

It wasn't until she saw his relaxed grin that it occurred to her it had been a while since she'd really seen him happy, but she willed herself not to think about that. As they made their way to the bed she realized it hadn't been a few days that she hadn't been feeling well, but at least a few weeks.

She pushed that thought aside as well, and just concentrated on being with him completely.

Craig's body was moving slowly, but his brain was still wrapped in the fog of a deep sleep. It registered the dark stillness of the room and the fact that it was not yet morning. His hand had picked up the phone so he must have heard it ring and answered, but all he could bring into focus was the sound of a woman's voice on the other end and words, "Somebody broke in."

"Again?"

"I-I'm scared and . . . again?"

He swung his legs over the side of the bed and shook his head. It wasn't his stepmother's voice. "Who is this?"

"L-Lisa. Lisa Harrington."

Things were starting to come into focus, although his body was still moving ahead of his brain. His pants were on and he was searching for a shirt before he even managed to reply. "Did you call 911?"

"Uh, no. Look—" A high note of panic hadn't just crept in to her voice, it had taken over completely. "Can you come? I don't want just any cop and it's . . . it's about Donny."

In the bed, Ashlyn rolled over and looked at him. He sighed. "Okay. Give me directions."

Lisa rattled off the address, but he stopped partway through writing it down. Same house. She'd never moved after Hope's murder. The directions were simple enough, although she didn't live in his jurisdiction.

"You know where I live, Lisa. It's going to be at least three quarters of an hour, maybe a bit more." She was south of Langley, and even at this time of day, without traffic, it would be a solid forty-five-minute drive.

"It's okay. I, uh, I'm sorry for phoning at home. I don't know who else to call."

His annoyance dissipated as he told her he'd be there as soon as he could and hung up. The waif he'd met not even twenty-four hours earlier looked barely capable of standing up, never mind fending off an intruder, and when people were scared they didn't think straight. He could call Langley RCMP—he should call them—but he'd spent enough time looking at the Harrington file. In a manner of speaking, he was even assigned to it. Zidani had ordered him to review the details. If Lisa was right, and this was connected to Donny's parole hearing . . .

But how would she know that?

Ashlyn sat up and started to climb out of bed.

"Go back to sleep."

"Where are you going?" she asked as he kissed her forehead.

"That case I was looking at files on earlier? There's been a break-in and it might tie in to that. I have to go check it out." A glance at the clock, which was back on, told him it was just after 4 A.M. "I doubt I'll be back before you've gone to work. Can we try for lunch or dinner today? Date at the mall, pick up the Christmas decorations? You said something about friends of yours getting a special ornament for every Christmas they share."

She nodded.

"Maybe we could do something like that."

"Sounds good." Ashlyn smiled, but her words were heavy with sleep. Craig gave her another kiss and left.

When Craig arrived at the Harrington residence, even in the predawn light he had a clear impression of a tiny house that had grown tired of standing at least a decade earlier, and that was probably being generous. The roof sagged, the screen door was partially unhinged, one of the steps leading to the small porch was cracked. The light was one of those motion-sensitive wall-mounted, battery-operated lights, and the bulb inside must have been the lowest wattage possible, because when Craig turned off his vehicle he couldn't see much more than a faint glow on the metal screen door, which dangled ineffectively in front of the entrance.

He skipped the broken step with ease. Lisa opened the door before he even raised his hand to knock. Her right hand was wrapped in a towel that was covered with blood.

"What happened?" he asked. When she didn't answer, Craig said, "We should call for paramedics or get you to a hospital."

"No. It looks worse than it is. I just cut it on some glass."

"At least let me take a look."

"I'll take care of it." Lisa held up her hand to stop him from following and disappeared down the hall. When she returned her hand was clumsily wrapped in a bandage. "See? Fine."

He wasn't convinced, but he decided not to push it for a moment. "Tell me what happened, from the beginning."

"I was asleep on the couch." She rubbed her forehead with her left hand. "I heard a crash and then a thud. Took me a moment to realize it wasn't coming from the TV." She nodded at the thirty-six-inch flat screen that dominated the small living room at the front of the house. A well-worn sofa, dim wallpaper, end tables that looked liked '70s leftovers and shag carpet clashed with the sleek TV set, satellite receiver, DVD player and surround-sound speakers.

Ones considerably more expensive than the pricey set he'd had his eye on.

She was leading the way down the narrow hall, which had similar worn wallpaper. It was the kind of generic pattern the eye overlooked because it just faded into the background. All that mattered about it was that it was old, like the house. It was also poorly lit, so Craig had to move slowly to avoid stepping in the drops of blood she'd left on the lino.

"By the time I got back here whoever it was had gone." Lisa nodded at the room at the back of the house, to the left. He guessed she'd call it a mud room, because it had a door beside the large window that had been broken. Lit by a single naked bulb, he could see the room held a washer and dryer, which both looked as though they predated the first human footprints on the moon, and an old table with a broken leg, propped up on that side by a stack of boxes that didn't quite match the height of the table legs still functioning.

Contents of another box were strewn on the floor. As he knelt beside it Craig could see why Lisa had assumed the break-in had something to do with Donny's case. Newspaper clippings covering the trial were mixed in with a diary, loose photos of Hope, a charm bracelet, teddy bear, things that clearly belonged to the girl, whose name was written in marker on the side of the box.

He stood up and moved to the window, careful not to disturb the items on the floor, or the glass scattered by the window. A pool of blood surrounded a large piece of glass. Craig found himself wishing for his flashlight, because all he could see looking out from the lit room was the darkness, but as he turned to ask Lisa if she had one he could borrow he saw what she was doing.

"Don't touch that!"

She looked up as she dropped a handful of papers into the box, but didn't say anything.

"Lisa, that's evidence. We need to call the local police—"

"No!" She sprang to her feet, cheeks red, uninjured hand clenched. "I called you."

"This is out of my jurisdiction, and without bringing out a team to search for evidence there's no chance we'll find out who broke in. If you want me to help you—"

"Just go." Hollow words, lacking the energy of her outburst seconds before. Lisa crouched down, finished repacking the box, picked it up and set it on a shelf on the far side of the washing machine. Craig had a split second to decide, and reached for a tissue from the container on the desk and dabbed it in the blood. He slipped it into a plastic bag he'd pulled from his coat, and stuck his hand in his pocket just as Lisa turned around.

When Craig had entered he'd noticed the open shelves, followed by the washer, a sink, the dryer and then the outer wall. He hadn't really picked up on the empty spot on the shelf. The upper shelves were filled with towels that matched the one she'd wrapped around her hand after cutting it, bedsheets, clothes, the usual things you'd find in a laundry room. A separate shelf above the sink had laundry detergent, bleach and stain removers. It was the lower three shelves of the original shelving unit that stored the boxes that weren't stacked under the ailing desk.

Hope's box had been taken from the middle of the second lowest shelf, with boxes on the shelves above and below appearing unmoved.

Craig stepped closer and what he saw confirmed that. The boxes were dusty, as though they hadn't been touched in some time. Only the box that had been dumped on the floor had been disturbed, which again, supported Lisa's suspicions that the break-in had something to do with Hope.

"I know you're frightened and upset, and it's understandable." She put her hand on her forehead, blocking her eyes as she looked down and shook her head. "You don't understand."

"And I'm not going to if you don't level with me about what's going on." She dropped her hand from her face and looked up at him, but he didn't stop. "Did you know about the lawsuit before you came to see me today? Did you tell anyone you were going to talk to me?" He didn't need to hear the answers to know the truth. "Why didn't you tell me what was really going on?"

For a moment she stood staring at him. Then all the color drained from her face as she slumped back against the wall by the door. "How'm I s'posed to know I can trust you?"

Craig lifted his hands for a second before dropping them in frustration. "I guess you don't, but you called me. You want my help, fine. But I'm not here to play games."

She looked away as she fiddled absently with a locket around her neck and stared at the boxes on the shelves beside the washer. Then she drew a breath and said, "I-I think I know who broke in here."

He stepped toward her and gently took her arm, prompting her to meet his gaze. "Then we call the police and tell them, and make sure it doesn't happen again. Who was it?"

"I—" Lisa's eyes widened as she slid along the wall until she reached the doorway, then turned, steadied herself and started walking down the hall. Craig followed, and she almost started to run. Like her earlier outburst the display of energy was short-lived. She collapsed against the wall in the living room, quivering. Craig reached out to touch her arm, and she whimpered as she slid down onto the sofa, wrapped her arms around her body.

"I don't know what to do," she whispered.

Craig knelt by her, careful to keep enough distance so that she wouldn't feel threatened. "You're upset and frightened and if someone broke into my house, I would be too. I want to help you if I can. But that's up to you."

It didn't seem like anything would break the stalemate that followed. She stared at him silently, and he was beginning to wonder why she really came to talk to him the day before. If she already knew about the lawsuit and was so scared of the police, why talk to Craig?

A pack of cigarettes and a lighter sat on the coffee table. It wasn't something Craig liked to encourage, but he picked them up and passed them to her, then stood and turned. She was already slipping a cigarette between her lips, the injury to her hand not even slowing her down.

"You have my number." Craig covered the distance to the

front door with a few quick steps and reached for the handle. "If you change your mind—"

"The guy who broke in, the reason I'm scared to tell you . . . he's a cop."

CHAPTER SIX

"Give me some good news."

Part of him wanted to laugh. There was his partner, perky as ever—although she'd smack him if he said so—sitting on his desk, hair in a ponytail, color in her cheeks, simmering with energy.

The other part of him hated to be the one to bear the bad news.

She seemed to sense what he was thinking, because her smile faded. "What's wrong?"

"The blood on the sweater was a match for Jeffrey Reimer, but . . ."

"But what?"

Tain passed her the report.

Ashlyn opened it and skimmed the contents. "And here I thought I might beat you in this morning."

"I stopped by the lab on the way in, so technically you did get here first."

That earned him one of her wide-eyed glares as she closed the folder. He knew she didn't care about technicalities. She cared that he knew about the results before she did.

"What about the bat?"

"The report isn't done, but the prelim says it's most likely the murder weapon. They need more time because they're processing fingerprints." He nodded toward the door. Ashlyn put the folder on a tray on her desk, slid off the table, grabbed her coat and followed him. "Where are we going?"

"To talk to the neighbors, see what we can find out about the happy Reimer household."

"Do I detect a note of cynicism in your voice? How unlike you." She smiled as they stepped outside. "Seriously, you care to connect the dots, or are you going to keep me in the dark?"

They got in the car. "The lab found two types of blood on the bat, and both of them match blood found on the clothes. They're doing some tests to confirm everything before we jump to conclusions."

"But?"

"The blood was from someone related to Jeffrey. We've seen Christopher, Richard and Tracy Reimer, and none of them had any obvious injuries." He backed out of the parking lot and headed for the road.

"Zidani's going to love this." Ashlyn shook her head, at first with the slow shake of disbelief, then with the more emphatic motions of someone who's reached an unpleasant conclusion. "Do you think Christopher hurt Shannon?"

Tain glanced at her, but before he could say anything she continued, "Maybe he tried to stop her from hurting Jeffrey."

"You think he feels guilty?"

She shrugged. "Assume he told us the truth yesterday and Shannon killed Jeffrey. Christopher doesn't just see it happen, he's there. He grabs the bat, he hits her and hurts her. But he's not strong enough to stop her. She kills Jeffrey. He feels like a failure because he couldn't protect his little brother."

"And he knows he assaulted his sister, so he's scared." Tain thought about it for a moment. "It's possible."

"But?"

He almost smiled. "But it could be he lied to us. It wasn't Shannon who killed Jeffrey, it was Christopher. He was found not far from where we recovered the bloodstained sweater. If that bat came from the Reimer house, then he had access to it."

"And if he managed to get a hold of the bat long enough to injure Shannon, how did she get it back from him to kill Jeffrey?"

Tain paused. "Unless he hurt her after the murder."

"But then why let his sister flee?" Ashlyn asked. "And why leave the bat in the woods, away from the crime scene?"

They were silent for a moment. Tain knew concealment was usually an indicator of guilt. What they lacked for both suspects was motive. Unless they could locate the witness, question Christopher or find Shannon, for now all they really had were theories.

"Nothing about that family felt . . . right yesterday, you know what I mean?"

Tain nodded. "I agree."

They lapsed into silence again. Tain glanced at Ashlyn and saw the slight twist of her jaw, which meant she was turning things over in her mind. After a few moments she sighed.

"Now we can't even be certain Shannon Reimer's a suspect," Ashlyn said. "She may be a second victim."

"Perhaps you can sweet-talk Mr. Smythe into letting us chat with the family."

"I'd have to conceal my loathing and contempt."

"Can I ask you something?" He glanced at her, just to get a sense of whether it was safe to continue. "What is it about guys like him that pisses you off so much?"

"You mean you think I should drop to my knees and thank God there are sexist pigs like Parker and egotistical jerks like Byron Smythe taking up valuable space on the planet?"

He grinned. "You sound like me."

She groaned. "I do, don't I? And 'unhealthy partner influence' isn't covered in the insurance plan."

"And I'm the product of extensive therapy. If that's your only hope, you're screwed."

That was met with silence. He doubted there was even a debate in her mind. Ashlyn wouldn't ask. She never pried, not about his past.

She probably just assumed he was talking about the incident when they'd first worked together anyway.

"You want to know what it is about guys like that, Tain? I'm not about putting guys down. Sure, I'll joke around with my friends, people who know I'm kidding, but I don't need to take shots at men to feel better about myself. They remind me of peacocks, strutting their stuff, but the only way they seem important is by attacking others. Specifically, women. I figure anyone who's so insecure they have to pull others down in order to feel good about themselves is pretty sad. They should save the pissing contests for the locker room. It's a real turnoff."

"You couldn't stand me when you met me."

"Who says anything's changed?"

"Touché."

"I know you were only joking about having me try to finesse the info out of Smythe, but I don't think he'd give in. We didn't even get to look through Shannon's room yesterday." She paused. "Let's run wild with the theories for a second. If either Shannon or Christopher killed Jeffrey, don't you think the parents would know which one did it?"

"There would probably be a history of violence, so yeah, I guess so."

Ashlyn looked at him. "That means if Shannon isn't a killer, but could be another victim, her parents probably know."

"Which means either she's guilty and they're protecting her, or they know she's innocent and they're protecting Christopher."

"Or this has something to do with Richard Reimer's business dealings and someone else was in the park yesterday," Ashlyn said.

"You know, Christopher's statement never did sit right. Without any of the physical evidence to consider, something still seemed strange."

That was what lingered on his mind as he parked the car. He knew that there was no one way people acted when they got shocking news, but everything about the Reimer family was wrong. Christopher had seemed nervous, agitated and been an unusual witness from the beginning. The physical altercation between Christopher and his father, the way Christopher just dumped the news about Jeffrey's death on his parents . . .

Parents who then promptly called a lawyer. Was it because they knew more than they'd let on? Did they have reason to suspect that it wasn't Shannon who'd murdered Jeffrey, but that she, too, was a victim? Is that why they'd never asked where their daughter was?

They followed the sidewalk to the door, and he rang the bell. When a woman answered he raised his ID.

"I'm Constable Tain, and this is my partner, Constable Hart. We were hoping you could answer a few questions for us."

"Eleanor Pratt. Is this about the people next door?" She looked like a pragmatic type. Hair cut in a short and tidy fashion, the wisps of gray uncorrected, clothed in blue slacks and a red blouse, no makeup.

"We were wondering if you noticed anything unusual yesterday morning, maybe even the night before?" Ashlyn asked.

"The better question would be when didn't I notice something unusual. The incident you witnessed yesterday morning between the older boy and his father, that is normal." She gestured for them to come inside and shut the door behind them, but didn't invite them past the landing. "The only thing odd about it was that the woman didn't get involved."

"You've witnessed regular physical confrontations between Christopher and his parents?" Tain asked.

The lines around her eyes deepened as she frowned. "Well, let's put it this way. Both parents get physical with their children, but Christopher is the only one who fights back." She paused. "He didn't always. But one day, he got big enough. I used to see the parents . . . with Shannon. I was surprised you didn't come asking questions yesterday."

"Normally we would have," Tain said. "Did you happen to see any of the family members leave the house yesterday before we arrived?"

She nodded. "They all left. It was still dark, and I was upstairs. I heard some shouting and looked out the window. Shannon was running down the driveway. Her father went after her and grabbed her arm. Christopher came out then and grabbed his dad. The little boy was crying and clinging to his sister. She ran down the road, with her little brother running after her, and Christopher ran after them."

"What did Mr. Reimer do?" Ashlyn asked.

"He went back in the house."

"And Mrs. Reimer?"

"If she was outside, I didn't see her. It wasn't until about ten minutes later that I heard the door slam and saw the parents leave. They were heading in the same direction their children had gone."

"Could you tell if they were carrying anything?" Ashlyn asked.

Eleanor Pratt shook her head. "Not that I could see."

"What about Shannon?"

"She had a bag with her."

"Big? Small? Color?"

"I'm sorry. It was dark. I can't be more specific. Blue or black would be my best guess. It was a large duffel bag."

"Not a knapsack?"

"No."

"Could you tell if anyone was wearing a dark hooded sweater?" Ashlyn asked.

The woman paused. "Now that I think about it, the parents looked like they'd just pulled on jogging pants and sweaters, but I think they had coats on. It's hazy. All of them were wearing dark clothes. I wasn't really paying attention to their clothing, just the fact that none of them looked like they were dressed for school or work."

Tain glanced at Ashlyn, who was writing something on her notepad. "Is there any chance you could be more specific about the time you saw this?"

"Well, normally the alarm goes off at five thirty. My husband prefers to beat the rush-hour traffic. He left shortly after six A.M. I never went back to sleep yesterday. He'd brought me a mug of tea, and I was sitting by the window drinking it when Shannon ran out of the house. I confess, I watched them. I do know that when the parents left the house it was about six forty because I had my alarm set for that time, and it had just gone off."

"Mrs. Pratt, did you ever call the police about the problems next door?" Tain suspected he knew the answer.

"I did. And I phoned social services."

Ashlyn's head snapped up then. "Any chance you remember who you spoke with, or if they ever followed up?"

A distant and thoughtful look crept into Eleanor Pratt's eye and then she said, "Just one moment," and disappeared down the hall. When she returned she handed Tain a card. "This woman came out to speak with me. I assumed it was all fairly straightforward, because they just had me cover what I'd said on the phone and thanked me for my time. As far as I could tell, nothing came of it."

"When was this?" Tain asked.

"Thanksgiving. The shouting was so loud inside their house we could hear it from here."

"And yesterday?" Ashlyn tapped her notepad with her pen. "Could you hear what they were saying?"

"I'm sorry. It was jumbled. 'Let go.' 'Leave me alone.' 'Don't touch her.' What you'd expect, I guess."

Ashlyn nodded. "Thank you very much for your time." She paused as Tain passed Mrs. Pratt one of his business cards. "If you think of anything else, please let us know."

Once Mrs. Pratt had closed the door behind them and they'd put some distance between themselves and the house, Ashlyn said, "It doesn't exactly match up with what Mrs. Reimer said yesterday, does it?"

Tain shook his head. "But nothing about that family adds up."

None of the other neighbors was as helpful. The Pratt house was closest to the Reimers, so it made sense that they would be more aware of any problems or incidents, but one resident farther down the road did add that they'd seen Shannon and Jeffrey Reimer running toward the paths the previous morning, before 6:30. That had been the time on the clock in their car when they'd left their house shortly afterward, but they hadn't seen Christopher, or his parents.

"It's something," Ashlyn said as they returned to the car. Her cell phone rang, and she fished it out of her pocket. Tain didn't have to ask who she was talking to; he was pretty sure he knew.

Her face clouded and she said nothing more than "We're on our way" before hanging up.

"There's no prize for guessing who that was." She opened the passenger door and got in. "However, you get brownie points for good effort if you can guess why we've been called in now."

"Don't tell me they found Shannon," he said as he started the car.

Ashlyn laughed. "Since when did you become an optimist? Nothing quite so helpful. Mr. Smythe would like an update on the status of our search for Shannon Reimer."

"Shame you aren't sick today. I'm sure it really would have pissed him off to come in to a police station on a weekend and not even get the consolation of seeing you."

"You were expecting me to be sick?"

Tain glanced at her and hesitated. He wouldn't have been surprised if she was annoyed by his remark, but instead she looked hurt. "You haven't been yourself lately. I thought maybe you were fighting off the flu or something."

"I'd have to be pretty sick to call in in the middle of a case like this."

"I know. I didn't mean anything by it. We had a long day yesterday and . . . Look, forget it. I just wish you didn't have to deal with Smythe today."

"That makes two of us."

When they arrived at the station Smythe was waiting in an interview room, looking relaxed. He was in casual attire, pants and a sweater instead of the custom suits he was fond of, and sipping an overpriced coffee that did not come from their staff room.

"Constable," Smythe said as Tain entered. When Ashlyn joined them a moment later Smythe smiled. "Ms. Hart. It's always nice to see you. Makes up for coming in on the weekend."

Tain saw the shadow flicker across Ashlyn's face as she sat down. "I can't say the same, Mr. Smythe. This is taking valuable time from our investigation. Unless your clients are willing to consent to interviews, or to allow us to search—"

"Not at this time." Smythe took a sip of his coffee, apparently undeterred by her brusque tone. "They want to know what's being done to find Shannon Reimer."

"Everything that can be done is being done."

"And by everything you mean . . ." He held up a hand, inviting her to elaborate.

Instead, Ashlyn stood. "This investigation is being hampered by your clients' unwillingness to speak with us. We have limited information about Shannon's friends, associates and family members, don't have access to her diary or any information from her family about her state of mind before Jeffrey's murder yesterday."

"My clients are not going to make any statements that may be used to help support a murder charge against their own daughter."

"Christopher Reimer already has."

He waved his hand dismissively. "Statements that will be thrown out as inadmissible. He was in shock, he wasn't afforded legal counsel, he's eleven years old."

Ashlyn glanced at Tain. He knew what she was thinking. Every exchange with this lawyer would be a cat-and-mouse game, wondering when to play certain cards. Revealing that Shannon was not necessarily their prime suspect now might be enough to persuade Smythe to get his clients to cooperate with them . . .

But not if one of them was guilty. Then it would tip them off, let them know they were under suspicion.

"Just remember, Mr. Smythe, that a young girl is out there somewhere. She may be injured, frightened, alone. Trying to get status reports from us is only going to make it take longer for us to find her. To be blunt, I don't have time for this."

Ashlyn turned and started walking to the door as Tain stood up.

"Wait." Smythe remained seated, but he didn't look quite as confident as he had when they'd first entered the room. He reached into his pocket and removed a small address book. "Shannon's. I expect it's bought me a bit of goodwill." He slid it across the table, toward Ashlyn.

She paused, blew out a breath, stepped toward the table and reached out for the book.

"If you expect to get information from us you'll have to do better than that," Ashlyn said as she reached for the book.

Smythe put his hand over hers. "And if you expect me to help you, you'll have to change your attitude."

The cocky grin slipped back into place as he stood, let go of her hand and walked out the door, leaving his coffee cup behind.

Craig sat in his vehicle, parked behind a Tim Hortons. He doubted parking behind a Tim Hortons at any time of the day was a good choice if you wanted to find a quiet place to think, but morning was especially bad. All the people who had to work needed their morning caffeine fix, and all the parents being dragged to the malls needed something to compensate for noisy kids and jostling with strangers in crowded stores as they tried to get their holiday shopping done.

It wasn't until a cruiser pulled up beside him and the officer got out and knocked on his window that he glanced at the clock and realized how long he'd been there.

He held up his ID. "Sorry. I'll go in, get my breakfast and be on my way."

"A little out of your jurisdiction, aren't you?"

"I'm not here on a call. Not really."

"You don't have to worry about it. Look, your sergeant called my sergeant and asked us to keep an eye on the Harrington place, just let him know if anything unusual came up. Apparently you didn't show up for work this morning, so he asked us to keep an eye out for you."

Craig pushed his irritation aside. How could Zidani know he was here? "Have you noticed anything out of the ordinary at the Harrington residence?"

"Not until you showed up there this morning."

After a moment of silence the officer slapped Craig's door and stepped back. "Well, I did my bit."

Craig passed the officer his card. "If anything unusual does happen at the Harrington house can you let me know?"

The man shrugged, said, "Sure," took the card and went back

to his car. Craig waited until he drove away, then reached for his phone.

There was no answer at the first number, so he tried Steve Daly's office. It was a weekend, and that seemed like a long shot, but this time of year everyone was trying to get things done before Christmas break. He was in luck.

"Steve Daly, please."

"I'm sorry, he isn't in."

"Do you know when you expect him?"

"Can I ask who's calling?"

"Constable Craig Nolan, Coquitlam RCMP." Silence. "His son."

"Oh, right. Sorry I didn't recognize your voice, Craig. You should be able to reach your father at home by now."

"I just tried his residence there."

"I meant home in BC. He flew back yesterday."

"Are you sure? I knew Alison was back . . ."

"Um hmm. Mrs. Daly flew back yesterday morning. Steve left a few hours later, around noon."

He hadn't asked Alison when Steve was due home, but she'd given him the impression that his father was still in Regina. Craig wondered if she knew. If Steve had flown back midday, he should have been home about the time an intruder was breaking in to his basement. "You don't happen to know why they flew at different times, do you?"

"Your father was supposed to leave tomorrow, but he made a last-minute change to his flight."

They went through the formalities of wishing each other happy holidays and he hung up. Then he started his vehicle and headed for the highway.

He was beginning to wonder if he should have insisted Zidani give the Lockridge review to someone else. Zidani, who'd been so quick to point fingers and assume Craig had been given a free ride by his dad when Steve had been his senior officer, had assigned Craig to review a case that his father had worked on years before. Something wasn't right about that.

It took longer than usual to work through the Saturday traffic. With only a few weeks of holiday shopping left Saturdays were hell on the roads. It was over an hour before he turned down the road his parents lived on.

There was an unmarked police car in the driveway, just like the one he normally drove. It was empty.

He parked and jogged to the door, barely stopping to knock before he opened it and called out. "Alison? It's Craig." He went in and started up the stairs.

"Craig?"

He reached the landing just as she entered the hallway from the living room.

"I tried to call you."

"When?"

"About an hour ago."

When he'd been on the phone, talking to his dad's secretary. He looked over Alison's shoulder. "What the hell are you doing here?"

Luke held up his hand. "Relax. I answered the phone at your desk. Nobody knew where you were so I came out myself."

"I've been on a call since before dawn." Craig turned back to his stepmother. "Could you make some tea?"

She returned his gaze for a moment, then nodded and gave one of her looks that told him she could see right through the flimsy request. He wanted her out of the room and she knew it, but at that moment he really didn't care. Once she was gone he walked right up to his partner and pointed a finger at him.

"You should have called me."

"She said she tried."

"The phone was busy, not out of the service area."

"What's your problem? I'd think you'd be happy someone came out here to check on her."

"The problem is, I don't want you anywhere near my family without me here."

"So that's it? You're going to talk about lack of trust when you're out on a call and don't even let me know?"

"A call that has nothing to do with you," Craig said. "It's something Zidani ordered me to go through yesterday."

"Yeah, the boxes you took home. Just in case your partner decides to snoop around, I guess."

"Messages have been going missing from my desk."

"Who do you think answers your phone and puts the messages there to begin with? What do I want with your messages?"

Craig stared at Luke. He had to admit that Luke had a point. He'd always thought Zidani had been the one, rifling through the garbage, rummaging through his desk drawers. He thought back to the day before, when he'd seen Luke lock his desk.

Alison entered then, carrying a tray with a teapot and three cups. They all sat down and went through the pretense of civility. Luke recapped what he knew, which wasn't much more than they'd learned the day before. Whoever it was hadn't even gotten inside this time. A neighbor had been walking their dog and the dog went crazy, broke free and ran into the Dalys' backyard. It wasn't until the dog's owner caught up with his pet that he saw a dark form dashing through the trees. The dog's leash had gotten tangled, which was the only reason he hadn't caught the intruder.

"Description?" Craig asked.

Luke shook his head. "Generic. Too far away to tell if it was a man or a woman or give a good guess on height. The neighbor couldn't say for sure, but his glasses are as thick as Coke bottles. Dark hair hidden by a ski cap, dark jacket, sweatpants as far as he could tell."

"When's Dad coming back?" Craig asked Alison.

"He flies home tomorrow."

She didn't avert her gaze, her cheeks didn't redden, she didn't flinch or hesitate. Craig had never known his stepmother to lie to him, and he didn't think if she tried now she could do it so convincingly. Which meant that wherever his dad was, Alison didn't know.

"You should stay at our place tonight. I'd feel a lot better, knowing you're okay."

Alison shook her head. "I'm not going to be chased out of my own home."

"You can't stay here! It's not safe."

"I have a gun."

"Since when?"

"It's licensed and I know how to use it."

"Alison . . ." He thought back to the day before. The unexplained blood on the floor.

"I haven't used it. I hope I don't have to. But once you start running, when do you stop? Could be it was just some kid, cutting through the yard this time. It happens."

"Then why run?"

"If a rottweiler came charging at you, wouldn't you run?"

He tossed up his hands. "But if anything else happens, you call me right away. And if you can't get me you call Ashlyn. Or Tain."

Craig stood, paused to bend down and kiss her on the cheek, then started down the stairs. When he reached the bottom he felt someone grab his arm.

"Should I be asking for a new partner?" Luke asked him as he turned.

"If you want one."

"You're a real piece of work. I heard Tain was a son of a bitch, but he's got nothing on you." Luke brushed past him, yanked the door open and slammed it behind him.

Craig went down the hall to the room where the boxes were stored. A break-in at his dad's home and at Lisa Harrington's and another attempted break-in, all in less than twenty-four hours? It was quite a coincidence.

He opened the closet. The day before he'd been forced to leave the box where the intruder had left it, pulled out and set to one side. It took less than a second to confirm it wasn't there now, and he scanned the rest of the boxes.

It hadn't been put back either.

Craig walked through the lower level, rechecking everything. It didn't appear that anyone had been in since the break-in the day before, but somehow someone had stolen the files the intruder was after.

His dad's work files. Files that dated back to the time of Hope Harrington's murder investigation.

CHAPTER SEVEN

Ashlyn hung up the phone and got to her feet. "Let's go."

Tain stood and reached for his coat. "Where?"

"Anywhere but here, preferably before Zidani finds us."

She'd called social services and after restating her request three times had been assured she'd get a call back when the case worker was tracked down. All she could do was thank them and leave her cell number.

Once they were inside the car she pulled out the address book Byron Smythe had given them and started leafing through it. "Wonderful."

"What?"

"She lists everyone by first name only. Nurani, Jody, Matt. And you can hardly call it an address book. All it lists are phone numbers. Cell phone numbers."

"And here I thought our buddy Byron was trying to be helpful. That's useless." Tain started the car. "He must really like you."

Ashlyn smacked him on the arm with the address book. She didn't like Byron Smythe, but she also didn't take him for a fool. Coming in on a Saturday, insisting on a personal update on the search for Shannon under the pretext of providing useless information . . . She could charge him with interfering with a police investigation. It might not stick, but it could still hurt him.

And he'd be off the Reimer case. Conflict of interest.

She doubted that was what he wanted. Smythe could pawn

the case off on one of the other lawyers in his firm with the snap of a finger. She opened the address book again, this time at the very first page and started reading everything.

Ashlyn whistled. "I changed my mind. Let's go talk to Zidani."

"Are you nuts?" He looked at her for a moment, but didn't argue. Instead, he pulled back into the spot he'd just backed out of and parked the car.

Ashlyn got out and shut the door. Once she was beside Tain on the sidewalk she held out the book.

"I guess BS isn't completely useless after all."

Zidani's door was open when they got there. She knocked, but didn't wait for him to respond before entering. "Sir, we—"

"Sir?" He smirked. "What's the occasion? Don't tell me you just want something and you think playing nice is the way to get it."

Ashlyn could feel her cheeks burn, but she didn't let that stop her. "Actually, I have bad news. We have reason to believe that Shannon Reimer didn't kill her brother. She may be a victim." She gave Zidani a quick recap of what they'd learned from the evidence and the statements the neighbors made. "What we do have is this," she said as she set the address book down on his desk. "Shannon's cell number and billing information."

"You want to put a trace on the phone, see if we can track her location that way?"

"Not just that. I want to clone it so that we can monitor any incoming calls. It might help us establish motive and piece together what happened."

"And if she's dead it won't help you at all."

"Unless the phone is active and someone leaves a message." Ashlyn shrugged. "There's no guarantee we'll even get her location. But right now, we don't have access to the family and without more to go on, I don't know how we're going to find Shannon."

"You could end up spending hours in office, wasting time, getting nothing useful."

"Put Sims on it, and one other officer. Skeleton crew working on a long shot."

Zidani reached for his phone. "Have you tracked down that other witness who saw the kids at the park?"

"Not yet," Tain said.

"Then get to work."

"Don't forget to take that book to the lab. They might be able to get Shannon's prints. I've touched it, you have, Byron Smythe and who knows who else, but it's still worth a shot."

Zidani nodded and jerked his thumb in the direction of the door.

Once they were in the hallway Tain said, "I guess that's Zidani for 'dismissed.' "

"He can't be feeling well. We just had a whole conversation with him without an argument."

"Well, if I didn't know better I'd swear you're seriously ill. You called him 'sir.' "

Ashlyn suppressed a grin. "Could be proof miracles still happen. Might restore your faith in a divine power in control of the universe."

"Best it could get me is belief in Santa Claus, and even that's unlikely," Tain said as he followed her out to the parking lot.

"So you don't believe in . . ." She considered her words. "Whatever your people believe in?"

"Why this sudden curiosity?"

Ashlyn shrugged. "You ever think about it when we're on a call? Like yesterday."

Tain looked down as he opened the car door. He didn't get inside, just stood there silently, one hand resting on the hood of the vehicle, gaze lowered. Then he said, "Sure. I think about it," and got in the car.

She got in the passenger side. "Why don't you ever let me drive?"

"Whatever's waiting on the other side of death, I don't want to find out just yet."

It was the kind of smart-ass comment she expected from him, but it lacked its usual underlying humor. There was a tension that had settled in his forehead and his neck, something about his bearing that told her the question was weighing on his mind.

"You'd think with all the cases we've had, with that big one back in the summer, that this wouldn't bother me so much," she said. "If anything, it's gotten harder."

He glanced at her as he pulled out onto the road. "You handle it well."

"C'mon, Tain. You saw me yesterday. It rattled me, more than I like to admit."

"You're human. What matters most is that you put your feelings aside and did your job. And you do it well. There were some guys there who've been with the department longer than you or I who were pretty shook up yesterday."

"Sometimes I wonder what good we're doing. Maybe it makes more sense to be a social worker, to intervene before stuff like this happens."

"Yeah, social services did a helluva lot of good for this family."

Most of the time, Ashlyn felt she and Tain got along extremely well. He could be harsh and unforgiving, as Sims knew, but she always felt she understood Tain. Deep down, they had a level of trust and respect that formed the foundation of their working relationship.

But every now and again she caught a glimpse of a side of him that he kept shut off from her, things he didn't share. Either because he thought it would affect her ability to work with him or because there were still things he didn't trust her with.

The way he spoke about social services, the venom in his words, surprised her. It wasn't an offhand remark or even the criticism of someone who felt the system had let a family down with devastating consequences. No, something in his words felt . . . personal. And private.

"Sometimes we have to let killers go free, Tain. No system is perfect."

He parked the car at the address of the witness, but he didn't get out right away. "Look, I'll try to keep an open mind until they call us back, but a child is dead. There was a history of abuse, and that was reported. Right now, the thing I want to know is why any of those children were still in Richard and Tracy Reimer's care."

He got out of the car, and once she'd closed the door she held up her hands. "I agree with you."

"Then let's drop it."

"Because this really isn't about Shannon and Jeffrey Reimer."

Tain turned and glared at her. She'd known the moment the words were out of her mouth that she'd crossed a line, and the look on his face made her feel as though someone had just weighed her heart down with a brick.

"I'm sorry. You're right. It's none of my business."

He turned wordlessly and walked up the driveway to the house.

When they reached the front step he held back, so she rang the bell. After a moment, when there was no answer, she rapped on the door.

Ashlyn turned around and scratched her forehead. "So much for that." She walked back to the car, conscious of Tain behind her and his silence. When they reached the passenger door he handed her the keys, but refused to meet her gaze.

As she climbed in the driver's side her cell phone rang. She answered it.

"How are you feeling today?" Craig asked.

"Good. What happened with that call this morning?"

There was a pause before he answered. "It's complicated."

"I thought you were on routine stuff, babysitting duty. How complicated can it be?" She ground her palm into her forehead, instantly regretting her words. "I didn't mean it like that."

He was silent for a moment, then asked, "Did you still want to meet up later?"

"If you're free. Craig—"

"Six thirty? At the food court."

"Unless something comes up with this case."

"Call if it does."

"Sure. Craig—"

"I can't talk right now. I'll see you later."

He cut the call before she had a chance to say anything else.

Craig tossed his cell phone on the passenger seat. Then he started his Rodeo and drove to the highway. What he wanted to do could be done from his own desk, but he didn't want to deal with Luke Geller. With any luck, by the time he did show up at the office, Luke would be reassigned to another partner.

If Zidani would let him. For a second, he almost felt bad for Luke. It wasn't fun to be on the receiving end of Zidani's contempt, granted, but what had Luke done to deserve being stuck shadowing an officer who was basically on desk duty?

It was Zidani who helped Craig decide which station to head to. Langley RCMP knew he'd been out at Lisa Harrington's that morning. Technically, Lisa lived in Langley Township, but the Langley RCMP covered policing in the entire area. She wasn't far from Aldergrove, which was where Hope's body had been recovered. His boss had ordered him to review a case from their territory; coming to ask for their input was professional courtesy, not stepping on toes.

He was also hoping that Zidani's interference that morning had been limited to the main station, in Langley, so the officers in Aldergrove wouldn't worry about speaking to him.

Before he got inside the building he bumped into an officer older than his father. "Constable Klassen? Isaac Klassen?" He gestured at the name tag, which betrayed the surname and rank.

"Yes. What can I do for you?"

"Constable Craig Nolan, Coquitlam RCMP." Craig shook Klassen's hand. "I've been assigned to review an old file, the Hope Harrington case."

"Ah." The lines in the man's face deepened. "Crime like that, you never forget it."

"I recognized your name from the case notes. You viewed the crime scene?"

Klassen nodded. "Called in to help search for evidence. It really wasn't my case. Steve Daly and Ted Bicknell were the ones who worked it."

"I can't find any record of Ted Bicknell. No phone listed in the province for him."

Klassen hesitated, as though he was considering how much to say. "I didn't know him well myself, but one of the other officers might be in touch. He's on holidays until Tuesday, though."

"It would be a real help if you could ask him if he knows where Ted is."

"Sure, but you can talk to Steve Daly yourself. He's inside."

Craig tried to keep the surprise from registering on his face as he followed Klassen through the building to the staff room. But when they got there it was empty. Klassen looked out the window and tapped it. Craig only saw the blur of a dark green sedan driving past. "Just missed him."

"That's okay. I'll catch him at home." He hoped his voice didn't sound as tense as he felt. "I don't suppose you'd have time to show me where Hope's body was found."

Again, Klassen shrugged. "Suit yourself. You can ride with me."

"If it's okay with you, I'll follow."

When they arrived at the alley Craig parked behind the cruiser. Klassen led him several yards down from the road. "It was right here." He pointed at the pavement. "She was found faceup."

Klassen walked him through the basics, nothing the files hadn't already told him. No blood trail and little blood at the scene, suggesting she'd been killed elsewhere, her body moved. The lab had found fibers that matched a blanket from the Harrington home, one from Hope's own bed. Lisa Harrington had noticed the blanket was missing when the police had searched Hope's bedroom. They'd matched fibers from the blanket left on the bedspread. A dog the family had looked after for a few days had chewed on the hem, causing it to fray.

It was enough to suggest someone who had access to her house and to justify searching the property, which was when they'd found the murder weapon.

The case had weaknesses, though. They'd never located any

eyewitnesses, despite five times canvassing the area where Hope's body had been found.

"Why did you guys cover the same ground again and again?" Craig asked.

"It was a bad case. Bad timing. Another young girl had been murdered only a few weeks before, in Surrey. Not our jurisdiction, but nobody wanted to think this was an epidemic. The public needed reassurance. I remember thinking I was glad I wasn't Bicknell or Daly, with all the pressure they were under to make an arrest, and do it fast. Me, I've always been more interested in community policing. Working murders, rapes, this kind of a case?" Klassen shook his head. "Not for me. Even now I can't get the bad taste out of my mouth. Kind of call that really gets to you and then won't get lost later. I mean, s'pose that's as it should be. I've got my own kids. Have you got kids?"

Craig shook his head.

"You have kids you'll understand what I'm saying. I knew Hope. Not well, but she was a nice girl. There wasn't much in her life to be happy about, but she was still a sweet kid. Me, I went home and hugged my kids so tight I thought they'd break. But Bicknell and Daly, they closed the case. Daly made rank as a result. Bicknell retired a few months later. I suspect it took a big toll on him. Never really figured him for the type to handle an investigation like this, and it wasn't as though he'd been working with Daly all that long, but they still put it down. Never seemed to rattle Daly, though, but then he didn't have kids of his own."

Something told Craig that if Klassen knew of his relationship to Steve Daly, he'd stop talking, so he didn't set him straight.

Craig shook Klassen's hand. "Thanks for taking the time to walk me through it." He pulled out a card and passed it to Klassen. "If you think of anything else, anything that didn't sit right with you about the case . . ."

Klassen's eyes narrowed. "You doubt they got the right guy?"

"I'm trying to make sure it's airtight. You haven't heard about the civil suit? Donny Lockridge is going after the department."

"Well, you'd best talk to Steve Daly, although if I were him I wouldn't be too happy to have you digging around in one of my old cases like this."

"Believe me, I'd feel the same if it was me, but I'm the lesser of two evils here. The media's already all over this."

"Ah, now I know why your name is so familiar. That case a few months back." Klassen nodded, as though that bit of information helped him reach some conclusion about Craig. Then he got in his cruiser and drove away.

There were two piles of reports on Ashlyn's desk. She thumbed through the ones stacked on her lap as she leaned back in her chair, feet propped up on a lower desk drawer that was open. Down to the last few pages.

She'd been deluding herself with the idea that in the mounting piles of reports from all the classmates and family members who'd been tracked down she might find some that contained promising leads. Instead she had a stack she called "Grasping at Straws" and another known as "Hope to Hell This Person Never Needs to Be Questioned Again in My Lifetime." "Useless" for short.

Tain's phone rang and he answered it. She snuck a glance, half hoping there was a promising lead they could follow up on. Ever since they'd returned to the station he'd been silent. The shadow she'd seen cross his face had turned into a cloud that had settled there.

If anything, when he answered the phone his face darkened.

"We already talked about this." Tain's voice was low, but not low enough that she couldn't hear what he was saying. When he was angry he spoke with a sharpness. Some people muddled their words, but with Tain, each syllable became crystal clear. "I don't want her there." His faced tightened. "Don't talk to me about rights. She lost that right when she—"

Tain looked up and stopped cold as he stared at Ashlyn. She felt a chill creep up her neck and settle in her skin.

"I'm not talking about this." He slammed the phone down, got up and stomped out of the room.

For a moment Ashlyn felt numb. Whatever was going on with Tain, he was keeping it bottled in, and it was eating at him. Had she been so preoccupied with her own concerns she just hadn't noticed it, or had this only been going on the past few days? Ashlyn turned back to the last few reports. More of the same. Seemed fine. Seemed unhappy. Family who hadn't seen Shannon in ages.

She lowered her feet and sat up after tossing the last useless piece of paper down. After labeling two folders and filing the stacks of papers appropriately, she got up and wandered down the hall to the room where Sims had been assigned to work. Zidani had approved her request and used the fact that they were searching for a missing teenager to expedite the process.

"Anything?" she asked as she sank down in a chair.

"Constable Hart." Sims flashed his perfect smile, but reined it in before answering. "Nothing so far, I'm afraid."

She shrugged. "Pretty much sums up this case. I just went through all the interview reports, which was a waste of time."

"You should pass that on to me. I'm stuck here anyway, and I may as well be of some help. Save yourself the time."

"Thanks, Sims. But sometimes it helps you wrap your head around a case. Besides, it isn't like there's anything else to go on right now. The family isn't cooperating. Their lawyer—" Ashlyn frowned. It was just one of the things that had been bothering her from the beginning, that she hadn't had a chance to check up on yet. "Do you have access to all our records through that computer?"

Sims nodded. "And the Internet and Mahjong if I'm really bored."

"You really want to do something to help me out?"

He nodded again. Almost eagerly.

"Byron Smythe is representing the family. Can you do a background check, see if anyone in the family's been charged before? Lawyers like Smythe usually stick to rich criminals, the kind who finance drug operations but never get their hands that dirty. I want to know what use Mr. and Mrs. Reimer have for him."

"Sure." Sims moved the laptop in front of him.

"Also, can you check out all their bank accounts? I know we've been monitoring Shannon's local accounts, but this family has a lot of money. Make sure she doesn't have access to anything offshore, and check them out."

"That shouldn't be a problem. If we have probable cause for cloning her phone, Sergeant Zidani should be able to clear any legal hurdles."

"Let me know if he can't."

"Anything else?"

"Can you get your partner to check on something for me? I want to know if either Mr. or Mrs. Reimer was having an affair, if either of them had anything . . . unusual going on. We're looking at that as well, but . . ."

"Fresh eyes." Sims nodded. "I'll let you know as soon as I find something, Constable Hart."

"Thanks." She stood, turned to leave but paused at the door. "And drop the 'constable' bit. Ashlyn."

He smiled. She walked away.

Craig had filtered out all the chatter, footsteps, the sound of the door opening and closing. It was all just background noise, nothing important, something he'd converted into an inconvenient hum in his mind.

Which was probably why he hadn't realized someone was approaching him until she sat across from him, mug in hand.

"I had a feeling I'd find you here."

He didn't need to look up. He recognized Emma Fenton's voice from their encounter the night before. "Unfortunately for me."

"Well, this is the closest coffee shop to the crime scene, and it was where Hope worked part-time before she died. I figured if you hadn't been here yet, you'd end up here sooner or later."

He looked up. Emma smiled. "Can I get you a coffee?"

"You can get lost."

She arched an eyebrow, but didn't really look annoyed. Bemused, more than anything. "We'll forgive that. Especially since you were up so early, dealing with the break-in at Lisa Harrington's home."

He felt his shoulders tighten. "How did you know about that?"

"That's not really what's important, is it? Although it's interesting." She tapped her index finger on her chin and looked thoughtful. "First there's a break-in at your parents' home. Then Lisa Harrington's. Then another attempt at your parents' house. I can't imagine what the intruder is after."

"You're assuming there's a connection. It's just a coincidence."

"And is it a coincidence that Steve Daly was transferred to Langley just before Hope Harrington's murder and that he made rank when he closed the case?"

"You tell me. You seem to have everything else about this case worked out." He stood up and walked to the door. Craig knew she was following him to his vehicle, but she waited until he was beside his Rodeo before she spoke again.

"You know, the most interesting thing about this case is you."

He spun around. "What the hell is that supposed to mean?"

"Think about it. Your dad gets transferred suddenly. Word is, his new partner was under suspicion by his own department. A local girl gets murdered and he and his partner catch the case. High profile, not just because it's a girl but because of a recent case, just across the township lines in Surrey. Your dad's under a lot of pressure to make an arrest, fast. Now the man convicted is suing for malicious prosecution, wrongful conviction and whatever else his lawyer can dream up. And who does the RCMP assign to check up on the details of the case? Steve Daly's son, the somewhat dishonored cop who some say got his partner killed last year. Why you, Craig? Zidani's hardly a card-carrying member of your fan club. Did he give you a rope to hang your dad with? Is that what you have to do to get back on the streets?"

Craig turned away from her and focused on unlocking the door and getting in his vehicle. He didn't trust himself to speak. His head felt as though it was stuck in a vise that was being screwed so tight, it might explode.

One thing was for sure. If Emma thought she'd win him over as an ally, she'd played the wrong cards. She had to have a source in the department to know about him and Zidani, and whatever she was after, it wasn't just a story about Donny Lockridge's conviction and his civil suit. Craig drove away and didn't look back.

When he finally located the house he was looking for he pulled over and killed the engine, but didn't get out. He didn't expect a warm reception, but he didn't know where else to look for his father.

His grandmother answered the door and almost slammed it in his face before he had a chance to speak, but he was too quick for her. He wedged his foot in the opening and used his body weight to push the door back open.

"What do you want?" she demanded.

"I'm looking for Dad."

"He's not here. Now go."

"Grandma—"

She was one of those tough, older people who hadn't softened around the edges with age but had sharpened. Maggie Daly bristled as she pointed a finger at him. "Don't you call me that. As far as I'm concerned, the only parent you've got is that slut of a mother who raised you. Nothing but a bastard, and if my son had any sense at all he would have left well enough alone."

"Whether you like it or not, I'm the only son Steve's ever going to have."

"More's the pity. Now get out before I call the police."

He took a step back, and she slammed the door so hard the windows rattled. The one good thing he could say about his grandmother was that she was honest to a fault. If she said his dad wasn't there, he didn't doubt that was the truth.

Which meant he'd have to make it a real family day and try his grandfather's.

Thomas Daly took off his reading glasses and stepped back. "Come in." Steve Daly looked so much like his father it disappointed Craig. Thomas had just a bit more gray in the hair and deeper lines around the eyes. Anyone could look at them and tell they were related.

Craig, on the other hand, didn't have the same striking resemblance, no obvious physical connection. A fact that probably made Maggie Daly happy.

"Sorry to bother you."

"It's no bother. You're family."

Tell that to your ex-wife. Craig didn't need to say the words. His grandfather smiled a sad smile, tinged with bitterness.

"She's a cold woman. Blames herself, you know."

"How do you figure that?"

"If she'd raised Steve right he would have been perfect. Never would have had any youthful indiscretions." Thomas Daly led him inside and sat down at the kitchen table.

"You know, I pulled the marriage records and the birth records. It's really amazing Dad survived, considering Grandma was only pregnant for six months. Today, that's possible, but back then . . ." He shrugged.

"And back then you did the right thing. Got married." He shook his head. "I spent a lot of years regretting that. Steve was what made it bearable. But you're not here to talk about your grandmother."

"I'm looking for Dad."

Thomas Daly's brows formed a solid line. "I thought he was still in Regina, teaching."

Craig shook his head. "Apparently he's back. But not at home."

"Alison?"

"She's at the house, but as far as I can tell she still thinks Dad's in Saskatchewan."

"Well, he hasn't been here."

Craig tapped his fingers against the table. "Grandpa, have you ever known Dad to get in any trouble?"

"You mean, besides the mess with your mother?" Thomas Daly shook his head. "No."

"Can you think of anywhere else he might have gone?"

"Sorry, son. Going to make Christmas dinner a real mess if he's having problems."

"You're going for dinner?"

"Heard they invited Maggie too."

"Gluttons for punishment." Craig stood up. "Thanks. I'll see you in a few weeks."

The only thing left for Craig to do was start running credit card checks, and that was where he drew the line. Whatever was going on with his dad, as far as he knew it wasn't criminal and possibly didn't even have anything to do with Craig's assignment.

It was already dark, and he was in Richmond. After the third beep cut into his thoughts he pulled out his cell phone. It took only a few minutes to confirm he'd forgotten the car charger, so he switched off the phone and tossed it on the front passenger seat. With the traffic it took quite a while for him to reach Port Coquitlam and his parents' home.

Alison asked who was there before opening the door to check. She had the chain lock engaged.

"Any more problems?" he asked once she let him inside.

She folded her arms across her chest. "Not unless you count the phone call I just had from my mother-in-law."

"What did she have to say?" Craig could see the answer in his stepmother's eyes and groaned.

"The break-in here, does this have something to do with why you're looking for Steve?"

"Do you know where he is?"

Alison stared at him for a moment, then shook her head. "I thought he was still in Regina."

She turned and walked upstairs, and he followed her.

"You don't seem very upset."

Alison led him into the kitchen. She was peeling potatoes in the sink and adding them to a pot on the stove. "From time to time, Steve gets called away for work."

"To do what?"

"I don't know. He doesn't say."

"Most women wouldn't be so trusting."

She gave him a stern look. "I'm not most women."

He sighed and scratched his head. "I know. Just . . . how come you've never mentioned this to me before?"

"I don't answer to you. And neither does your father."

"But you're here alone. Someone's broken in twice—"

"Once."

"They tried a second time. What if they come back again? What if they don't stay downstairs next time?"

"I'm not going to let fear drive me out of my home."

"Funny, you seemed pretty shook up yesterday. Or have you forgotten locking yourself in your bedroom and all the harassing phone calls?"

She continued peeling potatoes and didn't even glance at him. Her expression had hardened, and he knew she wasn't going to tell him anything useful now. Whether she was angrier at Steve or himself, he couldn't be sure, but he was the one standing there. If she lashed out, he'd take the brunt of it.

Craig reached out and touched her arm, which prompted her to turn and meet his gaze. "I really do need to talk to Dad. It's important."

"If I hear from him, I'll call you."

"Thanks. Now come dead bolt the door behind me."

Ashlyn glanced at her watch. She'd dialed Craig's cell phone three times. Each time it automatically had gone to voice mail, and finally, she broke down and left a message. It had taken a bit of effort to keep the edge out of her voice, but she'd tried. She'd said something thoughtless and annoyed him earlier. Maybe he was trying to get back at her by being late.

What was he working on? He hadn't told her. Whatever it was, he'd been so absorbed the night before that he'd brought work home. And then he got a phone call before dawn and had to go out and was gone all day. It didn't make any sense.

She left the food court and wandered past the window displays, the sparkling lights, boxes wrapped with shiny paper and big bows, overflowing stockings, stuffed toys and train sets and all the things you expected to see during the holidays, Elvis Presley's version of "White Christmas" battling with Bing Crosby's.

So much for peace on earth. They couldn't even agree on music without turning it into a competition. She wondered if Britney or one of the other soulless pop stars had done a Christmas album yet and shuddered. She hoped not. It would just be more noise pollution to tune out at the mall.

Which reminded her of the one album she really wanted to buy. Boney M's Christmas collection. She went to HMV and found a copy, but failed to produce Michael W. Smith's *Christmas*. When they'd made the list of things they needed for the holidays Craig had mentioned losing his CD and wanting to replace it.

Ashlyn continued wandering through the mall until a display of tree ornaments finally lured her inside one store. There was a nativity set, and she wondered if that was something Craig would be interested in. She tried to be supportive of his church background, but he didn't seem to know how important that was to him anymore. It wasn't something he liked to talk about.

She moved on to the tree ornaments. One caught her attention. It was perfect. As she touched it with her fingers she had a feeling, like a cold hand had just run a finger down her spine, and she shivered.

The clock on the wall said it was 7:45. Craig was more than an hour late and not answering his cell phone. What if something had happened to him? Tears welled up in her eyes, threatening to spill over. What if he was in the hospital, and she was here in the mall, annoyed because he'd missed their date while he was in surgery . . . or worse?

Don't be ridiculous. It's just your hormones and all the stuff about Christmas and family that's getting to you.

If Craig had been in an accident someone would call her, wouldn't they?

She took the ornament she'd chosen, got in line, tried not to think about Craig at all and failed.

Maybe she should call again. Or try the house. Once she'd paid the cashier and left the store she keyed in the number, half of her hoping he'd answer and the other half ready to throttle him if he did.

Damn. Craig had watched his stepmother peeling potatoes and convinced himself it wasn't as late as he thought. He should have known better. Alison always started preparing Sunday dinner Saturday night. Old habits died hard.

Despite the fact that it was almost 8 P.M. the parking lot was packed. He finally settled on a spot and tried out a dozen excuses in his mind on his way to the food court. None would do.

She wasn't there.

Why wouldn't she call?

He reached for his cell phone, but his coat pocket was empty. Where had he . . . ? Then he remembered it had been dying. He'd turned it off and tossed it on the front passenger seat.

Ashlyn must have gone home. He couldn't blame her. Even after he'd left Alison's, he'd had Billy Klippert on the stereo, turned up so loud he could have missed a call. Definitely too loud to hear any beeps alerting him to a missed call or a waiting message.

He turned to leave. Just when he thought things couldn't get much worse . . .

"Long day?"

"I'd rather not discuss it with you, Ms. Fenton."

"Emma." She smiled. "And if you insist on using my surname, it's Miss Fenton. Look, I know I was over the line earlier, and I'm sorry. Let me make it up to you. Something to eat, five minutes of your time. You don't have to say anything, just listen. And the sooner you agree, the sooner you get rid of me." She was silent for a moment. "Come on, my treat."

He sighed, and looked at his watch. "Fine. Five minutes."

Ashlyn felt her face flush as she watched Craig take a tray from Edo and follow the woman to a table. Why had she waited all this time? To watch him meet up with someone else?

As much as she hated feeling jealous, their relationship was past the initial euphoric stage, where everything was new. She'd never been the type to be lovesick over a guy or sit and moan over a broken heart for days on end. But things were different with Craig. Especially now.

Half of her wanted to walk over and join them, and the other half wanted to turn on her heel and run. She wondered which side was the more rational one. Her legs wobbled, and she suddenly realized how tired she was. If going over to that table meant getting in a fight, she didn't have the energy for it. She turned to leave.

"Well, well. I didn't expect to see you here." Byron Smythe smiled.

"Don't you have clients to shield?"

"Don't you have a case to solve?"

"For some reason all my suspects are hiding behind their lawyer. Can't imagine why."

"All your suspects? What about Shannon?"

"For all I know you have her stashed with her folks."

The grin slipped from his face. "You really do have a low opinion of me."

She felt a stab of guilt when she saw how his expression changed. "I always thought the first thing law firms did when they hired someone was remove their heart."

"And when you're out there at a crime scene, standing over the body of a dead child, are you any use to the victim if you let your feelings get in the way of processing the evidence?"

"It's different. I follow the evidence, wherever it leads. You use loopholes to keep criminals on the streets."

"Funny, I would think with what's going on with your boyfriend these days you'd have more appreciation for the fact that it's lawyers who keep cops honest." Before she had a chance to say anything, he continued, "Or hasn't he told you his dad framed an innocent man and sent him to prison?"

Her cheeks burned. "It's pretty pathetic when you need to slander good people to feel better about yourself." She started to walk around him, but he grabbed her arm.

"You look at the evidence."

"I don't need to. I've worked with Steve Daly."

"Oh, that's right. Keeping it all in the family. I understand you knew him before you got to know his love child."

It felt so good to smack Smythe, although the skin on her hand stung from the impact. The lawyer's eyes widened with shock and then narrowed as he grabbed her free hand. He still had a firm grip on her other arm.

"I could have you arrested."

She tried to wrench her arm free. "And I can sue you for the insinuations you're making about my personal life. So much for keeping people honest. You've got no leverage on someone so you have to make it up."

"I don't have to make up the fact that your boyfriend is having dinner with another woman though, do I?"

That was when she realized a bit of a crowd had gathered around them. "You have two seconds to let go of me."

"Or what? I'll regret it?" He moved his face closer to hers. "I like it when you're angry. Brings out your passion. I bet it's a real turn-on."

Ashlyn kicked him in the knee with all the energy she could muster, and heard a sickening pop. Smythe's face went a chalky white, and he let go of her. "You bitch!"

"If you ever touch me again I'll aim higher and kick harder."

She left before he had a chance to say anything else.

Ashlyn put the box in the drawer of her nightstand and sank down on the bed. She thought about phoning Tain. After talking to Sims, she'd returned to her desk just in time to see Tain heading out the other door, coat on. She hadn't said anything, and now she regretted it. The last time things had been so tense between them was when they'd first worked together, when she still thought he was a complete asshole.

The sound of the front door closing was distant but distinct and it carried through the silence. Craig was home. The rhythm of his movements, his pattern of stopping to check the mail or the messages on the table in the hallway before going to the closet to hang up his coat, was unmistakable.

A lump rose in her throat.

She caught herself, almost holding her breath, waiting for Craig to come upstairs. Instead, she heard the muffled footsteps heading for the living room.

Straight to the case materials he'd brought home. Her curiosity and irritation battled with her anger, until she finally took a deep breath and forced herself down the stairs. When she entered the room he was studying a report. She hadn't tried to walk softly, and she found it hard to believe he hadn't heard her.

"Where were you?" Ashlyn tried to keep her voice calm, but she felt the wobble of emotion in her words.

He didn't look up. "My cell phone died. I'm sorry."

It was on the far end of the coffee table, plugged in to the wall, the same outlet as the Christmas tree.

"And it didn't occur to you to borrow your friend's?"

Craig looked at her then. "You were there?"

She didn't trust herself to speak. The part of her mind that preferred to deal with practicalities, with reason, told her to go to the kitchen. She forced herself to turn away from him and walk to the other room. Once there she started scanning the cupboards, looking for something simple to make.

Craig had followed her. "What are you doing?"

"I haven't eaten."

"Ash." He moved closer to her and reached for her arm. "What the hell happened?"

Her arm was already starting to show the bruises. "I didn't realize he grabbed me so hard."

"Who?"

"I handled it." She grabbed a granola bar and started to walk past Craig.

"You call that dinner?" He followed her down the hall and up the stairs. "And I asked you a question."

"So did I."

"What?"

"It never even occurred to you to borrow a phone to let me

know you couldn't make it. Only, apparently you could make it. Not enough that I have to watch you have dinner with her, but that damn lawyer has to rub my face in it."

"Is that who did that to your arms? That son of a bitch Smythe?"

"This isn't about him."

"He hurts you and I'm just supposed to shrug that off? What else did he say?"

"It's none of your business."

Craig stared at her. "He said something to you about Dad, didn't he?"

She looked away.

"Ashlyn, what did he say."

Her gaze met his. "You really want to know? He seems to think I traded in for a younger Daly model."

The color drained out of Craig's face as every muscle tightened. For a second, she thought all his rage was directed at her, but he turned and ran down the stairs.

"Craig," she started down the stairs after him, "I told you I handled—"

The door slammed so hard the chandelier in the hallway rattled. Ashlyn sank down, leaned her head against the wall as the edges of the stairs blurred and the tears spilled over and trickled down her cheeks.

CHAPTER EIGHT

The morning sun was unusually bright and warm for December. Or it was an illusion, contributed to by exhaustion. Craig rubbed his eyes, opened them, looked at his watch and groaned.

It hadn't been hard to stay awake most of the night. If anything, it would have been impossible to sleep after what had happened. Last he remembered it was just after 4 A.M. and Lisa's house appeared to have remained undisturbed.

The tapping sound prompted the conscious part of his brain to catch up to his subconscious. That's what had woken him up: the sound of someone knocking on the window.

"Some guard I am," he said sheepishly after rolling down the window. His breath made white puffs in the air, and with the window down a burst of cold rushed into the Rodeo. The kind of cold that cut right through you.

"You want some coffee or tea or somethin'?"

"Really, I don't want to inconvenience you. I just wanted to make sure nobody bothered you again."

"Well, it's no trouble." She pulled her sweater tight around her body. "Bring your mug in and I'll fill it for you."

He followed her to the house and gave her the mug, which still had the remnants of cold tea in the bottom. On the shelf in the corner of the living room there were photos of girls he presumed were Lisa's other daughters. They didn't look much like Hope. They had strawberry-blond hair, like their mother. Freckles instead of Hope's creamy skin. The girls' faces were rounder, the shape of the eyes and nose more like Lisa's but filled out.

Lisa returned and passed him his beverage. "My other girls. I'm glad I had girls. Never had much luck with men." She glanced at him. "No offense."

That reminded him of something he'd wanted to ask about. "Mrs. Harrington, I don't mean to pry—"

"Lisa."

"What about Hope's father? I didn't see anything in the file about him. He didn't attend the trial?"

She walked over to the couch slowly, with her back to him, fiddling with the chain around her neck. "I kept Hope away from him." She turned around then. The look in her dull eyes was like someone had just snuffed out her soul. Mouth settled into a hard line and her shoulders sagged, as though a weight had just been dropped on them. "It's not easy raisin' kids even with two parents these days. But I've managed." She sank down on the sofa and sighed. "You worry about so much sometimes it seems like that's all you do. I spent years worryin' he'd come and take Hope away from me. Seems crazy now."

Lisa was leaning forward, arms resting on her legs, fidgeting as she stared off vacuously at the floor. He felt a surge of anger, only a shadow of what he'd felt the night before but still undeniable. Some women used men and drove them away.

Women like his mother.

And some did their best and still got shafted. What kind of man wouldn't even attend the trial when his daughter was murdered?

"I don't mean to upset you," he said as he sat down across from her, "but what about the father of Hope's half sister? There's no chance Destiny's dad . . . ?"

Lisa blinked, then shook her head. "He was long gone by then."

Craig nodded. "I'm not saying I think Donny's innocent. I just have to be thorough. It'll help if I review everything and show nobody else could have done it. His lawyer will exploit any avenue we don't pursue and use it to create reasonable doubt."

"But he's been convicted, and he lost his appeal."

"The legal process is complicated."

She swallowed. "They called and said he was getting released."

"I thought they hadn't had the parole board hearing yet."

"Apparently the lawsuit changed things. They sent that letter and it took a week to get to me, but he'd already had his meeting Thursday. He's supposed to get out tomorrow."

Craig thought about that. Lisa's testimony had been crucial, and was the main reason Donny had been convicted. "You should take the girls, stay in a hotel for a few days."

Lisa raised her hand. "No. I'm not leavin' my home. It ain't much, but it's what I've got and I can protect us. You mean well, but if we start runnin' how will we ever stop?"

Part of him could understand how she felt. He stood.

"You don't have to worry. I won't let him anywhere near me or my girls."

Craig nodded as the sound of footsteps approaching drew his attention. It was obvious from the photos they were Lisa's daughters.

"Destiny, Desiree, say hello to Constable Nolan."

The older girl, Destiny, did as she was told while averting her gaze. Shy. Quiet. Reserved. That's what struck Craig about how she carried herself.

Desiree was lively and exuberant. "Hi," she said, then turned and ran down the hall. Destiny followed, and then Craig heard the sound of doors closing in the distance.

"Can I use your bathroom?"

Lisa nodded and gave him directions. It didn't take long to establish they shared one primary bathroom, with their toothbrushes and hairbrushes all present and accounted for. Plus a bonus: every drawer was labeled. Destiny and Desiree each had her own place to put her stuff.

He slid the drawers open and sifted through the contents. Once he'd located what he was after he bagged and labeled samples, then quickly flushed the toilet and ran some water. Oldest trick in the book, but effective.

Lisa was waiting by the door when he returned. "It was"—she cleared her throat—"good of you to keep an eye on things."

"I'm just glad everyone's okay." After he thanked her he went back to his vehicle. He started the Rodeo and began to drive back to Coquitlam. Before long he was surrounded by the remnants of an early morning fog that hadn't burned off yet. It wasn't until he got to the Portman Bridge that the sky completely cleared, gold rays shimmering on the Fraser River, making it look prettier than it was most days. Blue sky surrounded the mountains to the north.

There were a number of things still bothering him. The fact that nobody had tried breaking in to Lisa's could mean the intruder had found whatever they were looking for. Lisa hadn't said whether anything was missing, but he'd seen the way she put everything back in the box, as quickly as possible, without really sorting through it. She might not have noticed.

It could also mean they'd returned to his parents' home, but the box they were after was gone. That was what convinced him of the connection, although he wouldn't admit it to that reporter. He'd only needed a quick look to realize that the files disturbed were from the same time as the Harrington murder investigation. That couldn't be a coincidence.

And then there was Emma Fenton. She knew more about this case than she'd even hinted at, and every time he turned around there she was. At the station, at the coffee shop . . .

At the mall.

As he drove along the Lougheed Highway, he switched lanes. Checking up on his stepmother would have to wait; he needed to talk to Ashlyn. He stopped at a grocery store, pretty much the only option at that hour on a Sunday morning, and searched through the bins for a bouquet of flowers that didn't look picked over or lifeless. Since it was close to Christmas there were also shelves of stuffed bears and skiing snowmen, ornaments and tinsel.

Flowers or a bear? Or both? Did the size of the gift reflect how sorry he was? He knew it wasn't actually the gift that mattered. It was the effort. Coming home with a bouquet that hadn't been hastily thrown together after pulling flowers out of a neighbor's garden meant he'd actually thought about her long enough to go to a store and buy something.

Maybe he should get some wine as well. The pasta she liked?

Once he'd spent more time and money at the store than he'd planned he drove to the lab and dropped off the samples, then went to the house.

Her car was gone.

"Thanks for covering for me," Sims said when he returned to the room where he'd been working, monitoring a cell phone nobody was using. Just one more futile effort to make headway on a case that was filled with dead ends. He set a cup down in front of Ashlyn. "Isn't it a bit early for ginger ale?"

"You're drinking that sludge."

"You don't like coffee?"

"I just can't stand the smell of it right now."

"Ah." Sims nodded. "You should really take a day off, get over the flu."

Ashlyn fought to keep her eyes from narrowing. "I have a murder to solve, and I'm fine. I just don't want to drink any damn coffee."

Sims picked up his own mug and took a sip. She almost smiled. He was wisely avoiding eye contact.

"I did start looking at Byron Smythe." Sims set down his mug. After rifling through a short stack of papers he removed a folder and passed it to her.

She'd felt her heart rate escalate just hearing the name, and her jaw clenched. As she took the papers from Sims he flinched.

Inside, he'd started to put together a list of high-profile clients and cases and other dealings. Ashlyn whistled.

"I thought he was just on speed dial with the drug dealers and importers."

"Real estate can be quite profitable for lawyers. That seems to be what ties him to Richard Reimer."

"That, and a lot of money. Any way to know if these deals aren't legit?"

"I'll keep looking, see if I can turn up anything, but I'm not sure how I'd prove that."

"Maybe check the history of the ownership of the properties? Reimer's flipping a lot of land." She pulled up one paper and passed it to him. "Third down. Isn't that where that huge condo complex is being built?"

Sims nodded.

"There's a lot of money in condos."

"I'll check the building permits and dig up whatever else I can on the lawyer."

"Thanks, Sims."

He looked as though he was about to say something, then nodded.

"What is it?"

"Are you just looking for dirt on Reimer, or do you want to take this lawyer down?"

Ashlyn stood. "Right now, I'm just looking for information. Smythe is known for dealing with a lot of drug suppliers. There's a strong possibility Shannon didn't kill her brother, and is a victim. For all we know, someone else was in the park, someone who wants a piece of whatever Reimer earns a living from. It explains why Christopher Reimer would lie about who hurt his brother, because he'd be afraid. And it explains why the parents would call their lawyer."

"It's a good theory."

"But that's all it is. Just a theory. Two days ago it seemed pretty reasonable to think Shannon killed her brother. Now I'm not even sure she's still alive. Theories are useless without evidence to support them. That's why I need to know what connects Reimer and Smythe." Ashlyn paused. "Any word on the footprints?"

Sims shook his head. "Not yet."

She left Sims and wandered down the hall. Tain was standing at her desk, looking at a file, his jacket on.

"Hey," she said.

He turned and stared at her for a moment. "You look like shit."

"That's how I feel. Look, about yesterday—"

"I saw you looking through the reports. I'm going to re-interview these ones." He held up the folder. "Unless you've got something else."

"I'll get my coat."

"I can handle it." He walked away.

Craig had put a roast in the oven and while that cooked he did the laundry, cleaned the house and chopped vegetables, with Blue Rodeo's *Lost Together* on the stereo. Then he'd put the flowers for Ashlyn in a vase and left it on the kitchen counter with the bear beside it.

After that he'd picked up some lunch and went to his parents' house, parking close enough to have full view of the driveway. He shut off the engine, reached for his copy of *The Fever Kill* and got comfortable.

It was supposed to be his day off, but he was running out of options. Unable to locate Ted Bicknell, he figured the best chance he had for answers was still finding his dad.

Assuming Alison was correct, Steve would arrive home that afternoon. If he did, Craig planned to talk to him before anyone else had a chance.

His stepmother was expecting Dad to fly in, and that gave Craig one moment of doubt. Since he'd moved to the Lower Mainland, whenever Steve flew in Craig had always picked him up. Alison didn't like driving to the airport.

There'd been no call from his dad to make arrangements, but he realized under the circumstances Steve would be handling the transportation home himself.

After almost three hours a taxi pulled up in front of the driveway. Craig put the book down and got out of his vehicle.

Steve passed the cab driver a few bills and as he put his wallet away he looked up. His eyes widened with surprise at first, then settled into a questioning look.

"If you were coming for dinner you would have parked in the driveway."

"I'm here to talk to you."

"Whatever it is, can't it wait? I just got home—"

"Home as in your house. But you flew back to BC two days ago."

Steve's expression hardened, but he held up a hand and spoke calmly. "Where I've been is none of your business."

"I suppose it's none of Alison's business either? Even when someone breaks in to her home and I've got to answer Zidani's questions about that?"

There was a slight hesitation as Steve's mouth opened, but no sound came out. "What happened? Alison's okay?"

Craig nodded. "I came out here and tried to handle it quietly."

Steve picked up his bags and started walking to the door. "Why? Someone broke in. It happens. Even to RCMP officers." He set the bags down and reached in his pocket for his keys.

"It's what they were after that was the problem. Some of your files. Specifically, your personal notes on the Hope Harrington murder investigation."

Steve paled and actually dropped his keys. "What do you know about that case?" he asked as he bent down to pick the keys up.

"Zidani ordered me to go over the files. Lockridge is up for parole." *And out for blood.*

"And Zidani has you reviewing the investigation?" Steve stared at him for a moment, then looked down at the keys in his hand, fumbling with them until he found the right one.

"Someone broke into Lisa Harrington's home as well. Only a few hours after the first break-in here."

"First?"

"There was a second incident here yesterday." He didn't want to elaborate. Without knowing who'd taken Steve's files, or when, all he had was speculation. If Steve wanted answers, he was looking in the wrong direction. Craig didn't have them, and he'd been hoping to get the answers from his dad. All he had were suspicions, and sharing those would only make things worse.

"Why'd they come back if they already had the files?"

"Maybe because they thought you had something else that

they wanted. But you knew about Lockridge. You were at the station in Aldergrove yesterday."

Steve exhaled. "Look, your sergeant may have ordered you to check up on the original investigation, but I don't answer to you."

"What is it everyone's hiding about this case? First Lisa Harrington calls me, looking for answers. Then Zidani orders me to review the files. I can't find Bicknell, and you're AWOL. Someone breaks in here and at Lisa's, Alison and I are being hounded, first by lawyers, then reporters—"

Steve turned and pointed a finger at Craig. "I'll handle that. You just stay away from them."

"How am I supposed to do that? With Lockridge's lawsuit pending against you, accusing you of setting him up for the murder charge, anything I learn will become evidence." Craig paused. "Is there anything I should be worried about here?"

Steve was still pale, but his face hardened, and the look in his eyes was one Craig had seldom seen before. From inside the house he heard the dead bolt turn back and the sound of the chain lock being undone. Alison opened the door.

"Craig, are you staying for dinner?" she asked. "We can call Ash—"

"Never mind," Steve said. "Craig's leaving."

He picked up his bags and walked inside as Alison stepped back. She gave Craig a puzzled glance before Steve shut the door, leaving Craig on the other side, listening to the sound of locks sliding back into place.

When Tain had decided to conceal his name for his career, he hadn't realized what a smart decision it would be.

Knowing his full name would make it easier for people to search out his past. One thing about the RCMP: They didn't like scandals. If they could avoid them, they would.

They'd been willing to let him use his surname alone. It meant he'd had a chance to handle the lawsuit privately.

And all this time, he'd felt certain Ashlyn didn't know.

Her comment the day before had still rattled him, more than

he wanted to admit. It had been a while before he could calm down enough to go home, venting the anger on a punching bag and lifting weights until his muscles burned.

And now, he closed his eyes and saw the look on Ashlyn's face that morning, when he'd made it clear he was working alone. Her eyes were sunken, dark smudges standing out against her unusually pale skin.

It's her own fault. That's what he'd told himself. Ashlyn never meddled, never stuck her nose in where it didn't belong. But he had to admit he'd opened the door, comment after comment, letting his guard down more and more because he trusted her. It made sense that she'd say something eventually.

The way she probably saw it, he'd been dropping hints because he wanted her to ask about his past. He didn't want her to ask; he wanted her to care, without anything else changing. That was the problem. It didn't matter how many cases they worked, how many times they handled a murdered child and he didn't let it get to him. Jeffrey was different. He was four, and everything was fresh in Tain's mind with the court case looming.

But if Ashlyn knew, somewhere in the back of her mind she'd be worrying about him instead of focusing on the case the next time their victim was a kid. He didn't want that.

It made him think of Lori, desperate not to be branded by what had happened to her. He should have been more sympathetic. Of all the people in the department, he should have understood. He hadn't been there when she'd died, but he felt responsible.

Ashlyn never knew the guilt he carried over her death.

Christmas was a time of family and celebration, and he couldn't help thinking this year, Lori wouldn't be celebrating with her family. Tain hated this time of year for other reasons, though. It wasn't just the commercialism, although that bothered him. It went beyond the religion, though the scars missionaries had left on his people lingered in the way that scars on the psyche did. The mistrust ran as deep as the bitterness.

What he really hated was how artificial the season was. Everything about it rang false. Families posed for photos and passed out presents and spent the rest of the year fighting or not speaking. He was one to talk; for three years he'd avoided home, kept what family he had left at a distance.

Until they'd threatened that if he didn't come back they would come to see him. They were expecting the judge's ruling, and they wanted him there to hear it.

Ever since he'd booked the time off and bought his plane ticket he couldn't shake the image of his daughter. He could hear her laugh, as though she was in the room with him, see her smile . . .

Hear her call him daddy. She was so alive . . . and omnipresent.

When he'd found himself standing over the beaten body of Jeffrey Reimer, what he'd considered a curse, the haunting image of his daughter that he couldn't get out of his mind, had abandoned him. For months he'd longed for the visions to stop, for the memories to go away. He hadn't realized it would be like losing her all over again.

Hadn't realized how it would bring back all the hate.

Tain tried to focus on the job as he went from house to house, reinterviewing everyone, keeping as busy as possible so that he didn't have to face his memories or the pain.

Three times Ashlyn had picked up the phone to call Tain, and three times she'd dropped the handset down without dialing.

Tain was reinterviewing everyone remotely connected with the investigation, and she was happy to let Sims look at Byron Smythe's connection to the Reimer family.

She double-checked everything else. News clippings of all the major Reimer family milestones hinted at nothing unusual. She checked the entire family, as well as Tracy Reimer's maiden name, and still came up with no arrest records for the family. Although part of her was upset that Tain had gone out on his own, because she knew he was angry with her, part of her was relieved. The nausea was back, worse than before. She was thankful it was Sunday so that she couldn't go to Christopher's school.

The time dragged by with little to show for it.

"Day's pretty much shot, Hart. You may as well head home."

"I don't know. Part of me thinks we should charge the family just to be done with it." She turned her chair so that she was looking at Zidani, who had perched on a nearby desk, one that was currently unused. "In some cultures parents take responsibility for the actions of their kids."

"But we don't know that Shannon murdered her brother."

"If she didn't, one of them probably did it." She leaned back, propped her feet up on the open drawer, and rubbed her forehead. "Don't mind me. I just have a bit of an issue with parents who put protecting themselves ahead of finding their child." She frowned. "And I thought the standard line was to work 'round the clock on high-profile murders. Shouldn't you be yelling at me for not having a suspect in custody instead of telling me to go home?"

"The press got wind of the fact that we're looking hard at the family."

She groaned and rubbed her temples, as though that would hold off the headache she felt coming on. "Have they done us damage?"

"Not as far as I can tell. Story won't run until tomorrow, but they are naming Shannon Reimer as a suspect."

"Fantastic. If she's innocent she'll be even less likely to come home now."

"But it might be enough to get her talking."

Ashlyn stared at him for a moment. "You leaked this?"

"Don't bite the hand that feeds you."

"You'll be hearing that from the reporter you used, soon enough."

"Look, even I have to say you've done everything that could be done. Followed up with family, friends, interviewed potential witnesses, neighbors. Tain told me you went through all the reports yesterday and reinterviewed people today."

Ashlyn put her feet down and started tidying her desk. "When?"

"Just a few minutes ago, just before he left." Zidani paused, then said, "Look, we've got her cell cloned and we're monitoring it 'round the clock. If she uses it, hopefully we'll get enough information to find her. It's not like the family is pressuring you for answers, and the public will be reassured. They don't care if there isn't an arrest, as long as they know it was a domestic."

"As long as they know it isn't some crazed serial killer who might go after one of their kids, you mean."

"Exactly."

"Am I going to get in trouble if I speak freely?"

"Would that stop you?"

Ashlyn thought about the past few days, how she'd upset her partner, and within minutes, Craig. "No, I suppose not." She stood, pushed the drawer shut and reached for her coat. "It's going to take me a while to get used to you being civil."

"You won't have to worry about it."

"You'll be back to being an asshole in the morning?"

He laughed. "Look, I came in here with a job to do and not the one you think." Zidani slid off the desk. "I'll be gone soon enough. You've got nothing to worry about with me, Ashlyn. For what it's worth, I think you're a good officer. Learn to keep your mouth shut on occasion and you'll make your way up the ladder, as far as you want to go."

There had been a time when Ashlyn had been motivated by the idea of making rank, putting the job first. She thought about that as she walked outside. Lazy flakes of snow were drifting through the night sky on their way to earth. For the parking lot of a police station it was unusually quiet. The past few years she hadn't really enjoyed Christmas. It was supposed to be a family time, supposed to be a season of warmth and good cheer. Instead, it had been a reminder that her life didn't match the Hallmark cards. It hadn't really bothered her in the way it got to others, because she was young, but it had still reminded her that she wanted more than a career.

She wanted a family. Not all at once. Things had happened faster than she would have expected. Six months earlier Craig hadn't even been part of her life. It wasn't that she'd wanted to rush into marriage and have kids right away, but she'd never thought of staying single.

Now she was on the verge of having everything, which presented different problems. She'd been so distracted by her own happiness that she hadn't really thought much about how frustrated Craig must be. Her career hadn't been derailed by the shooting in the summer, but Craig's had. And she expected him to just ride it out.

They'd never really talked about it.

There were a lot of things they'd never really talked about. They'd decided to continue living together, and she'd given up her apartment. Their commitment was inferred, not stated, but she'd never wanted to ask where things were going, to get ready to cut bait if there wasn't a ring in sight.

A van pulled into the lot and her cheeks flushed as she realized her hand was resting over her stomach. She dropped it to her side and went to her car.

The roads weren't bad and traffic was light. When she parked in front of the house she sat in the silence, flakes of snow still lazily drifting to the ground. The house was filled with a warm glow, and Craig's vehicle was there.

All day, she'd refused to think about what she'd do if he didn't come home. After he'd walked out and slammed the door behind him, she'd lost track of the time as she waited for him to come back. Eventually, she'd gone to the kitchen and dialed his cell number, only to hear it ring. Craig had left it charging, giving her no way to reach him. She'd dragged herself upstairs and after tossing and turning for hours had taken a blanket to the couch, turned on the tree lights and let the hypnotic flow of one color giving way to another over and over again lull her to sleep. The phone had woken her around 4:30, but the caller had hung up when Ashlyn answered. She'd gotten up long enough to check; Craig had not returned home. Part of her had hoped he'd be sitting in his Rodeo, unsure about whether to come inside after leaving the way he did, but the only vehicle at their house was hers. She'd returned to the couch and remained in a fog, half asleep, half listening for the sound of a key turning in the lock.

What she hadn't realized was that she'd expected to be home

first, for it to be her waiting for him to come back, to apologize. To make the first move.

Now it was up to her to walk to that door and open it. He was the one who'd walked out on her, and she had to make the first move. Was she really going to be so childish that she'd refuse to work things out unless it happened on her terms?

Ashlyn got out of the car and walked to the door.

Inside, the house was quiet. The living room was dark except the shimmering lights reflecting off the walls, which meant that the tree was on and judging from the shadows, the fireplace as well. She went to the kitchen.

Craig's back was to her, but she could still see the half-empty wineglass in his hand, complemented by the open bottle on the counter. There were two plates of food ready, which sat beside a vase of flowers and a stuffed bear. Another glass of wine.

His apology. Said with gestures rather than words.

When she looked back at him she realized he'd turned and was watching her silently. All day, even in the minutes when she'd been lecturing herself not to think about this moment, her brain had rushed ahead and tried out things to say.

Most of those things that had gone through her mind had been hurtful, biting, layered with insinuations meant to make him feel guilty.

"Where did you go?" She surprised herself. It was something she'd never consciously considered asking, and the words came out with a detached calm that didn't match the knot in her stomach.

"Does it matter?"

He set the wineglass down on the counter.

"No. I suppose it doesn't." She leaned against the doorway but forced herself not to cross her arms. Her gaze drifted back to the flowers, the bear. Proof he was sorry. Or proof that he knew he should apologize. The part of her that had been unable to rationalize his decision to walk out the night before wanted to punish him, to make sure he suffered for the agony he'd put her through, the sleepless night, the heart-pounding fear about what he was doing and the gnawing worry about how they'd work past this.

But the rational side knew that was pointless. She'd heard once that holding on to bitterness was like swallowing poison and hoping someone else died, although she couldn't remember where that was from. That didn't matter either. What mattered was that it was true. Whatever regret, whatever pain Craig felt, it couldn't undo the way he'd hurt her.

"Ash." He almost choked on her name. The look in his eyes was muddled, a mix of sadness and confusion, shadowed by fear.

She turned her gaze to the floor so that she could focus on her words instead of his feelings. "Are you in some kind of trouble at work?"

"Did Zidani say something to you?"

Ashlyn looked up. "Byron Smythe did."

"Son of a bitch. If I'd known that last night—" He picked up his glass and drained it, then reached for the bottle.

"What was he talking about?"

"I want you to stay away from him."

"That's a bit difficult, considering he represents the family of my murder victim."

"Then give the case to someone else. Take some sick days or tell Zidani it's a conflict of interest."

"A conflict of what interest? I don't even know what the hell he's talking about." She crossed her arms. "And I'm not sick. I just didn't get a lot of sleep last night, and that had nothing to do with Zidani or Smythe." Ashlyn realized then she hadn't eaten all day either. The only thing she'd had was ginger ale. "Craig, I'd be lying if I said I wasn't upset, but I really don't want to argue with you."

He started to lift his glass but stopped and set it down. Craig turned, braced his hands against the counter and lowered his head.

"I was late. I was there, looking for you, when that damn reporter showed up. I thought you'd already left."

"I called you. I left a message."

"I—" He lifted his head, although he didn't turn to face her. "I know. And I'd left the cell phone in the Rodeo . . ." Craig turned and met her gaze. "I'm not trying to make excuses. Just explain."

"You were pretty angry last night."

"At myself."

She paused. "Just yourself? Nobody else?"

He was quiet for a moment, but he didn't look away. "Okay, yeah, I was angry at myself, and I was mad at Luke for bothering my stepmother and that reporter for following me around all day and Zidani for sticking me on desk duty and Lori for shooting me, and—"

"And me, for killing her."

"You did what you had to do."

She rubbed her forehead as a thin smile spread across her lips. "You keep telling yourself that. All this time, we haven't even talked about it, and I really thought you understood that she would have killed you if I hadn't fired. She murdered a suspect and as it was, you almost died. But you do blame me. Why don't you just say it? It's my fault you're stuck on desk duty."

"No. It's Lori's. And Zidani's."

"Zidani is just following orders. They just sent him in to push us, to see if we were really okay."

"That's what the shrinks are for. I went to my sessions and was given the green light to go back to regular rotation."

She tipped her head toward the counter. "And look at you now. You're drinking."

"It's just a glass of wine."

"A glass?" Ashlyn walked over and picked up the bottle. "Try three."

"I thought you didn't want to fight."

"That doesn't mean I'm going to turn a blind eye. We need to work through our problems. Pretending they aren't there won't solve anything."

He leaned back against the counter, hand over his face. She could tell his eyes were closed, see the anger in the twist of his jaw. When she'd first known him she thought his ability to keep a lid on his temper was admirable. Now she wondered how healthy it was. If he bottled everything up inside, sooner or later he'd blow.

Maybe that was what this was really about. Not Byron Smythe or Luke Geller or a missed date or even Lori's shooting.

She walked over to him, reached up and pushed his hair back from his face. "I thought Zidani would tie you down and shave off this mop himself, the way he carried on about the regulations at first."

Craig lowered his hands and opened his eyes. Then he took her face in his hands. "I don't blame you." Said without blinking or a tremor in his voice. "I blame me."

"How can you blame yourself for what happened? You did everything possible to keep her away from that case."

He shook his head. "Not for what happened to her. I shouldn't have taken you on the arrest. If you hadn't been there—"

"You might not be here now." She thought back to when Craig was in the hospital. "I'll be honest. If I could turn back time and find another way to save your life, I would. But I can't. You have to let it go."

Craig shook his head. "Sometimes things happen on cases. You make choices, maybe even think you've done the right thing. Or maybe you just need to believe that, while deep down you're hoping nobody calls your bluff. Ten years from now what if—" He let go of her face.

"Ten years from now we're still following the evidence and on our way to arrest the man who raped several women, including your former partner, Lori Price. Ten years from now Lori's still using the fact that she was sleeping with a senior officer as leverage, to find out about the arrest. Ten years from now she's still choosing to load her weapon and show up at the suspect's house. She's still putting a bullet in him and killing him. And she's still pointing her gun at you and shooting you. And I still raise my gun and shoot her. Ten minutes or ten years, this still stands up because that's what happened."

He looked away.

"Unless there's something you haven't told me," she said slowly. "Is that what this is about?"

Craig shook his head.

"Then it's about something else." She watched him, the lack of response enough to convince her she was right.

"Just over ten years ago, Steve worked a murder case."

"I'm sure he worked a lot of murder cases."

"That call yesterday morning? It was the victim's mother. Someone broke in to her house."

"They didn't catch the killer?"

"No, they caught him. Guy's still in prison. He's up for parole this week." He paused, thinking about what Lisa had told him. "I mean, he got parole. He's out."

She held up a hand. "So you're thinking . . . ?"

"Someone broke in to my parents' house as well."

"Aren't they still in Regina?"

"Alison wasn't at the time. Steve was supposed to be, but—" Craig scratched his head. "The guy who was convicted? He's suing Dad, his partner, the department for wrongful conviction. Steve was supposed to be in Regina until today, but he flew back Friday."

She waited for him to continue. When he didn't speak she said, "So? He changed his mind."

"He didn't tell Alison. Someone messed with his files on the case at the house, then broke into the victim's mother's house and was looking through a box of the victim's stuff there. And Alison still thought Steve was in Regina. The only reason I found out he wasn't was because I called his office, looking for him. Then I go to talk to the cops who worked on the case out in Aldergrove, and I'm one step behind. Dad had just left the station."

Her head was starting to spin with the overload. "Wait. You mean, you think there's something to this? That they screwed up the case and now he's trying to cover his tracks?" She thought about what Byron Smythe had said the night before. Lawyers keeping cops honest. "You don't really believe that, do you?"

"I—" He shook his head. "I don't know what to believe."

"And is that why this reporter's following you around? She was at the station Friday night, then the mall yesterday." She turned away from him. "So that's what this is all about? The case file, you disappearing for hours on end, not showing up for work yesterday?"

"I was working."

"Digging up dirt on a case ten years old, for what? To prove that your father made a mistake?"

"You think I'd do that? You think I want to investigate this?"

"Then why are we even having this conversation?"

"Zidani ordered me to review the files."

She looked over her shoulder at him. "He wants . . . *you* to handle this?"

"I guess it will look better if Steve Daly's son is the one who destroys his career. A sure way to restore public confidence in the RCMP." He smirked as he picked up his glass and drained it. "We're so honest we'll take down our own family members."

"Craig, you don't really believe that Steve . . . planted evidence or railroaded a suspect, do you? If you're suggesting what I think you're suggesting . . . Why would he break into his own house?"

"I don't know Ash, but something isn't right about this."

"You have to go to Zidani, insist he take you off this."

"I can't do that. This is the last thing, then he's putting me back on the street."

"So that's your price? You'll sell out your own father to get out from behind a desk?"

"How can you say that? I'm just trying to get to the truth."

"And you really think handing in a report that says Steve is clean is going to cut it? You're screwed. If you don't implicate Steve of wrongdoing they'll just say it's because he's your father."

"So the only way I come out of this okay is if I hurt Dad."

"Why did you even agree to this? You should have refused."

"It's my fault? How am I supposed to know? Zidani tells me the case is going before a parole board and they just want me to check the files, make sure everything's solid. It isn't until later that the reporter tells me there's a pending civil suit."

"How did Smythe know about this?"

Craig's laugh carried a sharp, cynical edge. "He's representing the guy who was convicted."

"You have to go to Zidani. Go over his head if he won't listen. You have to pass this on to someone else, do the right thing."

"I have to do the right thing? This is a test, Ashlyn. To see if I'm willing to face the truth that my dad is a dirty cop."

"I don't believe that. I've known Steve for years, longer than I've known you. Why are you so convinced he's dirty? Couldn't he have just made a mistake? We did everything by the book and two people ended up dead and you were in the hospital. Is it really so hard to believe that if something went wrong with the case that it wasn't intentional? You're going to have a real problem with this if you've already made up your mind about what happened."

He put the glass down on the counter. "Then why won't Dad talk to me?"

"If you went to him with accusations like these I don't blame him. Cops don't like other cops sticking their nose in their old case files, digging up dirt."

"Damn it, Ash, it's not like I wanted to do this!"

"That's not the point. You are doing it, and you're his son. Don't all fathers want their sons to look up them, to respect them?"

"Maybe someday if I have a son I can answer that, but I don't see how he can expect me to respect him if he's lied to me."

"So this is all about you? This isn't about how he's a human being, capable of making mistakes, and it isn't about the fact that maybe he messed up on the job. Either he didn't, so he gets to still be perfect in your eyes, or he's dirty and you're a victim because your hero dad isn't the man you thought he was. Either way it's got nothing to do with this case or the victim or the guy who was convicted. This is all about you."

He brushed past her and she turned and followed him to the hall. "So what now? You're going to walk out again?"

Craig stopped. His hands were balled into fists at his side, and she could see the tension in his neck and shoulders. "I thought you'd understand."

"I understand this is difficult for you, and that's exactly why you should insist that Zidani reassign this to someone else. Stop looking at Steve as a cop who happens to be your father. Just let him be your dad."

"It's not that simple." He walked up the stairs and she let him go. The problem was, she did understand. Craig didn't just want his dad to be perfect; he needed to believe Steve was an honorable man. There wasn't a doubt in her mind about the kind of person Steve Daly was, but for Craig, it was so important that his fear of being disappointed overshadowed his faith in his father.

CHAPTER NINE

"Look, Daddy, look!" She giggled and then swung her arm for the next rail. The monkey bars, her favorite. Noelle's dark eyes sparkled, and her smile showed off her dimples. "See, Daddy!" And then her hand slipped and she was falling, her arms reaching out as she called for him, but the earth had opened up beneath her and he could still hear the echo of her screams as she fell beyond his grasp, out of sight.

Tain sat upright. It took a minute for him to get his bearings and then he shut off the alarm clock and got out of bed.

Despite the early hour Ashlyn was already at her desk when he arrived, on the phone. The hollow cheeks and chalky skin was augmented by a look in her eyes that could only be described as despondent.

He sat down across from her, but she kept her gaze lowered. One by one, he went through the messages on his desk and the slips of paper he'd taken from his mailbox and threw them all in the garbage.

Ashlyn was still on the phone, but hadn't said anything. As far as he could tell, she hadn't looked up either. She had left a report on his desk with an update on all the dead ends she'd exhausted the day before. He started to look through it, images of Noelle swinging from the monkey bars burned in his mind. Half of him didn't want to push the images away. They were all he had.

The words on the report blurred. It wasn't just the memory

now, but the sound of her laughter, teasing him with the lie that if he closed his eyes she'd be right there, so real he could touch her.

The smack of the handset hitting the receiver jolted him back to reality. Ashlyn's head was propped up by her hands as she looked at some papers on her desk.

"No new leads?"

She shook her head. "You?"

"Nothing." Tain stood up and grabbed his coat. "Come on."

Ashlyn looked up but remained sitting. "Where are we going?"

"To follow up on a hunch."

She walked to the car with him silently and offered no comment as he drove back to the park where Jeffrey had been murdered. He drove along Murray Street, to Ioco Road. Ioco Road was one of the main routes into the northern part of Port Moody. It led to the main shopping area, the adjoining roads that took thousands of tourists, hikers and movie crews to Buntzen Lake, and it also wound its way around the inlet, to where the Reimer family lived. That wasn't the direction he followed.

On the other side of Ioco Road, Murray Street turned into Guildford. Just past Eagle Ridge Hospital, Guildford left Port Moody, entered Coquitlam, and eventually led right to the RCMP station.

Tain didn't return to Coquitlam. Instead, he parked outside the hospital.

"This is where the anonymous 911 call was made from."

A smile flickered on Ashlyn's face as she rubbed her forehead and groaned. "All I was given was a street address on Guildford. I should have checked it myself."

"Fits with the idea of Shannon being injured."

She'd slumped back against the headrest, as though she was too tired to hold her head up, and she rolled it to the side just enough to look at him. "If we're assuming she's the one who made the call."

Tain wasn't sure who he thought had called 911, but if it was Shannon it opened up some interesting possibilities. The hospitals should have been checked in the initial canvas. He called Sims to find out who had handled Eagle Ridge, then hung up.

"Well?" Ashlyn asked.

"Sims says he sent two Port Moody police officers to check the hospital. No prizes for guessing who." He made another call, then hung up. "Well?"

She undid her seat belt. "Let's go have a chat with the staff."

The emergency room was packed, indicative of the chronic problems health-care staff faced. Too much demand, not enough resources. The media railed about people dying in waiting rooms and all it did was sell papers and prompt politicians to make promises they broke right after the elections.

After showing ID to three nurses who barely glanced at them Ashlyn blocked a nurse's path. "We really need to speak to someone who was treating patients Friday."

The woman nodded at a doctor a few feet away, busy going through charts. "Dr. Hughes. He might be able to help."

"Thanks." She walked up to the doctor and showed him her ID. Dr. Hughes looked about fifty, still with a full head of hair that was speckled with gray, but enough lines around the eyes to know he'd seen his share of pain and suffering over the years. "I know you see a lot of faces here." Ashlyn passed him a photo of Shannon.

"She was here on Friday," he said.

"You treated her?"

He nodded. "And you know medical records are confidential."

"Look, do you watch the news?" Tain asked. "Friday, a boy was beaten to death at Rocky Point Park." He waited until the doctor nodded. "That girl is the older sister. We have reason to believe she's another victim, and until now, we thought she might be dead. Can you at least confirm she's still alive?"

"I'm not promising you that." The doctor started walking down the hall, where there weren't as many people. "Look, I treated her."

"But?" Ashlyn prompted.

He drew a deep breath and glanced around before he spoke.

"I'd like to think she's still alive . . . How was the boy killed? Internal injuries caused from a severe beating?"

"The blow to the back of his head killed him first," Ashlyn said.

"And if it hadn't, without proper treatment he would have died from the internal damage? Hell, even with proper treatment he might have died?"

Tain glanced at Ashlyn and nodded.

"Then there are no guarantees that girl is still alive."

"But you let her walk out of here?" Ashlyn asked.

"I didn't let her do anything. I left to consult with the staff about her case. We were waiting on X-rays, but I suspected we'd find a history of old injuries suggesting long-term abuse."

"Why?"

The doctor nodded at a nurse scurrying by, then looked at Tain. "You ever pick up a kid you know is being beaten? You know that look. I see it in your eyes. Some stuff you can't run from, can't change. A lot of people who work here have to shut off from it because it's too much. I used to work in Toronto. Patch them up, send them out until they get stabbed or shot again. Here, we just send them home and let them be used as punching bags, and there's not a damn thing we can do about it."

"Look, I know you can't give us her file," Ashlyn said. "But we've been looking for her for days. If there's anything you can tell us, unofficially, that might be helpful . . ." She shrugged.

"My suspicions were correct. And she hadn't just been beaten. She'd been stabbed. When she came in, she had a pair of track pants wrapped around the wound, and she had the knife. I scolded her for pulling it out, but she said she hadn't, just that when she'd grabbed the pants the knife was there." He shook his head. "That was all she said. She wouldn't tell me what happened. I left that room for ten minutes and she managed to sneak out." He nodded down the hall, at the staff bustling from room to room, patients being wheeled down the hall for tests, X-rays, or to be taken to long-term care. "Hard to believe anyone can leave unnoticed around here."

"Actually, that's why it's easy to get out. What's one more person?" Tain said. "Look, I'm not trying to jump down your throat. You're busy and you're doing your best, but you never reported this?"

"When I came back there were two police officers talking to the nurses. Honestly, I thought that's why they were here."

Tain looked at Ashlyn and saw her jaw clench. "That's why they were supposed to be here." He passed the doctor his card. "Thanks. If you think of anything else . . ."

The doctor nodded. "Sure."

Tain followed Ashlyn to the car. "How many donut shops can there be in Port Moody?" he asked.

"Not donuts. Starbucks."

It was close, and when they arrived they could see the cop cars outside.

After he got out of the vehicle he leaned down and looked inside. "You coming?"

She paused. "I'm not sure I trust myself."

"It's up to you."

Ashlyn undid her seat belt and followed him.

Parker was laughing with his partner, but when he saw Tain and Ashlyn he reached for his cup and drained whatever was left of his beverage. When he set it down he wasn't smiling. "Time for us to go," he said as he stood.

"Leaving so soon?" Tain asked.

Parker looked at Bennett, who stood and glanced at Ashlyn, then Tain, then settled on looking at the floor. "We're a bit busy this morning," Parker said.

"I can see that."

Parker was sitting by the window, and Tain was standing directly in his path. Unless he wanted to crawl under the table Parker couldn't get out without Tain moving. "Excuse me," Parker said.

"Not so fast. The other day Constable Sims sent you to Eagle Ridge Hospital to do a routine check for Shannon Reimer."

From the corner of his eye he could see Bennett look up. Parker's scowl deepened. "So?"

"You learn anything helpful?"

"If we had we would have told you."

"How hard did you look?"

"I did my job."

"You checked on anyone without ID."

Parker was standing nose to nose with Tain. "Nobody matching Shannon's description was admitted."

"What about anyone treated and released? Or being treated while you were there?"

"Get out of my way."

"Or what? You'll make me get out of your way?"

Parker pushed him, hard. Caught off guard, Tain bumped into Ashlyn, who grabbed his arm.

"I told you to move," Parker said. "Next time, I won't ask twice."

Ashlyn let go of Tain and stepped forward to keep Parker from leaving. "He asked you a question."

Parker sneered. "Listen, sweetie, I don't answer to you either." He looked her up and down. "You looked better the other day. He must be running you ragged."

Ashlyn smacked Parker on the face so hard he twisted away from her. She used his momentum to grab his arm and pushed him facedown on the table. "I don't like your insinuations, your attitude and I don't like you, Parker. But on this case, I'm in charge. You had a job to do and you were asked a question. You either answer it, or I'm off to chat with your commanding officer." She let go of him.

Parker's face was as red as a Santa suit. He shoved Ashlyn into Tain, hard, and while Tain tried to steady himself and Ashlyn, Parker barreled past them to the door. His partner followed.

"You okay?" Tain asked.

"I will be after we see that son of a bitch's boss."

After Ashlyn had left the house, Craig had gone downstairs. He'd folded the blankets she'd left on the couch and set them with the spare pillow she'd used, made tea and pulled out the Harrington case folders.

Hours later, he had to admit that most of the loose ends of the case had been tied off nicely. Donny Lockridge's fingerprints were found on the murder weapon. So were Lisa Harrington's, but since it was her crowbar that was to be expected. Donny had legitimate access to the crowbar as well, his defense had countered. He had, after all, been the victim's boyfriend and been hired by Lisa Harrington to do some work around the house and clean out the garage. His fingerprints were on all of the tools.

Donny and Hope had been seen arguing a few days before her murder.

And Donny's alibi for the time of Hope's murder had fallen through. He'd refused to provide another explanation for his whereabouts, raising suspicions he was involved.

The prosecution had established that Donny had access to the murder weapon. They'd also pointed out that Hope's body had been moved from wherever she was murdered. The crime scene had never been found, and although Hope had been a slim, petite girl, it was still hard to believe her mother could have moved her alone.

The only other person with access to the blanket from Hope's bed and the murder weapon was Hope's younger sister, Destiny, and she'd only been six at the time.

Donny Lockridge had no alibi. Although no witnesses had seen him move the body, and there were no traces of DNA found in his vehicle, Donny had lost his temper on the stand. That fact, combined with his access to key physical evidence and Lisa's testimony had been enough to persuade the jury.

A locket Hope always wore had never been recovered, and it was assumed it was lost at the actual crime scene.

The other thing Daly and Bicknell had never explained was the DNA found under Hope's fingernails. It didn't match Donny Lockridge, and it was clearly not from someone Hope Harrington was related to. The defense argued that it suggested someone other than Lockridge had killed Hope.

The prosecution had countered by pointing out the severity of the crime. It was personal, they argued. Hope played sports at school. She could have tripped and grabbed a friend, and accidentally cut them with a fingernail. Since the defense could not prove beyond a shadow of a doubt that the DNA got on Hope during her murder, they couldn't use it to exonerate their client.

Craig leaned back in his chair. It had been circumstantial, but it still sounded solid. He'd been through half the interview notes and found nothing to suggest there was another viable suspect. Lisa Harrington's testimony had sealed Lockridge's fate. According to her, Hope had decided to end their relationship just days before her murder. Donny had been angry and had hit Hope. Lisa thought he was just upset and that he'd get over it. She said she always thought Donny was a "good kid."

Lisa had cried on the stand and blamed herself.

The profile that had been put together on Lockridge pegged him as an average kid, destined for a blue-collar job. He didn't have the grades for university or, as far as Craig could tell, the interest. Lockridge wasn't a big guy, but he'd been fit and strong and done a lot of jobs involving manual labor. As far as the case against him went, they had motive, means and opportunity. The physical evidence was thin but not nonexistent.

Yet Donny Lockridge had persuaded a lawyer that he'd been railroaded and that there was a case against the RCMP, the prosecutor, everyone involved. What could Lockridge have that would persuade a lawyer like Smythe to take legal action? And why against the RCMP? As far as Craig could tell they'd followed the evidence. It wasn't airtight, but it wasn't all smoke and mirrors.

Unless Lockridge knew who had the missing locket or the source of the mystery DNA, Craig couldn't even see grounds for an appeal. He leafed through the folders and eventually found what he was looking for. Donny Lockridge had appealed his conviction.

The appeal had been denied.

Craig took his mug to the kitchen and filled the kettle. As he plugged it in he heard a knock on the door.

His father was on the front step, and he didn't wait to be invited in. Craig followed him down the hall, toward the living room, but Steve caught a glimpse of what was spread across the dining room table and stopped.

He picked up a photo of Hope Harrington and stared at it. The kettle whistled, and Craig went to the kitchen.

When Steve entered a moment later Craig reached for an upper cupboard. "Tea?"

"I want you to drop this."

Craig let go of the cupboard door and turned around. "Why?"

"Is it really so hard for you to understand?"

"Do you have something to hide?"

"How can you even ask me that?"

"Then what difference does it make if I check the files or if someone else does? It's still the same truths or lies that will be found."

Steve's face lengthened. Not much, but paired with how his shoulders sagged it was noticeable. He turned away from Craig and then walked over to the counter and picked up the bottle. "You're drinking?"

"Don't start."

For a moment, Steve stood looking at the bottle, then set it down. "Seems there's nothing I can say to you."

"That's on you. If there was nothing to hide I can't imagine why you'd be upset about this. Even if Zidani took me off, someone else would be ordered to go over these files. I already have. I still have to find Ted Bicknell—"

Steve looked up then. "You haven't talked to J.T.?"

"J.T.?"

"His first name is John."

Craig hadn't pulled their service records. In part, because he'd hoped his dad would tell him whatever it was he needed to know so that he wouldn't have to go digging.

"That's what I still need to do. Talk to Ted, talk to you."

Steve turned abruptly and headed for the door. Craig followed him. "I think it would be a good idea for you to stay away from your old partner. It looks bad enough that you aren't cooperating—"

"I'm doing what I have to do." Steve turned and pointed a finger at Craig. "There are some things that should be left alone, and this is one of them."

"So you are trying to keep yourself out of trouble?"

Steve shook his head. "The only thing I'm trying to protect is you." He yanked the door open and walked out.

Ashlyn and Tain hadn't even reached their desks or taken their coats off before Zidani appeared in their work area, the cantankerous glare back in place.

"My office. Now." Then he paused and pointed at Ashlyn. "Just you."

As soon as he was out the door Ashlyn pulled off her coat and tossed it over her chair.

"Don't have too much fun without me," Tain said.

"I'll try not to."

When she arrived at Zidani's office he wasn't waiting at the desk. He had his hand on the door and as soon as she was inside he slammed it. "What the hell happened this morning? I've just had a call from the Port Moody police."

She rubbed her forehead. "Parker and his partner were sent to Eagle Ridge Hospital as part of the canvas, to make sure Shannon Reimer hadn't gone there. They only looked at anyone admitted. Shannon was treated Friday afternoon."

Zidani grunted. "At least we know she's not dead."

"Actually, we don't know that. The injuries were consistent with a severe beating, and she'd been stabbed. The doctor left to discuss the case with a colleague and we know how overworked nurses are. Shannon snuck out."

"You have her file?"

Ashlyn shook her head. "Legally, our hands are tied here. With the Reimers already having a lawyer on the case, it could take days to get the records. The doctor did tell us he suspected long-term abuse." She thought about what he'd said to Tain about the look in his eyes. "He hinted that the X-rays had supported that conclusion."

Zidani sighed. "What you're saying is, if they hadn't messed up, we might have found her."

"Worse. The doctor said when he returned about ten minutes after leaving Shannon, she'd disappeared, but there were two police officers talking to the nurses. We double-checked. If these guys had done their jobs we could have had Shannon on Friday afternoon. The reason we figured it out was because Tain checked up on the address where the 911 call came from."

"Eagle Ridge Hospital."

She nodded. "Can you imagine how long she must have been there for, waiting for treatment? And we still managed to get officers there in time to practically cross paths with her. If they hadn't messed up, if they'd done their job properly . . ."

"Christ, what a mess." He sank into his chair. "None of this changes the fact that you got physical with Parker."

"Not before he pushed Tain."

"So you let Tain get in his face and get him angry, and basically accuse him of incompetence."

"He's worse than incompetent. Parker's reckless and he's a sexist asshole."

Zidani pointed at a chair, and she sat down. "Makes me wonder why you partner with Tain."

"He's a good cop. I know he gives other people a hard time, but that's not how he is with me."

"So that's all that matters to you? If you don't have a problem with somebody, nobody else should?"

She was starting to wonder where this was going. "I didn't say that. If Parker has a problem with women, it's his problem, but if I'm in charge of an investigation and he's working on it, I expect him to do his job. And I don't think that's too much to ask."

Zidani nodded and leaned back in his chair. "So what do you want to do about Parker?"

"I don't want him on this investigation."

"You realize he's filed a complaint against you."

"What?"

"You deny hitting him?"

"Not for a second. He shoved Tain into me, and then . . ." She took a deep breath. "What's going to happen now?"

"Nothing. I already told his commanding officer that Parker's an arrogant asshole and a sexist pig. If you say it, you sound petty, even if it's true. If I say it, it's harder for him to argue with. It isn't Parker I'm concerned about. It's Byron Smythe."

Her annoyance had produced some heat in her cheeks, but Ashlyn felt that dissipate. "What are you talking about?"

"Someone worked him over. Good. Bruised ribs, split lip, sprained wrist. And a dislocated knee." He looked at her quietly for a moment. "Is there something you want to tell me?"

She closed her eyes for a moment. Craig . . . *What have you done?* "Smythe got physical with me at the mall."

"When was this?"

"Saturday night."

"So you kicked the shit out of him?"

She shook her head. "No. Just kicked him in the leg. I–I'm probably responsible for the knee injury. But the rest . . . It wasn't me."

Ashlyn rolled up her sleeves and Zidani was quiet for a moment as he looked at the bruises.

"Smythe grabbed you and you kicked him, and that's all that happened?" He nodded at her, looking at her arms. "Did you show those bruises to Tain?"

"No. It happened Saturday night and yesterday we barely saw each other."

"Nobody knows about this?"

"I didn't broadcast it in the office, if that's what you mean."

Zidani picked up his phone, dialed and relayed instructions. Within minutes there was a knock at the door. A woman came in, carrying a camera case.

"Take your shirt off and let Lucy photograph you. If Smythe files a complaint it's going to make this thing with Parker harder to shake off."

"I told you. It wasn't me."

"I'm not taking any chances. A guy like Smythe, it could have been any of ten dozen scumbags. Guys he represented who feel he let them down when they still got time. Guys he's trying not to represent who won't take no for an answer. Word is, Smythe took a bit of a beating a few months back, but I never saw it myself." Zidani walked to the door and opened it. "The thing is, he can produce witnesses, people who saw you kick him. If he needs a scapegoat he could lie to save his own ass. And if your problems with Parker come out, well, it won't look good, will it? Just do what I say and I'll cover your back, okay?"

Ashlyn knew there was no point arguing, knew he was right, but when he closed the door and she reached up to undo the buttons she felt her hands shake.

When she'd finished buttoning her shirt Ashlyn thanked the photographer, who let Zidani in as she left.

"You okay?" he asked.

She nodded, and started unrolling her sleeves just as Tain came in.

"We've got—" He stared at her arms.

Ashlyn yanked the sleeves down. "What is it?"

"Byron Smythe just phoned. The family received a call this morning from someone claiming they kidnapped Shannon Reimer."

Zidani's face had registered shock and disbelief initially. When he turned his gaze to Ashlyn he asked, "What's your gut telling you?"

"Not impossible."

"That's not exactly helpful, Hart."

"Look, there's motive. I've had Sims looking at the family and their connection to Byron Smythe. Richard Reimer does a lot of land deals, worth a lot of money. Sims is checking the history of all the properties, looking for any links to organized crime or drug trafficking."

"Because?"

"Because most of Smythe's clients have connections to criminal enterprises." She took a breath and then gestured for Tain to close the door. "Look, I've got nothing to back this up, and it may be a wild-goose chase, but from the beginning things were wrong. I've interrogated career criminals who've volunteered more during questioning than Christopher Reimer did. He blames the murder on his sister, who's conveniently missing. At the house there are photos of Shannon and Jeffrey, and they looked close. Like they adored each other. Maybe the reason Christopher lied was to get us looking in the wrong direction. It's not uncommon. Christopher's a kid, so he thinks if we realize his dad's a criminal we'll arrest him, and Christopher's scared. On the other hand, if Richard Reimer has ties to drug trafficking the family may have been threatened. Now we know Shannon was hurt. If I was the type to place bets on such things, I'd still put my money on someone in the family killing Jeffrey, but if someone really did kidnap Shannon Reimer . . ."

"It would explain why the Reimer family phoned their lawyer immediately and hasn't cooperated with the investigation," Tain said.

"We thought it wasn't much to ask to search Shannon's room, but if she'd written about anything in a diary or on a computer it could expose the truth," Ashlyn added. "Of course, that's assuming there's truth to expose here. Right now, it's just a theory. I don't like working off theories, but this case . . . it feels thin."

"And this theory fits the facts. And it suggests possible avenues of investigation." Zidani scratched his head. "Why didn't you mention it sooner?"

"That's not how I work. Initially, there was nothing to contradict the evidence we had that made Shannon our main suspect. What we've learned since then still makes me suspect someone else in the family. Sims can monitor the cell phone and dig for background. If there's something there, we follow up on it. Meanwhile, we pursue the most likely leads we have."

"What about the kidnapping?" Zidani asked. "How do you want to work it?"

"Like we would any other case. The family will have to give us access if they expect us to track the callers." Ashlyn looked at Tain. "Did Smythe give you anything to go on?"

"The call came in on their cell phone, but don't count on complete cooperation. According to Smythe, Richard Reimer had the presence of mind to tell the kidnappers not to use his primary cell, in case the police were monitoring it. He gave them a number for a pay-and-talk phone."

"Pay and talk," Zidani said. "The phone of choice for teenagers and criminals."

"He just happened to have a pay-and-talk phone hanging around that he could offer exclusively to his daughter's alleged kidnappers?" Ashlyn threw up her hands. "Unbelievable. But we're still monitoring a cell phone, which means we can bring them here and wait it out."

"Wouldn't it be better to take the opportunity to go to the Reimer house?" Zidani asked. "This gets you in the door."

"But they aren't even staying there. We don't know where Smythe has them. And if the kidnappers are watching the house they'll see us."

"What if we set up a safe house?" Tain asked. "Someplace neutral."

Zidani drummed his fingers on his desk for a moment. "I don't know. We don't know if there's a kidnapper, but we do know there's an alleged kidnapper. If that person's serious, they may be watching the Reimer family already. They have their cell phone number, so it's possible they know they aren't at home. The only place Richard and Tracy Reimer can go that you can access without raising suspicions is their lawyer's office."

"Can we at least do a check on Richard Reimer's cell phone to see if there's anything useful for us to track the kidnapper?"

Zidani shook his head. "Look, we could go ten rounds in court with Byron Smythe, and we might eventually win. He's got nothing to lose, but we simply don't have the resources or the time. If the parents are involved in Jeffrey's death, Smythe will use every loophole possible to keep them out of jail. My gut tells me we have to prove this without forcing cooperation. Or at least try." He looked at Ashlyn. "Tain can handle this if you prefer."

She shook her head. "This is still my case."

He raised his hand. "I know. But under the circumstances—"

"I'm going to do my job. If Byron Smythe doesn't like it, he can hand his clients over to another lawyer."

She didn't look away. After a moment Zidani nodded. "Okay. Go talk to Smythe. I'll get a team together and we'll monitor the cell phone. We treat this as though it's legitimate, but we don't stop looking for Shannon."

"Til I Am Myself Again" was on the radio as Craig merged into the traffic on the Trans Canada highway, heading east to Langley. The morning had brought with it clear skies and a biting cold, a blanket of white still covering the earth from the night before. To the north the mountains shimmered in the winter sun, which reminded him of home. He'd grown up in the interior, so he was used to snow-covered mountains and a crisp, winter chill in the air. The image was so strong he could almost smell the pine from when he'd gone skiing. That was the only thing about home that he missed. Real winter.

It was late enough that the roads had been cleared as well as could be expected, but snow was rare enough in the Lower Mainland for the average resident to forget how to drive in it. There were those who saw the winter conditions as an invitation to drive a lot faster than normal and those who drove dangerously slow. It took longer than he expected to reach the Harrington house, and when he arrived there was no answer at the door.

The school Hope had attended was his second option. After speaking to the secretary and principal, he navigated the hallways until he found Ms. Hill's room.

"You look a bit old for remedial English, and I don't recognize you as one of my parents," she said when he knocked on the open door.

He held up his ID. "Constable Craig Nolan, Coquitlam RCMP."

A murmur rippled through the classroom, gasps of shock, and one boy in the back called out, "Whaddya do, Ms. Hell?" which was rewarded with laughter.

She sighed, pushed her graying hair back behind her ears, shuffled into the hall and pulled the door shut behind her. "How can I help you?"

"You taught here ten years ago?"

"And then some." She smiled wryly. "What's this about?"

"You remember this girl?" Craig passed her a photo.

The corners of her mouth sagged. "Of course. Hope Harrington. Just terrible what happened." She passed the photo back. "Hope's boyfriend was convicted of murder. It was such a shame."

"I was wondering if you remember any of Hope's friends, students she was particularly close to."

"Well, let me see. Wendy Burns. They talked a lot in class. And I caught her passing notes with . . ." Ms. Hill pinched the bridge of her nose for a moment. "Brandy Hicks."

"You wouldn't happen to know if either of those girls still lives around here?"

Her eyes narrowed. "Sorry. What's this about? Are you finally going to do something about Donny?"

Craig looked up from jotting the names down in his notebook. "What do you mean by that?"

"Donny was a sweet boy. He wasn't going to find a cure for cancer, and he wasn't going to be a political leader or win an Olympic medal, but he seemed nice. Some kids"—she nodded at the window to her classroom, which betrayed the students throwing paper planes in the back of the room, the ones passing notes and giggling, and the few attempting to do classwork— "are nothing but trouble. Donny was never going to change the world, but he carried Hope's books when he walked her down the hall and always spoke to teachers with respect, which is more than I can say for most of them. I never believed he killed her."

She reached for the door. "Is that everything?"

Craig nodded. "Thanks for your time." He passed her a card. "If you think of anything else."

The sound of chaos in the classroom spilled into the hall as the door opened. As Craig walked away he could hear the teacher trying to restore order.

Donny Lockridge had a good lawyer now, and Byron Smythe wouldn't leave any stone unturned. Witnesses like Ms. Hill would strengthen his case, but her description of Donny Lockridge didn't match the testimony given at trial. Donny had been seen fighting with Hope a few days before her murder.

He flipped back through his notebook. Lisa Harrington had claimed she saw Donny hit Hope.

When he got to his vehicle he phoned directory assistance and kept them busy until he had three phone numbers to follow up with. After a few calls he had an address.

Wendy Burns answered the door hastily, one baby slung on her hip, another crawling down the hall and two preschoolers chasing each other around the dining room table. The dining room was to the right. To his left there was a small living room with an old couch, an older chair and a rug covered with so many toys Craig wasn't sure what color it was.

"Max! Tyler! I warned you already. Stop it right now."

"Eeeeeeeeeeeeeeee!"

Wendy grabbed the screaming boy's arm. "That's enough, Tyler. To your room. Now."

Max ran by and thudded Tyler on the back of the head, which made him really start crying.

Wendy thrust the baby into Craig's arms and started chasing Max around the table. "Get over here right now, or you're gonna get a spanking."

A crash from down the hall was followed by a split-second silence and then the wailing of the other baby.

"Look what you've done," Wendy muttered as she dragged the boys down the hall. Now all three children were screaming. It was a Tylenol commercial in the making.

Craig looked at the baby in his arms. A girl. Dark hair, dark eyes. A little dimple on her cheek. He extended a finger, which she wrapped her hand around.

Doors shut down the hallway, which muffled some of the crying. "Sorry about that," Wendy said as she scooped up the toddler in the hall and disappeared into the kitchen. When she returned the boy had an arrowroot cookie he was sucking on. Wendy grabbed a tissue and wiped the snot from his nose.

"Constable Craig Nolan," he said to Wendy as he smiled at the little girl in his arms.

"Sorry to leave you there like that."

"It's okay. Four kids. I imagine that's quite a handful."

"Fifth one's at school. You have kids?"

"No."

"They're wonderful." She said it like she meant it, then laughed. "When they're sleeping, anyway."

"I was hoping to ask you some questions about Hope Harrington."

"Wow. Hope. That one in your arms is named for her, you know?"

"She looks like her. Except for the dark eyes."

"What do you want to ask me? I never witnessed her murder or anything, and they sent Donny away."

"Do you think he killed her?"

Wendy didn't look confused or surprised. Her expression was blank. "Well, I mean, the jury said he did. Back then, I guess I figured they were right."

"And now?"

"Donny didn't seem that bad. He treated Hope nice."

"But if they'd argued? Maybe he wanted something and she refused?"

Wendy shook her head as she set the toddler down. "I never saw them fight. Actually, Donny's family was movin' away. Buying a business in Kelowna. Donny wanted Hope to go with them." She paused. "That's what Hope said, anyway."

"His parents were okay with that?"

"Who knows? Hope lived half in a dream world. Thought Donny was Prince Charming, you know?"

"Did Donny ever get in fights at school, ever show he was capable of getting violent?"

Wendy shrugged. "Not much. But there was once, someone said something about Hope's mother. He messed that guy up pretty good."

"Why would school kids be talking about Lisa?"

"Hope's mom was what you'd call friendly, if you know what I mean." She looked away, hand on her hip, then sighed. "There were some guys from school who used to score off her. And from what I heard, with her. Sometimes Hope would stay with Brandy, just to get enough sleep for school. Her mother partied more than she did."

Craig considered that. It was obvious Lisa had cleaned herself up, and Hope's murder might have been the reason . . . But hadn't Lisa said Hope had broken up with Donny? "Did either Hope or Donny use?"

Wendy turned away, tidying up the lunch dishes still on the table.

"I'm not here to judge," he said. "Just trying to figure out what happened."

"Not Hope."

"Donny?"

She carried the dishes back to the kitchen and when she returned her arms were folded across her chest. "I never saw him. But . . ." Wendy looked away and shrugged.

"But you thought maybe he was."

"He hung out there sometimes, even if Hope was working or at my house."

"And when was the last time you saw Hope?"

"Just after school, the day she was murdered. Check your files. I told the cops all this back then."

"Do you remember which officer you spoke to?"

"Dale, Daly, something like that. When I saw Hope she told me she was either going to get married and move to Kelowna with Donny's family or break up with him. I thought she was nuts."

"Is that where Donny's family is now?"

"Yeah. They moved after the trial."

"Any reason for the breakup plans? Did she tell you why she was giving him an ultimatum?"

Wendy shook her head as she lifted the boy off the floor and set him down on the couch with his cookie and tossed a few toys into a pile on the far side of the room as she cleared a path to the door. She took Hope from Craig's arms.

He handed her a card. "If you think of anything else."

"Donny's lawyer's already been here. I know about the court case."

"Let's say Donny didn't kill her. Is there someone you can think of, someone who was violent with Hope or who was obsessed with her who might be upset that she was moving away, anyone at all that the police overlooked?"

"The only person who ever had a problem with Hope was her mother. My mom wouldn't let me go to their house. Lisa was always hitting Hope, yelling at her, telling her she was no good." Wendy paused. "Once, she said she made a mistake when she took Hope away from her father."

"I thought Lisa had always had custody of Hope."

"Sorry. I have no idea. I know Hope had been asking questions, and she couldn't find any pictures of herself under the age of three. Lisa brushed it off, said her dad had kept them all. Then Hope started asking about him and Lisa got pretty mad. 'After all I've done for you, after all I've sacrificed you'd just run off? No good for nothin', ungrateful little bitch.' You get the idea."

Craig understood the questions and the reaction. It reminded him of his own fights with his mother before he'd found out about Steve. "Did Hope keep asking?"

"Far as I know she gave up."

"And Lisa was using back then?"

"I guess. I don't know. But I'd known Hope all my life. Broken arms, cuts, bruises. When we were kids that wasn't that unusual, you know?" She looked Craig straight in the eye. "Most of us knew how to duck fast when we had to. You know what I mean."

He nodded. "I'm not saying it's right, but you know there are lots of parents that smack their kids that aren't murderers."

"Yeah, but Lisa had been convicted for assault before."

Another thing that wasn't in the file.

"And what about Brandy Hicks? Are you still in touch with her?" he asked.

Wendy looked away, then held up a finger as she went to the kitchen. "Not really," she said when she returned. "But Brandy married Donny's older brother."

She passed him a photo, a young couple who looked happy, the girl holding up an engagement ring. And around her neck was a locket, one that looked familiar.

"Do you remember when this was taken?"

"A few months after Donny went to jail, I guess. Brandy and Darren got close when Hope was killed. We all went to support Donny, you know?"

"And when he was convicted Brandy kept seeing his brother?"

"Brandy never thought Donny did it. Even when he went to jail."

"Any idea what made her so sure?"

Wendy shrugged. "She'd had a crush on Donny. Had chased him around for years. Donny wasn't interested. Brandy had been so jealous. At first, well, anyway, she never thought he did it. Donny got arrested, and Brandy and Darren ended up together."

"Are Brandy and Darren still married?"

Wendy nodded. "Last I heard, anyway. Living in Kelowna."

"Any chance I can borrow this photo, make a copy?"

She hesitated, then shrugged. "Just drop it in the mailbox."

"Thanks for your time."

"Sure."

Craig smiled at the baby. "Bye, Hope." The girl burrowed her head into her mother's body. Craig thanked Wendy again and stepped outside.

Wendy shut the door behind him.

Just focus on the job. That was the mantra that had played over and over in Ashlyn's head as they'd set up the equipment needed at

Byron Smythe's offices. Smythe had been shielding the family as much as possible in an adjoining room.

"Do you figure he lost an important case?"

"Hmmm?" Ashlyn turned to look at Tain.

"Someone did a number on him."

She looked away. "Did he file assault charges?"

"Apparently not."

"Then who cares?"

She could feel Tain watching her, and her cheeks burned.

"You don't really mean that," he said.

How could she tell him that she was responsible? In her mind she'd seen Craig slam the door behind him a hundred times since Zidani had told her about Smythe's beating. He'd been so angry . . .

Through the open doorway she could see Tracy Reimer reaching for her son. Christopher pulled away from her and finally stomped across the room and sat down in the corner on the floor. Tracy slumped back against the couch and stared blankly at some spot on the wall. Richard paced behind her, looked at his watch, stopped with his hands on his hips, paced some more, looked at his watch again.

She nodded at the family. "What do you think?"

Tain watched as Richard continued his pattern. "What is it about him that tells me he thinks we're wasting his time?"

"That's what I've been trying to figure out. Something about all of them seems . . . off."

Richard Reimer stopped pacing and stared straight at them. Then he marched around the couch, pointed a finger at Smythe, face darkening as he spoke. Richard brushed past Smythe, almost knocking the lawyer down in the process, and slammed the door.

"You know, that's it," Ashlyn said. "It's like he isn't waiting for a phone call. Shouldn't one of them, at least, be in this room, where the phone is?"

"Smythe is still trying to shield them from us."

"Yeah? Then why even have Christopher Reimer here?" Ashlyn asked. "What good does that do him?"

"Maybe they're afraid to let him out of their sight."

She folded her arms across her chest. "You really think that?"

A distant look crept into Tain's eyes. "No. But having him with them makes it look like they're unified. Like they're still a family." He was silent for a moment. "That's what they think, anyway. In reality, they don't seem like a family going through a crisis together. They seem like three individuals stuck together."

"I know what you mean. I keep seeing Tracy reaching for her son, which should be a very natural thing to do. But it just seems . . . wrong. Forced." Ashlyn paused. "Like she's doing what she thinks we expect her to do."

"It was the mechanical way she moved. If it had been an impulse, a need, he wouldn't have just slipped from her grasp."

"She didn't look surprised when he got up. Just leaned back against the couch and let him go."

Tain nodded. "That's why the family image isn't working. Putting them in the same room only emphasizes the tension between them."

The door opened and Byron Smythe hobbled into their room. He carefully reached back and pulled the door shut behind him, cast a glance at Ashlyn and Tain and then looked away. Whatever he said to the officer at the desk was muffled and low enough that Ashlyn couldn't make it out.

When he turned around again his gaze met Ashlyn's.

"If looks could kill," Tain murmured.

There'd been a ferocity in Smythe's eyes. The way he'd frowned, the flare of his nostrils, the hard edges of his jaw . . .

"Guess he doesn't handle rejection well," Tain said as Smythe disappeared into the other office again.

Ashlyn closed her eyes. Smythe had argued that, since his offices were located in Burnaby, the Burnaby RCMP should handle the kidnapping investigation. Zidani had refused to budge on the grounds that the murder had occurred in the Tri-Cities and that if Shannon had been kidnapped that's where she'd been taken from as well.

Something had been lacking in Smythe's arguments. He'd gone through the pretense of protesting, but hadn't pushed it further when Zidani didn't budge. Smythe could be filing motions, could try to force Zidani's superiors to reassign the case, could even press charges against Ashlyn just to get her off the investigation. Part of her expected Smythe to use any means necessary to get his way, which left her wondering why he hadn't.

If Smythe did make his move, Tain would be caught in the cross fire, unaware.

"Part of me wishes we could hand this off to someone I trust," she said.

"What about Craig? Do you think Zidani would let him handle monitoring Shannon's cell phone, at least, so that Sims could come here?"

Ashlyn swallowed. Craig. "No. Zidani has him on something else right now."

"Someone steal a tricycle?"

"There's no way Zidani is going to let Craig anywhere near an investigation I'm supposed to be in charge of. And he's right."

"If not Craig, what about Luke Geller?"

The other door opened, to the outer office, and Luke Geller entered.

"Speak of the devil," Ashlyn murmured.

He walked up to her. "Zidani sent me over."

"For any special reason?"

"He doesn't want you tied down here. This way, you can go back to the station."

Ashlyn forced a smile. "You won't be offended if I check on that."

"I expect nothing less."

Said with a grating edge to his words. As she moved across the room to use her cell phone Ashlyn glanced at her partner. There was a slight twist to his mouth that she'd seen from time to time when Tain was irritated. Most people overlooked the subtleties of his expressions, but that's where the truth of his impressions lay. After partnering with him for months, Ashlyn knew that. The more people who were around, the more guarded his reactions.

She slipped her cell phone shut and walked back over to them. "No answer. We'll have to wait."

Luke offered a warm smile and managed to finesse the edge out of his tone. "I wouldn't lie to you, Constable Hart. What good would that do? You'd find out and I'd be in a helluva lot of trouble."

"And I'm responsible for this investigation. If Sergeant Zidani is satisfied you can handle this, I'm happy to pursue other—" The door to the adjoining room opened again, and Byron Smythe reappeared. Ashlyn lowered her voice. "Leads. But right now, the possibility Shannon's been kidnapped is our top priority. And to be blunt, if Zidani felt I needed more manpower I'm surprised he didn't put you on monitoring at the station so that he could send Sims here. You're supposed to be a rookie. Why would I leave a high-profile kidnapping investigation that ties to the murder of a four-year-old child in your hands?"

"Just because your boyfriend wouldn't give me a chance doesn't mean I'm not capable."

"This has nothing to do with Constable Nolan."

"Bullshit. I'm sick of this attitude. There's a break and enter at your boyfriend's parents' home and he's nowhere to be found, hasn't shown up for work, so I go out there to handle it quietly and when he shows up he practically throws me out. Tells his stepmother right in front of me that if she can't reach him to call you."

"Whatever problems you've got with Craig, don't take them out on me. I have enough to deal with right now, and my priority is getting Shannon Reimer home, alive, and finding the murderer of Jeffrey Reimer. Now, if your ego is going to get in the way of you doing your job you can walk right back out that door. I don't want anyone on my team who feels they've got something to prove."

"Is that it? Or is it just that you don't want to be upstaged?"

"I don't want to knock on your parents' door and tell them your pride got in the way of doing your job so you got yourself killed."

"Is that how you explained it to Lori Price's parents? The way her boyfriend keeps calling and threatening Craig, I'd say he didn't take it too well."

Ashlyn swallowed. Craig hadn't told her about any calls. "What happened with Constable Price has nothing to do with you." He opened his mouth to speak, but she didn't give him a chance. "And if you want to prove yourself on the street you're going about it the wrong way, Geller. You can start by showing you're capable of following orders."

Luke's face darkened, but he drew a breath before he spoke. "I didn't come here to get in an argument. I'm just doing what I was told. I'll wait until you confirm it with Zidani." He walked over to the desk, where they'd set up the equipment, and introduced himself to the other officers.

"Call Zidani," Tain said. "Get him to send Sims here instead."

Ashlyn considered that. Her first instinct was to have Luke kicked off the case, but she realized that was just to assert her authority. "Sims is doing some background checks that he wouldn't be able to bring here. And after this little incident I don't want Luke anywhere near that stuff. It doesn't make any sense to lie about being sent over here, but something about that's odd."

"Geller's in Zidani's pocket."

She looked at him. "What do you mean by that?"

"Look, I've seen them talking a few times. Like they know each other. If it wasn't for the fact that Craig's been pretty much on desk duty for so long I'd swear Geller's a plant, that his real job is to check up on Craig."

Tain's gaze met hers, and after a moment she looked away.

"Look, it's none of my business—" he said.

"You're right." She pulled out her cell phone and dialed Zidani's number. "It's none of your business."

Ashlyn forced herself not to look at Luke Geller during her phone conversation with her sergeant. When she hung up she leaned back against the wall, cell phone resting against her chin.

Tain's cell phone rang and he answered it. After a moment he thanked the caller and hung up. "Sims says he found a bank account in the Cayman Islands in Shannon's name with over two million in it."

Ashlyn frowned. "Any word on the shoe prints?"

"They have them, but they need something to match them against to be more helpful."

There was no doubt in her mind that her partner was waiting for her to tell him what Zidani had said. And from the other side of the room she could see Luke's glances.

"Well?" Tain finally asked.

She moved her hand to the side of her face, to keep Luke or anyone else from making out her words. "It seems Luke Geller was reaching just a bit. Zidani sent him over here to assist us. It's my call if we feel we can leave this in Luke's hands. Until then, we're babysitting."

Tain's eyes widened just a touch. "So why would he lie when he knows you're going to check up on him?"

"It won't be long before the second shift is here." Ashlyn looked at her watch. "Maybe he thought I wouldn't bother checking up so late in the day." What Luke had said kept running through her mind, about Vish Dhaval making threatening calls. How would Luke know that? It wasn't something Craig would tell his partner. Or anyone, it seemed.

And Craig hadn't shown up for work. Steve's old case was becoming an obsession. It didn't make sense that Zidani would pick Craig to review the case when one of Zidani's biggest complaints had been nepotism. Zidani had been convinced Craig had gotten an easy ride because of his relationship to Steve, and that was the main reason he'd given Craig such a hard time.

What Tain said about Luke and Zidani made a certain amount of sense as well. Put Craig in charge of someone who's supposed to be a rookie, and use him to spy on Craig. See if he works by the book, see how he handles cases.

But it still didn't explain this case review. If Zidani had been looking for an Achilles heel, he may have found it.

"Ash?"

"Hmm? Sorry. What?"

"I can handle this."

"I know." She straightened up. "That's why I'm leaving you in charge."

Ashlyn glanced at Luke Geller to make sure he'd heard that, and left.

The older farmhouse was in need of a fresh coat of paint. Streaks on the windows made the curtains inside appear dingy or at least, Craig guessed, more worn than they actually were. It was the kind of property that with just a little work would be enviable. Instead, it looked like the owners were in the early stages of letting it go.

Craig got out of his vehicle, walked up the concrete steps to the front door and knocked. He had his ID ready, but when the door opened he lowered it. "When we met the other day you never mentioned your name."

"You didn't ask."

"And Ted Bicknell?"

"My father."

"You know who I am?"

Jim Bicknell stepped outside and pulled the door shut behind him. He was average in most respects except for his bulk. Brown hair, brown eyes, a jagged scar on his chin that suggested he'd been cut with a knife or a bottle. When Bicknell had pulled up next to Craig's vehicle two days before, Craig hadn't been paying much attention. He'd been distracted by what the visit represented, the knowledge that Zidani had been checking up on him.

"You're the guy looking at the Harrington case files to see if my dad screwed up."

Craig shook his head. "That's not—"

"Save it, pal. I know what you're up to."

"Look, Lockridge is planning to file a lawsuit for wrongful conviction."

"He already did file the suit. The RCMP, my dad, the prosecutor, my dad's old partner. Lockridge is going after everyone."

"I'm just trying to get to the truth. As far as I can tell, Donny still looks good for this, but hiding only makes your dad look guilty."

"You sell it to yourself any way you want, I got no use for cops who investigate other cops."

"That's not my job. My boss asked me to look at the case, make sure they had nothing to worry about with the parole-board hearing. I didn't even know about the lawsuit until after he handed me the files."

"Look, buddy, my heart breaks for ya. But if you think you're gettin' anywhere near my dad so you can dump this on his lap, you can think again. Now get off this property. I won't ask twice."

Bicknell's hand clenched into a fist, but the move was so subtle Craig had to rethink his opinion of Jim Bicknell. Seeing him out of uniform, on his home turf, Craig had thought he'd be the type to use brute force. But his reactions were more measured than that. Bicknell wasn't reckless. He was controlled. And the look in his eyes was cold and hard.

"Look, I know you—"

"I'm warning you."

"Jim, I don't think you know everything—"

"I know enough. Now get off my property before I throw you off myself. And don't think I won't."

Craig raised his hands and backed down the steps, then turned and walked to his Rodeo. He was running out of options. With Ted Bicknell unreachable and with his own dad not talking, he had only one strong lead to follow other than talking to Donny Lockridge.

And talking to Donny meant another encounter with Byron Smythe.

He got a copy of the photo of Brandy made at Staples and bought an envelope for Wendy's picture. When he reached Wendy's house he put her copy inside, then wrapped the envelope in the plastic bag, walked up to the front door and slipped it in the mailbox.

Craig added his copy to his file.

He looked at his watch. It was late afternoon. Already the light was dissolving. He could head east to Kelowna and talk to Brandy Lockridge first thing in the morning, be home Tuesday night.

Or he could go west and talk to Zidani, get approval before going to Kelowna. That meant he'd have to leave in the morning.

Craig started driving to the highway, still weighing the choices in his mind.

"Constable, er, Ashlyn." Sims's face reddened. "I thought you were dealing with the kidnappers."

"Alleged kidnappers. I left Tain in charge."

"There hasn't been any activity on Shannon's cell phone. Another day or so and I think Zidani will shut it down."

Ashlyn nodded and sank into the chair beside Sims. "I know. And face it, if it turns out she really has been kidnapped, it won't matter if we pull the plug here."

"If you think it would be better for me to deal with—"

"No. I want you here, without the family lawyer looking over your shoulder. That's actually why I wanted to talk to you. Any luck with Richard Reimer's business contacts?"

Sims passed her a file. "He has more money than he should, but as far as I can tell, most of his business dealings are pretty straightforward. He's been opportunistic, buying land in areas where there's been a lot of crime. Once he gets a block of properties together, he hires a security firm to clean things up."

"Rent-a-cops?"

"Sort of. Look here." Sims flipped the file open and pulled out a map. "He buys up a bunch of houses in this part of New Westminster. Now, at the time he bought the properties, these were the stats for auto theft, break-and-enter calls, robberies. This area here has a problem with drugs and prostitution."

"Which explains the auto thefts and robberies. Some guy jonesing for a fix who's desperate is more likely to steal to get the money to support his habit."

"Reimer's guys cracked down on the robberies." Sims pulled out a second map. "Look at the numbers."

"A ten percent drop in auto thefts and fourteen percent in robberies?"

"Now, if you look at this"—Sims pulled out another map—"you can see that the auto thefts and robberies increased in these areas and so did the number of drug-related calls."

"Reimer forced them off their patch. I bet whoever's running drugs in that area wasn't too happy with him. What it doesn't explain is why he has Smythe as his lawyer."

"There's a lot of money in real estate. Wouldn't that be enough for Smythe?"

Ashlyn smiled. "You really think the rest of Smythe's clients are okay with him working for guys like Reimer?"

"You're right." Sims picked up another file. "Some of the drug dealers Smythe has represented have a habit of breaking bones when they don't get their way. And you remember that young guy who disappeared in New West a few years back, just after leaving a casino? Never found? He's got a tie to one of those dealers. New West is on the river."

"They must have weighed him down good."

"A friend of mine is on the fire department there. They got called out for a guy who'd had both his legs broken while in the comfort of his own home. Nothing missing."

"Let me guess."

"He didn't get a good look at his attackers."

"Right. Somehow failed to get a good look at them as they were breaking his legs." She stood up with the files in hand. "Looks like I need to go have a chat with the New Westminster PD."

Ashlyn went to Zidani's office, but it was empty. Craig's desk was also unoccupied.

Craig wouldn't tell Luke anything about Vish Dhaval. There was no doubt in her mind about that, which meant that either Luke was lying about the threats, or he'd seen something at work. Luke hadn't exactly been straight with her earlier, and he could know Vish's name from the newspaper reports about Lori's death.

Despite the strain of being on restricted duties for months

and living with uncertainty about what was going to happen to his dad, Ashlyn had thought Craig was handling things. The lack of discussion about Lori and what had happened had been taken as a sign that he was putting it behind him, but now . . .

I don't want to do this. But she knew she had to. If Vish had been threatening them, she needed to know.

And she needed to know if Craig was keeping things from her.

She sat down at his desk. For a moment, she felt as though her heart might burst through her chest. Not once, ever, had she snooped through his things at home or pried about something this serious that he hadn't seemed ready to talk about. Her insides twisted just at the thought of crossing that line. Luke had planted a seed of doubt that had taken root so quickly she couldn't ignore it, and a part of her hated him for that. She didn't know him at all and he'd stuck his nose into something that was personal.

No wonder Craig had never warmed up to the guy.

Close her eyes and she could go back a week in time and see how happy she'd been. Had her own happiness been nothing but an illusion? Was it based on denial and wishful thinking more than reality? A week ago she never would have believed Craig would walk out on her and not come home all night.

The image of Byron Smythe hobbling around his office, visible bruises, casts and crutches on display went through her mind.

Craig had been enraged. She didn't think she'd ever seen him so angry.

Ashlyn drew a deep breath. Then she opened the top desk drawer. Nothing unusual.

Notebooks and folders filled the second drawer, all of which were clearly labeled and linked to a case.

The bottom drawer revealed a sea of pink message slips and she felt her heart sink as she reached down and grabbed a handful. She read a few, then tossed them back in the drawer and pushed it shut.

Her hands trembled as she set them on his desk. After a moment, she trusted her legs enough to stand up and slowly walked around to where Luke sat.

She didn't hesitate to open the drawers of Luke's desk. The top one was locked. The second one was filled with legitimate work files and notebooks. The bottom drawer had a few pink slips in it, and she picked them up and read them.

Then she ran her hands under the desk, looking for a key. Her search turned up nothing, and after checking everything on the desk she gave up. Ashlyn picked up the files Sims had given her and went to get her coat.

Once Craig was sure that Ashlyn had left he went straight to Luke's desk and pulled open the bottom drawer. After he read the messages he slammed it shut.

It took less than two minutes to place the calls he needed to make, one to check up on who'd been visiting Donny Lockridge in prison, another to follow up with the lab on the samples he'd dropped off, letting them know he'd likely be out of town for the next day or two, and they should call his cell phone as soon as they had anything.

Then he marched down the hall.

Zidani was at his desk. Craig didn't hesitate after he knocked, just walked right in and shut the door.

"Why did you give me this case?"

"I told you. We needed to make sure that there wouldn't be any surprises at the parole hearing." Zidani didn't even blink. He barely looked up long enough to confirm it was Craig before he yawned.

"Cut the crap. You've been griping about how I got a free ride, with my dad as sergeant here, since the day you arrived. Then you hand me a case to review when you know my dad was the primary investigating officer."

"All this time you tell me you're capable of doing your job, being impartial. Well, do your damn job."

"And if I clear him you'll be okay with that?"

Zidani slammed his hand down on his desk. "Believe it or

not, I want the truth here. You come back and say we've got a liability issue, the department will move to settle. Nobody wants a scandal right now."

"And if I come back and say Dad and Bicknell are clean the department will fight it?" Craig was starting to see what was going on. "You're hanging them out to dry."

"They're doing that to themselves. Neither of them will talk."

"How do you know? I haven't given you an update." Then it hit him. "You've got someone else covering the same ground."

"No. Not exactly. Look, like it or not, you're in this. Best thing you can do is a thorough investigation and give us your report. Surely you've had enough time to review the case."

"There are gaps. I need to talk to a witness."

"You mean there are gaps in the initial investigation?"

"I mean there are things missing from the files. When I took the boxes from this office there was a folder in there about Desiree Harrington. I get a call from my stepmother and when I come back, that file is gone. You only gave me two boxes, but I checked the records; a third box is missing. The break-in at my parents' house? Someone took my dad's files on the case. You know how it works. Legal will have advised him to keep his mouth shut, and without his notes and with incomplete records I'm screwed."

"So you're what? Interviewing everyone again?"

"Just following up on legitimate leads."

"Fine. Talk to your witness."

"I have to leave town. They don't live here anymore."

"Who's the witness?"

"I'd rather not say."

"Constable Nolan, I don't think I like what you're implying."

"That's too damn bad. You put me in this situation, Zidani. Now, I've reviewed the files. I've talked to people from Hope's school, her friends, her mother, seen where she died and talked to one of the other officers on the case. I tracked down Ted Bicknell, but his son won't let me anywhere near him. And when you assigned me this case, you didn't exactly come clean with me. I have to find out when Lockridge's lawyer leaves phone messages and a reporter starts following me around that there's a civil case in the works, so don't you point fingers. That file on Desiree disappeared from this police station, and Lisa Harrington believes the person who broke in to her house the other night was a cop. If you really want answers on this case, you let me go talk to this witness. Otherwise I'll hand you what I have now."

"Which is?"

"A bit of room for doubt, but a solid circumstantial case that was upheld in the appeals process. The courts put an official stamp on the investigation not once, but twice. Unless you know something else about this that you aren't telling me, then the department should fight Lockridge's lawsuit."

Zidani leaned back in his chair. Craig had no idea what he was thinking, but he really didn't care. The more he thought about the case, the more he wondered what he was caught in the middle of. The department could have settled quietly right away if they'd been worried about their image, but the lawsuit was already in the papers. The damage was done.

Settling now would be an admission of guilt. As Craig looked at Zidani, he wondered if that was the point. Bicknell was retired, already on a pension, and the department would cover the suit. If this was a witch hunt, it wasn't about him. They couldn't really hurt him now.

He'd pinned Zidani between his own rock and hard place. Almost as though Zidani knew what he was thinking, he nodded.

"You'll leave in the morning?"

"Yes."

"And you'll be in the interior for one night, two at the most?"

Craig nodded as he reached for the door handle.

"Just remember something, Nolan. A lot of people are watching you."

"That's good."

"Why's that?"

"They'll know I've been thorough and honest." He opened the door and then paused and looked at Zidani. "You want to know why I never minded working for my father? I never needed to hide anything from him. Even my mistakes."

Craig walked out of the office before Zidani had a chance to say anything else. He'd baited Zidani and done it without playing the one card he was still holding back.

Smythe pointed a finger at Tain. "I'm telling you, this is a waste of time and an unnecessary strain on my clients."

"And if someone really did kidnap Shannon Reimer and we do nothing to pursue this, you'll file another multimillion dollar suit against the RCMP for negligence."

After Ashlyn had left, Tain had sent someone to get him a sandwich and a newspaper. The pressure his partner had been under and the reason Craig wasn't available to help on their case was starting to become clear, and he felt a pang of guilt for being so hard on her.

"Look, I understand all the blue wall crap, how you cops look after your own, but my client is innocent. And that has nothing to do with this case."

"Just because the kidnappers haven't phoned back yet doesn't mean they won't. Right now our top priority is finding Shannon Reimer. Preferably alive and well. If we have to babysit this phone until the New Year that's what we'll do."

"Suit yourself. At least that bitch left."

Tain grabbed Smythe's arm as he turned away. "Don't you ever speak about my partner that way."

The lawyer wrenched his arm free. "Or what? I'll get another beating? You just keep her the hell away from me."

Smythe hobbled over to his desk, and Mrs. Reimer ran in from the other room, Mr. Reimer behind her.

"How much longer do we have to put up with this?" said Richard Reimer, pointing a finger at Smythe.

"Look, I don't like it, but the cops have a job to do."

"I can't take much more of this!" There wasn't just a lone,

quiet note of hysteria in Tracy Reimer's voice: There was a full orchestra performing.

Tain took one look at them and made a decision. He slipped into the other room and gently nudged the door shut. Christopher was still sitting on the floor in the corner, slumped against the wall.

"Can I get you anything?"

Christopher snorted, but didn't look up.

"Come on. You must be hungry." Tain looked at his watch. "It's almost time for dinner."

No response. Christopher's tousled hair framed a pale face with a hard edge to it. He didn't fidget, didn't look around trying to make sense of what was going on. Suddenly, sitting in the corner made sense to Tain. Christopher was in control of his world, he could see everything coming at him. That gave him a sense of security and empowerment. Although the logic was flawed Tain could understand why the boy would embrace it.

"We know Shannon didn't kill Jeffrey."

Christopher's head snapped up then. After staring at Tain for a minute his mouth formed a hard line.

"Don't you want to help us find her?" Tain asked.

"If you know so much why haven't you found her already?"

"We're working on it."

Christopher leaned his head back against the wall and stared up at Tain. "Haven't you heard? She's been kidnapped. What the fuck do I know about that?"

The boy's lip curled and he looked away.

"You sure I can't get you a burger, tacos, anything?" Too late. He heard the sound of the door opening and footsteps behind him, even as he said the words.

"We'll look after him. You leave him alone!"

Richard Reimer had his hand on his wife's back and was pushing her toward the couch. He glanced at his son, then looked at Tain. "Get out."

Tain glanced at Christopher. The boy never flinched or

smiled. His expression was set in stone. As Tain walked through the doorway he took one look back and saw no indication that Christopher was even aware his parents had returned. He had disconnected himself from the world around him.

CHAPTER TEN

First they'd been held back by the family, unable to get straight answers or assistance that might help them find Shannon. Then police incompetence had been a contributing factor, prolonging a search that should have been over within hours instead of dragging on for days.

Most avenues of investigation had been stalled by the weekend. What limited information they did have from the parents, including the name of Christopher's school and the day care Jeffrey attended, had done them little good. They'd been set on the back burner, something to follow up on Monday.

Now most of Monday was gone. Only a few hours remained of the day, and it was far too late to talk to school staff. The alleged kidnapping was either the breakthrough they needed or a threat that could derail the entire investigation.

If Ashlyn believed it was a legitimate possibility . . .

That was the root of the problem. She was beginning to wonder if Byron Smythe was smarter than she gave him credit for. He'd turned over an address book, so smudged and manhandled that they couldn't get any useful prints off it. The only thing it contained that seemed helpful was the billing information for Shannon's cell phone.

And they'd begun monitoring her calls.

Maybe Smythe had figured Ashlyn would do that herself. That providing one small piece of useful information would stall the investigation from the outset. And when it failed to keep them from questioning the neighbors they had to come up with another plan. Another way to stretch the police to their limits.

What better way than to have an alleged call from someone claiming they'd kidnapped Shannon Reimer?

And Richard Reimer had handed over a pay-and-talk cell number. No chance they'd accidentally monitor a call with a business associate or stumble across an address book in his phone. They couldn't even trace the alleged call from the kidnappers.

Part of her understood why Zidani wasn't pushing the family hard. And part of her wondered if they'd painted themselves into a corner and if it was already too late to come through this clean.

"The guy over there bought this for you."

Ashlyn looked up at the guy who'd brought her the drink. "He should have saved his money."

The waiter—who she judged to be a few years younger, probably a Simon Fraser University student working his way through a degree—gave her a wry smile. "I'll be sure to tell him you said so."

He turned to take the drink to the man, but Ashlyn's would-be companion had gotten up and walked toward them. He took the drink from the waiter, who looked at Ashlyn. She lifted her hand just enough to signal him to hold back as the man sat down at the table and pushed the drink toward her.

She pushed it back, and he moved his hand to stop her. When he struck the glass some of the alcohol spilled over on Ashlyn's hand.

"I'm just leaving." She grabbed a napkin to mop up the booze, then pushed her drink aside. Before she had a chance to say anything else, he grabbed her arm.

"Aw, c'mon darlin'. What's the rush? We're just getting to know each other."

"If you don't let go of me, you'll get more than you bargained for."

The waiter hadn't left, and Ashlyn figured he was hovering between calling security and trying to play hero himself. She twisted her arm around to free it from the man's grasp, grabbed his wrist and pulled it behind his back as she stood up and pushed him toward the table.

"We never got to introduce ourselves." She pulled out her ID and held it in front of him. "You can call me Constable Hart."

Ashlyn let go of him. He was your average guy, dark hair cut short, maybe an extra twenty pounds that wasn't all muscle, and his face was flushed. She smiled at the waiter, put some money on the table and walked outside. It was a cold night with a clear sky, and Ashlyn pulled her jacket around herself. Her breath warmed her hands. After fiddling with the radio for a moment she pushed in a CD. Springsteen's *Tunnel of Love*.

How could so much change in such a short time? All she wanted to do was go home, soak in a hot bath and go to bed, but that wasn't an option. Too many things were left unsettled between her and Craig, and she knew maintaining the stalemate would only make it harder to work them through.

But she also knew that the root of their issues remained elusive, just beyond her ability to grasp. The misunderstandings had exposed mistrust, and that made her uncomfortable. Her working relationship with Craig had forged a strong bond between them. He'd proven himself to her through the job, and it hadn't been until after the case where she first worked plainclothes, the case where she first met Tain and Craig, that she realized just how much she'd come to depend on Craig.

She'd thought it would be hard to find her feet on a big investigation, working with other officers who had more experience. Instead, what had been brutal was when it ended and they'd all been reassigned. Tain had been disciplined and they'd both been transferred out to different detachments, and she had felt the loss of her partners deeply. She'd relied on them more than she'd admitted to herself at the time, and had to learn to stand on her own in her new assignment.

And then they'd all been transferred to the Tri-Cities and ended up working together again.

It wasn't as simple for her and Craig now that they weren't just colleagues. Their relationship made what happened to them on the job more personal. She couldn't be objective about his assignment or his willingness to investigate his own father. The doubts and concerns she had would have been the same for any other cop, but it was hard to extract the emotion when the person you were worried about was someone you loved.

There was no perfect situation waiting for her at home. A cold fear was barely being held at bay, waiting to be unleashed if Craig wasn't at the house. She didn't know what that would mean for them, and she didn't think she had the strength to look for him. Another part of her was tired and hoped he'd be asleep so that they wouldn't have to fight. With all the tension between herself and Zidani over the past few months, and the spats between herself and Tain over the last few days, she was desperate to sort things out.

The problem was, she knew she couldn't fix things on her own.

When she pulled in the driveway she could see dim lights on inside. She knew as soon as she opened the door that Craig was there, because she could smell the food.

He came into the hall as she slid off her coat. "You came home."

She opened the closet and reached for a hanger. "Zidani has a second shift monitoring the kidnapping angle."

His voice was quiet. "That wasn't what I meant."

Ashlyn pulled her shoe off and dropped it on the closet floor, but said nothing.

Craig exhaled. "It's pretty late."

"You know this is a crazy case." She dropped the other shoe and slid the closet door shut, still not trusting herself to look at him.

"Tain called here looking for you hours ago."

Her head snapped up then. "Why? Did he have a lead?" She reached in her bag for her cell phone. It was still on, fully charged. "You could have called me."

"So it's my fault that I didn't know where you were and you didn't call to tell me?"

"We're not going to get anywhere blaming each other."

"Then why don't you tell me where you were?"

"I needed some time to clear my head before I came home."

"Why?"

"Because of this. I knew if you were here we'd end up having another argument."

"If I was here? Where else would I be?" He disappeared into the kitchen, and she walked down the hall.

"You didn't come home the other night."

Craig poked a fork in the contents of a pot and turned off the burner. "So that's your excuse to justify doing whatever you want now?"

"Where'd you go?"

Part of her dreaded what he'd say. It wasn't even the question that was weighing on her mind, but she couldn't ask that one. She wasn't sure she could bear to face the answer.

"You first," he said.

"I needed to clear my head."

"Yeah, I can smell how you cleared it from here."

Ashlyn felt her cheeks burn as she glared at him. "I wasn't drinking. And you're one to talk." There was a half-empty bottle of wine on the counter.

"Sure, you smell like a brewery, but you never touched a drop."

"Craig, look." There was a knock at the door, but she ignored it. "I know you were upset—"

"Upset?" He pushed his way past her, moved down the hall and opened the door, but didn't stop to greet their guest. Craig turned around and walked back to the kitchen. "Upset would be a bit of an understatement, Ash. Don't you think I had the right to be angry?"

Tain shut the door. From where Ashlyn stood in the hallway, outside the entrance to the kitchen, she could see both of them, depending on which way she turned. She faced her work partner. "Did something come up on the case?"

"Craig called." Tain glanced at the entry to the kitchen. "You hadn't come home and he was worried."

She turned to look at Craig. He was leaning against the

counter, fingers within reach of a wineglass. "You call around checking up on me, but don't even try my cell phone? I don't believe this."

"Well, at least I cared enough to phone. Now you want to know where I went the other night, but you didn't call me then, did you?"

"You left your cell phone here. How the hell was I supposed to call you? Don't you dare turn this around as though it's my fault."

"No, it's all my fault, isn't it? I'm late and I think you've gone home, but because I talk to that reporter I must have been up to something."

"Don't be ridiculous. You want to know what bothered me most? Do you? When you came home you didn't even come looking for me. You went straight to the living room, back to your case files."

"You've never been distracted by a case? And you know this is personal. There's a lawsuit against my dad over this investigation."

"Which is exactly why you shouldn't even be involved with it. The way you were talking made it sound like you were convinced your dad did something wrong. You're way too close to this to be objective. Can't you see what you're doing? You've been on light duty for months because the bosses thought you let your feelings cloud your judgment and you're proving them right."

"Zidani's the one who ordered me to investigate. You think anyone else cares about finding the truth? If my dad did something wrong, I'll be the first to stand up and say so."

"And you'll be back on the streets while his career is ruined."

"If that happens, he did it to himself. It isn't my fault. Besides, I may have evidence that will help dig him out of this mess."

"And people will really trust that. 'Steve Daly accused of wrongdoing, but don't worry, his son says he's clean.' How can you honestly think anyone will take you seriously? You're only making things worse."

"No. I haven't done anything. Whatever happened on this case, it had nothing to do with me. All I'm doing is making sure it was done right. If something bad comes out of it, it's on Dad, it's on his partner, and it's on the department."

"And what about your dad? What if you're right, and you get the proof that he's innocent. You think he's going to just pat you on the back and say he knew you were just doing your job?" she said. "You doubt him. Can't you imagine what it would be like to have a son doubt you, how much it would hurt? Hasn't he earned your trust and your support?" Ashlyn paused. When Craig remained silent she continued. "You accused Zidani of being after his job months ago, and now he hands you a knife to stick in your own father's back and you're willing to do it?"

"You don't understand."

"You're right about that. I don't."

Craig grabbed the wineglass, drained it, and put it back on the counter. "There's chicken in the oven." He started down the hall, toward the stairs. "I have to pack."

The cold fear inside her spread through her body. "Wait—"

He stopped and looked at her. There was a hardness in his eyes she hadn't seen before. "I have to go to Kelowna to question somebody. I leave in the morning."

His footsteps were heavy on the stairs. Once she heard the bedroom door shut she looked at Tain and choked down the lump in her throat. "I'm sorry."

"I'll go. Let you two talk."

"No." She put up her hand to stop him. "Have you eaten?"

He shook his head. Ashlyn walked down the hall to the dining room and turned on the light. She stopped cold.

The table was covered with the crime-scene photos and files. She took a step forward and looked at one of the pictures. Hope Harrington's body, beaten so badly what little skin was left untouched was covered in blood. Her stomach twisted violently and she stood still, willing the nausea to pass.

"Ash—"

She covered her mouth and ran to the bathroom. There was so little in her stomach that it wasn't long before she was sure the worst was over, but she still shook a bit as she stood. Once she rinsed her mouth, she flushed the toilet and opened the door.

Tain was tucking the last photo into a folder. He looked up as she slowly walked back to the table. "I guess this means dinner's off?"

"You should eat something."

"So should you. Sit. I'll get you a plate." He put up his hand. "Don't argue."

When he returned he had two plates and utensils. "Do you want a glass of wine?"

"No. But help yourself."

He left and when he came back he had two glasses of water.

While Tain ate she poked at the food and finally tried a bit of chicken.

"How's your stomach?" he asked.

Ashlyn reached for the water. "Seems okay."

"That's good. Go slow, though. Just in case."

She swallowed and set the glass down. "Craig said you'd called at first."

"I just wanted to touch base. Smythe got in my face after you left. I had a chance to talk to Christopher, though."

"Really?" She knew the look on Tain's face and wasn't about to get her hopes up. "How'd you manage that?"

"Luck. He's completely shut off. I told him we knew Shannon didn't kill Jeffrey."

"How'd he respond?"

"He was startled, but in control enough not to say much. I tried to persuade him to help us find her, but he completely shut down."

"Maybe he doesn't want us to find her."

"What do you mean?"

"Well"—Ashlyn reached for her water again and took another drink—"we have the statement from the neighbor, which supports the idea that there's been long-term abuse at the Reimer house. Maybe Christopher wants her to stay away. You know what Mrs. Pratt said, about Jeffrey clinging to his sister and crying that morning, then chasing her down the road. Shannon's had enough, decides to run away, which is what her friends tell us as well. Somehow Jeffrey finds out and follows her. Christopher goes after them. Maybe he's after Jeffrey, not realizing Shannon's picked her little brother up. The parents pursue them. Maybe they catch them. Jeffrey ends up dead, Shannon injured and on the run." She shrugged. "The doctor said she'd been beaten. Maybe she tried to protect Jeffrey and couldn't save him. Christopher thinks if his sister comes home his parents will finish the job."

"But why lie and tell us she did it?"

"Don't abused kids often lie to protect their abusers?"

"Are you asking me as a person or as a cop?"

He stared at her for a moment, until she looked at her plate. "Tain, I never—"

He put his hand over hers. "It's okay."

"No, it isn't. I have no right to pry."

"Getting back to your question"—he let go of her hand—"a lot of kids do lie to protect their abusers. Especially parents. They feel if the parent is taken away it will destabilize their life, and they're conflicted by a sense of obligation. They're supposed to love their parents. Christopher's eleven. Old enough to know things aren't right and old enough to be afraid of what will happen to him if his parents go to jail."

"Do you really think he'd rather live with his parents if he knows they killed his brother? Wouldn't he be in constant fear?"

"Maybe he thinks he can take care of himself. After all, the neighbor said he was the one who fought back."

"And if Shannon knows the police think she killed Jeffrey, it's one sure way to keep her from coming home, so in a weird way, Christopher's protecting her." Ashlyn shook her head. "This whole case is such a mess."

"You didn't learn anything promising?"

"Actually, I did." She gave him a quick recap of what Sims had discovered about Richard Reimer's businesses. "I'll chase it down tomorrow."

"You sure you wouldn't rather keep an eye on Luke Geller?"

"I think I'd be too tempted to throttle him."

Tain nodded and stood. She followed him to the kitchen with her plate and glass.

He set his dishes in the sink. "Ash—"

"I'll be okay."

"You're sure?"

She nodded and forced a smile as she put her dishes on the counter. "We have to deal with this sooner or later."

He walked to the door and she followed. After he put his shoes on he said, "Give me a call. Let me know what you find out tomorrow."

"I will." Ashlyn shut the door behind him. There was silence from upstairs. She returned to the kitchen to rinse the dishes and put the food away. Just another way of avoiding the real problems in her life. Craig would leave in the morning and be gone for at least one night.

She closed the refrigerator and stopped to look at one of the photos of them together. She could cover the physical distance between them in half a minute, but what would it take to overcome the uncertainty she now carried? Whoever said time healed all wounds didn't know what they were talking about. Time let infections take hold. Wounds festered. In the few days since their argument the tension had distorted her judgment. The threads of doubt were undermining the strength of her convictions about the person Craig was, about their relationship and their future, and she knew if they didn't try to sort things out before he left it would only make it harder to work through the issues.

Fighting with him was just so exhausting.

Another photo, of her in a kayak just before they went on a camping trip in September. Craig had said that was one of the best things about her, she never stood still.

He'd said that was why she'd been able to save his life. She could process a situation in a moment, make a choice and act on her decision automatically. Maybe that was the root of their current problems: too much thinking.

She went into the pantry off the kitchen and pulled out a

storage bin. Once she'd removed the items she was after, she left a few of them in the downstairs hall closet and carried the rest upstairs.

When she reached the bedroom she paused. Should she knock? It seemed ludicrous that something that would never have been a consideration for her before now weighed on her mind. She opened the door.

Craig stood beside the bed as he folded a shirt and placed it in his carry-on suitcase.

"You'll need these." Ashlyn walked over to him and set the scarf and gloves down. "I left your boots and coat downstairs."

He zipped up the suitcase but didn't look at her. "Thanks."

She watched him pick up the case and leave the room. His response had sounded choked and forced. Ashlyn followed him downstairs.

When she reached the landing he glanced at her as the color crept up from his neck into his face. Everything he needed was together: suitcase, boots, coat, keys.

He straightened up but still didn't look directly at her. "It's not the same."

"I know."

Craig turned and walked to the dining room, then stopped.

"Everything's in the box," she said as she walked down the hall toward him.

He grabbed the box from the floor and put it on the table. "Everything's messed up," he muttered as he started to sort through the files. "Couldn't you just leave it?"

Within minutes he had the files emptied and the photographs and reports reorganized. Craig had always kept the house neat and tidy, but she'd never seen him so anal about case files before. Instead of arguing about it or blaming Tain, she leaned back against the doorjamb and murmured, "I'm sorry."

He stuck the folders in the box and stood still. "Do you think I was wrong?"

The hesitation was unavoidable. Was he talking about walking out or staying on the case?

Craig turned then and looked at her. "You saw these photos."

She nodded.

"How hard do you have to grab someone before you bruise them?" He walked over to her. "And if they're wearing a coat?"

"I told you I took care of it."

"How could you expect me to just let it go? The whole thing was my fault. If I hadn't been late, if I'd called, if I hadn't been sidetracked by that reporter, none of this would have happened."

"Look, if you want to beat yourself up over this, I can't stop you. But Byron Smythe made his own choices. When he grabbed me I kicked him so hard I think I dislocated his knee."

Craig's face was tight. "Guys like him need to be taught a lesson."

"So you tracked him down and gave him a taste of his own medicine?"

"No. I'm just saying—" He stopped and turned back to the table, hands on the box.

She looked at him. *What are you saying?* That's what she wanted to ask. "Bruises, a sprained wrist. Smythe was worked over pretty good."

"He deserved it."

"Craig, you don't mean that."

He grabbed the box off the table and brushed past her without meeting her gaze. Once the box of files was put down beside his suitcase, Craig turned and walked back to her. He reached for her arm and pulled up her shirtsleeve. "Look what he did to you."

When she didn't look at her arm or at him, he cupped her face with his hands. "You don't expect me to let him get away with that?"

"And what if he presses charges? Even if he doesn't, you put this on me?"

His brow wrinkled. "Wait. You think . . ." He let go of her. "How could you think that?"

"What am I supposed to think? Listen to yourself."

"You actually think I'd assault him."

Half of her felt like crying, the other burned with anger. "I think you've gotten used to handling things on your own, without even consulting me. Treating me like a damsel in distress you need to protect."

"Where the hell do you get that from?"

"Vish Dhaval."

Craig's jaw went slack.

"Why didn't you tell me about the phone calls, the threats?"

"Who told you?"

"What difference does that make? You don't respect me enough to tell me what's going on?"

"So you go through my desk. Doesn't explain why you were snooping through Luke's, though." His eyes blazed and he held up a hand before she could say anything. "Yeah, I saw you."

"You're avoiding the issue. If you'd told me yourself I never would have been put in that position."

"You could have come to me." He tapped his chest. "Why didn't you just ask?"

She closed her eyes and shook her head. "That's not fair. You made a choice to keep this from me."

"I'll tell you what's not fair. I used to think you trusted me. Maybe sometimes I'd screw up, and maybe sometimes I'd have to own up to that, but deep down I thought you knew me better than this. You've been carrying so much guilt over Lori's shooting and you won't even admit it to yourself. Every time we talk about work, my cases, my problems, it's always there. I didn't want anything else hanging over your head."

"You talk about me not trusting you, but you didn't even give me a chance to work through this with you. All this time with you not talking and I'm left thinking you blame me."

"Ash, if you want to be mad at me for trying to protect you, fine. You go right ahead. Hate me for it. I'm the bad guy here. Can't be too hard for you to believe that. I mean, you're so sure I beat up Smythe."

"You stormed out of here and you never came home. Next time I see Smythe he's . . ." She swallowed. "Zidani called me into his office. He had someone photograph my bruises. If Smythe decides to file an assault charge . . ." She stopped.

"Did Zidani tell you about Vish's threats?"

"No. How—"

"Then who was it?"

"Craig, it doesn't matter."

"Maybe not to you, but it does to me. Unless you're the one who's been going through my desk for months now, taking things."

"Why on earth would I take things from your desk?"

"I saw you go through my desk today. You could have asked me anything, Ashlyn, anything. Instead you go behind my back and sneak around."

"That's not fair, Craig. We've barely been speaking. Luke tells me about the threats—"

"Luke." He walked past her and headed up the stairs. "Big surprise."

She followed him to their bedroom and the master bathroom. "This isn't about Luke or Vish or Lori. This is about us. If I could take it back I wouldn't have gone through your desk. I just want us to get back to where we were."

He zipped the bag of toiletries and walked past her to the bedroom door. "It's too late for that."

"Wait a minute. You keep things from me for months, and I'm supposed to give you the benefit of the doubt because your intentions are good? I make a mistake and that's it? No second chances?"

"You don't even understand why I have to finish this investigation. Admit it. You don't want me to go to Kelowna."

"Honestly, no. I don't want you to go. But I can accept that this is important to you."

"You think digging out my boots and gloves makes up for everything? You doubt me, Ashlyn." He pointed at her, then looked away, balling his hand into a fist. "The one person I thought I could count on for support, and you doubt me." He turned back to face her. "Do you have any idea how that feels?"

"Probably the same way Steve feels about you investigating him."

If she'd smacked him across the face he couldn't have looked more stunned. "Good night, Ashlyn."

He opened the door and shut it behind him and she listened to the sound of his footsteps moving away from her as she sank down on the bed. For the first time in days no tears threatened to spill over. She felt too numb to cry.

CHAPTER ELEVEN

Despite the early hour, Craig knew Lisa would be up. The girls would need to get ready for school.

He stepped out of his Rodeo and removed the materials he had in the back. As he walked up to the house he could hear the fighting from inside.

"As long as you live in this house you'll do what I tell ya to do!"

Someone started to cry.

"I mean it. You better smarten up. How many times do I have to smack some sense into you before it sticks?"

Silence.

A minute later the door opened. Destiny and Desiree appeared, heads bowed. They came down the steps one at a time, careful to skip the broken one, and then Lisa stepped out on the porch.

"You walk your sister right to class, Destiny," she said, the threatening edge still in her voice.

The older girl took her sister's hand and barely glanced at Craig as they walked by. What he saw in her eyes was a hollowness, reaching up from inside her and threatening to swallow her whole. She had a mark on her cheek, as though she'd been slapped across the face.

He looked up at the house. Lisa had seen him, and started to pull her housecoat closed. He'd already seen enough to know she didn't have much on beneath it.

"I remembered your broken step, thought I could fix that for you."

Lisa stood speechless for a moment, then said, "Thanks. That's really nice of you."

"No problem."

It didn't take him long to pry up the rotted boards, and since he had a good eye for measurements, in part because of his job, he had wood that was almost a perfect fit, just a few millimeters short on one end.

"There. A fresh coat of paint this spring and nobody will know the difference," he said after he'd nailed it in place.

"Really, that's very nice of you," Lisa said. She hadn't moved from the porch while he'd worked. As Craig gathered his tools she said, "Guess you heard us fightin'."

He didn't want to make a big deal about it, or draw attention to the seed of doubt taking root in his mind. "Families argue. It's normal," he said. "I'm sure you argued with Hope."

Her eyes narrowed. "What's that supposed to mean?"

"She was a teenager. Isn't arguing with your mother part of the teenage girl job description?"

Lisa stared at him for a moment. "I . . . I guess. Not that anyone likes to talk about that when their kid is dead."

"No, I suppose not. Did you get along with most of her friends from school, or were there some bad influences?"

There was a slight hesitation before she said, "Her friends were good kids. I liked them."

"I guess that explains why you'd been visiting Donny at the prison." He watched her eyes widen, a look of pure shock settling on her face. "Funny, when we first talked, I got the feeling you never wanted to see him again."

She didn't answer, just stared at him.

"I made a few calls on the weekend."

"Look, I just wanted to get him to say sorry for what he'd done, make him see how much he'd hurt me."

It was the first time Craig was absolutely sure Lisa was lying to him. She'd visited Donny regularly for the full ten years.

According to the guard he'd spoken with, she'd even taken her daughters with her.

"I can understand, Lisa," he said softly. "He was the last person to see Hope. And Donny wasn't such a bad kid. There probably hadn't been a single day since her death that you didn't blame yourself."

"Yes, that's right," she said as she turned away from him. "It's like it's my fault."

"Look, I have to go out of town today," Craig said. "I should be back sometime tomorrow. With Donny out now just be careful."

She turned her head to the side so that he could see the profile, but didn't face him. Lisa nodded. "Thanks. I will."

When Ashlyn opened the door the next morning she almost walked right into the person coming up the steps, and almost spilled her ginger ale on the woman.

"Sorry."

"I wasn't expecting anyone to be there." Ashlyn took a breath of icy air. She knew who her unexpected visitor was, and would have described her as cute, in a nauseating way. There was an aura of innocence that Emma Fenton projected, but something about it struck Ashlyn as being contrived.

"I, uh, I'm looking for Craig."

"He's not here, Ms. Fenton."

The reporter flashed a smile. "Okay, I'll call him." Emma Fenton's eyes narrowed just a bit. "Didn't I see you the other night?"

"Where? At the police station or at the mall?"

Emma's cheeks were already rosy, but the color deepened. "I'm sorry I bothered you. I'll try his cell." She turned and started walking to her car.

"He's driving. You likely won't get him for hours." Ashlyn could have kicked herself. Emma Fenton had made the classic move, told Ashlyn she had direct access to Craig, and how had Ashlyn responded? By taunting her with information she didn't have. As much as she regretted it, it stopped Emma in her tracks.

"Do you . . . ?" The reporter hesitated as she turned around. Her expression was serious, partly apologetic, but there was curiosity there as well. The carrot Ashlyn had dangled was too tempting for Emma to resist. "Can I ask where he's gone?"

"Of course you can ask," Ashlyn said as she walked to her own car. She set her travel mug down on the roof as she unlocked her door. "Just don't expect an answer."

The reporter grew an inch and she turned around and walked behind Ashlyn's car, smile gone. Emma glared at Ashlyn through narrow slits, her wide-eyed-innocent routine clearly over. A gloved hand swept her hair back over her shoulder, and Emma's chin jutted out.

"I'm trying to help Craig."

Ashlyn opened her car door and picked up her mug. "I'm sure you are."

She got in her car and for a moment thought she was going to have a problem. The rearview mirror betrayed the fact that the reporter remained behind the vehicle, her gloved hands clenched into little fists. Ashlyn looked back, as though to shoulder check, and gestured for Emma to move. Finally she did.

The drive south to New Westminster didn't take long. New West was an interesting city, with a high population density and a high crime rate to go with it. Access to the Pattullo and Queensborough bridges was through New Westminster, and the Port Mann ran right past a major exit to New West as well. The volume of traffic that went through the small city every day was staggering.

The name Sims had given her was for a Liam Kincaid, a detective constable in the Criminal Investigation Section. She stopped at the front desk and asked if he was in and didn't realize until she heard the front desk officer say there was a woman there to see him that she hadn't identified herself.

A few minutes later a man entered the lobby, and the desk officer pointed at Ashlyn. Liam Kincaid was easily six feet tall, fit, with dark hair, brown eyes, and a dimple on his cheek that needed no encouragement to show itself off. She smiled apologetically as she held up her ID.

"Constable Ashlyn Hart, Coquitlam RCMP. I was hoping you might be able to help me with something I'm working on."

The easygoing smile didn't waiver. "Sure. Sign in and come on through."

They went through the formalities, and he led her to a desk that was what she'd call semiprivate. Plenty of other people visible, but distant enough to not be able to overhear their conversation without making an obvious attempt.

"Would you like a coffee? Tea?"

"No, thanks. But don't let me stop you."

"You're sure? Well then, to what do I owe the pleasure?" He leaned back and smiled.

She set the folder down on his desk. "Richard Reimer purchased these properties and brought in a security firm to clean up the area. I understand he made a few enemies."

Liam picked up the maps and nodded. "The rent-a-cops usually do. Heavy-handed tactics. It isn't that they stop the criminals, they just move them over a few blocks, displace them temporarily." He looked up at her and smiled again. "But you don't need me to tell you that."

"I'm investigating the murder of Jeffrey Reimer."

"Didn't the papers name his sister as a suspect?"

Ashlyn nodded. "Shannon's still missing, but we're pretty sure she didn't kill Jeffrey. Yesterday someone called claiming they kidnapped Shannon. I'm not convinced it's legit, but right now, we can't afford to ignore any possible lead. The family's hiding behind their lawyer, Byron Smythe—"

"Smythe." Liam's face clouded. "Doesn't he usually represent organized criminals and drug importers?"

"That's why we were suspicious. We arrive at the family home to notify the parents, tell them their son is dead, and the first thing they do is call their lawyer. We're left wondering why they have a lawyer like Smythe on speed dial. So far all we can turn up is more cash than he should have and a trail of what seems to be valid real estate deals."

"And you're wondering if anyone Reimer might have pissed off would threaten his family."

"Not just him. Someone worked over Reimer's lawyer." Craig wasn't the only person with motive, and if she found out someone else was guilty it might help her mend fences with him.

"I heard. Banged up pretty good, sprained wrist, dislocated knee."

Ashlyn felt her cheeks flush. "I dislocated his knee."

Liam grinned. "When word gets out you'll be a hero around here. Unfortunately, I'm not sure if I can help you. Most of the players in this part of town are pretty small time, not well organized. In New West we have three basic types of criminals: organized, disorganized and just plain stupid. This part of the city is where the disorganized and stupid overlap."

"You can't think of anyone?"

"We can go ask around, see if anyone was holding a grudge." He sat forward in his chair, as though he was about to stand. There was no hesitation in his movements. Liam was prepared to hit the streets with her on a hunch and a thin thread of hope.

"I actually have to follow up on a few other things this morning, then check up on the kidnapping angle."

His smile dimmed. "Well, I can make the rounds myself."

She stood. "Or if you have time this afternoon we could go then?"

"Tell you what." Liam passed her the file. "Meet me for dinner and I'll fill you in. If you think there's anyone worth looking at, we'll pay them a visit tomorrow. Deal?"

All she could see was the look on Craig's face the night before, when he'd said good night. Something about his expression had knocked the wind right out of her. It would be good for her to go out, instead of spending the evening at the house alone. A welcome distraction from her problems. "Okay. When and where?"

"You're in Coquitlam? How about Charlie's in Port Moody? Mexican."

"It's close to where I live. Seven?"

"Sounds good."

They traded cards. Once she was out of the building she

opened her cell phone as she walked back to her car and dialed Tain's number. "Having fun?"

"Laugh a minute. You?"

"So far, Richard Reimer's business dealings aren't looking promising, but someone on the New West department is going to dig a bit deeper for me. I'll have a better idea tonight."

"There was no activity on the phone here last night, and I called Sims. Nothing there either."

"How's our friend doing? Is he nosing around?"

"Not yet."

"Let me know if he gets ambitious. I'm on my way to the schools now."

After Ashlyn hung up, Tain closed his cell. As he slid the phone in its holder he caught sight of Luke watching him. Undeterred, Luke walked over to him.

"Is there any background you want me to run down, anything else you want me to follow up on?"

"We've got it covered, thanks."

"Seems like overkill to have so many of us standing around. If I was you I'd be anxious to get out there, chase down more leads."

"Ashlyn can handle it."

A shadow flickered in Luke's eyes. If Tain had blinked he would have missed it, but he'd seen it, despite the fact that Luke turned to look over his shoulder at the other officers monitoring the equipment.

"Look, I know she's your partner and I'm sure she's a good cop, but, well, her and Craig have been having some problems, and she's seemed . . ."

Tain felt his shoulders stiffen and didn't try to hold back the scowl. "Constable Hart has my full confidence, and her personal life is none of your concern."

"It is if it's going to get me killed."

Tain leaned forward. "Nobody's keeping you here. You don't want this assignment, there's the door. I'm the one who goes out on the streets with Ashlyn, and I trust her with my life."

"You know, maybe if you weren't all so closed off about what happened the rest of us wouldn't feel so nervous about it."

"The rest of who? The only person I see who's still obsessing about what happened is you."

"Maybe because it was Craig's partner who got killed," Luke said, "and I got to fill the vacancy."

"Lori was a danger, to herself and others. She wasn't even supposed to be there, and she killed a suspect and shot her own partner before Constable Hart returned fire. She saved Craig's life."

"Well she would, wouldn't she? Would she do the same for you?"

Tain didn't even blink. "Yes."

He stared at Luke until he saw the man back down. There was a subtle shift in his expression, as though he finally believed Tain was telling the truth.

"Okay. Sorry. It's just if—"

"If I ever hear you obsessing over this again, criticizing my partner, I'll give you something real to worry about. You may be more interested in investigating cops than criminals, but if you point fingers without proof there won't be a cop in the department who'll have your back. You just remember that. The rest of these guys have worked with us for months and none of them has a problem."

"Yeah, well, trust goes both ways," Luke said. "I don't see you handing me the files or talking over the case with me. I have a laptop here and I'm just as good as Sims at digging up background information."

"Believe it or not, this case isn't about you or your pride."

"I know that. I'm just—"

"Like I said, it's covered."

Luke looked like he was about to say something else, but Tain's gaze turned to Byron Smythe, who'd entered the room from the side door. Through the opening, Tain could see the family. Different clothes, but otherwise unchanged from the day before, Christopher still sitting in a corner. Smythe glared at Tain as the other officers told him there was no news, as though he wouldn't be the first to know if a call had come in, and Smythe retreated, closing the door to the adjoining office.

Tain's gaze shifted back to Luke, who was still looking at the door Smythe had just shut.

Luke's mouth twisted into a forced grin. "Okay. Fair enough." He went back to where he'd been sitting and pulled out the laptop anyway.

The only good thing about Luke's overconfidence was the fact that he was probably letting his ego get in the way of his understanding. Either that, or he was a very good actor.

Tain flipped his cell phone open and keyed in a text message. He was aware Luke was watching him, but didn't look up or react in any way.

Ashlyn had sounded more herself this morning, energetic and on top of her game. He hoped she wasn't putting on a front just for him. Before Ashlyn he'd preferred to work alone, had always resisted any attempts to make him partner with someone long-term. It had spared him from times like the night before, where he was confronted by personal problems that could get in the way of the job. Working solo had made it easier for him to be objective.

Did he really believe his partner had things covered? Maybe she'd worked things out with Craig the night before, but even that thought left him uneasy. Ashlyn had been more emotional than usual lately. Possibly because of the problems she was having with Craig. The fact that she hadn't been feeling well probably didn't help. But Tain didn't like the idea that her performance on the job might be tied so closely to her personal life.

He'd let his personal life cloud his judgment before, and it had cost him. He didn't want to see it happen to her.

But he also knew he couldn't carry her problems for her. And given the choice, he'd put his life in her hands before he'd turn his back on Luke Geller any day of the week.

For him, that faith was enough.

The day care Jeffrey Reimer attended was bright and spacious, clearly for families with money to pay higher fees for all the little extras.

"We maintain better ratios than the minimum government standards in every room," the director told her.

"It's very nice," Ashlyn said as she watched a staff member separate two boys who were fighting over a paint easel. The blond boy had painted the hand of the boy with the curly red hair. The redhead had shoved the other boy, who'd started to cry. "Do you have someplace private we can talk?"

"Certainly." Mrs. Wu was a petite woman, no more than 5'1", trim and without a trace of an accent. From what Ashlyn had seen on the tour, the day care featured a multicultural clientele, as well as an ethnically diverse staff, but all the employees had perfect English. Born in Canada. The brochure she'd been given listed optional exposure to French and Mandarin for children "in the early developmental stages."

The director led the way back toward the entrance, to a spacious office that had multiple paintings and crafts tacked to bulletin boards on the walls. It was a nice gesture, one that suggested the administration really cared about what the children did every day. Mrs. Wu motioned for Ashlyn to have a seat. "Jeffrey was a sweet little boy," Mrs. Wu said as she tucked her skirt under her legs and sat down. "We were devastated by the news."

"Did any of your staff ever see bruises on Jeffrey, anything unusual?"

The director's face lengthened. "Constable, I assure you, we run one of the best facilities in the Lower Mainland."

Ashlyn smiled and put up her hand. "I don't doubt that, Mrs. Wu. The reason I'm asking is because a little boy was murdered. He was beaten to death." Mrs. Wu flinched. "I had to go to a park and stand over his body and look at what someone had done to him. I just want to find that person and make sure they don't hurt another child."

"You think the parents . . . ?"

She shook her head. A day care could be a hub for gossip, and Ashlyn did not want the staff speculating on their suspect list. At least not because of anything she said. "I have to ask these questions. Unfortunately, Christopher told us Shannon killed Jeffrey. I can't ignore that allegation."

Mrs. Wu looked away. "I saw that in the newspapers."

"Did you know Shannon?"

Ashlyn could tell that Mrs. Wu was fighting with herself, conflicted by her need to maintain confidentiality for her patrons and her sense of duty to Jeffrey Reimer. Finally, she nodded. "Yes. She was authorized to pick up her brother."

"And I'm sure you wouldn't have allowed her to take Jeffrey if you'd had any concerns about his safety."

"If I had any concerns I would have addressed it with the parents."

Ashlyn nodded and smiled again. Part of her effort to appear supportive, like she was on Mrs. Wu's side. "And I understand completely that you would never reveal the substance of any concerns you did raise with Jeffrey's parents, if you'd needed to address anything. I'm actually expecting my first child. With all the stories in the news about children unsupervised, or centers not meeting the licensing requirements, I've been concerned about finding quality care."

"We have a waiting list here. The best centers do."

"Is there a screening process for the families?"

"Our preference is to focus on children with devoted parents who have their own careers."

"And your staff?"

"They have the highest level of training. We require that they take additional courses each year. All of our staff members have criminal records checks, of course, and their first-aid certificate."

Ashlyn nodded as though she approved. She did, but that wasn't the point. "I heard some centers have cameras installed so that parents can watch their children online. Does your center offer that?"

Mrs. Wu smiled. "We do. We have a transparent staff. Our center welcomes the parents as visitors during the day. This allows parents to have complete confidence in the quality of the care their children receive."

"With the parents able to monitor their children and the staff all day, what would you do if you suspected a child was being abused?"

Mrs. Wu pushed her cheeks up into a forced smile. "That's what this office is for."

Ashlyn nodded. "And let's say, hypothetically, that a staff member suspected a child was being abused. What would happen?"

"Our staff would begin a journal." Mrs. Wu stood, removed a key from her top desk drawer and crossed the room silently. She opened a cabinet, removed a notebook, and locked the cabinet again. "Such as this one." She tapped it as she sat down and replaced the key. "Any visible bruises, cuts, signs of emotional distress, change in appetite, anything questionable is written down. I keep a full shelf of blank books and hope we never need to use them, Constable Hart. With most of our families, this isn't an issue."

Ashlyn nodded. "And I assume that you would call social services?"

Mrs. Wu paused. "Not right away. I'm sure that, as a police officer, you can appreciate how difficult it can be to prove child abuse. Our parents hire us to provide a service, and that does not include accusing them of a crime. As you know, children fall and have little accidents all the time."

"There was a case last year where social services in Ontario removed all the children in the home after a report was filed. It was proven the child had bruises from falling off her bicycle." Ashlyn heard her cell phone ring, but ignored it.

"Exactly. We document first. If it is something extreme, I make a decision about phoning social services and the police. Otherwise, we wait until we feel we've established evidence that supports an accusation of abuse."

"Do you ever ask the parents about the injuries?"

"Initially, yes, with the first incident. No matter what the parent says, we document for a full two weeks, just in case. If there's no further evidence of abuse and we're satisfied with the parent's explanation, we file the book. You must understand that we cannot be sure any abuse is by the parents. It may be a babysitter or relative who visits occasionally. Normally, when we approach the family we address it as though we're bringing this to their attention, assuming they'd like to know that someone could be hurting their child." Mrs. Wu smiled again. "Of course, that isn't something we deal with often. Most indications of abuse turn out to be an older sibling who is a bit rough when playing with a younger child."

"Or an accident."

"Precisely." Mrs. Wu looked at her watch. "If you can excuse me, I promised to visit the French teacher this afternoon. Do you have any further questions for me?"

Ashlyn stood and took out her card. "You will call me if you think of anything else?"

Mrs. Wu nodded. "Certainly. Please feel free to look around as long as you'd like. I'll shut the door so that you can return your call in privacy, and I'll tell my assistant not to disturb you. Please feel free to use my desk."

"Thank you." Ashlyn shook her hand and waited until Mrs. Wu had closed the door behind her, then moved behind the director's desk as she pulled her cell phone out.

The journal was a hardcover notebook with nothing except a label with a date, room number and the letters *J A R* attached to the spine. Ashlyn read the message on her cell phone and hit speed dial with one hand while opening the book with the other.

"I'm at Jeffrey's day care. They've been documenting suspected abuse for weeks."

"Let me guess," Tain said. "Starting around Thanksgiving."

"You really are more than just a pretty face."

"Any chance you can get a copy?"

Ashlyn glanced around the office, confirming that she had not overlooked a copier. "I'm going to take photos on my cell phone and e-mail them to you. Can you go over to the office and enlarge them and print them off?"

"Where will you be?"

"I'll meet you there shortly. You can start moving before I start snapping. Tell Luke you'll be back after lunch."

"It's a bit early, isn't it?"

"You'd rather order in and eat with him?"

"Forget I said anything. I'll see you soon."

Once she'd photographed all the pages and e-mailed the pictures to Tain, she leafed through her notebook until she found the number she was looking for and dialed. Eventually she left a message. Then she put the book back where Mrs. Wu had left it and thanked the assistant before she left.

When she reached the office Tain was waiting, a sheaf of papers in hand. "I'm surprised they turned this to you."

"Turned what over? The director graciously let me use her office to make a phone call after our discussion."

He frowned. "Ash."

"Look, if we need the documents from the day care, we'll get them legally. Right now, this is just to help us figure out the truth." She met his gaze. "The parents aren't going to talk. I've called social services three times now and still haven't heard back. Come on. I'm buying lunch."

Once they'd reached the restaurant and ordered, Ashlyn reached for the folder. "Did you read it all?"

"There's no way the day care will hand over that book, Ash."

"Why? They let me see it today."

"Let you?"

"She took it out of a locked cabinet and left it on her desk before offering to let me use her office undisturbed. It wasn't like I snooped around." Ashlyn looked up. "I'm serious."

"I just wonder why they didn't report this."

"The director explained the process. She said that in the rare cases it's necessary, they often approach the parents as though they're innocent, because it could be a sibling or babysitter who's abusing the child."

"Makes sense, but this had been going on for almost two months. Won't there be questions about why they hadn't called social services?"

Ashlyn skimmed the final pages, which were the ones she hadn't read in the office. "Maybe they had." She turned the page around and showed it to Tain.

"They had a meeting with the parents one week before

Jeffrey's murder." He collected the papers and put them in the folder, directing his gaze past Ashlyn for a moment, and put the folder aside.

The waiter set their food down. "Is there anything else I can get for you?"

"Not for me," Ashlyn said.

"No, thanks."

Ashlyn waited until the petite blonde was out of earshot. "They can still prove due diligence. Since none of the abuse happened on their property they have little more than suspicions, which have been clearly documented. Even if they didn't call social services, the neighbor did, and social services hasn't returned my messages yet." She saw Tain's eyebrows lift and the slight tilt of his head. "If anyone will be covering their ass after this, it will be them."

"Not if Jeffrey wasn't killed by a family member."

"Kidnappers are really anxious to get their money, aren't they?"

Tain smiled. "We'll make a cynic out of you yet." The smile faded. "I know it's none of my business—"

"We didn't sort things out."

He reached for his drink and didn't comment.

"If anything, things got worse," she said.

"Are you okay?"

She sighed, turned up her palm. "Every relationship has its ups and downs."

"You're going to work it out, then?" When she didn't answer right away he continued, "All that matters to me is you're okay."

"You don't have to worry about me."

"Ash, that comes with the territory. You're my partner."

She poked at the potatoes with her fork until he took her hand. There was a rush of heat in her cheeks, but when she looked up at him she could see the genuine concern on his face.

"Yesterday, in Zidani's office . . ." He paused. "Then last night. I've seen Craig angry before, but he's drinking."

Which was a problem. Craig knew he couldn't handle it. Then she realized what Tain meant. "Oh, it's not what you think. It was Byron Smythe who bruised my arms."

He let go of her hand and sat up straight. "Smythe. What the hell?"

"I was at the mall Saturday night, waiting for Craig. Smythe showed up." She took a breath. "We had words."

For a moment there was complete silence. She didn't need to ask what Tain was thinking: she knew. "I was the one who dislocated his knee. He wouldn't let go of me."

Tain nodded, but remained silent. There was no judgment in his eyes.

"When Craig found out he—" She took a drink of water and a deep breath. "He took off."

"And you don't know where he went."

"He never came home. The next time I saw him was Sunday night and he was working his way through a bottle of wine."

Tain nodded again. "Have you told Zidani?"

"Not about Craig."

"Don't."

"You still don't trust him?"

"Until a few days ago, neither did you. What's changed?"

Ashlyn paused. "We talked."

"When?"

"Saturday night." She covered her face with her hand. "You think he tried to get me on his side to help drive a wedge between me and you?"

"Or you and Craig. Zidani ordered him to go through those case files, and he knew that meant Craig was checking up on an investigation his father handled. With everything Zidani had to say about Craig and Steve's relationship when he transferred in, it doesn't make sense."

"And you're sure about Zidani and Luke?"

He reached for his fork again. "I have my suspicions."

Ashlyn watched him eat for a moment. One of the reasons she didn't talk through cases to the same extent other people did was that voicing a thought sometimes made it sound ridiculous, or it seemed to give weight to it that wasn't always warranted. "Tain, do you trust Craig?"

"That doesn't matter. The question is, do you trust him?" He looked up at her.

"I'm pregnant."

Tain was silent for a moment. "That's not an answer to the question."

"I know. That's why this is so complicated. Morning sickness, hormones. I've probably cried more in the last five days than I have in the past five years, if you don't count when Craig was shot. I don't even trust my own judgment right now. And of all the cases . . ."

"I'll tell you what I know. If someone bruised my girlfriend . . ." Tain looked at her arms, then met her gaze. "And you're pregnant."

Her face burned. "I haven't told Craig. It's crazy, I know, but I wanted to wait until Christmas."

"I'd still have words with the guy. I know, okay, but if he tracked Smythe down I wouldn't blame him."

"You've seen the bruises, his wrist."

"And I've seen Craig. He doesn't look like he's been in a fight."

That was the niggling bit of logic that had been trying to break through the cloud of doubt weighing on her mind. Normally she wouldn't jump to conclusions without some physical evidence to back it up. Then again, she hadn't seen Craig for almost twenty-four hours, he was fit and he knew how to take care of himself. Just because he hadn't come home and stuck his fist in a bucket of ice . . .

"If you're right about Zidani . . ." Ashlyn rubbed her forehead. What was it Craig had said to her when they'd argued? "Craig's being set up. He said something about things going missing from his desk for months."

"Luke Geller's been his partner since the summer."

"And Zidani's had them on a short leash, keeping a close eye on them. What am I going to do?"

"First, eat. You need to take care of yourself. Second, talk to Craig."

She picked up her fork and speared a potato. "He's in Kelowna. He won't be home until tomorrow, at the earliest."

"Meanwhile this is eating you up inside."

There was no way to deny that. She picked up her cell phone and keyed in a text message. "There. Better than nothing."

They finished eating in silence. After they'd paid they headed to the front entrance. "I'm going to grab a newspaper."

"I've had my fill of reporters for one day," Ashlyn said as she paused at the door.

Tain glanced at her with a puzzled look. "Have they been harassing you about this . . . ?" He stopped as he looked down at the paper.

"What is it?"

"Nothing," he said, without picking up a copy. He started to walk toward her.

"I thought you wanted a paper." The look on his face betrayed him. She moved to walk around him.

He reached for her arm to stop her. "Ash, don't."

It was too late. She could see the headline.

Tain watched Ashlyn digest the contents of the news article. For a moment she looked pale, as though she was about to faint. Then she squared her shoulders, folded the paper and walked to the car.

"What's next for you?"

"Christopher's school," she said as Tain's cell phone rang.

He glanced at the caller ID. "Luke," he told Ashlyn, then flipped it open and answered it.

"They called."

"And?"

"We got a trace."

He glanced at Ashlyn. "We'll be right there. Wait for us." He snapped the phone shut without saying good-bye. "They called."

"Finally."

It didn't take long for them to reach the lawyer's office. The scene had changed. Richard and Tracy Reimer were now in the main room. Tracy looked peaked, and Richard's face burned with anger as he paced the floor behind the desk. Through the opening to the adjoining room Tain could see that Christopher remained on the floor in the corner, where he stared blankly into space.

Luke met them near the door. "They called. The voice was disguised. They said they have Shannon and they want half a million dollars to let her go."

Ashlyn's eyes widened. "You're kidding, right?"

"Do I look like I'm joking?"

She frowned. "Get the recording and bring it to the lobby so we can listen to it."

Tain followed her out of the room. "I think he missed your point."

"And he wonders why I'm not leaving him in charge here."

The door clapped shut behind them, and Tain turned to see Luke already approaching Ashlyn. "Here's the copy." He passed her a CD player and set of headphones.

Once she'd processed the recording she looked at Tain. He looked at Luke.

"You said you had a trace?"

Luke passed him a slip of paper. "I phoned you from the bathroom. Smythe is watching them like a hawk. He doesn't want us to do anything to jeopardize this."

Tain looked at his watch. It was quarter to one. "Let me guess. He wants to do just what the kidnappers demand."

"They're going to phone back at four P.M. to make sure they have the money, then give the instructions for the drop."

"And the money?"

"Smythe says they already have that much here." Luke looked at Ashlyn, who'd removed the headphones. "How do you want to play this?"

"We'll check out the address. You wait for the call."

"You're leaving me without a babysitter?"

Tain saw the way Ashlyn's eyes blazed and he put his hand on her shoulder, gently. "Look, Luke, half a million dollars? These people own a boat that costs more than that. Whoever made this call is either an idiot or knows exactly how much money the Reimers can put together on short notice. Funny, Smythe never mentioned before he had a safe full of cash ready for this call."

Luke's mouth twisted as his cheeks reddened. "Okay. So this looks like an inside job."

"Or a complete amateur who's just been very, very lucky, and I'm not buying that," Ashlyn said. She glanced at the receptionist and lowered her voice. "These people are still suspects. Wait for the call but meanwhile, you watch them. If any of them try to leave, insist on a police escort."

"Ash—" Tain said. She raised her hand to stop him and looked at Luke.

"Just tell them there's been a threat made against the family."

"Since when?"

"Since I just told you that if any of them leaves here unsupervised, I'll personally make them regret it." She glanced at Tain. "Okay, seriously, we still don't know if this wasn't someone Reimer pissed off with his business dealings. I already have the New West PD checking that out, but right now the kidnappers seem to be our best lead for finding Shannon, and I'm not taking any chances. If she's alive and someone has her, we're not going to let them screw that up. Understood?"

Luke nodded. Ashlyn handed him the CD player and he went back to the office. Tain followed his partner to the elevator.

Once they were in the car she pulled out her cell phone, then held it on her lap while she stared out the window.

"Craig?" Tain asked.

"Hmmm? No. No reply. Do you think we should call?"

"This is recon, right?"

"Yeah."

"Then no."

"Are you thinking what I'm thinking?" she asked.

He nodded. "New Westminster. Interesting."

It didn't take them long to track down the address where the kidnapper's phone call had originated. The sagging two-story house was faded and worn. The interior was completely obscured from view by bland drapes that were so heavy it was impossible to tell if there was even a light on inside. Tain pulled over a block down, so that their interest in the house wouldn't be obvious.

Ashlyn flipped her phone open and dialed. "Sims, it's Constable Hart. I want you to check on something for me." She relayed the address. "See if it has any connection to Richard Reimer or anyone he's been doing business with. Call me on my cell if you find anything."

After she thanked him and hung up she turned to face Tain. "If we talk to neighbors we risk tipping them off."

"And we can't sit here," he said as he put the car into drive. "What do we do now?"

He watched her fish a card out of her pocket. "Call the police," she said.

They met in a parking lot at Royal Square Mall on Eighth Avenue. Ashlyn introduced them and gave the address to Liam. "What can you tell us?"

"No tie to Reimer, or any of the people he's pissed off. Not as far as I know." Liam leaned back against his car. "What's the connection?"

"Shannon's alleged kidnappers placed a call," Ashlyn said.

"From this address?" Liam laughed. "Dealing with real pros here?"

Tain met Ashlyn's gaze, and he watched her hesitate, then give the tiniest shrug of her shoulders.

"They demanded half a million," Tain said.

Liam's eyes widened. He looked at Ashlyn, then Tain, and then his brow furrowed. "Junkies, maybe? Any chance Shannon used?"

"The family isn't cooperating, so we're limited by what friends have told us," Ashlyn said.

"And they aren't going to voluntarily fess up and admit their good friend did drugs." Liam scratched his head. "What's your plan?"

"We'll need to watch the house." Ashlyn looked at her watch. "In a few hours they're due to phone again. If there is any kind of sophisticated phone relay that call might tip us off. My gut says amateurs. No way pros would ask for five hundred thousand dollars. This doesn't even hurt the family. Anyone who kidnapped Shannon to extort money would have picked her because the Reimers have money, and they would have asked for three or four times as much, at least."

"More like ten times that amount," Tain said.

"Agreed. You want to babysit with me? I can have patrol on standby to follow anyone who leaves the house. What do you say?"

Tain saw the flicker of doubt in Ashlyn's eyes. "Go. I'll handle the monitoring," he said.

"You're sure?"

"Just update Zidani."

She grinned. "I could delegate that responsibility, you know."

"Me dealing with Smythe and Luke isn't enough?"

The smile slipped from her face. "Yeah, yeah, all right, I'll call."

Ashlyn gathered what she needed from the car, then called Zidani. She watched while Liam gave Tain a card, and they attempted to make small talk. When she was finished on the phone she got out and walked over to Liam's vehicle.

"What did he say?" Tain asked.

"Words of profound insight and inspiration, sure to warm even your heart. 'Proceed as planned.'"

Tain watched Ashlyn and Liam get in the car and looked at the card in his hand. The urge to stop them and insist Ashlyn trade places with him was overwhelming, but he held back and watched them drive away, unsure of whether his gut was telling him something about Liam Kincaid, or if he just wanted to avoid the Reimers and what they reminded him of.

CHAPTER TWELVE

It was a basic motel room—beige carpet, a nondescript bedspread, generic wildlife painting on the wall. A simple dresser had a large TV on top, a small table and two chairs were positioned close to a short counter with a kettle, mugs and everything needed to make tea or coffee. Thick curtains obscured the midday light, making the room seem unnaturally dark for noon.

Craig flicked on a light, pulled off his boots and mitts, set his bag down by the closet and then picked up the box with the case files. The daily newspaper was lying on top. He set the box down on the bed and picked up the *Sun*.

The lawsuit was official, and it had made it into the public domain with a splash, along with the news of Donny's release from prison. Not only had Donny Lockridge sued the department and everyone involved in his conviction, but Lisa Harrington had also filed a suit against the department "for misconduct." She alleged that the police had focused on Donny while refusing to consider other evidence that suggested someone had broken in to the Harrington home and abducted Hope, which explained the missing blanket and the fact that the killer had used a weapon taken from the victim's house.

It also explained the DNA found on Hope, DNA that was not a match for Donny Lockridge. What remained unexplained in her scenario was how the murder weapon had been returned to the house, which Lisa's lawyer dismissed as "a minor detail."

"What better place to hide it? It cast suspicion on others and effectively allowed the guilty party to go free."

None of that, however, was the big news. What had landed in the headlines were Lisa's allegations that one of the RCMP officers working the case coerced her, made her believe Donny was a danger to her and her other daughter, and pressured her into a sexual relationship and a pledge to lie on the stand about Donny hitting Hope in order to guarantee they'd find sufficient evidence to ensure Donny was convicted. She'd been scared and manipulated by the people she trusted to protect her. Now she wasn't sure Donny was guilty.

And approximately nine months after Hope's murder Lisa had given birth to a little bundle of alleged proof.

Emma had warned him. While the article didn't name Steve Daly as the accused, he had been in charge of the investigation.

Craig's cell phone beeped and he pulled it out. A text message from Ashlyn. He scratched his head for a moment, looked at the phone but didn't open it or read the messages before he put it away.

He felt like he was a piece in a Jenga game. The lawsuit, investigation, Dad, Smythe, Emma, Zidani, the break-ins, Ashlyn . . . It wasn't like someone piling on. Each thing felt like another piece of his foundation being pulled out from under him, just one more thing and his world might come crashing down. Whatever Ashlyn had to say, he couldn't face it. Not now.

What if . . . ?

He squeezed his eyes shut and dug his elbows into his knees as he clawed his head with his fingers. No. He refused to think about it. *Just focus on the case. Do your job.* As though it could be that easy.

Brandy hadn't been home when he'd gone to the house, before he'd checked into the motel. The family business had been easy enough to track down, but he hadn't gone in to speak to them. With any luck he could talk to Brandy first.

Craig stopped at Subway before returning to the Lockridge home. It was an older house, but large and on a fairly big lot. He dreaded the thought of spending hours in a vehicle with nothing but his thoughts for company, and he looked at the book on the front passenger seat. During the night Ashlyn had obviously gotten up and brought it downstairs, because he'd forgotten to pack it. *The 50/50 Killer*. The premise made his stomach twist now, as he thought about the look on Ashlyn's face when he'd said good-bye and walked out, and the fact that she had still taken his book downstairs so that he would have it.

Close his eyes and he could see her as she was when they first met. Hair a bit shorter, impulsive, stubborn. From day one she'd made it clear she wouldn't take crap from anyone. He smiled. Some things hadn't changed.

If it wasn't for this case, if this hadn't happened now. A matter of days. What if he hadn't decided to wait for Christmas?

He opened the book. Music hadn't been enough to distract him from replaying the arguments over in his mind on the drive to Kelowna, and he needed something to block it out.

After a few hours a dark green Saturn Vue pulled into the driveway, and he didn't need to look twice to know it was Brandy. In ten years she hadn't aged much in terms of her appearance. Stylish leather coat, dress pants, hair pulled back into a neat ponytail, showing off the diamond earrings. What had changed about Brandy's appearance since the photo Wendy had showed him was the price tag of her wardrobe.

"Mrs. Lockridge?" he said as he approached the vehicle. She had the back door open and was removing a child from a car seat.

Brandy's head snapped around to look at him. When she saw the ID she exhaled. "You startled me."

"Sorry. Constable Craig Nolan. Coquitlam RCMP."

"Coquitlam?"

"I'm reviewing Hope Harrington's murder."

Her eyes narrowed and she turned to lift the child out of the backseat. "Hope was murdered in Aldergrove. Doesn't Langley RCMP handle policing there?" She pushed the door shut, propped her son up with one arm and took her purse off the driver's seat. Then she slammed that door shut and started walking toward the house.

"They do."

"So what is this about? You guys trying to make it look like an impartial investigation?"

Craig allowed himself the smile, since she had her back to him. Hardly.

"I met with Lisa Harrington last week, and I understand your brother-in-law is out on parole."

Brandy stopped, then turned around. "And what does this have to do with me?"

"You were friends with Hope. I wanted to ask you a few questions."

"I answered questions back then, when it happened."

"Sometimes, we see things differently later. Maybe back then you thought the cops must have got it right, since a jury convicted him. And maybe now you think they got it wrong."

"What difference does it make what I think? My brother-in-law still went to jail. He lost ten years he'll never get back."

"And what about the years Hope lost?"

Brandy shifted her son to her other hip. "Look, I'm sorry about that, all right? But it wasn't my fault and there's nothing I can do about it."

"So that's it? Even if a murderer is back on the streets?"

She rolled her eyes the way younger girls do to express irritation with a stupid adult. The curl to her lips, the way her hip jutted out just a bit, it suggested to Craig a petulant child. Brandy set her son down and unlocked the door. "Come inside, Donny. Let's get your boots off."

Donny.

Craig was surprised Brandy didn't shut the door on him. Once she had her son out of his boots and coat she turned and said, "Look, come in, ask your questions, then go. I don't want you here when Darren gets home. He wouldn't be too happy if he knew about this. Donny getting out . . . They spent last weekend celebrating."

Did that mean Darren had been in the Langley area over the weekend? He used to live there, he'd know where Lisa lived . . . Craig complied with Brandy's instructions, giving her space as she set her son on the couch with a blanket, a bottle, a plate of animal crackers, then turned on the TV. It was a sunken living room, three steps down from the main level, which gave it the appearance of a vaulted ceiling. The large windows on both sides of the room and white paint, offset with wooden trim and hardwood floors, made it look bright and spacious.

The kitchen, which was the first room on the main floor after the entry, was big but the dark wood cabinets were matched by dark green counters. On the far side, Craig could see an alcove opening to a dining room.

Brandy returned to the kitchen. "I honestly don't know what more I can tell you."

"Why don't we start with the obvious? You don't believe Donny murdered Hope."

"Of course not. Donny treated Hope like a queen. He was"—she shook her head a little too emphatically—"he is a wonderful person."

Craig noted the way she caught herself, but didn't comment. Ten years in prison was a long time. How much had Donny Lockridge changed from the person he was? "You liked him back then."

She folded her arms across her chest and leaned back against the counter. "So?"

"Maybe you weren't the most objective person." When she didn't respond he said, "Your husband gave you a locket when you got engaged. I saw it in a photo. Do you still have it?"

Her whole face clouded then. "What does that have to do with anything?"

"Do you still have it?"

"And if I don't? You'll be back with a warrant?" She uncrossed her arms and started down the hallway, putting up her hand to indicate he should wait there. After a moment she returned and passed him the necklace. "There. Satisfied?"

"Why did Darren give you a locket?"

"Why is that any of your business?"

"You're aware that Hope wore a locket that looked exactly like this, and it was never recovered after her murder?"

"And you think Donny would be so stupid he'd give it to his

brother? Go ahead, take it. Do whatever you want with it." She sighed as her hand landed on her hip. "Truth is, Darren said he had it made for me, but it creeped me out. Hope never took hers off. I wore it for the photo, but that's it. It reminded me of her a little too much."

Craig pulled a form from his pocket and had her sign it, giving him permission to run tests on the locket. The reason he'd come had been to get the necklace, but he hadn't dared to hope it would be so easy. Pushing Brandy's buttons wasn't hard, and she'd responded accordingly. He placed the locket in a plastic bag.

"Let me ask you something. If Donny's innocent, who do you think killed Hope?"

"I don't know. Her slut of a mother? One of her mother's boyfriends? That woman had so many guys going in and out of there, half the men around could have gotten their hands on the murder weapon. Lisa Harrington's one of those women who sleeps her way into pregnancy just to stay on the system and get the extra cash."

"Then why would she kill Hope? Wouldn't she want Hope to stay at home?"

"Hope wanted to move here with Donny and his family."

"Didn't Donny want her to come with them?"

Brandy shook her head. "Donny wasn't going to move. He was going to stay in Langley."

"Why?"

"Why don't you ask him? Look"—she glanced at the clock on the wall—"Darren will be here soon. You should go."

Craig nodded, took out his card and held it out to her. "If you think of anything else."

She glared at the card for a second, then snatched it from him. Once he had his boots on and stepped outside he thanked her again, told her where he was staying just in case she remembered something before he left town and walked back to the Rodeo.

Tain checked his watch and looked at Luke. Not much longer.

His cell rang and he looked at it. As though she could read his thoughts.

"Anything?" he asked as he answered the phone.

"No. We have the alley behind the house covered. The nice thing about hills is that it's easy enough to park someone a few blocks up and monitor their back door. I'm telling you, Tain, criminals should invest in trees. They almost make it too easy."

"How considerate of them." He paused. "You okay?"

"Of course."

"Any word from Craig?"

He heard her breath catch in her throat. "No. I can't imagine he's too happy."

"No, I suppose not."

"Call me as soon as they make contact."

The other cell phone rang just as Tain closed his. Luke was hovering over Richard Reimer's shoulder. Richard answered the phone.

"You have the money?"

The voice was muffled, but not in a consistent, professional manner. Tain frowned. It sounded tinny, as though someone was talking through a can. Audio analysis wasn't his strong suit, but despite the low tone there was something in the voice that made him think it was a woman.

Richard looked at him and he nodded. Tain had spent the past few hours coaching the man. Now it was time to see which rule book he was playing by.

"I want to talk to Shannon."

"When we get the money."

Richard paused and looked at his lawyer before he asked, "How do I know she's okay?"

Tain glared at Smythe, who averted his gaze. When he looked back at the desk he saw Richard wipe his brow with a shaky hand. "I want to talk to her."

"You pay or you never talk to her again."

"Fine, okay. Half a million dollars. I have it."

"One million now."

"Bu-but you said—"

"One million. Mrs. Reimer will leave it in a black knapsack at the water park at Rocky Point. She knows the place."

Richard's eyes widened and his lip quivered. It took two false starts for him to get the single word out. "When?"

"One A.M. Make sure she comes alone. No cops."

There was a click as the caller hung up, but Richard cried, "Wait!" and jumped to his feet. "What are we going to do?"

"You don't have a million?" Luke asked.

"What?" Richard blinked. "Of course." He walked over to his lawyer. "Byron, what if they get her killed? We-we never should have called them!"

Smythe nudged him toward the other room, and once the door was closed Tain went to the officer who'd handled the tracing relay. The man was about to pass the slip of paper to Luke, but Tain put out his hand.

"I'll take that and report to Constable Hart."

The officer didn't question him, and Tain was about to shut the office door behind him before he realized Luke was following him out of the office.

"Am I part of this investigation or not?" Luke demanded.

"Who's in charge of this case?"

"Your partner."

Tain nodded. "And that means when she's not here, I'm in charge. Do you have a problem with that?"

"I have a problem with everyone in this department shutting me out."

"Then you go home and cry to your mommy and don't come back until you're ready to stuff your ego and get to work." Tain stared at him for a moment, watching the heat rise in the man's face. "I mean it. Either get back in that office and do your damn job or get the hell out. I don't have time for your shit."

Tain's cell rang then, but he remained still, staring at Luke. Finally the constable backed off and returned to the office.

He flipped the cell open and heard the words before it was even at his ear. "What the hell is going on?"

"I told you I'd call, Ash."

"Well, I've already had a call from Smythe. He says his client is refusing to cooperate unless we stay out of it."

"Oh for Christ's sake."

"Didn't you talk to him?"

"No. I was too busy dealing with Luke."

"Luke? What his problem now?"

"I have a new appreciation for Craig's ability to put up with Geller's self-centered bullshit all these months."

"Tain . . ."

"What?

"Back to the point. Did you get a trace?"

"Yes."

"Same location?"

"Yes."

"Well, nobody left here, so that means whoever it is is either in that house or sophisticated enough to have some sort of relay system in place, routing the call source. Details?"

"They raised it to a million. One A.M. in a black knapsack, at the water park at Rocky Point."

"Makes a statement, doesn't it?"

"And guess who they want to do the drop."

"Mrs. Reimer."

"Smythe told you?"

"No. Just a hunch. We're going to have someone replace us here. Let's meet at the station in half an hour."

"What about Luke?"

"Buy him a candy and tell him he's a good boy."

"How can I do that after I threatened to send him home to mommy if he doesn't quit whining?"

She laughed. "You didn't." When he didn't respond she groaned. "You did. See, I always knew the old Tain was still alive and well under the polite veneer."

"It's your fault."

"Hey, don't hold back on my account. There's something perversely amusing about seeing you deflate a man's ego."

Ashlyn hung up the phone.

"The second shift is in place," Liam told her as he started the car. "You and your partner, you get along?"

She nodded. "I've known him a long time. Ever since I was in plainclothes."

He glanced at her. "And judging from your age that's been, what? Three months?"

"Almost two years. What about you? No partner?"

"I've been solo for a while. My partner was shot and killed during a call."

Ashlyn swallowed. Part of her didn't want to talk about it, but he seemed pretty relaxed. If she said nothing, would it make him wonder why? "Were you there?"

He nodded. "You can take every precaution and things still go wrong."

"Did you get the shooter?"

"Sure. We got her. Nine-year-old girl, freaking out because her mother was just shot by her pimp. Guy drops the gun to go through her pockets and the kid picks it up. Just our luck, we aren't even two blocks away. We're going in the front, another pair of officers are heading in from the back. John's in the door first and he's talking to her, real calm, but the pimp, he flips out and tries to get the gun and bang. Gets John right in the neck."

She remembered reading about it then. The other officers had just been coming in. Shot automatically. The pimp and the girl had both died.

"Sorry."

He looked at her. "Yeah, well, we all have our crosses to bear, right? Your partner looked at me like he wasn't so sure he could trust me."

"Yeah, well, Tain watches my back. It's nothing personal."

They made it to Zidani's office before Tain, and when he walked in the first thing Zidani said was, "Where's Luke?"

"Handling Byron Smythe," Ashlyn said automatically as she avoided Tain's glance. "The family's threatening to not cooperate if we're involved with the drop."

She ran him through the details quickly.

"Okay, those are the facts." Zidani looked from Ashlyn to Tain. "What aren't you telling me?"

Everyone was silent for a moment. Liam, who was leaning against the wall, arms folded across his chest, spoke first. "The callers specifically wanted Mrs. Reimer to leave the money. How does that tie in with the theory that this might be someone with a grudge against Mr. Reimer because of his business dealings?"

Ashlyn paused. "Well, it doesn't. At least, not that I can tell."

"But you knew it was the mother. I heard you on the phone," Liam said.

"Look," she sighed, "there's no direct proof, and I don't like to operate on wild theories. But when we went to notify the family about Jeffrey's murder Mrs. Reimer lied to us."

"Christopher Reimer lied as well," Zidani said.

"Which can be explained any number of ways. Shock at seeing one or both of his parents murder his little brother. We all know abused kids often protect their abusers, and he may have felt the need to lie to protect what was left of his family. That's one possibility. Another option is that it wasn't a family member. Someone was threatening the family, trying to extort money or get them to give up on a business venture. They took it too far and killed Jeffrey. That one has more holes in it. How did Shannon get away after being stabbed? Why demand Mrs. Reimer bring the money? That still doesn't make sense."

"What if Mrs. Reimer was having an affair?" Zidani asked. "Or even Mr. Reimer, and his mistress is planning to kill Tracy Reimer?"

"There's no evidence to suggest either Mr. or Mrs. Reimer was having an affair," Tain said.

"I've had Sims looking at the family hard and running checks on their finances. At least a hint of an affair should have turned up," Ashlyn said. "Nothing has."

"Even in the first scenario, with the murderer being a family member, it doesn't explain why they'd want Mrs. Reimer to bring the money," Liam said.

"But it does make sense if the kidnapper is Shannon," Tain replied.

Ashlyn nodded. "Everything makes sense if Shannon's the one demanding the money."

"You mean, you think she is guilty of Jeffrey's murder?" Zidani rubbed his jaw. "This case is such a mess. I'm beginning to think I should have legally compelled the Reimer family to co-operate with the investigation."

"We wouldn't be here now if you had," Ashlyn said.

"Obviously," Zidani said dryly.

"No, seriously. I think their behavior has pointed us in the right direction from the start. We've explored all the avenues open to us, but from the beginning it's been clear this was personal. We started off believing one member of the family killed another. We just didn't know why. I still think that's likely what happened, just that it wasn't Shannon. Remember, Shannon was planning to run away. Things went horribly wrong. Her brother was murdered. She was stabbed. Somehow she managed to escape and get treatment, and then she disappeared. Possibly she fled before Jeffrey was killed, which explains why she called 911. Not a guilty girl on the run but a girl running scared. The alleged kidnappers knew how much money the family could access on short notice. They knew the father's personal cell phone number. And they want Shannon's mother to deliver the money to the place her son was murdered."

"Blood money," Liam said. "Make her own up to her crime. Maybe that's the whole reason for the ransom demand. Not because they actually want the cash, but because they want to prove Tracy Reimer's guilty."

"Shannon could have turned herself in and done that," Zidani said.

"With the newspapers reporting that she's a suspect? She's injured, potentially traumatized from her brother's death and afraid she'll go to jail. You can't expect her to be rational about this," Ashlyn said.

"Speaking of newspapers, have you talked to Craig?" Zidani asked.

"No."

"And you haven't talked to any reporters, have you?"

"Not since this morning." Ashlyn glanced at Tain. "She was waiting on my doorstep."

"What did you tell her?" Zidani asked.

"Nothing."

Her boss stared at her for a moment, his eyes cold, but he nodded. "Okay. We need to decide how we want to handle this. I'm assuming you plan to monitor the house and take down any suspects once they leave."

"No," Ashlyn said. "I want them to do the drop."

"That's a hell of a risk, isn't it? Something goes wrong, the press will have your ass."

"We have to plan like the drop will go down. For one thing, it's still possible this is someone who knows how to reroute a call so that the tracing information is incorrect. The address could be bogus. If we monitor the house and don't do the drop we could lose our only chance to make contact, and if this is a real kidnapping they could kill Shannon. We can't risk that. This is why I don't like to waste time playing with theories when we have a clock ticking. Let's just deal with the facts. There's a ransom demand. We know the time and place. Shannon's missing, and injured. Those are the only absolutes we've got."

"Okay. We set up two teams, one at the house, one at Rocky Point," Zidani said. "I can pull Sims—"

"No. I want him monitoring Shannon's cell, just in case. If Shannon does try to take the money, this may be when she uses her phone. Plus, I want us to plant a wire and a video camera at the scene of the drop. Move everything Sims has into a van and we've got the site fully monitored."

"Where will you be?"

Ashlyn looked at Tain, then turned back to Zidani. "Liam and I will return to New Westminster. We have to assume if the kidnappers are there, they have a car. We'll time the trip and be ready to move. Tain will be in charge of the team at the park. I need you to get the van ready for Sims, get the surveillance equipment ready, and prep the team," she said to Tain. He nodded. She turned to Zidani. "And I need you to smooth things over with Smythe and make sure he understands if his clients don't cooperate, we'll charge them for obstructing justice, hindering a police investigation and whatever else we can think of."

"Okay. I'll have Luke report to Tain."

"Luke stays where he is." Before Zidani could argue with her, Ashlyn continued, "Look, at this point, we have no reason to assume the kidnappers will try to make contact again, but they've already changed the rules midstream. We can't take a chance that they'll try to change the time or the location. If we aren't monitoring that phone, Smythe might not notify us. I need Luke there."

"He's not going to like it."

"Too bad for him. We don't get to pick and choose our assignments. Sims has been on telephonic surveillance for days and he's not complaining."

After a moment, when she didn't back down from Zidani's stare, he nodded. "Okay. Everyone has somewhere they need to be." After they started moving toward the door he said, "A word, Constable Hart."

She exchanged a glance with Tain, ignored Liam's curious look, and waited until her partner had closed the door. "If this is about Luke—"

"It's about Craig. How's he handling things?"

"How does he seem to be handling them?"

He walked around his desk and sat down. "Is that your way of telling me to mind my own business?"

"Look, when we're on duty we're expected to put the personal aside and be professionals. You wouldn't expect your wife to be questioned about how you're coping with an investigation or an officer's girlfriend to be called in to talk about his mental state. If you want to know how Craig's doing, you ask him." She turned and reached for the door.

"But you don't blame Tain for sharing concerns about you, when he thought you were going to cross the line on an investigation."

How had Zidani found out about that? Steve had kept Tain out of the report. Zidani had dug deep, done his homework. She took a deep breath. "He's my partner. If I mess up on the job it can jeopardize his safety, maybe even cost him his life." She took a breath. "Is that all?"

"For now."

When Ashlyn shut the door behind her she noticed her hand was shaking. Had something happened to Craig that she didn't know about? Maybe that was why he hadn't replied to her message.

That overwhelming, irrational fear ran through the core of her body and chilled her to the bone. She took a deep breath. *Stay focused. Right now your priority is Shannon Reimer.* And on some level, she was already starting to come to grips with the fact that there wasn't anything she could do to help Craig.

CHAPTER THIRTEEN

Nothing softens the arrogance of our nature . . .

Craig stared at Ashlyn's text message. After ignoring it all day, along with several messages from Emma Fenton, now that he found himself staring at the seven words on the screen he felt his stomach twist.

He set the phone down and thought about what he'd put in the evidence bag hours before. The locket was such a small, simple thing, but so many lives were connected to it, like links in the chain the locket hung on, and the truths it might tell would affect them all.

Of course, it was also possible the locket would reveal nothing, leaving them with unanswered questions and enough lingering doubt to work on them like a slow poison.

It wasn't that he didn't understand why Ashlyn had wanted him to back off from this case. He just couldn't let it go. And now as he considered the words of her message he wondered how things had gotten so messed up so fast.

The half-empty glass on the table beside his phone bore witness to that.

And she'd know if he called, even though he wasn't drunk. The lie of evasion would weigh on him, and she'd sense it, just one more seed of doubt planted between them. No. When he talked to her, he needed to be as clear as a bell.

This was why he tried to read. To fill the void with distractions, to keep the demons at bay. The effort had been there before, but once Ashlyn moved in he'd pushed himself harder than ever, trying to settle down. It wasn't that he didn't want her—the box with the ring was waiting for Christmas. It was that he couldn't find a way to kill the anger gnawing at him from inside. As much as he tried, outer illusion wasn't effecting much internal change.

A sharp knock at his door interrupted his thoughts, and he hastily dumped the balance of the beverage in the bathroom sink and tossed the bottle in the garbage. All he needed was a quick glance through the peephole to confirm what he suspected before he opened the door.

"Constable Nolan? I'm Constable Williams." The man glanced past Craig's shoulder and surveyed the room. "I understand you were talking to Brandy Lockridge today."

"Yes, that's right." Craig remained in the entrance and didn't invite the officer in. Williams had a round face, was losing his hair and kept a ready smile close at hand, which Craig had already seen three times since opening the door.

"If you require any assistance we'd be happy to provide background, let you use our facilities . . ." Williams smiled again, this time a big, toothy grin. "Just let us know."

"I expect to be returning home tomorrow."

"Home. Langley, is it?"

Craig fought to keep his face blank. He hadn't gone to the local RCMP station to check in. An oversight, more than strategy. But here was an officer, who knew where to find him and seemed to have a pretty good idea what he was doing in Kelowna.

"Tri-Cities, actually."

The smile slipped for a second. "Well, Mrs. Lockridge only mentioned you'd been here about her brother-in-law, so I assumed."

Craig forced a polite smile. "Funny, I had the impression Mrs. Lockridge wasn't anxious to talk about her brother-in-law or his legal proceedings."

"Well, she's in the hospital. Says she fell down the stairs."

"And do we believe her?"

The smile was completely gone. "No. At least, I don't. I understand you've been instructed to review an old case. I can also understand that most police officers do not like someone checking up on their work. I can even appreciate that might explain why you didn't notify us of your intention to question someone in our jurisdiction. However, when that person ends up in the hospital a few hours later, I do need to ask some questions, and I hope that you can understand that."

Craig nodded. "You want me to come with you to the station?"

"The hospital, actually."

"Do you really think that if someone assaulted Brandy because I questioned her that she'll be willing to speak to me?"

"I think if the person who hypothetically assaulted her is at the hospital, he's more likely to react if I return with you."

Craig grabbed his keys, cell phone and coat. It didn't take long for them to reach the hospital. Williams's easy smile was firmly back in place as he nodded at doctors and greeted nurses. The city of Kelowna was approximately half the size of the Tri-Cities in terms of population. Add in the commuter traffic that flowed through Craig's jurisdiction and the proximity to other major cities, such as Vancouver and Burnaby, and it wasn't surprising that Kelowna felt more like a town to Craig than a city, although he knew from his own experiences working in the interior that locals would bristle at the inference. It wasn't meant as an insult, he just couldn't imagine knowing the local hospital staff by name. At least, not as many as Williams seemed to know.

As though he sensed what Craig was thinking Williams shrugged. "Born and raised here, and our church congregation is a fair size."

"How long have you known the Lockridge family?"

"It's been ten, eleven years now, since they bought the business up here. The parents were originally from here and the kids used to visit their grandparents for summer holidays." Williams nodded. "This is the room."

The nurse looked to be about Craig's age, with dark hair neatly pinned back, large brown eyes and olive skin. She was just smoothing the sheets as they walked in. "Julie, we're here to see Brandy Lockridge."

"Oh, sorry, Bob. You just missed them. They left about ten minutes ago."

"She was transferred to another room?"

Julie smiled and shook her head. "Discharged. Darren took her home."

Hard lines settled in Williams's face as his expression darkened. "Thanks, Julie," he said curtly. Williams set a brisk pace back to his vehicle. Once there, he clipped his seat belt, put the keys in the ignition, then grabbed the steering wheel and froze.

Craig fastened his own seat belt and waited for a moment before he asked, "Are we going to the house?"

Williams shook his head. "I was testing a theory." He started the engine.

For a few moments, Craig observed the lights of the buildings, the festive decorations that repelled the darkness, as he turned everything over in his mind. "You said the boys spent summers up here as kids. And you doubted Brandy's story enough to ask me to come to the hospital with you." Craig turned and looked at Williams. "Why?"

The Christmas decorations projected enough light to show the hard edges were still in place. Williams's neck, shoulders, arms were rigid. Then the gaps between lights widened, and Craig looked outside.

"This isn't the way to the Lockridge home, and it isn't the way to my motel."

Williams pulled off on a dirt road. The vehicle lurched over bumps, and only the headlights broke the darkness.

They came to a spot that was basically a wide bend in the dirt road, and Williams pulled over. One side was shadowed by trees, the other by the incline of the hill.

Williams undid his seat belt, opened the door and climbed out before bending down to look at Craig. "You coming?"

Then Williams shut the door and started walking. He was a silhouette in the beams of light from the car, which dispelled some of the darkness, and he stood with his back to the vehicle.

Once Craig got out of the car he slowly unclipped his holster. He waited with his door open. "What are we doing here?"

"Are you coming?"

After a moment's hesitation, Craig shut the door and approached Williams, although he kept some distance and stayed behind him. "Where are we going?"

"It's not far." Williams led the way through the brush, snow crunching under his steps.

They stopped at a small clearing. It wasn't far, but it was far enough that Craig could no longer hear the hum of the engine.

For a few minutes Williams stood, head lowered, back to Craig, hands on his hips. Without moonlight the snow was the only relief from the shadow of trees blending into the night sky, so Craig couldn't see Bob Williams's face, but he sensed the tension from the man.

When he'd first opened his room door to see Williams he'd had the impression of someone friendly but devious, someone who used the veneer of warmth and casual acceptance as a way to lure people into complacency. Another cop might have grilled that nurse. Instead, she offered up information to Williams with a smile.

It bothered Craig that Williams knew who he was, where he was staying and what he was doing in Kelowna, and the only guess Craig had was that Brandy had told Williams herself.

But why volunteer that information to a police officer when you're claiming you fell down the stairs? If Brandy had told Williams about Craig's visit—which was the only plausible explanation—then it was likely her husband had beaten her because she'd given Craig the locket.

The news that Brandy Lockridge had been taken home by her husband had dramatically changed Williams's mood and demeanor. He knew more than he'd told Craig. This wasn't about playing a hunch, but Craig was still a pawn. The only thing he wasn't sure about was whether he was on the same side as Williams.

"You ever have a case you couldn't let go of?"

The words broke the silence unexpectedly, and Craig almost

jumped. There was something in Williams's tone, the controlled rage, that did more to put a chill down Craig's spine than the coldness of the night.

"Maybe you haven't. Maybe you're too young."

Craig thought back to earlier cases, to being partnered with Ashlyn when they'd first met, on her first plainclothes assignment. "There are things that keep me up at night."

Williams turned to face Craig, although he was barely more than a dark outline blending into the black. "When Donny Lockridge went to prison, I slept better.

"It was twelve years ago. The day was hot, the kind of summer day where you can see the waves of heat rising off the ground. My children were pretty young then. Eric was six, and it was Ellie's fourth birthday. We'd planned to have a party on the weekend, so we put out a sprinkler in the backyard in the morning, just for something special. I was working nights, and we were going to take the kids out for lunch. It's hard to pin children that age down to put sunscreen on them." He shook his head. "We kept on them, but it wasn't enough. Ellie's so fair, and when the burn showed it was bad. I remember she cried at the softest touch, and it was nearly impossible for my wife to rub aloe on her skin."

Silence. Williams was a statue, his thoughts concealed, face unreadable.

"She was inconsolable. We couldn't hug her, she couldn't lie down on her back or side, and lunch was out of the question. Eric was frustrated, and he shoved Ellie. She put her hand out, as I expect anyone would do, and we heard the snap. It was . . . eerily quiet as she thudded on the ground. And then she screamed. And screamed. And despite the sunburn we could tell her face had gone white."

He paused again. Craig sensed Williams wasn't expecting him to say anything, just that whatever Williams wanted to share was difficult, a door to more painful memories he'd prefer to keep locked away.

"When you watch your child cry and realize there's nothing, not a single thing, that you can do to stop their pain it's like someone's reached inside your chest with an ice-cold hand and squeezed your heart. Ellie screamed all the way to the hospital. Once they'd set her arm and put the cast on, we brought her home, and she was still crying. By then it was the silent tears. Of course, she'd just turned four. Ellie still needed an afternoon nap. She was overtired and miserable, and we couldn't get her to sleep. I still remember telling my wife I could call in, stay home and help her out, but she said they'd be fine."

Williams turned away. "I wish to God I'd stayed home that day." He lowered his head for a moment, then continued his story.

"As cops we know people are capable of doing horrible things. But I never really *knew* it in the same way until I got the call. Kids in the bush. A girl was hurt. It's not unusual for the kids to head out of town for parties, and I thought a group must have gone drinking, and one of them had fallen, had an accident.

"She was right there." He pointed at a spot on the other side of the clearing. "I was the first on the scene. I thought . . ."

A tremor had crept into his voice. Craig heard Williams take a deep breath.

"I thought for a second she'd been skinned alive. All I could see was the blood. I was reporting in, about to say she was dead, when I saw her eyes move as she looked at me. It wasn't until then that I realized I knew who she was."

He raised his hand to his face. Then he took some controlled breaths and continued.

"I have a brother who's six years older than me. One of his friends had married pretty young. This was his daughter. My brother was Jessie Fenton's godfather.

"I knelt down and told her it was going to be okay. Help was on the way. I remember thinking that I needed to get the fear and the repulsion out of my eyes, you know? She took a breath . . ."

Williams lowered his head, the words barely more than a whisper. "And it was her last."

For a while, Williams was quiet. Craig's eyes had adjusted enough for him to see the rise and fall of Williams's shoulders, and he let him have some time.

When he was ready he turned back to Craig. "We knew she'd come out here with a group of friends. Darren and Donny Lockridge were staying with their grandparents, just down the street from where Jessie's family lived. She'd invited them to come along. The other kids said they left early. Darren and Donny were drinking more than the others. They'd brought extra alcohol in their backpacks. That was one of the things that was odd. The kids all admitted they'd brought clothes for later, as well as food, because they were going to hang out until that night, but Darren had tried to start a fight. Jessie didn't leave with her friends because she felt responsible for inviting Darren and Donny.

"The last time they saw her, she was here, alone with them."

Williams was quiet again, and finally Craig asked, "What happened with the case?"

A cold, hard, staccato laugh escaped from Williams. "Boys that young don't *kill*. Don't you know that? Oh, they swore she'd been fine when they left her. Why did they leave her alone? She insisted she wanted to spend some time in the woods by herself, so they walked back without her.

"She'd been beaten. Every inch of her, to the point where the skin was ripped and torn and dangling in shreds. A few weeks later Darren and Donny went back home. It was to be expected. School was starting. By then we could only prove that there had been a few times other kids had seen them be mean or a bit aggressive, but nobody had ever seen them beat a girl. Nothing close.

"We knew they'd been with her, and Darren admitted right away they had sex. Smart. She was a virgin, according to her friends, so that made it harder to prove it was rape. And besides, her skin was so broken and torn from the beating it was impossible to prove beyond a shadow of a doubt that she'd been held down and forced. We never could find a conclusive murder weapon. The coroner said a branch, most likely. We turned these woods inside out, looking for any trace of blood, anything.

"We knew they'd had a change of clothes with them, but it was all circumstantial. There wasn't enough to make a case, and considering how young they were even if we did convict them they'd get nothing more than a slap on the wrist."

Williams shook his head. "That day, I went to tell Randy his daughter was dead. At first he cried. Then he put his fist through a wall and broke his hand. That's the stuff that really gets you. It wasn't just Jessie who died that day. It destroyed her whole family. A few weeks later, Jessie's brother and sister came home to find their mom in the living room. She must have swallowed all the pills just after they went to school. Randy was killed in a drunk-driving accident not long after that."

Craig paused. "What happened to the kids?"

"There was no family, so my brother took them." Williams walked up to Craig. "I know you're just doing your job, but when I read about that girl my hands shook. And when I heard Donny Lockridge was a suspect, I knew. I knew he'd done it, just like I knew Darren and Donny had killed Jessie."

Craig swallowed. "The reason I came here to see Brandy was that I thought she had something that could prove that Donny killed Hope."

Williams's head snapped up. "Did she?"

"I think so. A locket that matched the one missing from Hope's body when she was murdered. Brandy said Darren gave it to her, and that it was a replica."

"But you think tests might prove otherwise."

Craig nodded.

"The time he served, it isn't enough."

Craig hadn't needed to hear Williams's story to know that. The photos of Hope Harrington's body had been enough, and Williams's story confirmed in his own mind that Donny Lockridge was guilty, but . . .

It also left him with a question.

"Why didn't you contact the investigators and tell them about the case here, that Darren and Donny had been suspects?"

"I did."

Williams walked past Craig, who turned and started to follow him back to the car. He stopped for a moment and looked back at the clearing, trying not to imagine the suffering that girl had endured. It was starting to snow. The first flakes had drifted lazily to the ground while Williams had told his story, but now they were coming down thick and fast, and the wind was picking up.

He hoped the weather would pass so that he could drive home in the morning.

Craig pulled out his cell phone and flipped it open. It only took a moment to reply to Ashlyn's text message, and then he put the phone away. On some level, he'd always known life was fragile, that at any moment something could happen that would destroy a person. He'd been doubting his father and had been so wrapped up in his own problems he hadn't even thought about her case, and how it might be affecting her. He'd been looking at photos from years before. She'd actually stood over the body of a four-year-old just five days earlier.

And he'd been so weak he'd started to crawl into a bottle.

The drive back to the motel felt slow, slush pulling at the tires and the windshield wipers on high to keep the snow from obscuring their view of the road. When Williams pulled up at the motel Craig gave him his card. "If you think of anything else."

Williams reciprocated.

"Does Brandy know about Jessie?" Craig asked as he opened his door.

"I told her."

"She doesn't believe you?"

A cynical smile spread across Williams's face as he shook his head.

Craig got out and shut the door. He watched Williams drive away, then fished the key out of his pocket and unlocked his room door. As he reached for the light he felt the thud on the back of his head and saw the burst of stars against the black in his eyes before everything went dark again.

"You know, I'm surprised you wanted to stick on this surveillance."

Liam's voice cut through the darkness. A faint glow from the streetlights pinpointed his profile, but it was one of those black nights that engulfed people, objects, houses. For some reason, the darkness emphasized the cold.

"Being stuck in a car with you in the middle of the night when it's freezing out isn't so bad," Ashlyn said.

"That wasn't what I meant."

She heard the humor in his words and smiled. "Truth is, I feel the answer to this whole case is in that building. Or at least, the information that will lead us to the answers. Where else would I rather be?"

"I'd settle for bed."

Was he flirting or just sincerely tired and making conversation? It was becoming obvious to her she'd spent so much time with Tain and Craig she forgot the subtleties of interacting with other men. With Sims it was so expected she only noticed when he wasn't being pleasant, and she'd had plenty of practice ignoring other men in her department.

She decided to play it safe.

"Cases like this are pretty demanding."

"And you've been at it for days, but I'm the one whining."

"It's okay. One of the things I love about the job is that it's never predictable."

"Yeah. It's hell on your social life, though. I suppose the thing to do is to date cops."

"That's what I do," Ashlyn said.

"Really? And how's that working out for you?"

"Some days better than others."

They lapsed into silence again. As soon as she'd heard her own words she knew he'd either prove he was interested by pushing it, or back off because of the tone of her voice. She hadn't meant for the words to come out as hard as they had, but it was too late to take them back.

All day, part of her had hoped for a response from Craig. Every time the phone buzzed there was that flutter, followed by disappointment. Now it was almost 11 P.M. and she still hadn't heard from him.

Sometimes no answer was an answer, but she didn't want to believe that.

"Not that it's any of my business . . ."

Liam let his voice trail off, a way of opening the door. She knew he wanted her to invite him to ask. It was a safety net. You couldn't get angry at someone if you'd encouraged them to speak their mind.

She gave him his opening.

"But?"

"You and Tain?"

Ashlyn started to laugh, and she had to put her hand over her mouth to muffle the sound. Once she felt in control enough to maintain her composure she wiped the tears from her eyes.

"I didn't realize it was that funny," Liam said.

"I'm sorry. It's just . . . he's Tain." She chuckled. "It feels like I've known him forever. Why on earth would you think we were involved?"

"Just a feeling I got when he looked at me. Like if I crossed any lines he'd take me apart, limb by limb."

"He probably would."

"So, is that why your dating isn't working out so well these days?"

There it was. He'd circled back around to the original question, and there was just enough of a lilt in his voice to tell her he was fishing.

Her cell phone beeped.

She pulled it out. A text message, and it only took a moment to confirm it was from Craig.

Talk later. That was all it said.

She'd texted him the first part of a quote she loved. "Nothing softens the arrogance of our nature . . ." The second part was, ". . . like a mixture of some frailties." Funny how a few words could evoke such a strong memory, but she could almost taste the salt air and feel the sun on her skin as they lay together reading on a gorgeous September weekend when they'd gone sailing and stayed out for a weekend, just a little ways up the coast.

She'd discovered the quote from Sir George Savile and loved it. It reminded her that life was fragile, that everyone made mistakes and that recognizing your own weaknesses helped you forgive the shortcomings of others.

They'd used it as a way to apologize, or extend an olive branch, to each other ever since.

Ashlyn closed the phone and put it away.

"About the case?" Liam's question cut through her thoughts.

"Hmmm? No. Personal."

Her phone rang and her heart skipped a beat. She hoped it was Craig, hoped the reason he hadn't finished the quote was because he actually wanted to talk instead of text, but the call display betrayed that it wasn't him. "Constable Hart."

"Ashlyn, it's Sims. I managed to track down who owns that house. It was tricky. The house is owned by a company, which is owned by another company."

"And?"

"The family name is Patel. They live in Anmore."

"Do you know if there are tenants in the house currently?"

"It's supposed to be vacant."

"Have you told Tain?" she asked.

"Yeah, he said to let you know right away."

"Thanks, Sims. I take it things are still quiet there."

"Not a creature stirring."

Ashlyn groaned. "How festive of you. Bye."

As soon as she hung up she dialed Tain's number.

He answered. "Constable Tain."

"You didn't want to share the news with me yourself?"

"Why should I have all the fun?"

She laughed. "I'll remember you said that next time I order you to do something you don't like."

"Changes things, doesn't it?"

Ashlyn thought back to the day when they'd followed Matt Lewis to Nurani Patel's house. The girl's body language had suggested arrogance, which Ashlyn had attributed to the obvious family wealth. Now she wondered how much of that had concealed her guilt. "I'd love to get a search warrant for the Patel home."

"First things first," Tain said.

"Sims says this house is supposed to be empty."

"I'm sure the Patels would be most displeased to find out someone's using the phone there."

Ashlyn smiled. "And using it for criminal purposes."

"Then again, perhaps they won't mind. A vacant rental that will suddenly find itself in the news. They won't even need to pay for an ad to get a new tenant."

"And who says you can't find the positive in every situation?"

Tain laughed. "I'll call you if anything happens."

"Same here."

"I take it the house is a link to someone in the case," Liam said once Ashlyn had hung up.

"The family that owns the company that owns the other company that owns the house has a daughter who just happens to be good friends with Shannon Reimer."

"Let me guess. She insisted she had no idea where Shannon was."

"Better. When we talked to her and Shannon's boyfriend, he said Shannon had been planning to run away and that Shannon wouldn't say where she was going so that they couldn't be forced to lie to the police or Shannon's parents."

"Kids these days. They're so considerate. Always looking out for their friends."

"Really warms the heart, doesn't it?"

They were silent for a moment before he asked, "Do you think Shannon's in that house?"

Ashlyn paused. "I don't want to hope for that and be disappointed. The only thing I'm sure of is that Nurani Patel knows more than she told us."

"This makes it look less likely that it's related to Reimer's business interests."

"True. I'm afraid you're missing out on bed for nothing."

"The pleasure of your company makes up for it, even if it means we missed out on dinner."

She turned and looked at him. "I think I should tell you, I'm involved with someone."

"It's serious?"

"It's complicated."

"Huh. Isn't it always?"

"A few days ago it actually seemed pretty simple, in a good way."

"That's who the message was from?"

Ashlyn nodded.

"And that's this Craig guy, the one your sergeant was asking about?"

She hesitated.

"Hey, if it wasn't Tain, it had to be him, right? No chance it was Luke." Liam smiled. "He's in some hot water right now?"

"Not exactly. It's . . ."

"Complicated."

Neither of them tried to break the silence until it was half an hour until the drop.

"They should be leaving any time," Liam said.

Ashlyn nodded. She had her cell phone in her hand and could feel her heart pounding. After all this time, she just wanted to feel they'd made some progress.

And for things to go well, so that she wouldn't have to second-guess her decision to handle the money exchange this way.

"You made the right call, you know. We had grounds for a warrant, but if the people involved aren't in that house it might have blown the whole thing."

"Still could. They said no cops."

"We both know nobody was going to play it that way," Liam said.

"Still, it's a risk."

"That's part of the job. And part of the uncertainty."

"Yeah, well, it's not the part I like."

"Ah. You like the challenge but not the responsibility."

She thought about it. "I guess you could say that. This case has been tough. A dead child always is, but right before Christmas. It gets to you."

"Must really get to your partner."

Her head snapped up then. "What are you talking about?"

"See, after you left this morning I checked you out. Plenty to work with, because of the shooting last summer. I guess you stopped at the front page when you saw how your old boss had been smeared in the press today. You had to dig deeper to see your partner's name in print today."

Ashlyn was about to ask what the hell he was talking about when her cell rang. "Constable Hart."

"We've got movement," Tain said.

"We've got nothing."

"What are you going to do?"

Ashlyn glanced at Liam. "Move someone else to our position and head to the park. The house isn't going anywhere, and apparently neither is anyone inside."

She hung up as Liam radioed for a car to replace them.

Tain snapped the phone shut. He'd already ordered everyone to hold their positions.

"There she is," Sims said.

In the bottom corner of the screen, Tracy Reimer had entered the picture. It was the first time Tain had really seen her on her own, independent of a hovering husband or the family lawyer. She was as skittish as a newborn foal. One hand compulsively twisted the knapsack's strap as she cradled the bag with the other, holding it tight against her chest. Tracy Reimer glanced over her left shoulder, then right, and back over her left again. Her foot snagged on a branch as she turned and backed toward the spot on the concrete where she'd been told to leave the money. Her one arm flailed wildly until she regained her balance.

"Two minutes until the drop," Sims said as Tracy looked at the watch on her wrist, then cautiously set the bag down. "You'd think there was a bomb in there, the way she carried that bag."

"She showed more affection for that bag than she's shown for her own son in the last five days," Tain said.

"It probably isn't the bag. It's the money."

Tain grinned. "We'll make a cynic out of you yet, Sims."

"One o'clock. What's she waiting for?"

Tracy Reimer smoothed her sleeves, looked at her watch, turned slowly and looked at her watch again. She stiffened and stared off into the darkness, toward the trails through the woods on the other side of the playground.

After a minute Sims asked, "Are you going to radio for a visual?"

"If anyone spots something they're supposed to call it in." Tain frowned. "I don't like this."

As he reached for his radio Sims said, "Hold on. She's leaving."

Tracy Reimer went back the way she came, this time moving with more confidence. Her arms were wrapped tight around her body, and she didn't hesitate or look back even once.

"I thought she was going to blow it," Sims said.

They spent the next ten minutes watching the bag. The only call they received confirmed Mrs. Reimer had returned to the vehicle she'd arrived in.

Someone knocked at the van door, and Sims checked before opening it.

"Nothing?" Ashlyn asked as she climbed inside.

Tain barely took note of Liam following her in. "Not so far." Then he noticed movement on the screen that displayed the wider shot. It was still in the edges, where it was dark. "Okay, I think we have something."

"Why aren't they radioing in?" Ashlyn asked.

"You can ask yourself after I kick their asses," Tain muttered. Then he whistled as the figure came into view. "Well, well."

He radioed for some of the teams to hold their positions and then followed Liam and Ashlyn out of the van.

"How—" he started. Ashlyn held up her hand.

"This is your show, your call."

He gestured for her and Liam to approach from the other side of the washrooms, and radioed for two officers positioned near the beach to approach with caution.

Once he got to the corner of the building he took a quick look. Matt Lewis was almost at the bag. He hadn't even tried to disguise himself with a hoodie or a hat, and he wasn't looking over his shoulder.

Tain edged along the building and then moved forward decisively. "Police! Stop and put your hands in the air slowly."

From the corner of his eye he could see Ashlyn moving in from her side, Liam beside her. Matt froze for a moment and started to raise his hands. Then he started to run.

"Hold your fire," Tain called into the radio. He raced after the boy. The darkness worked against Matt, and he couldn't see he was running straight toward one of the officers near the playground. The officer jumped out and Matt tried to change course, but the hesitation was enough for Tain to tackle him.

After he got to his feet and pulled the teenager off the ground, Tain said, "Matthew Lewis, you're under arrest."

Once he'd determined Matt was unarmed and had handcuffed him, Tain escorted Matt to the parking lot. Ashlyn had the bag of money.

Sims had driven over and slid open the side door of the van. "Nothing so far."

"Stay on it, Sims," Ashlyn said. "Just in case." She turned to Matt Lewis. "Looks like we need to have a little chat."

"Walking in the park isn't a crime."

"Aw. And they say the youth of today are completely self-absorbed and unaware. I'm truly impressed by your legal knowledge, but extortion is a crime. And, of course, there's the little matter of hindering a criminal investigation." Ashlyn walked right up to Matt. "We gave you a chance to tell us where Shannon was. Instead, you tried to swindle her parents out of a million dollars."

"Wh-what?" Matt shrieked. "What are you talking about?"

"Oh, come off it, Matt. You really expect me to believe you just happened to come to this particular park, in the middle of the night, for a stroll? On the same night that your girlfriend's mother had been instructed to leave a bag filled with money at the spot where her son was murdered?"

"Wh-why . . ." Matt looked at Tain, then back at Ashlyn. "Why would Mrs. Reimer do that?"

"The callers claimed to have Shannon." Ashlyn unzipped the

bag and pulled out a bundle of bills. "They wanted a million dollars in exchange for her safe return. At least, that's what they said. Personally, I'm not convinced that's what they really wanted the money for." She looked at Tain.

"I agree. I don't think Shannon was kidnapped. I think she wanted the money to run away."

Ashlyn snapped her fingers. "You know, someone told us Shannon planned to run away. And they said they had no idea where she was. But then someone who knows the family and has Mr. Reimer's private cell number starts making calls, demanding a ransom payment. And look who shows up to collect." Ashlyn paused for a moment, her expression serious. "You better talk, Matt, because I'm in no mood to be jerked around. We're taking you back to the station and if you don't cooperate you'll be charged."

There was movement behind Ashlyn and Tain turned just as Tracy Reimer rushed up to Matt. "Where is she? Where's my daughter? Where's Shannon?"

She grabbed Matt's jacket, pulling at it frantically, and screamed the words over and over, even as Tain pried her off Matt and another officer grabbed her from behind.

"Control your client or I'll have her arrested," Ashlyn snapped at Byron Smythe, who'd appeared out of the shadows.

"She's clearly distraught—"

Ashlyn put up her hand. "Save it, Smythe. Here's your client's money."

He took the bag from her. "Do you want us at the station?"

"It would be a good idea. We may have information we need to confirm with the family if we're going to find Shannon."

"I only brought Mrs. Reimer."

Tain and Ashlyn exchanged a glance. "Where's Christopher?"

"With his dad. They were going to the house to pick up some things."

Tain exchanged a glance with Ashlyn before taking Matt to a cruiser to be transported to the station.

* * *

Ashlyn turned to Smythe. "Okay, you take Mrs. Reimer to the station and stay there. First call Richard's cell and find out where he is."

Smythe set the bag down and pulled out his phone with his one good hand. He was no longer on crutches, she noticed, but hobbling along independently. Tain had mentioned earlier that the knee injury wasn't as serious as initially thought, and she felt a mix of relief and regret about that.

After a moment he shook his head. "No answer."

Ashlyn held out her hand. "Give me the phone."

"I will not."

"You will, or so help me I'll charge you with assault for what you did to me the other night." Her voice was low, but she let her loathing for Smythe come through. Then she snapped her fingers at the officer holding Tracy Reimer. "Check her for a phone."

He did, then shook his head. "She's clean."

"Okay. Take these two to the station, put them in an interview room together and don't let them speak to anyone."

"You better have a damn good reason for this," Smythe said as he glared at her.

"Didn't your mother ever tell you your face would freeze that way?"

Ashlyn turned to Liam as the officer took Smythe and Mrs. Reimer to his cruiser.

"What do you need from me?" he asked.

"I need to question Matt, but I also need to know who's in that house."

Liam nodded. "Consider it done."

She turned to follow Tain, but Liam stopped her and squeezed her arm. "Hey . . . keep in touch, okay?"

Ashlyn nodded.

He offered a small grin, and she allowed herself a fleeting smile and a quick nod before she turned and walked away.

CHAPTER FOURTEEN

On the drive to the station Tain and Ashlyn had sat with Matt Lewis between them and hadn't said a word. With two officers in the front, as well as them sitting with Matt in the back, words weren't necessary. Ashlyn could see the sheen of sweat on the boy's face. At first, he'd appeared confused and uncertain, but when they pulled into the station his eyes widened with fear. By the time he was seated in an interview room he looked like he was about to cry.

"How do you want to play this?" Tain asked Ashlyn as they watched Matt through the glass.

"No games. Go at him hard."

Tain nodded. "He looks scared spitless."

"He should be. These are serious crimes." She glanced at her watch. "Before we do this . . ."

"You want to follow up at the Reimer house."

"Don't we have someone watching it still?"

Tain shook his head. "Pulled off for this tonight. Zidani had it handed over to Port Moody police."

"Shit shit shit."

"Come on." Tain ordered an officer to stay and watch Matt Lewis. "Let's go make sure everything's okay."

They didn't talk on the drive over. Ashlyn knew it was unusual for them to walk away from a suspect, especially under the circumstances, but ever since Smythe had told her he'd only brought Mrs. Reimer with him she'd felt as though a trapdoor in her stomach had opened up and everything had fallen through.

Their headlights revealed the status of the surveillance on the Reimer house, as Parker and his partner blinked and rubbed their eyes.

"Ash," Tain warned as he stopped their car.

She walked right up to driver's side window. "Are Richard and Christopher Reimer still inside?"

Parker yawned and swore beneath his breath. Bennett rubbed his eyes. "Yeah, they're still here."

"Unless they left while you were sleeping," she snapped.

Ashlyn marched past the Land Rover parked in the driveway and pounded on the door. The lights were on inside, but there was no sound of movement or sign of shadows. She rang the doorbell and then after a moment pounded again.

Tain pulled out his gun and nodded at Ashlyn. She reached for her gun first, then the door. It was unlocked.

"Mr. Reimer? It's Constable Hart and Constable Tain from the RCMP. We need to speak with you." She entered the house cautiously, doing a quick check to the left, into the living room.

"Oh God." Ashlyn froze.

A pillow with a gaping hole lay on the floor, the feathers scattered in the blood. Tain walked around, approaching from the other side where there wasn't as much seepage, and knelt by the body. He checked for a pulse and shook his head. "He's still warm," he said, then pulled his cell phone out and called it in. They checked the rest of the house. It was empty, and so was the garage and driveway.

"I guess we have access to the whole house now," Tain said.

"Small consolation." Ashlyn walked over to the gun. "We'll have to check and see if it belonged to the family."

It only took a few moments for more officers to arrive. Ashlyn snapped a photo on her cell phone and they handed the scene over to one of the secondary officers who'd worked the ransom drop with them.

"Make sure you have every room dusted," Ashlyn said. "This

is tied to another murder, so we want every print identified. I know it's a lot . . ."

The officer nodded. "We'll get it done."

Ashlyn walked outside. For a moment she stood silent, staring at the PoMo police car. Then she started to march down the driveway.

"We have to get back to the station," Tain said in a low voice.

"Not before I kick his ass."

Parker was out of the cruiser, leaning against it, grinning as he chatted with his partner and someone else.

"You no good son of a bitch." Ashlyn stopped right in front of him. "You can't even babysit a fucking house properly."

That cocky smile was gone in a heartbeat. "You're such a sanctimonious little bitch."

"I'm impressed, Parker. You used a word with more than three syllables. And when you write up your report we'll all get to find out if you know how to spell it."

He straightened up then and glared down at her. "I'd back off if I were you."

"Why? Big tough guy might take a swing at me?" She poked his chest. "Probably all you're good for, since we know how you rate at doing your job."

Parker shoved her back, and she felt Tain catch her and fluidly step in between. Parker was still moving forward, fists clenched, but he stopped cold as Tain looked him in the eye.

"That's the second time you've shown us you know how to push a woman around."

"She wants to play with the boys she has to take it. Equal rights means no special treatment."

"And I don't expect any," Ashlyn said as she got between him and Tain, clocked Parker on the jaw and kneed him in the stomach as he went down.

Tain grabbed her and pulled her back as Bennett went to help his partner.

"I'm not done with him." She struggled against Tain's grip. The surge of anger inside her was matched by the heat in her face.

Tain pulled her back, grabbed her forearms, and looked her in the eyes. "You are for now. We have to talk to Matt."

They drove back to the station in silence, except for Ashlyn's quick call to Zidani to fill him in, made once she'd calmed down enough to keep her voice level.

When they got to the interview room where Matt was waiting Ashlyn paused and looked up at Tain. "I could have throttled him."

"Ash, as a result of his incompetence a man is dead and a second child is missing. He's not going to walk away from that. Zidani seemed to take it well."

"It's when Zidani isn't yelling that I start to worry," Ashlyn said.

"Who's going to tell Smythe?"

She shook her head. "I assume we are. But first, we're going to see what Matt can tell us."

They entered the room and both remained standing. Tain moved closer to Matt, towering over him. "What have you got to say for yourself?"

"I—" Matt's voice squeaked like a prepubescent boy's would. "I don't know anything about a kidnapping!"

"Fine," Ashlyn said as she walked up to the table, put her hands down on it and leaned toward the boy. "Then let's talk about murder."

"Murder? Who— What— I-I don't know nothin' about a murder."

"Come on, Matt," Ashlyn said. "You knew Shannon was running away. We know the calls to Shannon's parents, demanding money, came from a house in New Westminster owned by Nurani Patel's family. And you showed up at the park right after the drop. You're in serious trouble here."

"But I-I-I didn't kill anyone! They just asked me to go to the park and pick up a bag. They said where it would be and when to go. That's it. I swear." He closed his eyes. "I thought . . . I thought . . ."

"You thought what?" Ashlyn asked.

He opened his eyes and looked right at her. "I thought it was clothes and stuff. I didn't know what was in the bag until you showed me."

"Who wanted you to go get it?" Tain asked.

Matt was shaking. He looked up at Tain. "Nurani."

"Where's Shannon?" Ashlyn demanded.

Matt moved his head from side to side, slowly at first, then at an almost frenzied pace. "I swear I don't know. You have to believe me."

"If you want me to believe you, Matt, you better tell me everything," Ashlyn said.

"I have! Nurani asked me to go to the park and pick up a black knapsack. She said to wait until about quarter, twenty after one."

Ashlyn frowned. "How did Nurani ask you?"

"Wh-what do you mean how?"

"Did she talk to you, phone you?"

"She called me."

"From her house or her cell?"

"Uh, her cell. Why?"

"What were you supposed to do with the bag?" Tain asked.

"Take it to some house."

"What's the address?" Ashlyn asked.

"It's on the paper in my coat pocket."

Tain checked the coat and removed the slip. "It's the house in New Westminster. The one Nurani's family owns."

"Well, that all fits, doesn't it?" Ashlyn said. "That makes our friend Matt an accomplice to extortion."

Tain nodded. "And murder."

"I didn't have nothin' to do with Jeffrey's murder! You've gotta believe me!"

"Oh, we're not talking about Jeffrey." Ashlyn pulled out her cell phone and found the picture she'd taken. "We're talking about this murder."

She turned the phone around so that Matt could see the photo. He'd seemed pale before, but his face went a pasty white and then he heaved and retched all over the table. Ashlyn had just enough time to pull herself back and avoid the spray.

Once his stomach was empty Matt sat there, sweat trickling down his face along with the tears. His voice was low and calm when he finally spoke.

"I didn't know. But I guess now Nurani knew more than I did. If anyone knows where Shannon is, it's her, but I swear I haven't talked to her since she disappeared."

"We'll get someone in here to clean this up, and get you some fresh clothes and something to drink," Tain said. "And we want to run a test."

"What kind of test?"

"One that will prove you didn't shoot Richard Reimer."

"Okay, sure, fine."

Ashlyn was already at the door and turned to open it.

"Where are you going?" Matt asked.

"To talk to Nurani."

"Sh-sh-sh-she'll kn-know I told you."

Ashlyn glanced at Tain. "Matt, I think that's the least of your worries."

"But what if she killed Shannon's dad?"

"Then she'll go to prison," Tain said.

It only took a minute to give an officer instructions about Matt. As they walked down the hall the sound of shouting grew, and when they turned a corner Byron Smythe was getting in an officer's face, demanding answers.

Smythe looked up as Tain and Ashlyn approached.

"You! You've kept us waiting here for hours. This is ridiculous. I'm taking my client home."

Ashlyn folded her arms across her chest. "So you can get her killed too?"

"What the hell are you talking about?"

"Why didn't you bring Richard and Christopher with you tonight? You've kept the family together for everything else. Tracy and Christopher didn't need to be at your office for days as we waited for a phone call from the alleged kidnappers—"

"Alleged? You've got the guy in an interview room!"

"Shannon's boyfriend. He hasn't seen her since she disappeared. And if you'd cooperated with us from the beginning,

Smythe, it's likely we'd already have Shannon, so don't you whine to me about having to wait here for a few hours." Ashlyn started to walk past him.

Smythe grabbed her left arm with his left hand and pushed her up against the wall. "I'm sick of your attitude."

"Get your hands off me."

She heard Zidani before she saw him. "Let go of her right now." Smythe was pressing hard, and she could feel the pressure of his weight pushing into her body. Then he let go and backed away as he turned to Zidani.

"I want to take my client home right now!"

He shook his head. "You two aren't going anywhere."

"This is outrageous! This"—he pointed at Ashlyn—"officer confiscated my cell phone and will not allow me to contact Mrs. Reimer's family."

"You can't call them." Ashlyn practically spat the words out. "Thanks to you, Richard's dead and Christopher's missing."

"Ashlyn," Zidani warned.

Smythe froze and turned pale. "What are you talking about?"

She stepped up to him. "Every second of this investigation you haven't let a single member of this family out of your sight, but tonight you leave Richard Reimer and his son alone. Now we've got two missing kids and two murder victims. This'll do wonders for your reputation. I'm sure everyone will want to hire a lawyer who lets his clients get killed."

"Don't do anything stupid." Zidani stepped between her and the lawyer, who'd raised a fist, his face burning and eyes flashing with anger.

"Come on, Ash," Tain said. "He's not worth it."

She felt her partner's fingers on her arm, took a step back as Zidani stepped forward and handed her some papers.

"Search warrants. You've got full access to the Patel house and a team waiting." He paused and looked at Smythe. "And full access to the residence of Byron Smythe, where the Reimer family was staying since Jeffrey's murder. Mr. Smythe and Mrs. Reimer won't be going anywhere. New West PD are holding for another half an hour, then they're going in."

Ashlyn reached into her pocket and pulled out Smythe's cell phone. She gave it to Zidani without a word and walked away.

When they got in the car Tain turned to Ashlyn before he started the engine.

"Don't start." Her words sounded flat and hollow. Somewhere between the confrontation in the hallway and their arrival in the parking lot all her anger had seeped out. "I feel like I've spent the last few days trying to control my temper, or bawling like a baby, and I'm frustrated."

"You can't beat yourself up, Ash. It won't help anyone."

She smiled wryly. "If you say it's hormones—"

"You're passionate about justice, about your job. Parker and Smythe both screwed up. You know the only reason I'm annoyed is because when you lose your temper I can't."

"That's how it works, is it? One of us always has to stay rational?"

"It keeps us from ever doing anything really stupid."

She was silent for a moment, then said, "I'm not so sure about that."

It didn't take long to reach the Patel house and get the team organized. Once everyone was in position Ashlyn pounded on the front door, identifying them as police with a search warrant.

Tain watched as first one light went on upstairs, then another, and then light spilled down to the main floor. They could hear footsteps and voices, but the murmurs were too low for him to make out the words. Ashlyn knocked again.

"Mr. and Mrs. Patel, this is the RCMP. We have a search warrant. If you don't open the door we're going to use force."

There was a moment of silence, followed by the sound of the dead bolt sliding back as the door was unlocked. When the man opened the door Ashlyn asked, "Are you Mr. Patel?"

He nodded. Mr. Patel was a thin man, not particularly tall, with dark hair, dark eyes, a lean face. He had a calm look about him. Ashlyn handed him the warrant and advised him of his rights, nudging him aside as officers entered the house.

"What is it you want?" Mr. Patel asked.

Tain could see Mrs. Patel, Nurani, a boy he assumed was her younger brother and a younger girl standing near the foot of the stairs. Nurani towered over her mother, and the girl's streamlined figure emphasized Mrs. Patel's round body. The boy and girl looked like they would be tall as well, and both were a healthy weight. Tain was struck by how quiet they were, despite being woken up in the middle of the night by armed police officers.

Ashlyn nodded at them. "Is this your entire family?"

"My older son is away."

"Nobody else lives in the house?"

Mr. Patel shook his head.

Ashlyn walked past him, down the hall, looking through doorways. "Mr. Patel, bring your family in here, please," she said as she gestured into one of the rooms.

Tain waited until they'd filed in, then followed Ashlyn.

"What is it you want?" Mr. Patel asked again.

"I'm sure you're aware that your daughter has a close friend from school who's been missing for several days," Ashlyn said.

Mr. Patel didn't even look at his daughter, just nodded. Tain noticed Mrs. Patel's eyes widened with fear.

"And I'm sure your daughter informed you that we spoke to her last week about Shannon," Ashlyn said.

That did provoke a response. Mr. Patel's eyes narrowed, and he glanced at his daughter quickly. "My daughter cannot help you."

"Can't or won't?" Ashlyn passed him a second document. He took it in his hands, and began to read it. "This is to inform you that the New Westminster Police Department is executing a search warrant at the residence marked on that document." She leaned forward and tapped a spot on the paper. "A residence owned by one of your companies."

"What is the reason for this?" Mr. Patel was starting to lose the look of calm he'd had when he first opened the door. The paper quivered in his hand.

"Someone at that residence placed a call to a private cell phone owned by Richard Reimer. They claimed they'd kidnapped Shannon and demanded a ransom of one million dollars."

Tain watched as Nurani stiffened. She was looking at the carpet, sitting on the far side of her father. Her mother and siblings were on his other side.

"And you think we have kidnapped Shannon? That is ridiculous! Look at our house. What is a million dollars to us?"

The room was lavish, silk cushions, imported furnishings, polished floors, not a speck of dust anywhere. A collection of elephant carvings in glass cases along the wall looked expensive to Tain's untrained eye. He wasn't an art connoisseur, but he knew the difference between professional products and cheap knockoffs. Just the fact that they lived in this part of the Lower Mainland, in a house bigger than some apartment buildings, hinted at how much money the Patels had. They were wealthier than the Reimer family.

"We don't think you kidnapped Shannon," Ashlyn said. "But we want to know who's in that house."

"It is vacant. Your police officers will see. We are having work done next month, and the property will be empty until the renovations are finished."

"I don't think it is vacant," Ashlyn said.

"You think someone is staying at my house and has kidnapped my daughter's friend?"

"We don't think she was kidnapped at all. We think Nurani knows where Shannon is."

Nurani didn't move. Mr. Patel sat staring at Ashlyn and didn't respond. Mrs. Patel averted her gaze as she fussed over the younger children, despite the fact they were sitting still.

"We have enough evidence to arrest your daughter, Mr. Patel," Tain said. "She could face criminal charges for extortion and hindering a criminal investigation."

Mr. Patel turned to look at his daughter. "Tell them whatever you know."

Her head snapped up. "Papa, I—"

"You will do as I tell you."

Ashlyn pulled a stool over in front of the couch and sat down right in front of Nurani. "We know Shannon was being abused. We know Jeffrey was being abused too. We also know Shannon didn't kill her little brother. She was injured, and she went to the hospital. She might still need medical treatment, Nurani. And we also know all her friends would be scared that if we found her she might go to jail, or be sent back home. I think you just wanted to help."

Nurani looked at her father, then back at Ashlyn.

A cell phone rang, and it only took a few seconds to identify it as Ashlyn's. She pulled it out.

"Constable Hart."

She was silent while she listened to the voice on the other end, then looked up at Tain and nodded. "Right." She paused. "Really. That is interesting. Can you do me a favor?" Another pause. "You read my mind. Thanks, Liam." Ashlyn closed the phone. "That was the New Westminster police."

Nurani buried her face in her hands and started to cry. While Ashlyn waited with professional calm, Tain wondered how she could be so patient with the girl. He knew part of her was still furious about the murder of Richard Reimer. Not because she blamed Parker or Smythe, although that was part of it, but primarily because she blamed herself. If they'd pushed Nurani and Matt harder, if they'd brought them in for questioning . . .

If, if, if. It was so easy to look back and tell yourself things would be better if you'd done just this one thing differently. On some level, he knew Ashlyn was asking herself if the reason they'd failed to find Shannon—and that another person was dead and another child missing—was partly because Ashlyn's emotions had clouded her judgment. He also knew nothing he could say would make much of a difference. For someone as levelheaded as Ashlyn normally was, she was pushed to the limit by the events of the past week.

Mr. Patel looked at his daughter but made no effort to comfort her. The first hint of anger crept into his features as he scowled. "And what do they say?"

"Maybe you should ask your daughter," Ashlyn said.

Nurani looked up then, tears still rolling down her face. "Papa—"

Her father raised his voice. "Tell me now! What have you done?"

Tain hadn't been certain if Nurani was faking her tears until that moment. Then he knew she'd been putting on a show, because she really started to cry. The selfishness of the teen rankled him, and he wanted to shake her by the shoulders and tell her to stop acting like a child. He couldn't put his finger on exactly what it was about her that convinced him she was only upset because she'd been caught, and that her tears were primarily for herself.

"When the alleged kidnappers contacted Richard Reimer, we were able to trace the call to the house you own in New Westminster," Ashlyn said as she turned to look at Mr. Patel. "We began monitoring the house to see if anyone entered or left the premises. Nobody did. Another call was placed, again from that address. The alleged kidnappers gave very clear instructions for Mrs. Reimer to leave the money in the park where Jeffrey Reimer was killed."

Mrs. Patel gasped, but her husband ignored her. "But if nobody left the house to get the money, what does this have to do with us?"

"The person who came to the park to get the money was Matt Lewis," Ashlyn said.

Mr. Patel's nostrils flared as he turned to his daughter. Whatever he was about to say remained unspoken as Ashlyn continued, her voice calm, her words measured.

"The police in New West found Jody Hoath at the property you own, along with a young man named Dan Patel and some substances neither have any business possessing. You know, when we question teenagers it's always interesting. At first they try to be so tough, but it never takes long for them to break. Now your son has been arrested in possession of illegal drugs. And your daughter"—Ashlyn gestured at the girl, who was still sobbing—"is an accomplice to murder."

"What?" Nurani shrieked, at the same time her father gasped and Mrs. Patel cried out. "You're lying! I had nothing to do with it. Is that what Jody says? That bitch." The teenager sprang to her feet. "I don't have to listen to this!"

Tain stepped in front of her to block her way and pulled out his handcuffs. "Then we'll arrest you right now for hindering a criminal investigation."

"We have Jody admitting you asked her to make the phone calls. That's extortion, Nurani." Ashlyn got up and stood behind the girl. "And we've already talked to Matt Lewis. We have enough to get a court order for your phone records, and our boss is already looking after that. They'll prove that Jody and Matt are telling the truth, that you asked them to do these favors for you.

"What threw me off was that I really believed Matt when he told me Shannon was running away, and that she hadn't told him where she was going so that he wouldn't have to try to lie to the police. I don't know, something about his face."

Tain nodded. "He seemed genuine. I believed him too."

"My mistake was thinking that extended to you. Matt said Shannon never told him, but when I think back to that day we chatted, you never said that. You never actually denied knowing where Shannon was. You just let Matt talk."

Nurani spun around, arms folded across her chest. "I won't tell you."

Mr. Patel sprung to his feet then. "For God's sake, Nurani, you will tell them right now. What have I raised you to be? Your friends are sluts who sleep with older men and do drugs? You are a criminal! You're a disgrace to this family!"

By then, the boy and girl were crying, and so was Mrs. Patel. She wrapped her arms around her younger children and shushed them quietly, wiping their tears as her own fell unchecked.

"Me, Papa? Ask your wife where Shannon is!"

"Nurani!" Mrs. Patel gasped, then said something in a foreign language.

Mr. Patel spun around then. "You are involved in this?"

His wife cowered as though afraid he would strike her. "She was being abused. For God's sake, she'd been stabbed."

Mr. Patel's face was so tight Tain thought he might have a stroke. The calm he'd shown earlier had been replaced by a consuming rage, complete with clenched fists, and spit flying from his mouth as he yelled, "You foolish woman!"

The sound of the front door opening and voices as people came inside interrupted them, and Tain turned to see an officer lead another woman into the room.

"Who's this?" Ashlyn asked as Mrs. Patel cried out. She clamped her hand over her mouth as the stream of tears turned into a flood.

"Our housekeeper," Mr. Patel snapped.

"I thought you told me only the family lived here."

"In the house. She lives in an apartment above the garage."

"And she wasn't alone," the officer said. He nodded at the entrance. Another officer appeared, leading a pale teenager, hands cuffed behind her.

Shannon Reimer.

Ashlyn watched Zidani tap his fingers on his desk. The sergeant had been silent for a few long minutes. Finally, he sighed and tossed up his hands.

"Go ahead. Just be careful."

As she reached for the door, Zidani stopped her. "There's one thing I want to know. Why have Mrs. Reimer do the drop? Aren't we thinking this was most likely a setup to get to Richard?"

"He was physical with Christopher when we first met him," Tain said. "Although I've never seen bruises on Mrs. Reimer, it's possible he abuses her as well."

"Their neighbor said Christopher was the only one who ever fought back," Ashlyn murmured.

"Maybe Jeffrey's murder changed that," Tain said softly. "It actually explains Mrs. Reimer's odd reactions."

"More afraid of her husband than scared for her children."

A quick glance at Tain was all Ashlyn needed to confirm he was wondering the same thing.

"I know it doesn't look good," Ashlyn said, "but I still think

Shannon's innocent in all of this. Okay, not innocent of running away or of trying to get money from her family. But I don't think she murdered anyone."

"She had enough time to get from the Patel home to her own house, kill her father, help her brother escape, and return," Zidani said.

"But why help her brother escape and not just go with him? And where would she help him escape to?" Ashlyn shook her head. "I don't know, something just doesn't seem right about this."

"Two people have been murdered. 'Right' doesn't have much to do with it," Zidani said. "Give me another scenario."

"I will when I figure one out," Ashlyn said. "But you know what's going to happen when Mrs. Reimer finds out Shannon's here. She'll want to see her daughter."

Zidani nodded. "That's our holdback. I want to be there for the reunion."

"You and me both." Ashlyn opened the door. "But first, we'll see what Shannon has to say."

The predawn quiet still lingered over the station, and they walked to the interview room in silence. Once there, Tain said, "We never did break the news about Richard's murder to the Patel family."

"What are you thinking?"

"Let Shannon lead."

The teen was sitting at the table, hands free. There had been no waterworks, no hysterics. There was a tension in the girl, a stiffness in the shoulders, that suggested she wasn't happy she'd been found, but no drama.

Her long brown hair framed her face, skin white, but her eyes weren't red or puffy. If anything, they were sunken, the dark smudges underneath betraying her fatigue. Otherwise, Shannon seemed calm.

They sat down across from her.

"You've had a few rough days," Ashlyn said. "The doctor was concerned."

"Mae, the Patels' housekeeper, she took good care of me."

"Did she pick you up from the hospital?"

Shannon shook her head.

"Do you want to tell us what happened Friday morning?"

"You already know."

Ashlyn deliberately wrinkled her face and looked at Tain as she shook her head. "No, Shannon. I don't think we do."

For a moment Shannon stared back. Then she slumped in her chair and looked down at the table. Ashlyn glanced at Tain, and he shook his head.

"We know you left the house that morning. It was early. We know Jeffrey ran after you, so you carried him in your arms as you went to the path that circles the inlet and leads to Rocky Point Park. We know Christopher followed you, and your parents followed him.

"And we know someone murdered Jeffrey."

Ashlyn let the silence linger as she watched Shannon and waited. Finding the girl had produced a feeling of disappointment she hadn't expected. It might have been satisfying, if it wasn't for the fact that now, once she was finished with Shannon, she had to find Christopher Reimer.

They also had to sort out how they'd deal with Matt, Jody, Nurani and her family. Mr. Patel had remained at the house with his younger children. Mae, Mrs. Patel and Nurani were all in interview rooms, charges pending.

It was hard not to feel conflicted about Shannon Reimer. There was no doubt in Ashlyn's mind that Shannon was a victim of abuse and that social services had dropped the ball. Hell, it had been days since she'd first called, and they still hadn't gotten back to her, despite multiple messages.

But that was the difference between systems and people. Systems could fail to fulfill their responsibility and face no serious repercussions. Social services wouldn't go to jail or be fined or face punishment of any real kind. They'd just carry on, helping some, failing others. Although Ashlyn knew it really wasn't any different from law enforcement, she still felt frustrated. With her own job, she knew her legal boundaries, and she knew that sometimes it meant murderers went free and criminals didn't face justice. With social services, she assumed the reason things fell through the cracks wasn't because of the limitations of the law, but because nobody cared.

It was easy to think nobody cared as much as you did.

"Shannon, I think you'd feel a lot better if you told us what happened."

"I did it." She lifted her head, but didn't look right at Ashlyn. Instead, her gaze went past her, a little above and to the left. "I'm responsible. I couldn't take Jeffrey with me."

"That's not what our evidence tells us, Shannon."

"Then it's wrong!" She smacked her fist against the table. "It's my fault."

"There's a difference between it being your fault, and you actually killing him," Ashlyn said quietly. "I saw the pictures at the house, in Jeffrey's bedroom. You adored your little brother."

Shannon's shoulders shook as the tears streamed down her face. She cried silently and made no attempt to hide her grief.

It only took a moment to go to the door, ask someone to get a box of Kleenex and have them return with it. Ashlyn slid the tissues across the table.

"I'll tell you what I think. You were running away. Something went wrong, Jeffrey saw you, and your parents figured out what was going on. They tried to stop you from leaving. Now you blame yourself, because Jeffrey was murdered, and if you'd just stayed home that morning he'd still be okay."

Shannon reached for a Kleenex and wiped her nose. The tears weren't streaming down her face as fast as before, but she remained silent.

"Only you know that's not true, Shannon. Jeffrey wouldn't have been okay. We know about the abuse."

As Ashlyn spoke she watched the girl deflate. The truth was, they were still guessing about the abuse. They had the indications, they had the eyewitness next door, they had what the doctor had told them, but they didn't know the extent of it. Shannon remained as still as stone, her gaze fixed on the table, but she was limp, and the energy she'd shown in her insistence that she was responsible for Jeffrey's death was gone.

"We want to help you."

Shannon's head snapped up and she stared at Ashlyn. "You can't."

"How do you know that if you don't give us a chance?"

The girl looked away.

"If you won't tell us what happened, why don't you tell us what you want?"

"What I want? I want Jeffrey to be okay. Can you fix that for me?" The words echoed in the room, the shrill note that had crept into Shannon's voice reverberating in the air. "I want to go to jail."

"Why?"

"Because I don't want to go home." The girl's mouth twisted as she looked away. "If you want to help me"—she brushed a stray tear away—"you won't make me go home."

Ashlyn looked at Tain. Then she stood.

"We'll see what we can do. Your mother will want to see you."

Shannon's jaw dropped. "I don't want to see her. Please! I don't want to see any of them! You can't make me talk to my parents!" She was out of her seat, yelling, her face almost purple.

"Whoa. Calm down. Okay, we won't make you see them." Ashlyn touched Shannon's shoulder lightly and the girl shrugged her off, but sat down. "Is there anything we can get for you? A drink, breakfast?"

Her elbows propped up on the table, Shannon's face fell against her hands. Her head moved back and forth.

"If you change your mind the officer will get you something, okay?"

As soon as they were in the hall, Tain nodded. "She's terrified of going home."

"And you heard what she said. 'Don't make me see my parents.' She doesn't know her father's dead."

"We still need to do a GSR test, to be on the safe side."

"We've tested Matt, and I gave instructions for them to test Nurani, then Shannon," Ashlyn said. "Jody Hoath and Dan Patel will be tested as well, although I don't see how they could have gotten out of the house. Sims is questioning them, and they're also taking all their fingerprints and DNA."

"Maybe that will help us sort this out once and for all."

"You are turning into an optimist. The way this case has been going, I wouldn't be surprised if elves from the North Pole were responsible for the murders."

He grinned. "That would be quite a headline."

"Seriously, though, what are we going to do? Social services still hasn't called me back from the weekend."

All traces of amusement vanished from Tain's face, and his lip curled with obvious distaste. "Unless we have charges pending against Tracy Reimer, I don't see how we can keep her from taking her daughter home. We could charge Shannon, but once we put her in the system we can't undo that."

Zidani stepped out into the hall.

"Do you think she'll change her mind once she learns her father is dead?" Ashlyn asked.

"We still don't know she's not involved in her father's murder. She might think because we found her that we prevented it, if she didn't pull the trigger herself." Zidani passed Ashlyn a stack of message slips. "No sightings of Christopher. Early estimate for time of death is approximately one A.M., give or take an hour."

"Which makes it look like the ransom really was a decoy for the murder." Ashlyn groaned. "You know, if we play that theory in court we can charge them as accomplices to murder, but where does that leave the extortion charge?"

"Sims uncovered an account in Shannon's name in the Cayman Islands that has more than two million in it," Tain said. "It's pretty easy to argue she didn't need the cash, but unless Nurani or the maid testify that she knew about the setup to murder her father, I don't see how that charge could stick based on what we've got."

"If we don't have a case against her on the murder, it will be almost impossible to get them to implicate her on the extortion charge. And if they argue it was an attempt to rescue Christopher from his abuser, these guys could all get a slap on the wrist." Ashlyn thought about the crime-scene photos from Craig's case, the extent of the beating, the way that girl must have suffered. And the boy had been about sixteen. Ten years later and he was out of prison with a civil suit for millions of dollars, and he just might win. Twenty-six years old and he could be set for life. No wonder Craig couldn't let it go.

"Ash?"

"Hmm?" She realized Tain was waiting for her to continue. "Well, it wasn't like Shannon was a wanted criminal. She was a suspect, but Mrs. Patel and the housekeeper could both argue they never saw the news. I mean, unless someone recovers a current newspaper in the house, how can we prove they actually knew we were looking for Shannon? We never spoke to the family, just Nurani."

"We have a dead child, a dead father, a teenager who's been stabbed and yes, who did have enough time to get to the house, commit the murder and return to the Patel residence before you found her there. If she pulled the trigger we can look at post-traumatic stress arguments and mitigating circumstances and the courts might call it a justifiable homicide. We still don't know where Christopher Reimer is," Zidani said. He nodded at the door to the interrogation room as a team entered. "They'll do the GSR test, which won't help us if she wore gloves."

"Goddamn Parker falling asleep on the job," Ashlyn muttered.

Zidani pointed a finger at her. "Rule Shannon in or out, based on the evidence. You know what that means." He turned and walked away.

"We could have sent someone else to do this," Tain said after the fifth house.

It had started to rain. With the temperature hovering just above zero, it was a cold rain, driven by a wind with an icy bite.

"I just don't want any more screwups," Ashlyn said as they approached the next house.

They'd started their canvas with the Patels' neighbors. So far, nobody had seen or heard anything unusual. Mr. Patel had insisted no vehicles had left his property that he knew of, and he'd been home all evening.

"Although it is clear that I do not know everything that happens in my own home," he'd said as he'd shut the door on them. They couldn't disagree.

"We could send Luke out," Tain suggested.

A devilish gleam flickered in Ashlyn's eyes, and her face broke into a smile. "Don't tempt me."

They knocked on the door, and when an older woman answered they repeated the process. No, she hadn't seen anyone come or go from the Patel house all evening, until the police arrived. No, she hadn't seen anything unusual at all the last few days.

Tain held up a photo. "Do you recognize this girl?"

The woman nodded. "She's been in the news, and I thought I'd seen her at the Patel home."

"Recently?" Ashlyn asked.

"No, not for a few weeks."

They returned to the car and repeated the process on the street near the Reimer house. Crime-scene tape had it marked off, and an RCMP car was positioned out front. After they confirmed that there hadn't been any other activity at the house, they started going door to door.

The results were the same as before: nobody had seen anything unusual, until the police had arrived. Not even Eleanor Pratt.

"It's going to make it a lot harder to prove Shannon did this, unless the GSR test is positive," Ashlyn said as they drove back to the station.

Tain glanced at her. "I thought this is the result you wanted."

"What I want is the truth. I know, I know. How cliché. This is all very good for my ego and confirming my gut's right about Shannon, but we didn't just cast doubt on her involvement. We have nothing to prove anyone entered that house last night."

"Who else would know about other ways to get on the property without coming on the road? If it wasn't Shannon it has to be one of her friends."

Ashlyn's cell phone rang. "Constable Hart." She listened for a moment, then said, "Thanks, Sims" and hung up.

"Jody and Dan have an alibi," she said with wry amusement as she looked at him, a sardonic smile tugging at the corners of her mouth. "Their supplier called and told them about the police surveillance, and that was just after midnight." She rubbed her forehead. "I'm sure Liam's thrilled to know we prevented a drug deal."

"And if we can't prove Shannon left the Patel house, we can't prove Nurani did either."

"Can we get the optimistic version of you back?" Said with a half smile, which soon slipped from her face. Ashlyn's expression grew serious, her look distant but not vacant. "What time did Smythe and Mrs. Reimer check in last night?"

"Around twelve thirty. I spoke to Smythe by phone a few times . . ." He glanced at her. "Tracy Reimer?"

"It doesn't explain Christopher."

"Unless she's the one who's stashed him somewhere."

"We still can't prove someone entered the house."

"We'll send Luke to explore all other ways onto the property. Unless you want to do it."

She was still staring at the dashboard. Tain had worked with her long enough to know that she was half listening to him, half working out scenarios in her head. "No, we'll send Sims." She looked up then, her eyes clear. "I want to talk to Tracy Reimer."

CHAPTER FIFTEEN

"I understand this is a very difficult time for you." Ashlyn set a file folder on the table and sat down across from Byron Smythe and Tracy Reimer. "I'm sorry we have to do this now."

Tain almost smiled. Her voice was soft and sympathetic; the sentiments sounded genuine. Even he almost believed her.

The woman across the table could only be described as a mess. Unlike the day they'd first met Tracy Reimer, when they'd told her that her son had been murdered, she had clearly been crying. Her eyes were red and puffy, her skin blotched with dried tears and her brown hair stuck out in all directions. The tissue in her hands was being shredded meticulously, a pile of white bits growing on the table in front of her, despite the fact that her hands were shaking.

Tain realized then that he'd been around this woman in a lot of stressful moments, but somehow she'd always seemed off, until now. He couldn't put his finger on it, but her emotions hadn't seemed to match, as though what was really upsetting her wasn't the death of her youngest child or her missing daughter. Normally, parents would be calling, anxious for updates about the investigation. Maybe his assessment had more to do with the fact that the Reimers had hidden behind their lawyer, who seemed more interested in protecting the parents than anything else.

He sat beside Ashlyn as she slid a photo from the file folder in front of her. "Do you recognize this gun?"

Tracy gasped and dropped the tissue as her hands flew over

her mouth. The wide-eyed look of shock betrayed the truth, although they still needed to hear it.

"Mrs. Reimer?" Ashlyn prodded gently, her voice quiet.

Smythe's eyes had narrowed, a dark shadow settling into his
face. He looked at the photo of the gun instead of his client.
"Answer the question."

Tracy nodded, but didn't unclamp her hands from her mouth.

After Ashlyn fished another document out of the folder she
said, "Your husband had permits to own two handguns." She
slid the paper across the table toward Tracy Reimer. "One of
the weapons he had registered is this gun"—Ashlyn tapped the
photo—"which we recovered at the crime scene."

"She already told you she recognized the gun," Smythe said.

Ashlyn kept her gaze focused on Tracy Reimer. "I need you to
tell me where the guns were kept and who had access to them."

Tracy's hands dropped from her face as she turned to look at
her lawyer. He exhaled and nodded.

"My . . ." Her face scrunched up like a pug's, in what Tain
suspected was an attempt to keep from crying. "We . . ." She
took a deep breath. "They were in the safe. In . . . in the den."

Her hands had gone back to the tissue, shredding it at a frenzied pace.

"And who had access to the safe?"

The tears started then. "My husband. Me. I suppose Shannon knew where the key was, possibly Christopher." Her voice
cracked as she said his name.

Tain saw Ashlyn's glance before she turned back to their suspect. "Anyone else?"

Mrs. Reimer's forehead wrinkled, as though she didn't quite
understand the question. "Our lawyer, maybe a few of"—she
swallowed—"Richard's friends knew where he might have the
key."

Ashlyn nodded and put the permits and photo back in the
folder. "Thank you. That's very helpful. Now, I know it's been
a long night, and I know you're anxious to leave. But it would
be very helpful to us if you could walk us through what happened last night."

"Why? You were there. I left the money, like you said to do, and then we came here."

"I meant before you went to the park. Go back a few hours earlier. Were you at the house with Richard and Christopher?"

Tracy's mouth opened as though she was about to answer, but Smythe put his hand over hers. "Don't answer that." He looked at Ashlyn. "Where's this going?"

"I need to get a working time line for last night. Were Richard and Christopher with you? Were you all at the family house? If not, when did they leave? As far as I know, next to the killer, you two are the last people who saw Richard alive." When they remained silent she continued, "You've done enough to hinder the investigation into Jeffrey's murder. Don't tell me you're going to screw us over on this one as well."

Smythe clenched his teeth, but didn't protest and removed his hand from his client's.

"We were at Byron's house," Tracy said, "until about eleven P.M. Richard and Christopher drove to the house together."

"Why did they go to the house?"

"To get some things. Clothes."

"They weren't planning to stay there?"

Tracy looked at her lawyer again, then shook her head.

"Mrs. Reimer, why would they go there so late at night? Especially when the ransom exchange was going to happen so soon?"

Tracy looked like a deer caught in the headlights. She glanced at her lawyer, who again nodded. "Richard didn't want to see any of the neighbors."

"Okay. What vehicle was your husband driving?"

"His Land Rover."

Ashlyn flipped the folder open again and leafed through the papers and photos. She passed one to Mrs. Reimer. "This vehicle?"

Tracy took the paper and then passed it right back. "Yes. Why?"

"What did you do after they left?"

As Tracy exhaled she slumped down in her chair. "Nothing," she murmured in a voice so low Tain could hardly hear her.

"You waited for almost an hour and a half, and just did nothing?"

"Is my client under suspicion?" Smythe demanded.

"I've already explained—"

"Save it," Smythe snapped. "Whether my client sat and stared at the wall, ate, drank, slept or paced, it has nothing to do with the murder of her husband and disappearance of her son, and you damn well know it. This interview ends now. Shouldn't you be out trying to find Shannon and Christopher?"

"Actually, we have found Shannon. She's here."

Tracy Reimer's head snapped up, but she didn't smile or say anything. She looked dazed, as though someone had just slapped her across the face.

It took Smythe a moment to recover. "Well, that's wonderful. Her mother wants to see her immediately."

"We'll be back shortly," Ashlyn said as she stood, the folder in her hand.

"No stalling. We want to see her right away. As her lawyer—"

"With all due respect, Mr. Smythe, shut up." Ashlyn turned, opened the door and walked away.

Once Tain had closed the door to the interview room and caught up to her, he asked, "What now?"

"I need a drink."

"Isn't it a bit early?"

"You're a laugh a minute, Tain," she said as he followed her into the staff room.

She stopped by the door, at the vending machine, vaguely aware of Tain moving farther into the room. "The news is on. I wonder if they've picked up on the murder yet."

"I'm sure they have," she said as she moved beside him, just as the story changed.

"In Kelowna, RCMP officers called to the scene of a vicious assault this morning were shocked to discover a colleague had been attacked in his motel room." The anchor's image was replaced by live footage of the motel, crime-scene tape fluttering in the breeze as snow fell and an officer entered the room behind the tape. "Constable Craig Nolan of the Coquitlam RCMP detachment was found unconscious when a guest in a neighboring room noticed the door was open." The image switched to a young man with short brown hair, telling his story about going to the reception area to ask for directions when he noticed the door was open and snow was blowing in.

"I just thought maybe I should close the door, you know, like someone had accidentally left it open but then I saw him lying on the floor and saw the blood, and I didn't want to touch anything so I called 911 on my cell . . ."

The man's voice faded as the anchor reported that Nolan had been taken to the hospital, and a photo of Craig appeared on the screen. "The RCMP has issued a statement, confirming that Nolan was struck on the head. No arrests have been made. RCMP also confirmed that Nolan was in Kelowna on police business but declined to offer more details at this time."

Ashlyn staggered back toward the door. She'd been pushing down her anger with Craig, her frustration that he hadn't called. Although she knew she hadn't had time to actually talk to him that hadn't been the point.

There were footsteps approaching from the hallway, and she was vaguely aware of Tain's hand on her arm, murmured reassurances that everything would be okay and Zidani's voice— distant and muffled, as though her head were underwater and the liquid was distorting the words—telling them to come to his office.

She'd had that moment, when she'd thought something had happened to him, and brushed it off. He'd texted his terse reply to her after that. The assault must have happened later. What had he even gone to Kelowna for? They'd been too busy arguing for her to pay much attention.

"Ashlyn."

Tain nudged her arm. He had an expectant look on his face, as though he was waiting for her to say something. A glance at Zidani showed he, too, looked like he was anticipating a response from her. Tain spoke before she could apologize.

"When was the last time you heard from Craig?"

"He sent me a short text message last night when I was still in New Westminster before the drop." It seemed like days ago now, when in reality it was only a matter of hours.

"Did he say anything to suggest he was in trouble?" Zidani asked.

"No. It was just a short message, saying we'd talk later. I never replied. We were busy with the case . . ."

"That's fine." Zidani sat down on his desk. "They're running some tests, just to be on the safe side, but he wasn't out for long."

"Do they have any idea what happened?" Tain asked.

Zidani drew a breath and looked away. The hesitation was enough.

"What aren't you telling us?" Ashlyn heard her words, and she knew she'd said them, but they still sounded far away, like they'd come from someone else. The calm, the lack of emotion, surprised her.

"We have Donny Lockridge's parole officer checking on his whereabouts. His family lives in Kelowna." Zidani's eyes squeezed shut for a moment, as he rubbed their corners. Then he sighed. Aware of her own fatigue, Ashlyn had forgotten that Zidani had also been working all night. "We understand he spoke to Donny's sister-in-law yesterday afternoon. A short time later, she ended up in the hospital. Constable Bob Williams informed Craig, and he said he spent a few hours with him last night. Williams dropped him off at his motel shortly before he was found." Zidani handed her a slip of paper. "There's the number where he can be reached at the hospital."

Once the paper was in her hand she said, "Thanks," and turned to leave.

"Tain and Sims can handle things from here. You can cancel your time off?" he asked Tain.

Ashlyn looked at her partner and saw him nod. Time off? He hadn't said anything.

When she looked at Zidani he was watching her. "Go home," he said. "Call Craig. Make sure he's okay, fly to Kelowna, whatever. Take a few days off."

"Is that what you'd tell Craig to do if I was hurt?"

"It's what I'd tell anyone here to do if their partner was assaulted. It's a family emergency."

"It's not that simple and you know it. Craig was hurt on the job. Maybe if he was a teacher or a mechanic I could see your point, but he and I both knew the risks when we joined the RCMP. You think he'll be happy if I drop everything and jeopardize this investigation so that I can hold his hand in the hospital?"

"If it was you—"

"It isn't me." She could hear the edge in her voice, the one that sounded like a barrier being thrown up in a desperate attempt to keep her emotions in check, but it wasn't succeeding. Ashlyn took a deep breath. "Look, I appreciate the offer. Really, I do. But you're telling me Craig's going to be fine. That is what you're saying?" She waited as Zidani glanced at Tain, then looked back at her and nodded. "Then I have a job to do here."

She held up her hand as Tain started to speak. "I know you could handle things without me, but nobody knows as much about this investigation as I do. We're running out of time before we have to decide what to do about Shannon. Just give me ten minutes to make a phone call."

Zidani kept his gaze on the floor as he folded his arms across his chest. Then he looked at her and nodded. "Okay."

She reached behind her and opened the door, turned and went back to her desk. Tain hadn't followed, she assumed to give her as much privacy as possible. It wasn't until she put the bottled water on the desk and reached for the handset that she realized her hands were shaking.

How could she be so furious with him and so afraid at the same time? She wondered if Steve was grappling with the same dichotomy of emotions.

"Shit. Steve." Did he even know? She sank into her chair, picked up the phone and dialed the hospital. Once they'd patched her through to Craig's room she listened to the phone ring and ring and ring. No answer.

Steve answered his phone on the second ring and listened quietly while she told him what they knew.

"Are you going to Kelowna?" he asked when she was finished.

"No. I have the Reimer murder investigation." She paused. "I don't think Craig would want me to drop everything when he's going to be okay."

"You're right. He knew the risks of the job when he signed up."

"Steve, we haven't really talked since you came back."

His voice was calm. "Ashlyn, this problem with this case he's on, it's between him and me. I'm sorry if it makes things tense—"

"It's not that, Steve. Well, not just that. Vish Dhaval has been making threats."

"How'd you find out?"

"Craig's partner said something."

"Ash, I don't know Craig's new partner, but I can't imagine Craig telling someone else about something like this."

"He didn't."

"So how do you know?"

Steve's voice was so calm, so quiet, it was comforting. There was no judgment in his words, though she had no doubt that he could guess the answer. She told him what she'd done.

"You feel you've betrayed his trust, but you're angry because he kept something from you. In a way, he's guilty of the same thing you're beating yourself up for."

"It's all become such a mess. I keep looking back over the last few days and wondering how we got here."

"I'm the last person Craig will listen to right now."

"I-I know." She managed to hold back what she was really thinking, her sincere shock that of all people, Craig didn't trust Steve.

"If it was the case, Ashlyn, I'd say he did the right thing. Facts first."

A sadness had crept into his words, and she knew what he was thinking. It was more than the case. That was the problem.

"I have to go, Steve. I haven't been able to reach Craig, and Tain's waiting for me."

"You take care of yourself."

"You too."

She cut the call, then dialed the hospital again. It took less than a minute for her to be connected to Craig's room, but again the phone rang and rang, and nobody answered.

CHAPTER SIXTEEN

He was aware of the light before he opened his eyes. A shadow passed over him.

What Craig could hear was the sound of voices, but he couldn't make out the words. They were muted, the tones hushed. There was a noise, like a bell ringing, over and over and over again. Finally it stopped.

Where was he? He knew he wasn't where he was supposed to be. Part of him didn't know if he should open his eyes until he'd figured things out. What was the last thing he remembered? Driving to Kelowna. Talking to that woman, the jewelry, the courier's office, a glass of alcohol on a table in a nondescript room. The ringing bell in the distance started again. He'd been in a motel room, looking at his cell phone . . .

That's what the ringing was. A phone. Suddenly it all snapped into place. The constable. The other case. Donny and his brother, suspects. Snow falling hard, and going back to the motel. Darkness pulling itself over his head from behind . . .

He was in the hospital. The blurry images of a man in uniform and a nurse standing at the end of his bed greeted him as he opened his eyes. They were both familiar, but it took a moment for him to access their names.

"Williams."

They both turned.

"I'll get the doctor," the nurse said.

"Julie," Craig said after she'd left the room.

Williams glanced at the door, then at Craig, then nodded. "That's right. That's good. Always a good sign if you remember who the pretty women are."

"What does it say that I remember you?"

Williams grinned. "Not sure." The smile faded. "How do you feel?"

"Like someone clocked me over the head with a sledge-hammer."

"What do you remember?"

Craig stared at him. In Williams's place, he'd be asking the exact same thing. It was crucial that Craig tell them anything that could help them find the person who'd attacked him . . .

"You don't know who did it?"

Williams ran a hand over his head. "Well, I can guess. I mean, it doesn't take a rocket scientist, does it?"

"They didn't take anything?"

"Not as far as we can tell. Your room was ransacked, but your cell phone, wallet, money, computer—none of that was touched. They were looking for something specific, and judging from the way they turned everything upside down, I don't think they found it."

Craig nodded and closed his eyes.

"Whoa. Don't go back to sleep just yet. The doctor wants to talk to you."

The nurse returned with the doctor. Introductions were a bit of a blur while the doctor checked Craig's vision, asked a few questions and nodded his approval.

"I think we'll keep you overnight just as a precaution." The doctor scribbled on Craig's chart, then left.

"Don't worry about the hotel," Williams said. "Once we've finished with the room all your things will be packed up and brought here."

"Thanks."

"Do you know what they were after?"

"Assuming it was them?"

"You have anyone else running around who might want to take a swing at you?"

"Well, maybe not in Kelowna." He wondered about Vish Dhaval, and how serious his threats were. Not serious enough to follow Craig 395 kilometers into the interior in the winter. "It must have been what Brandy gave me. The locket. It could prove Donny killed Hope."

Williams frowned. "Why would that matter now?"

"The lawsuit."

"What did you do with it?"

Craig closed his eyes. "It's safe."

After a moment, he felt Williams lean toward him. "I know you're tired. You want me to get you anything? We've got officers in the hall." Craig opened his mouth to protest, but Williams shook his head. "Don't argue. You're in my town and as long as you're here we want you in one piece. Next time you get beat up do it in your own city."

"Noted. Maybe a newspaper? Something to read?" Still looking for that distraction. He winced as he tried to sit up. How was it being hit on the head could make your body stiff? It must have been from falling on the floor. "Unless you've got any case notes you want to drop off."

Williams headed for the door. "I'll see what they've got in the gift shop."

"We handed Jody Hoath and Dan Patel back to the New West PD so they can talk to them about their drug dealer," Sims said. "But everything we have from the phone records confirms their story. Nurani orchestrated the whole thing, and the left hand didn't know what the right hand was doing."

They were gathered in the room Sims had used for monitoring Shannon's cell phone, Luke and Zidani sitting on one side of the table, Ashlyn and Tain on the other. Sims was at the end. Ever since Smythe had learned they'd found Shannon he'd been putting pressure on Zidani to release her and let Tracy Reimer see her daughter.

He was also under pressure from his bosses to close this case.

"She had to be planning it with Shannon. Why else?" Luke

said. "I don't think we should release Shannon. That girl is guilty."

"Says what? Your gut? That won't even get us to trial. We need evidence," Ashlyn said.

"You get to bank on your woman's intuition and that's okay, but the minute one of us guys relies on our instincts we're irrational?"

"That's not what I'm saying, and if you had half a brain you'd know it. We rely on instincts when we're tracking leads and looking at suspects, but when it comes to holding someone or charging them, we have to consider the law. I realize it's a real inconvenience to you that no judge is going to say, 'Luke Geller thinks she's guilty? Lock her up and throw away the key!' but most people go to jail on more than an opinion."

The chair Luke had been sitting on clattered to the floor as he jumped to his feet and pounded the table with his fist. "I don't know who's worse, you or that jackass of a boyfriend I've been stuck with all these months, but I'm sure sick of your attitude. If you weren't a woman—"

"Don't feed me your chauvinistic bullshit. The only reason you won't touch me is because I'd kick your ass."

"Enough!" Zidani glared at them. "Luke, sit down and shut it. Ashlyn is right. We simply don't have any evidence to hold Shannon."

Luke looked like he'd rather reach across the table and throttle Ashlyn, but he picked up the chair and did as he was told. He turned to Zidani and spoke calmly. "She confessed."

Ashlyn wondered how Luke knew that. She certainly hadn't filled him in on what Shannon had said during questioning. "To being responsible for Jeffrey's death. She doesn't know anything about her father's murder. And if you checked with your source, you'd know Shannon only confessed because she doesn't want to go back to that house."

"Have we heard anything from social services?" Zidani asked.

Tain shook his head. "I tried again after I left your office. Some song and dance about the case worker being off sick and playing catch-up. I told them if we didn't hear from them today we'd be in their office with a court order tomorrow and would personally make their lives hell."

Zidani frowned. "What did they say to that?"

"The woman laughed and said hell was just a different name for where she was already."

The thinly veiled loathing seeped through in Tain's words, and Ashlyn wondered again about his issues with social services, then reminded herself this wasn't the time.

"Okay, what's next? I feel like we're running out of options here," Zidani said.

"There's still that witness we weren't able to track down. We meant to get back there, but the kidnapping situation got in the way."

"And we were going to Christopher Reimer's school," Tain added. "Now that he's missing that's more than just background."

Zidani nodded. "Start there. We'll release Shannon and Tracy Reimer."

"What happens when we do have proof of her guilt? We won't be able to find her again." Luke swore. "Shannon already tried to run once."

"Then you can babysit her," Ashlyn said.

Zidani nodded. "Luke, you'll take the first shift. I'll make it clear to Smythe that for their own safety, we want police protection."

Luke scowled as Ashlyn stood and nodded at Tain. "We'll go break the news to Shannon."

It didn't look like Shannon Reimer had moved since they left her earlier. Her shoulders sagged, the stain of tears on her skin was still obvious, but her eyes had a resigned look of defeat.

As though she knew that things were completely out of her control now.

Tain watched as Ashlyn sat down across from her. "Your mother wants to see you."

"So?" The tone was flat, void of emotion, and Shannon didn't look up.

"She's had a pretty rough night," Ashlyn said.

"Oh, waah for her."

Ashlyn glanced up at Tain.

Shannon appeared to notice the hesitation and twisted her head to look at him as well. "If you're going to take a run at the fatherly advice crap, save it."

"You're pretty tough, Shannon. At least, you want to think you are," Tain said.

"Whatever." She turned in her seat, her back to him.

"We found your dad's body last night. Shot and killed in your living room." Tain paused. "Guess that doesn't bug you."

She was still for a moment, then shrugged.

"You know, all you're doing is wasting our time."

"Then leave."

Tain walked around and knelt in front of her. "You can sit there and pretend you don't care."

"I don't! He's dead, big deal. Not like it's a news flash."

"I think you do care," he said softly. "I think you just wish you didn't. That way, Jeffrey's death wouldn't hurt so much, but it's tearing you apart." He watched as a tear trickled down her cheek and dripped off her chin. "We want to help you."

She hastily brushed the tears away but still didn't look up.

"You know what else I think, Shannon? I think everyone's let you down. Your mom. Your dad. Teachers at school. Social services. Things got so bad at home that you couldn't take it anymore and decided to run away. But you never meant for Jeffrey to get hurt. Nobody blames you."

Her shoulders shook as she started to cry again, and she covered her face with her hands. "I do."

"Then help us make it right, Shannon. We need to find your brother."

She dropped her hands from her face as her head snapped up.

"Christopher's missing. We need to find him."

Shannon pulled back as she started shaking her head. "He's . . . missing. No."

"We're going to find him. We found you, right?"

The door opened and Zidani offered a hasty apology as Tracy

Reimer pushed past him. She stopped beside Tain. "You don't have to talk to them anymore, sweetie."

"I'm not your 'sweetie,'" Shannon hissed as she turned away and faced the wall.

"Come on. We're leaving." Tracy Reimer didn't reach for her daughter. The gentle tone she'd used at first had disappeared. "Now."

Shannon jumped out of the chair and turned to look at Tain as she backed away from her mother. "Do I have to go with . . . with her?"

Tain looked at Ashlyn, then Zidani, who looked at Smythe. The answer was clear.

Shannon's back was pressed against the wall as she screamed, "How can you make me go with her? I thought you said you wanted to help me?"

"Your mom wants to take you home," Smythe said as he walked into the room and stood beside Tracy. "She's your mother. Your family."

The girl bolted and went for the door, but Zidani stopped her. Smythe and Tracy closed in, each taking an arm. She wriggled and pulled, but with her fatigue was no match for the two of them.

"How can you let them do this to me?" she screamed. "I thought you wanted to help me! No, I don't want to go."

Tain looked at Zidani, who raised his hand. "Don't either of you start. Just find Christopher."

When Williams returned he was armed with a newspaper, a copy of *A Wicked Snow* and *Big City, Bad Blood*. "Wasn't sure what you liked to read, but you didn't strike me as the romantic type."

Craig had already skimmed the book descriptions. "They both look good, thanks."

Williams pulled up a chair. That easygoing smile that had irritated Craig so much at first was gone. "You know we went through your things, just—"

"Sure." Craig cut him off. "I know the routine."

The look on Williams's face seemed caught somewhere between indecision and regret. "I saw the photo in your wallet."

It took a minute for that to register with Craig as he tried to remember what photos he actually had in his wallet, and why they'd matter to Williams. "Look, Steve Daly is my dad. I—"

"This isn't about him. The woman. You're involved with her?"

"Ash? Yes. Why?"

"We tried your home number and couldn't reach anyone. I caught a bit of the news and I recognized her. She's working on a big case."

Craig's forehead pinched as he wondered what that had to do with anything, other than the fact that she wasn't home. "Looks like a domestic. One child murdered, another missing."

Williams nodded. "They found the girl, but the father was murdered last night and the other kid's gone missing." He stood. "Just thought you'd want to know. You can't make outgoing calls with the phone here anyway. They're in the middle of upgrading their system, so no incoming calls either for at least a few hours, and you can't have your cell phone. If you want I can keep trying her, give her a message."

"Did you reach my boss?"

"Zidani? Yes, we gave him an update already."

"He'll tell Ashlyn."

"Are you sure you don't want me to call her, give her a message?"

Craig hesitated. He'd planned to talk to her last night once he was back at the motel, but what was the point in asking someone Ashlyn didn't even know to call her and tell her what she already knew? He shook his head.

"Okay. Look, if you need me you'll have to get one of the officers in the hall to get in touch. Is there anything else I can get you before I go?"

"Signed release forms."

Williams smiled. "I actually did talk to the doctor. He said if everything looks okay he might let you out this afternoon."

"Where are you going?"

The smile faded. "To talk to Brandy."

Craig was sure the expression on his own face matched the sober look on Williams's. "Maybe there is something you can get for me. A full background check on Lisa Harrington, information about her conviction for assault." He paused. "Birth records for all her kids."

"Just covering your bases?"

"Something like that."

Williams nodded and left the room.

"Don't beat yourself up." Tain parked the car and looked at Ashlyn.

She stared straight ahead, looking at the school. "This is where he should be. Safe, happy, with friends. His whole life in front of him. Instead, he's . . . Well, we're assuming he's on the run, aren't we? For all we know . . ."

"Don't, Ash. That kind of thinking isn't going to help anyone."

She blew out a breath. "I know, I know. I just feel like we wasted so much time. First it was the weekend. Then the ransom demand. We should have been here two days ago."

He reached over and squeezed her shoulder. "We're here now."

Ashlyn offered him a rueful smile. "Let's just hope it isn't already too late," she said as she unclipped her seat belt.

They introduced themselves in the office, and the principal came out to speak with them. She was younger than Tain expected, midforties, dark-skinned, large brown eyes and long hair, with a warm smile and an aura of optimism that he wasn't accustomed to seeing in long-term educators either. "I'm sorry, but the family lawyer has given us explicit instructions not to speak with anyone regarding his clients."

"Mrs. Colton, Christopher is missing. Last night his father was murdered. Right now, we have three possible scenarios to consider. One, Christopher is already dead. The only thing we can do then is catch the killer, but until we know he's dead we have to act as though he's still alive. That means he ran, possibly after witnessing his father's murder, and is afraid for his own life. Or the person who killed his father has him." Tain let the words sink in. "To be blunt, I don't care about confidentiality or what the family lawyer has threatened you with right now. We've already stood over the dead body of one child from this family. Isn't that enough?"

The principal looked away for a moment as she folded her arms, then sighed. "We knew there were issues. Christopher's behavior was aggressive and increasingly disruptive."

"Did you contact social services, talk to the parents?" Ashlyn asked.

"We tried. There was no external evidence of abuse that couldn't be explained away. We sensed he was a troubled boy, but all we had were theories. Mr. and Mrs. Reimer would come in together for parent-teacher consultations. They seemed very involved, and we never had a reason to think they'd harm their son." She paused. "To be honest with you, the only altercation we witnessed was started by Christopher. He struck his father."

Ashlyn frowned. "How did Richard respond?"

"He tried to defend himself. All he did was try to make Christopher stop hitting him. It was completely unprovoked. Mr. Reimer had arrived to pick Christopher up from a field hockey game. He was early." Mrs. Colton took another deep breath. "Christopher struck his father over the head with the hockey stick, and his father suffered a concussion."

Tain looked at Ashlyn. He was thinking back to what had happened when they'd taken Christopher home. "Mrs. Colton, do you have any idea where Christopher might go if he was on the run?"

She looked from Ashlyn to Tain and shook her head. "I wish I did."

"If you think of anything." He passed her his card.

Once they were back in the car he said, "Are you thinking what I'm thinking?"

"We never did track down that witness. Maybe we should find out what they saw in the park," Ashlyn said.

When they reached the house, the man was just locking the front door. He turned and started down the front walk as they got out of the car, and when he saw them his face fell. He had a short beard, brown hair cut short enough to emphasize the fact that it was in hasty retreat from his forehead, which seemed enormous. Coffee mug in one hand, he twisted his other arm obviously and looked at his watch. "Whatever this is, can't it wait? I have an appointment in Richmond—"

Ashlyn held out her ID. "Mr. Townsend, we've been waiting for days to speak to you."

He rolled his eyes in a manner that suggested total exasperation. "Is this about that boy in the park?"

"What else would it be about, Mr. Townsend?"

It took him less than a minute to sidestep them, set his mug on top of the red Honda Civic in the driveway, and fish his keys out of his pocket. Just as he started to open the door Tain walked over and pushed it shut. He glared at the man and practically growled the words. "You saw something in the park last week."

Mr. Townsend looked at Ashlyn, presumably for sympathy. She moved beside Tain, hand on her hip. The man sighed, ran a gloved hand over his head and said, "Okay, sure. I was there Friday morning."

"What? You told the officers you saw something the day before." Ashlyn's face was flushed red.

"I did. And I didn't lie. I just didn't tell them everything. Look, I had reservations for the weekend. In Whistler. They came just as I was about to leave. You have to understand."

"What I understand, Mr. Townsend, is that you hindered a police investigation so that you could go skiing." Tain leaned toward him. "Or maybe you had some little hussy waiting for you? Another person is dead, and you might have been able to prevent that murder. You better start talking now, and tell us everything."

"You let him go around talking to people like this? This is borderline harassment," he said to Ashlyn.

"You think he's bad? I'm pregnant, hormonal and haven't slept in over twenty-four hours."

The man's jaw dropped open, and he raised his hands. "Look, I'm sorry. But I saw the police put the boy into the cruiser, so I figured it didn't matter, you had him."

Tain frowned. "What are you talking about?"

"The boy with the curly hair? I've seen them around the park before. That one, he's trouble. I tied my dog outside the bathrooms on Thursday and came out to find that kid throwing stones at her. Don't they say that's a sign of a sociopath or something? Look, what I saw was the girl and the young boy running across the park. He caught up to them and knocked her down. The girl pulled a bat out of her bag and tried to keep the little boy behind her, but the older boy grabbed the bat and got it away from her. She tried to shield the little kid . . ." He shrugged. "And before you ask, I was down by the water. I was just about to shout out when the little boy went down, and that girl, the way she screamed, I knew he was already dead. She took off running, and the boy chased her into the bushes."

"What about the parents?" Ashlyn asked.

"There was a couple, and they came out from the path, the one that goes around the inlet. He was pretty hysterical when he saw the boy. She dragged him away, and slapped him across the face, said something to him, and then they went back the way they came."

Ashlyn passed him her notebook and pen. "I want every place where you can be reached. Cell phone, work number. I want your mother's home phone number. I swear, we call, you come running, or you'll be up on charges."

"You're not going to take me to the station for a formal statement now?" he asked as he wrote his contact information in her notebook.

Tain shook his head. "We have to make sure that boy doesn't kill someone else."

"You mean you let him go?"

"We didn't know he killed his brother, no thanks to you!" Ashlyn snapped.

"Does this mean I can go to Richmond?" he asked as he reached for the mug on his car.

"Do whatever the hell you want," Tain muttered as he jogged to the car.

Ashlyn's phone rang just as they climbed in the car. "Constable—" She looked at Tain, and he could see the tension on her face. "We just talked to the witness." She paused. "No, he went skiing instead of sticking around to admit he witnessed the murder. It was Christopher." Another pause. "Isn't Luke there? What? We're on our way," she said as she clipped her seat belt and then snapped the phone shut.

"Shots fired at Byron Smythe's town house."

"Where's Luke?"

"He thought it would be best if he went back to the Reimer house to see if he could find alternate ways on to the property, and you don't even want to know who he left watching Smythe's place."

Tain swore. They weren't far from Smythe's fancy waterfront home, but by the time they reached his residence it was too late. Three cruisers were parked out front, lights flashing, and an officer was already rolling out the crime-scene tape.

They flashed their ID and went to the house, just as Parker led Smythe out. Smythe had a blanket wrapped around him, face as white as unspoiled snow, and his gaze was vacuous. Parker wasn't offering much in terms of support, but mustered a slight curl of his lip when he saw Ashlyn and Tain.

The living room had been immaculate. White walls, white marble floors, the only furniture in the room was black or metal. The pools of blood growing around the bodies stood out in stark contrast.

Tracy Reimer lay facedown, her head turned on its side. Shannon was on her back, staring straight up at the ceiling, two red spots on her chest leaving no room for doubt about how she'd died.

Footsteps behind them were followed by the sound of someone clearing his throat. Tain turned and saw Parker's partner. Bennett's skin was an unhealthy greenish gray shade, and his eyes looked like they'd been weighed down at the corners.

"Call just came in," he said. "Shots fired. At the Reimer house."

CHAPTER SEVENTEEN

It felt like time was moving in slow motion. Some moments in life seem to fly by, while others crawl. She couldn't run fast enough, that's what Ashlyn kept thinking. Why did the car still seem so far away? And even once they were in it, why wasn't Tain driving faster?

On some level, she knew he was driving fast, a fact reinforced when she had to put her arm out to brace herself against the dash as he slammed on the brakes to avoid a dog that ran out on the road. She could see everything clearly, but she could also see Shannon's lifeless body.

It all made so much sense now. How could they have missed it? How could she have even seriously considered any of the wild theories they'd discussed?

She was hardly aware of the car stopping when they reached the Reimer house, of opening the door, of the shout. All that stood out was the two people at the other end of the driveway. Luke was kneeling. His left arm didn't look right, but he still had his gun in his other hand, although it was lowered. She wondered how bad his wound was.

Christopher still had his gun as well. His arm was hanging at his side, his grip on the gun firm, but the weapon was pointed at the ground. He was laughing. "What are you gonna do? I'm eleven."

Luke pulled his arm up. He was breathing hard, his hand shaky as he pointed the gun at Christopher.

The boy laughed harder. "You wouldn't dare."

Boom.

For a moment, Christopher stopped laughing. He stood on the steps, wide-eyed. He looked down at his chest, then touched the blood with his hand. He stared at it, then laughed again as he staggered back. The gun slipped from his hand as he sank to his knees. With one last raspy laugh he fell facedown.

Ashlyn pointed her gun at Luke. "He wasn't a threat. He wasn't pointing the gun at you!"

A bitter smile filled Luke's face as he held up the good hand and lowered the other one, carefully dropping his weapon with a groan. "You heard him," he said hoarsely. "What were we gonna do? Just wait for the next time"—Luke coughed—"to scrape up more bodies."

She removed Luke's gun and looked over at Christopher.

Tain was checking for a pulse, but Ashlyn felt sure of the verdict before she saw the disappointment on his face.

He reached for his phone as she turned around. Luke was sitting on the pavement behind her, clutching his upper arm. She realized there was blood all over the body of his shirt.

Their gazes met. "Spare me the lecture," he said. "I think I've paid the price."

"You, Shannon and Tracy," she said, sirens screaming in the distance.

"Wh-what are you talking about? I left cops there."

"Christopher must have been waiting inside."

The realization hit home on his face. "They . . . Shit." He coughed, his good hand over his wound, the blood still seeping through. "Told you. Scrape up more bodies."

She saw the flashing lights from the corner of her eye and leaned forward. "He wasn't aiming at you when you fired." For a moment, she stared into his eyes, searching for some sign of remorse. All she got was a half-hearted smile. "You aren't judge, jury and executioner."

Emergency personnel arrived and started asking questions. Tain bagged Luke's gun.

They spent the next few hours giving statements, waiting as

they watched Zidani handle the investigators, the reporters, his bosses and his stress.

"You know, this will ruin Luke," Ashlyn said as they watched Zidani yell at a journalist who'd snuck behind the crime-scene tape.

Tain's face was hard as stone as he watched them wheel the bagged body of Christopher Reimer away. "Good," was all he said.

When the door to Craig's room opened, he'd just assumed it was the nurse. The doctor had been in a short time earlier, doing another examination, and he didn't expect him back. He only cast a fleeting glance toward the entrance and had to do a double take.

The smile was half sheepish, half apologetic. "I guess I owe you an apology."

"Were you the one who hit me over the head?"

Emma's face wrinkled with confusion. "No."

"Then it's not your fault, Emma."

"Uh-oh. Now I know it's serious. We're on a first-name basis." She set her coat and bag down on the chair and walked over to the bed. "I should have told you."

"You didn't owe me an explanation."

"But you thought I was just a pushy reporter, willing to make your life hell for a headline."

"Who says I don't still think that?" When he saw the startled look in her eyes he let a smile flicker across his face. "Couldn't resist. What are you doing here?"

"I saw the news this morning and got on the first flight I could."

"Emma, we still don't have anything that's going to solve Jessie's murder."

She held up her hand. "I had to make peace with that a long time ago. I just couldn't accept that Donny might win his case and get all that money."

"And part of you still can't accept that he got away with murder."

Emma sat down on the edge of the bed beside him. "I

looked at the crime-scene photos. I've covered criminal investigations and I've seen bodies, but what he did to Hope . . ." She shook her head. "Once I knew about your personal connection to the investigation I knew you'd be motivated to be thorough, and I pushed and pushed. I'm sorry."

"You weren't responsible for me being assigned this case."

She hesitated. "In a way, I was. Your sergeant is my mother's cousin."

That was how Zidani had known where he was going. He hadn't told him, but he'd still known it was the interior. "You're lucky."

Her brow wrinkled. "Why?"

"You take after your father's side of the family."

A quick rap at the door was the only warning they had that someone was coming in. When Williams appeared he looked happy, like he was already about to say something. He was carrying Craig's bag. Then he saw Emma.

"What are you doing here?"

Her cheeks colored. "I came to see Craig."

Williams paused, appeared to be thinking over what he'd been about to say, and then discarded it. "Well, I have good news. The doctor says he'll let you out of here."

"You mean I miss the rubber chicken and Jell-O lunch?"

"I'll make it up to you." He set the bag down beside the bed. "We'll wait for you in the hall."

They managed to beat the lunch-hour rush, and had ordered when Williams shifted the conversation back to Emma. "We've talked about this before."

"I'm not getting my hopes up," she said, chin jutting out.

In all their exchanges, Craig had never seen her that passionate. She was emphatic and yet somehow he sensed her disappointment, read it in the hurt in her eyes.

"Isn't there anything you can do?" Craig asked.

Williams hesitated as he glanced at Emma. "We could try to go back, interview the witnesses again, try to poke holes in the time line Darren and Donny gave us. The only reason Donny was convicted for Hope's murder was because of Lisa Harrington's testimony. From what I've read, it sounds like she's recanting." The waitress brought their food, and for a moment the conversation was set aside as she made sure they got the correct orders and had everything they needed. Then Williams continued, "It feels like it's now or never."

That made sense, from a certain point of view.

"The lawsuit makes it tricky." Emma lifted a fork full of salad. "If the RCMP loses or settles, and you reopen the investigation he could have a second suit."

Williams nodded. "They're watching this closely."

"Which is how you knew I was here." Craig speared a potato. "I didn't check in at the police station for a reason."

"Brandy told me where you were staying." Williams hesitated. "In front of Darren."

Craig remembered telling Brandy the name of the motel, just in case. He held up a hand. "It's not your fault."

They continued eating in silence, until Williams's cell phone rang.

As soon as he answered it his face clouded. "It took them this long?" he said as he glanced at his watch, then reached up with his free hand to rub his forehead. "Right. I'm on my way."

"They've brought Darren in for questioning," he said as he snapped the phone shut.

Craig exchanged a glance with Emma, and they both tossed their napkins down on their plates and started to push their chairs back from the table.

"Not so fast. I'll drop you off at your vehicle," Williams said to Craig. "I suspect you'll want to head back to the Lower Mainland. It seems Donny's parole officer has finally confirmed he's not at home, and he didn't show up for work today. A credit-card purchase puts him in the Lower Mainland." He looked at Emma. "What about you?"

"I'll get a flight back. If Donny's arrested, my editor will want firsthand coverage."

"I have to drive back anyway," Craig said as he stood up. "You can ride with me."

Her hesitation was barely noticeable before she nodded. "Let's go."

Ashlyn and Tain had just taken off their coats when Zidani stormed in.

"Now I have to meet with the deputy chief constable from the Port Moody Police Department about that witless wonder of theirs." He pointed a finger at Ashlyn. "Nurani Patel and Matt Lewis. Break the news to them."

"Are we pressing charges?"

"We're still looking at the Patel girl, but for now, cut her loose." He scowled as he turned and walked away.

"I can tell them," Tain said. "You call Craig."

She held up her hand. "It's okay. Let's go get this over with."

Tain took the lead with Matt. Any fleeting thought that the boy might be overcome with guilt and share anything he'd held back earlier disappeared when he started to cry. Ashlyn finally called his parents.

Then they went to talk to Nurani Patel.

When Ashlyn opened the door the girl stopped pacing the room and looked startled, for a moment frozen. She must have sensed their defeat because she straightened up and tossed her head. "It's about time."

"So sorry to keep you waiting." Ashlyn infused her words with a healthy dose of sarcasm. "We're still investigating, but you can go."

"Hmmmph. It's about time. I have things to do," Nurani said as she started to walk to the door.

"Shame about Shannon," Ashlyn said as she looked at Tain.

"So young. Matt's taking it pretty hard."

Nurani stopped. "What about Shannon?"

"I thought you had things to do," Ashlyn said.

"We wouldn't want to keep you," Tain added.

"Really, we're so sorry that a pesky little thing like Shannon's murder messed up your morning."

Nurani blanched. "What are you talking about?"

"You got her killed."

A flash of anger lit her eyes. "I tried to help her."

"Next time you want to help someone"—Ashlyn pulled out her cell phone and located the photo of Richard Reimer—"remember this. Remember just how valuable your help was."

Nurani gagged and ran past them, down the hallway.

"You'll be the parent who takes her kids to the morgue to show them the damage drugs can do, won't you?" Tain said as they walked back to their desk.

"Better than dealing with their death."

As soon as the words were out she regretted them, because she'd seen the look on Tain's face before. She could only describe it as haunted, a glimpse of raw pain that was normally concealed under the constructed mask.

It was a look she'd seen all too often on this case, usually when Tain thought she wasn't watching.

Before she could say anything he put up his hand and walked off.

As soon as she got back to her desk she tried to phone Craig. Although she'd left a message on his cell phone earlier, she knew he wouldn't be able to use it in the hospital. First all the lines were busy. Then she got through and asked for his room.

"That patient has been released."

"Really?" He hadn't returned her call. "Thank you."

She hung up and her phone started to ring. She answered it, thinking it might be Craig. When the caller identified themselves she almost laughed. Social services, after all this time.

The apology came out sounding like, "I'm thawwy I thook tho long," and Ashlyn rubbed her forehead as the woman bumbled through the explanation, interspersed with sneezing and coughing as though she was trying to emphasize just how severe her cold was.

"Please, can you just tell me the status of the complaint and investigation?"

To her relief, the woman offered to fax her a report. Once Ashlyn had it, she headed straight for Zidani's office. She paused long enough to knock, but didn't wait for an invitation.

"Constable Hart." Zidani frowned as she walked in and shut the door behind her. "I'm in a meeting at the moment." He pointed at the man sitting across from him, who Ashlyn quickly identified as the deputy chief from the Port Moody police.

"I know. You need to see this, sir." Sign of respect tacked on for good measure as she set the papers on the desk in front of him.

He skimmed the contents, then stopped, picked it up, got up and passed it to the deputy chief constable.

"It says there that social services spoke to Parker four times and have been waiting on a report from him for over a month."

The deputy chief glanced at Ashlyn. "Look, he's a young officer. He's made a few mistakes."

"A few? He screwed up the routine search on Friday. He missed the murder weapon. Then he wasn't thorough at the hospital. If he'd done his job, we might have found Shannon Reimer that afternoon, and it's possible four people would still be alive. He fell asleep while monitoring the family home."

"Hang on. Christopher was in the house with his father. Now that we know he shot him, there was nothing anyone could have done to stop that from happening."

"But he might have been able to prevent Christopher from leaving. Too late for Richard, but not too late to save Shannon and Tracy."

"Parker tells me you've been on him since day one because you didn't like the way he looked at you."

"That's Parker's excuse because he was responsible for supervising Christopher Reimer while we covered the crime scene. He failed to get Christopher food or water, and left him in the back of an unheated cruiser. The boy was numb and in shock. The fact that he was the killer doesn't change that. We didn't know that then."

The deputy chief hesitated, looked at Zidani, who held up his hand. "We can't bail you out here. Two people were murdered inside Byron Smythe's home. If he catches wind of Parker's track record he'll have a case for incompetence."

"And if we discipline Parker we admit our guilt."

"If you do nothing you're condoning his actions," Zidani

said. "We've got our own case right now. We can't afford to take some mud for you over this one, and from what I've seen Parker isn't worth it."

The deputy chief constable stood and nodded. "Suspended without pay, pending the outcome of an internal investigation."

He shook Zidani's hand, then Ashlyn's.

"Be sure to tell Parker I wish him happy holidays," she said.

The deputy chief glanced at Zidani, then opened the door and walked out.

"Was that really necessary?" Zidani asked her.

"I don't know, but it felt good."

They'd been driving for less than an hour when Craig's cell phone rang.

"Do you mind?" he asked Emma.

She answered it.

"Yes, this is his number." A pause as her cheeks colored. "Yes, I am. He's driving. Can I—" She nodded and started rummaging through her bag, extracting a pen and pad of paper. "Right. Thanks."

When Emma hung up she was still scribbling notes. Craig was trying to decipher them. "Is that shorthand?"

She looked up as she tucked her hair back behind her ears. "My own version."

"Who was that?"

"You spoke to a corrections officer at the prison Donny Lockridge did his time in. He confirmed that Lisa Harrington's visits were more than just guilt trips. When he was released from prison guess who picked him up?"

What did it say about his judgment if he'd presumed so much into Lisa Harrington that he'd missed the reality? That she was actually a calculated, manipulative woman who had an involvement with the murderer of her daughter? She'd filed a lawsuit against his father, his employer . . . Was she that good of an actress that most would have made the same mistake, or had he imagined the emotions he'd assumed he'd read?

At least one thing was clear: She'd played him from the beginning.

"But why me?"

"Excuse me?"

"Lisa Harrington came to speak to me before I was even asked to check into the investigation. Why? Why involve me?"

"She knew you were Steve Daly's son. Considering the allegations about their involvement, that would make her youngest child your half sister." Emma shrugged. "It gives you a personal stake in this."

"Only I never told her Steve's my father." He thought back to what she'd said when they'd first met, that she didn't remember him from the investigation. That he looked young. "She thought I'd been part of the original investigation."

Emma's eyes took on a faraway look and her mouth formed a hard line.

"What is it?"

"I talked to Frank to get you put on the investigation."

"You mentioned something about that back at the hospital."

She looked at him. "But didn't you wonder how I knew about Donny's planned legal action before it was public?"

"I had . . . I just . . ."

"You were too busy avoiding this pain-in-the-ass reporter to question it."

As he flicked the windshield wipers on he replayed their conversations, the details she'd shared before they went public, even the break-in at his parents' house . . .

His cell phone rang again and he nodded when she glanced at him questioningly. She answered it. After a moment of silence she thanked the caller and hung up.

"That was Bob. First, he said you asked him to check on the birth records for all of Lisa Harrington's children."

Craig nodded.

"He said the father's name is blank for both Destiny and Desiree."

"What about Hope?"

"That's the interesting thing. There's no record of a birth certificate for her."

"Hmmm. Sometimes records go missing, people make mistakes." It was too soon to jump to conclusions, although it was interesting.

"Well, that's not all. According to Lisa Harrington's arrest records, she's only thirty-nine years old."

Craig did the math, deducted the ten years Donny had spent in jail and Hope's age . . .

"He did have some good news. Brandy wouldn't change her story, but the neighbors heard the whole thing. They're charging Darren so that they can search the house."

"Hoping they'll find something that implicates him in my assault," he said as the phone rang again.

As she identified the phone as Craig's and confirmed they had dialed the right number he looked at the puffy snow that was plummeting to earth. It seemed misleading to refer to them as snowflakes when they were about the size of a quarter. The windshield wipers, on high, barely kept up with the downfall.

Emma covered the mouthpiece with her hand. "It's the lab. They'll only talk to you."

A quick glance failed to reveal the source of his headset for hands-free talking. "Can you hold the phone up?"

She leaned over and pressed the phone against the side of his head.

"Constable Nolan."

"It's Greg, from the lab. Sorry to be such a pest about it . . ."

"It's okay."

"Who says you're unreasonable? I thought you'd be ready to take my head off because it's taken so long to get back to you."

"People say I'm unreasonable?"

"Figure of speech."

"Right. But I just couriered the chain to you yesterday."

"First, about the blood samples from Steve Daly's house."

"Oh." It still seemed fast to him. No doubt pressure from the bosses was on everyone to produce results, which meant Craig's evidence had been expedited. "What did you find?"

"You also asked me to double-check the tests done in the Hope Harrington case."

"Uh-huh."

"We have a match."

Craig frowned. "On what?"

"DNA samples taken from under the fingernails of Hope Harrington? Matches the blood taken from Sergeant Daly's house. Same source."

"Shit."

"Shouldn't that help you?"

"They never identified the source of that DNA. All they knew was it wasn't a match for Donny Lockridge, and it wasn't someone Hope was related to." It didn't make any sense.

"Well, there's more. That other sample you gave me, blood from the Harrington house from Saturday morning?"

Craig was starting to see it. "A match."

"How'd you know?"

"Lucky guess. What about the other samples I gave you? The DNA . . ." He almost choked just saying the words. What if the answer was something he wasn't ready to face?

"Still working on it."

"Okay. Thanks."

Once Emma had taken the phone away there was nothing but the sound of the windshield wipers flicking back and forth. It was as though planeloads of cottonballs had just been dropped from the sky. Craig was beginning to wonder if they'd be able to make it back.

The phone rang again. She flipped it open. "Craig Nolan's answering service."

After a few seconds she said, "Hello?" and then clapped the phone shut. "Guess it was the wrong number," she said. "Do you have a charger? It's nearly dead."

"Should be one in the glove compartment." If he'd remembered to pack it. He turned the radio on and flicked around until he found a weather report. Heavy snowfall for the

Okanagan, which was the name of the valley Kelowna was located in.

"That doesn't sound promising," Emma said.

"It's just for the Okanagan. That might mean we're driving out of it." So much for catching up with Donny Lockridge. Even if they made it home, this had slowed them down. If anyone tipped off Donny about Darren's arrest he would have a significant head start. By the time they reached the Lower Mainland Lockridge could be gone.

Ashlyn cut the connection and then slowly set the phone down. Once she'd learned Craig had been released from the hospital she'd phoned the Kelowna RCMP and eventually tracked down a Constable Williams, who was investigating Craig's assault.

"He's on his way back to the Lower Mainland," Williams had told her once she'd identified herself. "You could try him on his cell."

Try him on his cell . . . Leaving her to wonder why he hadn't called her back. She'd called anyway.

He hadn't said anything about going to Kelowna with a woman. He was supposed to be working the case alone.

Her phone rang, and her heart sank. Part of her still wanted it to be Craig, and another part of her was certain she'd be disappointed when she answered.

"Constable Hart."

"Liam Kincaid." His tone was warm, though he sounded tired. "I just wanted to see if you're okay."

After the initial wave of hurt washed over her, Ashlyn actually smiled. "You heard?"

"Yeah."

The short silence that followed was a comfortable one, the kind where you felt the other person understood what you were thinking, without you saying a word. "I'm glad you called," she said.

"Jody and Dan gave us enough information to help with some other drug cases."

"That's . . . that's good. Listen, can I ask you something?

When we were on surveillance you said something, about Tain. About this case getting to him."

The silence that followed wasn't as comfortable. "Look, I shouldn't have said anything."

"But you did. I'm not angry. I just want to know what you were talking about."

There was a pause, and then Liam sighed. "His daughter was killed by her mother. She's out of jail now, barely got a slap on the wrist. There was an article in the paper about it, because the woman was white. Sparked a whole racial thing, about the courts not treating Aboriginals equally."

Ashlyn looked up as Tain sat down at his desk across from her. He was holding a book, one she hadn't seen before. Their gaze met and she felt her cheeks flush as Liam continued.

"Social services refused to take action, and the courts wouldn't give Tain custody, despite the fact that he had a stable career, suitable home and no reason to be deemed unfit. The RCMP must have worked overtime to keep this all quiet because there's an ongoing civil case against social services."

"I-I didn't know," she said into the phone as she stared at her partner.

"His little girl? She was four." There was a silence, and then Liam continued, "And, Ash, she'd been beaten."

No wonder this case had been so hard for Tain. And with a lawsuit pending, the mother just released from jail . . . Ashlyn remembered her own casual banter, poking fun at the idea of Tain raising more than his dog. How cruel she'd been.

And what kind of partner was she that she didn't even know about this?

"Listen, I have to go," Liam said. "Remember, if things ever get uncomplicated . . . well, you know where to find me."

"Stay in touch, Liam."

They said good-bye and she hung up. The tense phone calls she'd overheard, Tain's anger with social services . . . It all made sense now.

"Tain—"

He held up the book. "Shannon's diary." Tain set it down in front of her. "Read the marked passages."

She took the book from him and opened it to the first marker.

> *It's getting worse. At first, they seemed so happy with Jeffrey, too happy to bother much with Chris and me, but I guess that's the problem. He totally flipped out about how they love Jeff but not us.*
>
> *Dad got physical with him, and this time Chris hit him back. I couldn't believe it. Neither could Dad, but when he smacked Chris again, Chris punched him and knocked him on the floor.*
>
> *Then he said to Mom he'd do the same to her, just watch him.*
>
> *Now it never stops. Thanksgiving was horrible. By Halloween it was pure hell. I don't have to worry about backhanders from them all the time, I worry about Chris starting something. The slightest bit of attention to Jeffrey and he totally flips out. I've been trying to help, to keep Jeffrey away when he gets like that, but it's like once he hit back he was never going to stop, no matter who he's hitting.*

Ashlyn flipped to the next marked passage.

> *Okay, Chris totally snapped and he's lost it. Today, he punched me hard. It isn't the first time. I can't believe this. He's worse than they were.*

She turned the page.

> *I finally told Nurani and Jody and Matt. They said I have to get out. It's happening every day now, and this time he stuck his hand under my bra. Then he pulled out a knife and told me if I said anything to them, I'd regret it.*
>
> *I don't want to leave Jeffrey but I have to run away. Maybe I can figure something out, make the cops believe me, do something . . .*

She looked up at Tain. "Sure explains a few things."

He nodded. "I haven't read the whole thing. Just skimmed a bit."

"I'll go through it. You should—"

"You should go home, Ashlyn."

She opened her mouth to protest, but another voice cut in first.

"Actually, you have to go home. My orders," Zidani said. "There's nothing now that won't keep."

For a moment Ashlyn thought about arguing. Zidani was leaning against the empty desks near them, and Tain hadn't budged, but she could tell from looks on their faces that she wouldn't win an argument. As she stood and got her coat she glanced at Tain, but his gaze was on his desk, and he didn't look up. She took her time collecting her things, but he didn't make any indication he was going to leave with her.

"Craig's been released from the hospital," she said.

"You've spoken to him?" Zidani asked.

She shook her head. "Left messages. I'll see you tomorrow," she said to Zidani. Then she turned to Tain. "Can I call you later?"

He looked up then, and there was a hardness in his eyes, a warning look that seemed to say *Not now.* "Sure."

"You'll be at home?"

Tain nodded.

She'd felt the tension billowing off him, then wondered how much of it she was projecting, how much was her own guilt? Though logic maintained there was no way that she could have known he'd even had a daughter, a part of her thought back to when they'd first worked together and the moments when Tain's face had not been hard as stone, to when she'd seen through his mask to the breaking heart beneath the surface.

The moments that had convinced her he wasn't a complete asshole, despite how he'd first treated her.

Shouldn't she have been able to see there was more to it, that like everyone he projected a persona intended to conceal his pain? She'd misjudged him.

Part of her didn't want to go home, so she spent some time driving around before she returned to the house. Instead of feeling the sense of comfort that she was used to when she was at home, a cold chill passed through her when she checked the answering machine. No messages.

She locked up her gun and climbed the stairs as she started to unbutton her shirt. The adrenaline surge had worn off and initially been replaced by a numbing guilt that overrode her fatigue. There had been so many moments during the investigation she'd second-guessed herself, and an entire family was now dead. She kept looking for the moment in time that, if she could go back to it, would change everything, like being able to start a Mahjong game all over again from the beginning and make a different choice that would allow her to win.

Not so different from Tracy Reimer blaming the weather, even if it had been a lie. *If it had just rained today. I never let the kids out in the rain.*

A thousand "what ifs" that did nothing but remind you of all the moments you couldn't get back, all the things you can't undo.

Ashlyn walked over to her side of the bed and opened the drawer to her nightstand. Her purchase was still there, wrapped in tissue paper.

In reality it was such a small thing, but when she picked it up it felt like a weight in her hand. As she carefully peeled the papers back to reveal the empty crib she realized she was holding her breath. Why should an object matter so much?

For some reason, people sought out symbols to represent truths or values, and this small ornament was more than just a decoration for the tree, or a way of telling Craig about the baby. It now felt like the fabric of their relationship had been pulled apart and all that remained to hold them together were thin threads that rested on what a baby's bed signified.

She moved to the dresser and set it down, then fished the card she'd bought to go with it out of her nightstand drawer, found a pen and wrote the note.

One last roll of the dice that could no longer wait for Christmas morning.

A thud from downstairs caught her attention. She froze, strained to listen for further evidence something was wrong. It had sounded like something she hadn't heard in a long time, something she couldn't automatically place. Like snow falling off a roof.

Maybe Craig was home and what she'd heard was the muffled sound of him banging his boots on the step? Even as she told herself not to indulge in false hopes she felt a surge of optimism, and started down the stairs.

One look outside told her he wasn't on the front step, so she turned to check the backyard. Everything in the hall seemed exactly as she'd left it, but as she started to walk away from the door she felt the hairs on the back of her neck stand on end. As she walked by the entrance to the kitchen she had the strangest sensation that she couldn't shake, that someone was watching her.

Ashlyn turned as a gloved fist came straight at her. Her head snapped back, and she reached out to try to steady herself, but her attacker had already struck again. Her vision was blurry and she felt the blow to her chest, followed by a sharp pain in her stomach. As she doubled over a fist hit her side, followed by blows to her back.

Her body bounced against the floor when she fell, and the man towering over her started to kick her over and over, first the legs, then her arms, until her body was more exposed and he struck in the chest and abdomen. She thought he was done, because his steady rhythm broke, but then he swung his leg with such force that when his booted foot hit her stomach it lifted her into the air, sending a searing pain deep into her and up through her chest before her world went dark.

CHAPTER EIGHTEEN

"What is it you think you'll find?"

Craig had just been going on impulse, to get to Lisa Harrington's house and confront her, and hadn't really stopped to consider Emma's question until that moment. What *did* he expect? The truth?

Maybe a part of him thought that if he locked Donny Lockridge up, it would mend fences between him and his father. A definitive way of saying that Steve had been right.

As he turned the corner he saw the emergency vehicles, the flashing lights cutting through the darkness, an officer marking the area with crime-scene tape.

He parked the Rodeo and got out. There was no need to tell Emma to wait. As he showed his ID to the officer and was allowed to duck under the plastic band that represented the line citizens couldn't cross she held up her hand and nodded at him. He had to admire that restraint. First on the scene of what could be a significant story, and she hadn't even asked for access.

There were certain things you could learn just by the variables at a crime scene. A quick survey told him at least half a dozen cars were parked outside the property. An ambulance sat idling, emergency lights off. White flashes of light from inside the house suggested someone was taking photos.

It had to be a murder.

When he got to the bottom of the steps, Craig felt his breath catch. *What if . . . ?* He looked up.

"Constable Bicknell."

"Nolan," the man said gruffly.

"Lisa Harrington?"

Bicknell shook his head and stepped to the side to indicate Craig should go ahead. He walked up to the entrance.

Donny Lockridge, with his head spliced open in a way that made Craig question why anyone would even dream of calling an ambulance. Talk about positive thinking.

"Looks like Lisa did a runner," Bicknell said.

"Took off with her girls?" Someone must have tipped her off.

Bicknell shook his head. "Left them behind. They're in the kitchen."

Craig entered the house, which was when he saw a man standing in the far corner of the living room. The years had not been as kind to him. The skin on his face sagged and his belly protruded, but there was no doubt in Craig's mind. Ted Bicknell.

The girls were sitting in the kitchen, side by side, staring soberly at the floor.

After he showed his ID to the officers one of them said, "We're still waiting on social services."

Craig knelt down in front of the girls. "Hey. Remember me?"

Desiree nodded. Her green eyes hadn't taken on the vacant look that Destiny's had. Hopeless. Destiny knew that, as lacking as her life had been thus far, things were about to get worse.

"Have you girls had anything to eat?"

They exchanged a glance, and Destiny shook her head.

"What can I get for you?"

Once he'd taken a basic order he returned to where he'd parked. "I need you to do me a favor," he said to Emma as he passed her his keys. "Two bacon cheeseburger combos from Wendy's, with Cokes."

Her eyebrows rose questioningly.

"Donny's dead, and Lisa's on the run."

He watched those facts register on her face, the relief about Donny followed by the shock and then the confusion. "She abandoned her kids, Emma."

"I need to call this in, Craig."

He held up his hand. "I know. Look, I'll get you as much access as I can. Let me talk to them while you get the food."

Once the girls had dinner and Emma had her exclusive access to the crime scene, Craig went to the back room, the one Lisa had claimed someone had broken into. The box that held all that was left of Hope's short life was still on the shelf and he pulled it out.

Photos, a diary, birthday cards, concert tickets from a date with Donny . . . It contained all the usual things people collected. At the bottom a photo album began with her last school photo, was followed by an obituary, and then traveled back through the years, to Hope's childhood.

The photos stopped when she was about three years old. No baby pictures, no birth certificate, no lock of hair or hospital bracelet.

Some of the photos included a man, and there was even what appeared to be a family shot of him with Lisa and Hope, but Craig skimmed back through the photos and confirmed that he'd disappeared after a few months.

Hope's diary held more clues.

Craig skimmed the contents. There were the usual things he'd expect to find in a teenage girl's diary.

Donny wants more. He's always pushing. I tried telling him I wasn't ready, that I didn't want to get pregnant, and he just laughed and said to ask my mom for some condoms, 'cos she has plenty. When I asked him what he meant by that he told me to drop it.

So I looked through Mom's room while she was out. She has a whole drawer filled with stuff. Condoms and KY and stuff for sex. I don't even know what it all is.

Then there were these newspaper clippings in the bottom of the drawer about a little girl who was abducted about thirteen years ago. And she won't let me see my dad. Won't even answer my questions about him. I'm starting to wonder . . . Is she even my mother?

Her last few entries touched on her questions about her
father, Lisa's violent reaction when she said she wanted to move
away.

*I told Donny I didn't want to be like my mom, I didn't want to
end up alone and pregnant. I said if he wanted to have sex, then
we should get married and move to Kelowna with his parents.
He actually said he'd think about it.*

*Then he said he had stuff to do, so he'd see me later. I was
supposed to go shopping but forgot to tell him that my plans
with Brandy had been put off. Something had come up.*

*I went home, and I could hear the sounds from outside. Not
in my mother's bedroom, in the living room. Donny screwing
my mother . . .*

*I can't believe they'd do that to me. Maybe I should have
walked in, but I couldn't. I just went and hid and waited until
Donny left.*

*Picked a fight with my mother, demanding to know about my
dad again, and she was furious. I told her Donny and I were going to get married and move far away and never see her again.
Then I ran to my room and locked the door.*

*Should I call the police? Would they even believe me? I'm
just a kid, but I know she's having sex with other boys. After I
found the stuff I started asking around . . . Everyone knew. I
just didn't think she'd have sex with my boyfriend. How could
my mother do this to me? I hate her.*

*I'm going to talk to Donny tomorrow. Either he'll agree
about Kelowna or I'm dumping him. Maybe I'm being weak
even giving him a choice, but if he says no, I'm telling his parents. I've already written the letter, telling them about Lisa and
Donny having sex. He says no and I'm giving it to them. I
know they want us to go to Kelowna, and were worried he
might stay here because of me. Well, he's not blaming me for
staying.*

*Saturday I'll go to the library and see if I can find copies of
those news stories. Maybe I can find the truth about my dad and
get away from Lisa forever. I hate her, I hate her.*

Hope was going to confront Donny the next day.

The day she was murdered.

If Lisa had read Hope's diary . . . But why keep it? Why not throw it away? Had she really been so confident nobody would learn the truth? Craig thought about the night of the alleged break-in and the effect the box of belongings was meant to have.

They made him believe that Lisa had loved her daughter, missed her. That she'd kept Hope's things as a way of clinging to her memory. It was an illusion, but the presence of a diary hinted at innocence. It had suggested to him that Lisa had nothing to hide.

He hadn't even asked to see it.

Craig turned his attention to the other boxes. Most seemed to contain junk or old tax forms that were being filed away, and he felt the film of dust that lingered on them. The box that caught his attention was labeled *Hope—Court* and tucked away on the bottom shelf.

There was no need to blow the dust off that box. Most likely, Lisa had stored it carefully before she'd staged the break-in and called Craig. He slid the lid off and confirmed what he suspected: Lisa had been more than one step ahead of them from the beginning. Newspaper clippings, including the details of Lori's shooting, Steve's suspension, the revelations that Craig was Steve's son . . .

Enough of the history to make accusations of an affair believable.

A small palm-sized notebook that was more of a diary spelled it all out. Craig slid it into his pocket. Other clippings, ones that proved what Constable Bicknell was trying to protect his father from, what Lisa had been able to use to protect herself from being charged.

He'd wanted to believe in Lisa. Maybe part of him had needed to believe in her, to make her some sort of substitute for his own sorry excuse of a mother. A single mom who could actually care about her kids . . .

But he'd let that affect his judgment. What kind of father insisted on keeping all the photos of his daughter but never tried to see her, didn't go to court when her murderer was on trial? It didn't make sense.

He allowed his emotions to filter the facts.

"What are you looking for?"

Zidani was standing in the doorway, glowering at him.

"Shouldn't you be happy?"

The scowl deepened. "Why?"

"No Donny, no Lisa . . ." Craig shrugged. "No lawsuit."

Zidani forced his words out between clenched teeth. "You didn't answer my question."

"What am I looking for? Proof." Craig held up a pile of newspaper clippings. "You know those picture puzzles, where if you look at it just right you can see the hidden image? It's so clear once you know the secret. I just couldn't figure out why you'd have Luke steal files from my dad's house." He put up his hand as Zidani's jaw went slack. "Oh, I know it wasn't him the first time. It was Lisa."

"How did she know about them?"

"I told her. Steve always kept his own notes." It was all so clear now. "I said I'd check and see if there was anything helpful there that she could use for the parole-board hearing. And I said that Steve was away . . ."

"She broke in, thinking the house would be empty."

"And tipped you off. Luke knew there were files there. Files went missing from work." Craig dropped the clippings into the box. "The only thing I couldn't figure out was why." He set the lid on top of the box and patted it. "Lisa had the answer to that."

"Look what happened last year, with your partner, even your own father," Zidani said. "Good cops suspended, transferred, under a media spotlight. One dead."

"From what I've learned it looks like Bicknell was having an affair with a senior officer, so the department decides to save face. The press mysteriously caught wind of the fact that Lisa Harrington was allegedly having a sexual relationship with one of the officers involved in her daughter's murder investigation. Donny is charged, the investigation grinds to a halt. Steve gets transferred out as quickly as he was brought in. Bicknell and

Daly weren't incompetent. The department put its reputation ahead of a murder investigation, and they used Steve Daly as a pawn and the mother of a murdered girl to conceal Bicknell's sins."

"Lisa didn't deny the affair," Zidani pointed out.

It was a valid point. Why? So many things about Lisa hadn't added up. How had he missed it? "Maybe they were having an affair. Maybe she found out about the trouble Bicknell was in and seduced him. Hell, she abducted Hope as a child, and we don't even know why"

"Probably saw it as an easy way to get on the system, live off welfare."

"That isn't the point. The RCMP rushed an investigation, and as a result, may have sent the wrong person to jail. They compromised an investigation, and if it had been done properly then, Donny Lockridge might still be alive."

"You've got it all worked out, haven't you?"

Craig shook his head. "No. Just bits and pieces. Maybe nobody will ever know exactly what was going on that the department decided to hide, but it doesn't matter. Hope didn't have much in life, and because of the attempts of the RCMP to cover their own ass she wasn't afforded a proper investigation into her murder. If we ignore that, we're as guilty as they are. And you're okay with being part of this?"

"Let me tell you something, Nolan. Being a cop is the only chance you have of offering justice to anyone. It isn't perfect, but nothing is, and I don't always make the orders, but I sure as hell follow the ones I'm given." He reached into his pocket, pulled out an envelope that was already ripped open and tossed it down in front of Craig.

"What's this?"

"Proof."

He pulled the papers out and skimmed them. "The locket was Hope's" Craig replaced the report in the envelope and gestured at the boxes. "Guess the question now is, what happens to this? You going to bury it too?"

Zidani stared at him, lips twisted into what could only be

called a snarl. Then he put his hands on his hips. "We're putting together a team to search for Lisa. Every border crossing, ferry, checkpoints on the highway." Zidani looked at Craig's head. "I don't want you pushing it."

"I'm okay."

"They're meeting out front."

Craig hesitated, hands still on the box in front of him.

"Don't worry, Nolan. I'll make sure these boxes end up somewhere safe."

The look on Zidani's face was enough. Craig let go and walked past his boss without a glance. Zidani had been a plant since day one, there to investigate Craig, although the fact that Zidani had let Craig handle this particular case alone made him suspect they'd been looking at Ashlyn, Tain and Steve as well, because he had no doubt Luke was involved somehow. Craig was sure of that, even without concrete proof. In a matter of days, or even hours, Zidani and Luke would be gone, reassigned because Craig had caught on to what was happening.

Left in place long enough to clean up one old mess. Donny's death had provided another convenient opportunity to make sure the sins of the past were never revealed to the public.

Unless they could find Lisa.

Tain groaned as he reached for the kink in his back. Considering how many people slept in hospital chairs on a daily basis it was shocking they didn't get ones that were more comfortable, and more suited to their dual purpose.

For a moment he felt disoriented. He knew he was in the hospital from the moment that consciousness first started to pry him from his sleep. There was no confusion there.

What surprised him was that he hadn't been woken up by something external—a noise, a person, a telephone ringing. A glance at the clock was all he needed to confirm that his body had identified this as the usual time he woke, despite the fact that he'd hardly slept for the past two nights.

He got up, went to the washroom, swirled a cup of water around his mouth to clear the bad taste and washed his face.

There was no remedy for bloodshot eyes within his grasp, or for his dark, tousled hair, which was getting longer than he normally kept it.

As he returned to the room and stood at the foot of the bed he thought of how small Ashlyn looked, how vulnerable. Those weren't words he typically associated with her. She wasn't a big person, but she was strong and carried herself with confidence both on and off the job.

She would hate it if she knew what he was thinking.

Dark bruises stood out on her face in stark contrast to her pale skin. For some reason, the effect made her seem like a china doll, fragile, breakable.

He almost hadn't stopped by her house the night before. After she'd left, Zidani had spoken to him, about his own situation.

"Have you decided what you're going to say about social services and the police investigation?" Zidani asked.

He stood slowly and stared at Zidani as he said, "None of your fucking business."

No course, no seminar, no self-help book filled with wise words and the best of intentions . . . Nothing prepared a person to tell a parent their child was dead.

And nothing could prepare a parent to hear those words, to know that their child had been taken from them. Fathers were supposed to protect their children. Whatever he could say about the investigation, about social services, even about his ex-girlfriend, none of it changed the fact that he'd failed his daughter, and she'd paid the price with her life. He should have said to hell with the courts and refused to honor the custody ruling.

He walked back to the chair, pulled it up to the bed and placed his hand over Ashlyn's. She was cold. He got up, found another blanket from the empty bed beside hers and spread it over her gently, tucking her arms underneath. Then he sat down and reached under the blanket so that he could hold her hand.

Where was Craig?

At least half a dozen times he'd phoned and left messages on Craig's cell. He pulled out his phone and checked it, just to be sure. Still charged.

The worst thing about sitting there was the conflict. Should he try talking to her? What would he say? All the things that were going through his mind didn't sound like the right thing to say to someone who'd been beaten to a pulp and left unconscious.

He looked up when the door opened. Typical doctor, with a blue shirt, white coat, clipboard in hand, short dark hair graying around the edges and nondescript glasses. "How's she doing?"

"Hasn't woken up."

The doctor walked around to the side of the bed Tain was sitting on. "You're her partner?"

"Yes."

"She has a couple of cracked ribs, and the bruising you see on her face is nothing compared to what this guy did to her body."

Tain processed that. "What about organ damage?"

"I don't think we have anything serious to worry about there. So far, the test results are encouraging." He felt the doctor's hand on his shoulder. "But she lost the baby. I'm sorry."

That was when he grasped what the doctor had meant by partner, but Tain didn't correct him. "What happens now?"

"We gave her a sedative last night, so she'll probably sleep for two or three more hours. You should go home, get some rest. We'll call you if anything changes."

Tain thought about that. He didn't want to go home, but he should tell Zidani. As he stood he pulled out his wallet and removed a card, which he passed to the doctor.

"If anything changes or she wakes up, please call me right away."

The doctor nodded. "She doesn't know about the baby yet." He paused. "Sometimes it's harder for people to hear that kind of news—"

"I'll tell her."

"You're sure? It's not an easy thing to do."

He thought about how he'd felt, bracing himself to tell Mr. and Mrs. Reimer that their son was dead. "I know," he said as he bent down and kissed Ashlyn on the forehead, keenly aware that it was the only time he'd ever touched her that way, grabbed his coat and walked out the door.

Despite his desire to return to the hospital as quickly as possible, Tain stopped at home briefly to change. When he got to the office it was past his shift start time, but the building was unusually quiet.

He didn't know what made him angrier, the fact that Craig hadn't returned his calls or the fact that he still wasn't in the office. Three boxes were stacked on his desk, but there was no sign Craig had been in. Tain tried the house, and Craig's cell again. Still no answer.

Luke's desk was also empty. Not just empty, he noted. Deserted.

He walked down the hall to Zidani's office. The temporary nameplate outside had been removed, the desk completely cleared, all personal effects gone. He tracked down the duty sergeant.

"Transferred, effective immediately."

"Just Zidani?" he asked.

"Zidani and Constable Geller. You'll report to Rogers for now."

He filled Rogers in on Ashlyn's assault, then returned to the hospital.

The RCMP station was a hive of activity, and they were standing in the hallway, at a crossroads between corridors to interview rooms and offices.

Emma handed Craig a hot cup of tea. "You look like you could use it."

"It's been a long night."

"Anything?"

He looked at her as he took a sip.

She made a face. "Off the record."

"Well, a team has been searching for her vehicle, and an APB has been issued for her and the car. Personally, I've been to the airport to talk to security there, met with the border guards and

Washington State Police. She's wanted on suspicion of murder, so they're taking it seriously, but . . ."

"But what?"

He took another sip of tea. "My gut says she's gone." They were silent for a few moments and he wasn't sure what she thought of his admission. "You got your exclusive?"

"Yes. Small consolation."

The tinge of sadness in her eyes hinted at what he knew already. Without Donny it would be harder to prove the case against Darren.

A man was approaching from the side, and Craig looked up. Ted Bicknell.

"I just want you to know, I don't hold nothin' against you," Bicknell said.

Before Craig had a chance to respond Constable Bicknell appeared. "Everything okay, Dad?"

Ted nodded, then looked up and his eyes widened.

Craig turned and saw Steve Daly approach and extend his hand. "Ted. It's been a long time."

Ted didn't move for a moment, then nodded and shook Steve's hand, hesitantly at first, then vigorously as a grin broke out across his face. "Good to see you." The smile disappeared. "Hell of a thing having this case dredged up again." Ted gestured at Bicknell junior. "My son, Jim."

After Steve shook Constable Bicknell's hand he said, "And you've already met my son, Constable Nolan." He glanced at Emma, and then his gaze met Craig's. "I need to speak to you."

"I'm—"

"I'm not asking, Craig."

Constable Bicknell pointed down the hall. "First door on the right, there's an interview room there you can use."

Steve nodded and waited until Craig started to walk to the room before he followed him.

As Craig went inside he wondered how many bland interview rooms he'd sat in already, with generic tables and chairs, equipment for recording interviews and little more.

He realized how badly he wanted to bring Lisa in, to prove she was an accomplice in Hope's murder, but with each passing hour, as he'd thought about what Zidani had said about the evidence and the look on his face, he realized there was no way the bosses wanted that. Arresting Lisa now would mean exposing the truth they'd chosen to overlook all those years before.

"Any trace of her?" Steve asked.

"No," Craig said as he turned around to face him. "And you know there won't be." Craig leaned back against the wall. "Great smokescreen. Get me involved in the manhunt, so that when she isn't found they can call me up as a witness and say we left no stone unturned."

"What did you think you were going to prove? That the RCMP isn't perfect? We make mistakes?"

"When did you stop caring about the truth?"

"The truth?" Steve's laugh was bitter. "This isn't about the truth. This was about you and me. You couldn't let this go. And now you can't even admit it to yourself."

"Oh, I know you were clean. I found the evidence. God knows what Zidani did with it."

"Zidani's gone. Transferred, along with Geller."

"Figures." Craig looked his father in the eyes. "Does that leave you on the hook now? Who will decide what to do about Hope's real identity?"

Steve stared at him. "What are you talking about?"

"The DNA from under Hope's fingernails that wasn't from a relative? It matched Lisa Harrington." Craig shook his head. "I couldn't figure it out. She said some things that seemed strange, that she was always afraid Hope's father would take her away from her . . ." He looked at Steve. "Hope wasn't her biological child."

Steve's mouth hung open for a second. "I . . . I had no idea. We were about to start investigating her more thoroughly, and then suddenly she's ready to testify and the bosses are pushing us to arrest Donny . . ." His face was a mix of disappointment and frustration. "Why couldn't you just trust me?"

"Why didn't you tell me what was going on? You didn't give me anything to trust."

"Except me." Steve shook his head. "There are things in my job I can't tell anyone, including you, and I don't owe you answers for everything." He gripped the back of the chair, his gaze lowered. "Look, I know I failed you—"

"This isn't about that."

"The hell it isn't. That's all this has been about. You actually believed I could be involved with a murder suspect."

"You got involved with my mother. I'm proof of that."

"Years ago, Craig. Before I married Alison. I made a mistake. Despite having a clear conflict of interest you refused to drop this case because you had to know if I'd mishandled the investigation." Steve looked up. "You want to know what I think this was about? You can't handle the fact that I'm not perfect. In order for you to accept me as your father it's like you need to believe I'm a hero."

"Shouldn't it matter that you're a good person? Are you saying I shouldn't care? Don't tell me you don't judge my life, my choices, and that you're never disappointed."

Steve swallowed. "The difference is I love you. No matter what, Craig. You don't have to be perfect to earn that from me. You're my son."

For a moment they stood in silence, staring at each other. Then Steve cleared his throat. "Ashlyn was assaulted last night and taken to the hospital. Someone broke into your house and beat her up pretty bad. Tain's been leaving messages on your cell phone. He called me when I was on my way here."

Craig reached for it, only to find his holder empty. When had he last used it? Not for hours, not since Emma had asked about the charger.

"Where is she?"

"Royal Columbian, in New Westminster."

Emma was gone when he walked out of the room. He stopped long enough to ask and was told she'd found a ride with an off-duty officer who lived near her office.

Confirmed when he reached his vehicle and found her bag gone.

As he drove he thought about the things that had been said between him and Ashlyn over the past few days, about how much he'd hurt her.

He thought about the ring he'd bought and how much he'd wanted to surprise her Christmas morning.

He thought about Steve. Craig knew he'd let his pride get in the way of simply being there for Ashlyn, for his father. Maybe he didn't deserve her and this was a sign of what was inevitable, that sooner or later he'd hurt her so deeply he wouldn't be able to live with himself.

It was something he did every time someone got too close. He pushed them away. He'd let his pride come between them.

The darkness he carried inside, all the bitterness and anger he'd struggled to let go of, had just manifested itself in a different way. For once he could plainly see what his grandmother saw when she looked in his eyes and why she wanted nothing to do with him. He didn't deserve her acceptance, not when he could so quickly turn his back on his own father and the woman he claimed to love.

Instead of supporting the people who were supposed to matter most, he'd betrayed them.

Tain put his arm around Ashlyn as she took her first unsteady step forward, then stopped.

"Are you okay?"

A tear spilled over. "I guess I just went autopilot, you know? I shouldn't want to stay in the hospital." She reached up with her free hand and wiped her eye, then looked down at the ground.

"If you need more time we can turn around."

"No." Her voice was thick and hoarse. "It's not that." She looked up. "I don't want to go . . . back to Craig's."

"You can stay at my place."

"Tain."

"Seriously. I have to leave in the morning for a few days. You can stay until I'm back, or go . . ." He didn't say home. She was confused and hurt, the strain on her relationship with Craig compounded by the fact that she couldn't even reach him.

"I didn't go to Kelowna when he was in the hospital," she said as they slowly made their way across the parking lot. Her movements were jerky and labored, the result of the bruising and stiffness. "Can I blame him?"

"You called him when he was in the hospital."

"He was with a woman."

"What?"

"The last time I called someone finally answered. A woman. She confirmed it was his cell phone. He was driving back from Kelowna with her yesterday afternoon when Zidani sent me home."

Tain reached in his pocket and removed his keys. He kept his focus on opening the door, careful not to meet her gaze. Craig had been back for almost twenty-four hours? His house was a crime scene. Tain had left messages there and on his cell. The only way Craig wouldn't have known about Ashlyn's attack was if he never went home.

Once they were both buckled in he drove. From the corner of his eye he could see Ashlyn gazing out the passenger window, lost in thought. He didn't break the silence or push her to talk.

Craig had been debating about whether to try to intercept Tain and Ashlyn before they left when he saw them get in the car. Assuming Tain was taking Ashlyn home, he decided to follow them instead and managed to pull out a few cars behind them.

At first, the route was expected, but then he saw Tain turn off. Craig followed. Maybe they needed to pick something up along the way.

They didn't stop at any stores, and when Tain turned again Craig realized they were going to Tain's house. He followed, and when Tain's truck pulled into his driveway Craig stopped across the street, a few houses down.

Why would they go there first? Craig searched for some reasonable explanation, but even the idea that Tain needed to let his dog out sounded flimsy. Besides, whenever he worked a big case with long hours he left his dog at day care.

The CD he'd had on was a mix, and "One More Time" started playing. He watched Tain and Ashlyn and swallowed hard against the lump rising in his throat.

As soon as Tain helped Ashlyn out of the truck she asked, "What aren't you telling me?"

The doctor had done a good job of gently touching on her injuries and suggested they run some tests over the next few weeks to make sure everything was healing. Perhaps because Ashlyn had never been one to sit still, possibly because she didn't want to ask in front of Tain, she hadn't asked the obvious question. She hadn't pushed for anything, other than to be released.

Moments like this could be awkward. What was just the right way to reach out to her so that she felt supported but didn't feel uncomfortable? He gently took her hands in his and looked down at her.

"I'm so sorry, Ash."

At first, her eyes narrowed with confusion, then widened, and he felt her grip on his hands tighten.

"So, he, uh . . ." She drew in a deep breath and squared her shoulders. "That's what he wants to run tests on. To make sure there's no internal damage."

Tain swallowed, nodded, reached up and squeezed her shoulder.

"I knew," she said as she pulled a hand free and brushed away a tear. "It just wasn't real until someone said it." Her face went taut, as though she was fighting to govern every nuance of her expression, so that she wouldn't lose control.

"I didn't want you to hear from a stranger. All the times we go and knock on a door and tell someone we've never met before . . ." He swallowed. "I remember what that felt like. People say your whole world falls apart and it sounds so cliché, but it's like someone just cut your legs off at the knees and knocked you on the ass. You're in shock, you're in pain and you don't know how you're ever going to get up again, but you're trying to hold yourself together so that you don't lose it in front of some stranger." Tain reached up and put his hand on the side of her head. "You need to grieve. There's no shame in it."

Another tear trickled down her cheek, and he could tell she was still struggling to keep herself together. Even outside his house was too public, the day unseasonably bright and cheerful, as though the world was laughing at her. A reminder that life goes on for everyone else, even when your heart is breaking and you'd swear that nothing will ever feel right or good again.

"And if you want to wait until I'm gone it's okay. I can tell you how frustrated I am about a case or what I think about things we handle on the job, but I've never been good at the personal stuff." Even then, he couldn't bring himself to form the words, to say to her, *When my daughter died . . .*

It was like she'd said herself. It wasn't real until someone said it.

It wouldn't be completely real for her until she said it herself.

Her face crumpled and she leaned forward, her head against his chest.

Tain wrapped his arms around her and just stood there, holding her. Ashlyn's body shook. Although her cries were muffled they rang in his ears, echoes of the grief he'd pushed down inside himself.

It was so easy for him to remember his daughter then, to remember what it felt like to have her take his face in her small hands and rub her nose against his. Her laugh was infectious. Funny, he'd never wanted children, but from the moment he'd held Noelle in his arms he'd really understood what it meant to love someone wholeheartedly, unconditionally.

He rested his cheek against Ashlyn's head and didn't try to quiet her, didn't patronize her with pat answers and false promises that everything would be okay. In time . . . Tain had faith in her strength, and his own pain had changed over time. Still there, still powerful, but not all-consuming. It would be the same for her.

He held her and listened to her cry as he blinked back his own tears.

"Ruttan has a spellbinding style."
—CLIVE CUSSLER

SANDRA
RUTTAN

One year ago, a brutal case almost destroyed three cops. Since then they've lost touch with one another, avoiding painful memories, content to go their own ways. Now Nolan is after a serial rapist. Hart is working on a string of arsons. And Tain has been assigned a series of child abductions, a case all too similar to that one. But when the body of one of the abduction victims is found at the site of one of the arsons, it starts to look like maybe these cases are connected after all....

WHAT
BURNS
WITHIN

ISBN 13: 978-0-8439-6074-7

**HOW MUCH DO YOU OWE
A FORMER LOVE?**

WINDY CITY KNIGHTS

Against his better judgment, private detective
Ron Shade let Paula back into his life, but then
she left again, without so much as a good-bye
kiss. Now she's turned up dead. Paula's cousin
doesn't think her death was an accident, and she
wants Shade to find out the truth. But the truth
is hard to find, and every time he gets close to it,
someone gets killed.

MICHAEL A. BLACK

ISBN 13: 978-0-8439-6162-1

STACY DITTRICH

Detective CeeCee Gallagher is no stranger to high-pressure cases. But this one could easily cost her career…and her life. A macabre serial killer is on the loose, leaving the bodies of his young victims made up to resemble dolls. With only a Bible passage sent by the killer to guide her, CeeCee will have to sacrifice everything to find him and end his reign of terror before another child is murdered.

THE DEVIL'S CLOSET

A CeeCee Gallagher Thriller

ISBN 13: 978-0-8439-6159-1

LEE JACKSON

REDEMPTION

Even though he never had a trial, Homeland Security has labeled Ben Trinity a terrorist. Guilty or innocent, it doesn't matter. He's been forever marked. Free on parole, Trinity just wants to start over. And since it appears he'll be stuck there for a while, Redemption, Montana, seems as good a place as any. But everyone knows it's impossible to keep a big secret in a small town. And once the residents of Redemption get wind of Trinity's past, they have no intention of letting him have a future....

ISBN 13: 978-0-8439-6158-4

HAGGAI CARMON

It seemed like a straightforward case of money-laundering. Dan Gordon had seen his share of those since leaving Mossad, the Israeli intelligence agency, to work for the U.S. Department of Justice. But in the Byzantine world of dirty money and international crime, nothing is ever what it seems.

Gordon's once-routine case has now become a desperate hunt across three continents for a devastating bio-terror weapon. Unless Gordon can uncover the truth in time, the population of the world will learn the horrors of…

THE RED SYNDROME

ISBN 13: 978-0-8439-6041-9